BETRAYAL

Lorand's blood ran cold. There had been pumas in the hills beyond the farms of his county, and once he'd even sensed one in the distance. But to be *this* close . . .

"You can't seriously expect me to use Persuasion on an animal like *that*," Lorand protested. "I'll be killed!"

"That motivation is considered sufficient for those who qualify for this competition," the Adept replied coolly. "I would suggest that you attempt to take control of the beast now, before it attacks."

Lorand felt like ⬛⬛⬛ hysteria rather than a⬛⬛⬛ to the animal ⬛⬛⬛

. . . and ⬛⬛⬛ kind of barrier.

Something w⬛⬛⬛ him and the big cat—something determin⬛⬛ to keep him from even attempting to exercise control!

Other AvoNova Books in
THE BLENDING *Series by*
Sharon Green

CONVERGENCE: BOOK ONE OF THE BLENDING

DARK MIRROR, DARK DREAMS
GAME'S END
WIND WHISPERS, SHADOW SHOUTS

COMPETITIONS

Book Two of THE BLENDING

SHARON GREEN

AVON BOOKS • NEW YORK

AVON BOOKS
A division of
The Hearst Corporation
1350 Avenue of the Americas
New York, New York 10019

Copyright © 1997 by Sharon Green
Cover art by Thomas Canty
Published by arrangement with the author
Visit our website at **http://AvonBooks.com**
Library of Congress Catalog Card Number: 96-96952
ISBN: 0-380-78415-7

First AvoNova Printing: March 1997

AVONOVA TRADEMARK REG. U.S. PAT. OFF. AND IN OTHER COUNTRIES, MARCA REGISTRADA, HECHO EN U.S.A.

Printed in the U.S.A.

RA   10   9   8   7   6   5   4   3   2   1

This book is dedicated to my son, SPC Brian Green, and his platoon, all of whom had the "pleasure" of participating in Operation Joint Endeavor in Bosnia as part of the 984th MP Company. ("If Srebrenica only knew ... they would have shuddered.")

The 4th Platoon "Knights" are:

1st LT Matthew Metzel, PLT LDR
SFC Robert "Bosco" Branch, PLT SGT
SSG Dennis Mahaney, Operations NCO

1st Squad:

SSG Su-Lang "Mama Bear" Barabin, SQD LDR
CPL Sean Green, A Team LDR
SPC Jennifer Carnes, A TM
PFC Jason Schaur, A TM
SGT Michael Williams, B Team LDR
SPC Sharon Lyght, B TM
SPC Eric Larimer, B TM
SGT Russell Price, C Team LDR
SPC James Schwertfeger, C TM
SPC Chris Wall, C TM
SGT Scott Bennett, D Team LDR
SPC A. Scott Mears, D TM
SPC Jonathan Blair Hickman, D TM

2nd Squad:

SSG Marko Hakama, SQD LDR
CPL Richard DE Pauw, A Team ("Excaliber") LDR
SPC Todd Perkuhn, A TM
SGT Clint Vernieu, B Team ("Merlin") LDR
SPC Brian Green, B TM
PFC Christopher Videau, B TM
SGT Darryl Martinez, C Team ("Sir Lancelot") LDR
SPC Steven Estrada, C TM
SPC James Mayernik, C TM
SGT Todd Rundle, D Team ("Black Knight") LDR
SPC Mark Corriea, D TM
SPC Yesenia Garcia, D TM
And SGT Ron Rhodes as "The Doc"

All the members of the platoon would like to rededicate this book to their families and loved ones, whose unfailing support made it possible for them to accomplish their mission.

COMPETITIONS

You may be wondering why I broke off the story so abruptly, so I'll tell you: things have been happening. Those early days didn't seem quiet and peaceful when they were happening, but compared to what's going on now. . . . Well, letting you know what happened is one of the reasons I'm writing this, but telling you things out of order will just confuse you. Whoever you are, whenever you're reading this . . . and however things turned out. I'll just continue on as if I really believe we'll succeed in the end . . . and that we'll all survive. . . .

I'll remind you who the five of us are, and then I'll introduce you to our major opponents.

ONE

LORAND COLL—EARTH MAGIC

The day had warmed considerably, but it was still moderately cool under the canopy stretched across the area. Lorand sat at a table alone, finishing the last of the excellent lunch he'd been served. He'd worked hard all morning and had felt tired when he'd sat down to the meal, but now he felt a good deal better. And he felt more confident, something that was much more important than simple physical comfort.

Lorand poured himself another cup of tea and sat back with it, looking around while giving his food a chance to settle. There were thirty or forty people sitting in or moving around the area, some of them grouped together like friends but most as alone as he was. They were all practitioners of Earth magic like himself and they were supposed to be there to qualify for the competitions, but he'd been the only one practicing this morning.

A bird trilled happily from its perch atop the resin wall of one of the practice areas, and Lorand looked up to see that it was the same bird that had kept him company all morning. The feathery practicing-supporter had appeared right after Lorand's Adept guide, Hestir, had left him to his solitary practice, and it had really seemed to be there to support Lorand. It had chirped encouragingly when he'd hesitated, crooned reassurance when he'd made his tries, and had sung for all it was worth when he'd succeeded. It was as though it knew he needed support to get through the time, and had come just to give that support. . . .

"Well, Lorand, all finished with lunch, dear boy?" a voice asked suddenly, and then Hestir, his Adept guide, was sitting down at his table. Hestir was a man in his middle years, not as tall as Lorand and considerably rounder, with a round and friendly face, brown hair, and mild brown eyes. "Was the food as good as I said it would be?"

"It was better," Lorand answered after sipping from his teacup. "Truthfully, I was expecting the same sort of food served us during the qualifying sessions, and regretted how hungry I was."

"I don't blame you in the least, dear boy," Hestir replied with a laugh of true amusement. "They know that most of the applicants still attending the sessions won't qualify for the competitions, so they tend not to waste decent food on them. So tell me, are you ready yet to qualify in the areas where you've been practicing? You've been at it all morning, after all."

Lorand could see that Hestir was joking, teasing him in what he considered a gentle way. That meant it wasn't usual for people to qualify so quickly, but Lorand had very little choice. He had to get past what he had no trouble with, to give himself more time with what he *would* find hard.

"As a matter of fact I *am* ready to test in the first three practice areas," Lorand said, pretending not to see how quickly Hestir's amusement disappeared. "The silver din I get for each of them will let me pay for my food at the residence for another week, so I'll have the time to work on the last two areas. I don't expect those two to be mastered quite as easily as the first three."

"No, the last two aren't nearly as easy as the first three," Hestir agreed, as though reminding himself aloud that he himself had mastered them. "Well, then, let's go and see what you can do—unless you'd rather finish your tea first."

"I *would* like to finish the tea," Lorand said, telling himself he wasn't really stalling. He was still in the process of regathering his strength, something he'd be wise to finish along with the tea if he expected to move on to the more advanced practice areas. Hestir smiled and nodded and settled back in his chair, silently pleased with Lorand's hesitation. So showing a bit of nervousness might be the best thing Lorand could do. . . .

The conclusion wasn't a terribly certain one, but it would be typical of these people who worked for the testing authority. Lorand hadn't yet found one of them that he liked, but his likes and dislikes were secondary to the aim of staying alive. He and the others at the residence had noticed that none of them knew or even knew *of* anyone who had gone through the testing for High practitioner and had come back to talk about it. Failed applicants were . . . done away with? Sent somewhere to never return? No one knew, so he and the others had decided they *had* to succeed. Even though success itself wasn't all that certain to save them. . . .

"I'm ready now," Lorand said, after finishing his tea in a single swallow and then standing. The more he thought about what might lie ahead, the more disturbed he became. And he couldn't afford to *be* disturbed, not when he needed the gold he could win at the competitions. Getting there in the first place would be far from easy, and that would provide enough disturbance for three or four people.

Lorand let Hestir lead the way to the first practice area, which contained nothing but a pile of soil. The Adept stepped aside to give Lorand room to walk in, and then it was time to begin. After two or three false starts, Lorand had found the key to handling the mound of soil properly without needing to draw in more power than he'd already been using, a discovery that had come as a great relief. Using larger and larger amounts of power was very dangerous, and Lorand couldn't seem to get around picturing himself burned out and mindless, just as that little girl had been so many years ago. . . .

"You may begin at any time, dear boy," Hestir prompted, now back to sounding amused. "Of course, if you've changed your mind about trying for mastery right now, that's perfectly all right. Some of us are a bit more shy than others about performing in public, but it's something you do eventually get beyond. Would you like to postpone this until tomorrow?"

"No," Lorand replied after taking a deep breath. If he let himself postpone the test today, tomorrow there would be a different reason for postponing it again. He had to do it *now*, and get it quickly behind him.

So he looked at the mound of soil even as he reached out to it with his ability. Earth magic was his realm, everything and anything to do with the earth. Soil was the most basic part of that, and the first step to handling this practice problem was to spread his power around the entire area. Trying to contain things afterward just didn't work, and that was what it had taken him a while to realize.

Once his power filled the entire cubicle, Lorand used a portion of that power to grasp the mound of soil. Making it explode in all directions *looked* impressive, but basically he simply tore the soil apart with his strength. That caused the tortured grains to fly away from each other with great force, but they weren't allowed to go far. The net of power he'd spread out before starting caught the grains and contained them, especially keeping them from flying at Lorand with the force of their explosion. The first time he'd nearly blinded himself, and had had to waste some strength cleaning himself up afterward.

"Dear boy, that was marvelous!" Hestir enthused, his tone nevertheless sounding faintly hollow. "And not a single grain has escaped you. A true mastery without doubt."

"And the first of the three silver dins I need," Lorand deliberately pointed out. "If not for that, you can be certain I would be taking a good deal more time. Well, we might as well get on to the next one."

Even as he spoke, Lorand automatically gathered the scattered soil back into its original mound. He tended to be neat, and leaving the soil scattered every which way as Hestir had done after demonstrating the practice problem wasn't Lorand's way. Hestir muttered something Lorand didn't hear as he followed Lorand to the next cubicle, but it couldn't have been anything important. If it had been, the Adept would have repeated it, but he didn't.

Which meant there was no excuse to put off trying the second practice problem. An iron ingot stood in the middle of the cubicle, and Lorand reached to it with the fingers of his talent. He could feel everything about the metal that way, every smoothness and flaw, almost every grain of it. Of course, metal didn't come in grains, at least not after it was worked, but the memory of being ore seemed to be part of even a molded ingot. Strange, but not something to be worried about now. . . .

Instead he reached to the flaws in the ingot, exerted his strength, then watched the ingot fall to pieces just the way it was supposed to. As a boy he'd found the flaws in bent nails to crumble them in an effort to impress the girls, but here in the practice area his efforts were apparently even more impressive.

"That's really quite good," Hestir said softly, and Lorand could feel the tail end of the Adept's use of his own power. "You're considerably stronger than I'd realized at first, and I'm no longer surprised at the progress you've made. You've now achieved a second mastery, and I'm ready to witness the third."

Lorand nodded and walked to the third cubicle, faintly disturbed by Hestir's new attitude. Had he blundered by passing the tests so quickly, or was the other man simply impressed? It was so damned hard knowing which way to jump, or even if he should jump at all. He could feel the agitation making his control over his ability begin to slip, and then—

And then he heard the birdsong again, causing him to glance up. That bird was still there, a pretty little gold, black, and white chickadee, and it seemed to be encouraging him again. Silly or not its presence did hearten him, and that made him glad that the practice area was generally out-of-doors. If it had been in a building the bird wouldn't have been able to get in, and he might not have had the heart to continue what he'd started.

"Number three," Lorand said, now looking at the cage of rats in the middle of the cubicle. Again he reached out with his power, but this time much more carefully. The rats were living creatures, and were meant to stay that way. Very gently he began to urge the rats to leave the center of the cage, and just as they'd done earlier they responded more quickly than he expected. Once the center of the cage was empty he had to choose a single rat to return to it, and that was harder. Holding back all the others while coaxing just one to where he wanted it to go . . .

But after a couple of minutes it was done. The single rat stood alone in the center of the cage, and despite the sweat covering Lorand's face, he wasn't all that tired. Every time he repeated a new undertaking it became easier to do, just as if practice really did make perfect.

"Number three mastery, just as promised," Hestir said with a sigh, a comment Lorand took as his cue to release the rats. "You're really quite accomplished, sir, and I look forward to watching you climb to the heights. Please believe that I feel honored to be your guide during these first days."

Lorand was certain that the Adept was being sarcastic, but when he turned to look at the man, he was even more disturbed than he'd been earlier. Hestir no longer looked him in the eye, and his stance was all but subservient. Lorand had been fairly certain from the first that he was stronger than the Adept, and somehow he'd apparently proven it. He was no longer "dear boy," but "sir."

"I think I'm ready for another cup of tea now," Lorand said lightly, trying to ease the tension he could feel far too clearly. "Would you do me the favor of joining me, Adept Hestir?"

"The honor would be mine, sir," Hestir returned, clearly refusing to return to his former attitude. "And allow me to ring for a servant for you. . . ."

Hestir hurried ahead to call a servant and get the tea ordered, and Lorand followed rather quickly in order to add a request for a sandwich or something. He'd expended enough strength to be hungry again, and he wanted to get the food swallowed before Hestir's attitude ruined his appetite. It was obvious the round little man expected Lorand to become rather important, and wanted to start ingratiating himself as soon as possible.

Lorand sighed at that, having the distinct impression that he would hate being important. He hadn't expected to feel that way and it was disappointing, almost as disappointing as the fact that his little bird supporter had apparently flown away. The chickadee was nowhere to be seen, which left Lorand all alone among strangers . . . and possible enemies. . . .

TWO

JOVVI HAFFORD—SPIRIT MAGIC

The canopy above the tables in the eating area created a pleasant shade under the noon sun that Jovvi could really appreciate. Sitting out in the fresh air after spending the morning in a practice building felt good, and the lunch she'd just eaten had been more than simply adequate. The people in this area *did* believe in pampering themselves, just as her Adept guide Genovir had said.

Jovvi sipped at her second cup of tea, thinking about the morning and the Adept Genovir, and even about the people around her at the other tables. Genovir had been the first one she'd met there, and it hadn't taken long to notice that the other woman's talent wasn't particularly strong. An Adept was supposed to be one level below the strength of High practitioners, so the anomaly made Jovvi even more suspicious about what was going on than she had been.

And that suspicion increased when she considered the others sitting in the area having their lunch. There were more than thirty men and women, most of them eating alone as she had, and all of them were supposed to be there to qualify for the competitions to become a Seated High. But after spending all morning practicing with her ability, Jovvi was able to tell that most of these people weren't unusually strong. Oh, they were all *potential* Highs, just like the people in the practice sessions she'd attended before qualifying for *this* place, but they seemed just as stuck at this level as the other sessions people were at the lower level.

Which brought Jovvi to the question she'd been asking herself all along: when it came to surviving that time of tests and competitions, how strong was strong enough? It would be foolish to stand out as being *too* good, she felt, but it also would be less than wise to be too ordinary. She hadn't been able to answer the question this morning, but now she was getting a slightly better idea. . . .

"Did you enjoy your lunch, dear?" a voice came, and Genovir appeared beside Jovvi and then sat herself at the table. The Adept had taken her own lunch at a larger table with half a dozen others, people whose attitudes seemed to be just like hers. Genovir was perhaps ten years older than Jovvi and taller, handsome rather than pretty, brown-haired and-eyed, and projecting an attitude of wise patience and full balance.

"Lunch was wonderful, thank you," Jovvi replied with a smile, feeling Genovir's probes in her direction. The so-called Adept was apparently trying to be surreptitious about checking Jovvi's state of mind and balance, but Genovir wasn't strong enough to get past Jovvi's awareness undiscovered.

"I knew you'd enjoy it," Genovir said with a smile and a nod. "We do work harder here, so we deserve to be treated better than those who haven't accomplished what we have. And after half a day of doing that work yourself, I believe you understand now why it would be foolish of you to expect to reach the competitions very quickly."

"Actually, I realize more than that," Jovvi said with the same smile, still turning aside the woman's ever-strengthening probes. "I noticed a few of these others coming in to practice in the building this morning, but the rest seem content to rest on whatever they've already accomplished. Just like those others at the sessions, the ones who have been trying for weeks or months to qualify, but just haven't managed to do it.''

"What are you saying?" Genovir asked, clearly trying to fight away a frown. "That our people here are no better than those poor, useless souls of the lower level? But that's ridiculous, my dear, utterly ridiculous. Many of our people don't *have* to practice any longer, and some work better expending less effort. During the next weeks I'm sure you'll find your own best pace, and then—"

"Next *weeks*?" Jovvi interrupted to echo, raising one brow. "But we were told that no one will be allowed to try to qualify for the competitions beyond this week's end. Surely that means there's only a matter of days before the major competitions will be held?"

"Actually . . . more than just a few days," Genovir grudged, not terribly happy about parting with the information. "But that means nothing to someone at your level, my dear, and you shouldn't let it disturb you. Disturbance will hamper your ability, you know, so when it comes time for you to try for mastery you'll be at a severe disadvantage.''

"I think that achieving mastery will take care of any disturbance there might be," Jovvi said pleasantly after finishing her tea. "Just how do I arrange to go about that?"

"I—I ask one of the other Adepts to witness your performance," Genovir responded, her inner balance definitely gone now. "But you really should take more practice time first, to be certain . . . you. . . .''

The woman's words trailed off as Jovvi calmly and simply shook her head, refusing to hear Genovir's "words of wisdom." There was no longer any doubt that moving ahead as quickly as possible was still the right thing to do, and she'd have to tell the others as soon as they all got back to the residence tonight. Tamma, and Vallant Ro, and Rion Mardimil, and Pagin Holter—and Lorand Coll. Lorand especially. . . .

Genovir left the table abruptly, but Jovvi wasn't given much time to worry about how Lorand was doing. It took only a couple of moments before Genovir was back, along with a man who looked more supercilious than self-assured.

"Dama Jovvi Hafford, I present you to Adept Algus," Genovir said, all but curtseying. "Adept Algus will witness your attempt at mastery, and certify it if you succeed."

"*When* I succeed," Jovvi corrected, then rose to her feet to smile at Algus. "How nice that I'll have a gentleman accompanying me. I always do much better in the company of gentlemen."

"I don't doubt that for a moment, lovely child," Algus replied, his smile having grown interested. "Allow me to offer my arm for the short walk to the practice building."

Jovvi took the man's arm with her most charming smile of agreement, ignoring the roiling fuss coming from Genovir. The female Adept was furious over how quickly Jovvi had melted Algus's aloofness, but that was too bad about her. The tall, saturnine man would do much better on Jovvi's side, most likely missing entirely how he was being manipulated. Many men with power enjoyed letting beautiful women manipulate them, a fact Jovvi had learned during her time as a courtesan.

Algus wanted to talk as he escorted Jovvi to the practice building, so she obligingly chatted. He was an older man who was still in his prime, although obviously no stronger than Genovir. His attempts to unbalance Jovvi's emotions to his own benefit were easily deflected, so they walked into the practice room still chatting about nothing.

Six new subjects stood in the room, eyes dull from the drugs they'd been given, and Algus waved a languid hand at them.

"There they are, lovely child," he said, his smile more demeaning than amused. "As soon as I cue them, you may go right to it."

Jovvi nodded with a much better smile and walked to the center of the room, hiding her extreme distaste with the ease of long practice done elsewhere. The subjects they gave her to practice on here were all drugged; otherwise they'd never be able to maintain an almost constant state of unbalance for her to work with. Anger was the easiest thing to induce, with fear coming in a close second. She'd worked with both during the initial test and the sessions, but in this place they'd so far used only anger.

"Hear one who is authorized to command you," Algus said, obviously giving the subjects the keying phrase. "This woman is your enemy, and your anger at her is boundless."

The six people immediately grew furious, their raging emotions aimed directly at Jovvi. It had disturbed her for quite some time that morning to see the expressions and gestures that went with the emotion, but she'd finally gotten almost used to it. At least she'd learned to be less concerned over working with actual people, something everyone was raised *not* to do. The far from easy life she'd led as a child now helped her in that respect, and Jovvi was willing to take any help she could get.

She immediately spread out her ability, touching the hostile emotions of the people before her. They really were furious and weren't far from deciding to hurt her, so she quickly began to balance their hostility. Their emotions eased immediately. The drug's presence in their systems did nothing to stop her, and their shouting and fist-shaking ended just as quickly. They were completely mollified and under control, but Algus waited a moment or two before acknowledging that.

"Very nicely done, lovely child," he conceded at last, sounding more patronizing than approving. "One mastery accomplished, three to go. You people—division one."

At the command the six subjects divided into two groups of three, and then began radiating heavy anger again. It was slightly more difficult for Jovvi to divide her abilities as well, but only because there were individual sources of unbalance in each of the two groups. Beyond that she'd already divided her strength into more than two parts, so a pair of moments later the two groups were calm again. This time Algus waited longer than he had the first time, but eventually had to give in.

"Two masteries, then," he granted, his words on the cool side. "Quickly now, you people—division two."

One person came from each of the former groups, and now there were three groups containing two people each. Jovvi had to brace herself against the renewed anger, wondering if the testing authority realized that *this* was the hardest part of the problem. Multiple members of multiple groups was a very tricky exercise in balance, and small beads of perspiration formed on Jovvi's brow before she had all three groups calmed again. The beads of sweat grew larger while Algus made her hold the groups, but once again he was eventually forced to acknowledge her accomplishment.

"All right, that's three," he snapped, apparently finding it difficult to maintain his own balance. "But there's still one to go, so don't congratulate yourself quite yet. You people—division three."

The six people spread out to stand individually, which came as a relief for Jovvi. If Algus thought handling six individuals was harder than three pairs Jovvi wasn't about to correct him, but she did make something of a production of it. She let the ranting and raging go on for a moment before bringing it under control, then clenched her fists as she held the six with her power. She wanted her "struggle" to be clear to Algus, who would certainly wait as long as possible before ending the test. Again he waited longer, while Jovvi held the six with only a small amount of effort. Finally his voice ended it.

"Much to my astonishment, that's four masteries," he said, now sounding honestly surprised. "You have my congratulations, Dama, for showing yourself superior to most of those of the gentle sex. Would you care to rest now?"

"Yes, with a cup of tea, if you please," Jovvi replied faintly after releasing the six subjects. Actually she felt fine, but if Algus wanted to believe her exhausted, that was something else she wasn't about to argue.

"Here, take my arm," Algus said after hurrying over to her, his interest now a good deal more intense. "We'll have the tea together, and perhaps a sweet cake as well. Or anything else you might wish. Your company honors me, Dama, and it would please me to see to your needs."

Jovvi gave him a wan smile as she leaned on his arm, perfectly well aware of which needs of hers Algus would most prefer seeing to. It would be silly to tell him at once that he hadn't a prayer of making it into her bed, not when there were things she hoped to learn from the man.

But one thing she'd already learned, and the point was rather significant. Algus now called her "dama" rather than the condescending "lovely child" he'd *been* using, which meant quite a lot. Gaining those masteries had earned her another step upward, and one that was important enough to change Algus's attitude. If it had been a negative step he would have been a lot less ingratiating, which meant her theories about moving ahead being the best way were proving themselves.

Jovvi took a deep breath of fresh air as Algus led her outside, but still had to fight down a brief flash of frustration. So her theories had proven themselves so far; that didn't tell her how much farther they would take her. She still didn't know how good good-enough would turn out to be, but she'd better find out before everything fell apart. . . .

THREE
RION MARDIMIL—AIR MAGIC

Rion sat in the fresh air after enjoying his meal, a pleasant change from the circumstance found with the sessions he'd moved beyond. The food served for lunch at the sessions had been abominable, nothing a man of breeding and culture would accept for long. Here, though . . . the meal had been good enough that even Mother wouldn't have complained very much.

Rion realized that that was the first time he'd thought about Mother all morning, and the realization pleased him. Mother was doing her best to keep him under her thumb and completely dependent on her, but he'd already gained more of an advantage than he'd expected to. She'd tried to force him into changing his name back to Clarion, that awful joke she'd saddled him with, but it hadn't worked. Instead she'd secured him allies, which Padril had explained about.

Looking around showed Rion the place where Padril, his Adept guide, had taken his lunch, at a table with others who also seemed to be Adepts. Padril had assured Rion that he was much more potentially valuable to the Empire than Mother was, so as soon as he proved his worth he would have powerful friends to stand between him and Mother. And he needed those friends, no matter how strong his resolve was to find independence. He'd discovered that his resolve and determination began to crumble when Mother stood directly in front of him, and as abhorrent as the thought of returning to her domination was, he feared it would happen if he found himself standing alone.

A burst of laughter arose from those people sitting with Padril, momentarily making Rion believe that they were laughing at *him*. When he'd still been Clarion he'd been laughed at more than once, but he hastened to remind himself that he was now Rion and that didn't happen to Rion. Indeed, from the way Padril had spoken, Rion would be the last one anyone laughed at. Great things were expected from Rion, and Rion was ready to produce them.

Another burst of laughter came from the same tableful of people, and this time one or two actually glanced in his direction. Rion knew he was extremely unworldly as far as most things went, but being ridiculed was one state of affairs he was well familiar with. Those people *were* laughing at him, but he couldn't understand why they would do so. Padril had agreed about how special he knew Rion to be, how much better than all the commoners around him. . . .

Only then did the thought come, that there *were* just commoners around him. Clothing didn't enter into it, since all applicants wore the same white shirt or blouse and gray trousers or skirt. Bearing and attitude shouted that he was the only member of the nobility present, which could well mean that other members of the nobility were being handled and tested in some other place. Since he hadn't come across any of his peers at any time so far, the theory appeared to be more than sound.

Which meant that Padril hadn't believed his claim to be a member of the nobility, and the Adept's very solicitous concern and support had been a sham. He hadn't admired Rion and his potential at all, and possibly hadn't even believed in it. Padril had been pretending, making Rion the butt of a joke, and that was the amusement he now shared with his friends. *See the foolish young man who really thought he was important.*

Rion felt the definite urge to do violence, an emotion he'd

felt before but had never been so close to acting on. The nerve of that peasant, to make *him* the butt of his senseless joke! Committing violence would have felt marvelous, but Rion saw Padril rise and begin to walk toward him, and suddenly he had a better idea. Telling people things was never as good as showing them, and Padril had earned some showing. Besides, he now remembered that he and the others at the residence had decided to move ahead as quickly as possible, which fit in perfectly with his own plans.

"Ah, Rion, finished with lunch, I see," Padril remarked with his usual ingratiating smile as he reached Rion. "You must have had a strenuous morning, but you certainly look as if you've been restored."

"Completely restored, thank you," Rion returned, trying not to sound stiff with anger. There was no sense in warning the fellow, or making it impossible for the man to say the wrong thing.

"Ah, then in that case I must disturb your rest time to ask a most pressing question," Padril continued, his brown eyes showing veiled amusement. "We've already established that you'll be doing marvelous things, but I've been wondering just how soon you'll be doing them. My superiors will want to know. . . . Perhaps by the beginning of the new week? Surely that won't be too soon?"

"Actually, the beginning of the new week doesn't suit me at all," Rion drawled, fairly certain he knew what Padril was aiming at. "I wonder why you would think it did."

"I thought so because you were the one who wanted to forge strongly ahead," Padril reminded him, gentle admonition behind the words. "But surely I'm the one who is mistaken, and you would prefer to wait until the second new week before showing us your prowess. Better to wait a bit longer and be absolutely certain, eh?"

"I'm already absolutely certain," Rion said, ignoring the wink the man had shown him. "And I see no reason for a wait of any length. Whom do I have to see to arrange the testing right now?"

"Now?" Padril echoed, his vast and worldly amusement suddenly faltering. "You can't mean you want to—Now?"

"Yes, now," Rion repeated, taking a grimly pleased satisfaction from the man's sudden nervousness. "To whom do I speak about it?"

"Why, *I'm* the one assigned to witness your attempts at mastery, but surely you're simply joking with me." Padril had begun to sweat and squirm, for some reason Rion couldn't fathom. "You can't possibly be ready to test yet, not after only half a day of practice. It—isn't often done."

"I'm glad you weren't foolish enough to say 'never done,' " Rion told him as he rose to his feet. "Let's not waste any more time."

Padril's bearded face creased into a worried frown, but he said nothing further before turning to lead the way to the path that led across the grass to the practice building. The so-called Adept glanced at those he'd been sitting with as he walked, but made no effort to acknowledge their smirks and grins. He must have come over to add to the general amusement, Rion realized, but had found the joke ruined instead. And it would really be ruined once Rion passed the test.

The practice building was divided into a number of rooms, each of which was lit by lamps sealed behind clear windows of resin. In fact the entire room was capable of being sealed, which Padril saw to once the six people Rion was to work with had entered.

"When I pull this cord, smoke will be pumped into the room," Padril said as though Rion had no idea about what was going on. "The first mastery required of you is to keep yourself and those six people breathing freely, with them standing together in a single group."

Rion nodded curtly to show that he understood perfectly, and after a moment's hesitation Padril pulled the rope. Smoke began to billow into the room immediately, heavier smoke than Rion had worked with that morning. The difference wasn't all that significant, however, not when Rion reached out with the fingers of his talent. Air magic was his aspect, and in no more than a moment there was clean air for himself and the six subject people to breathe.

"Now they'll divide into two groups of three," Padril announced after another hesitation. "Remember that you must keep them breathing freely."

Padril had surrounded himself with his own clean air, of course, but Rion had the impression that the man wasn't holding it easily. But that was not important at the moment, and protecting his subjects was. Rion carefully parted the shell of clean air and sent it with the three people who moved away from the others, and not a wisp of smoke disturbed any of them.

"Very . . . impressive," Padril said after an even longer hesitation, his voice now trembling faintly. "Two masteries completed, two to go. May we have the next separation, please?"

The three people who had moved away now moved back again, but only in order to form three groups of two. Rion carefully separated his spheres of air again, but there wasn't much time left. The air that had started out clear was being used too far by too many people, and the pumped-in smoke had tainted whatever air was left. If Padril didn't stop taking his time admitting the masteries, the subjects would soon be coughing and choking from something other than smoke.

"Yes, well, that's three now, isn't it?" Padril asked after much too long a time. "Well, just one more to go, but it *is* the hardest. Places, please."

The Adept now sounded too pleased to suit Rion, so while the six people began to separate into six individually clear islands in the smoke, Rion thought about why. It took only a moment to come up with a guess, but it seemed rather likely. If one or more of the subjects began to cough from breath-tainted air, Padril could claim it was smoke causing them to cough, and thereafter deny him the mastery. It would fit well with the heavy man's twisted sense of humor, but Rion had a joke of his own to play.

It took an enormous amount of concentration and effort, but Rion did find it possible to steal the air from around Padril and distribute it among his six subjects. He didn't take all of Padril's air, of course, just enough to keep his subjects breathing freely. And the most amusing part of it all was that Padril never noticed the loss.

Or at least didn't notice it to begin with. The Adept seemed prepared to wait even longer than previously before acknowledging Rion's mastery, but then there was an abrupt change in his plans. It was Padril who began to cough and choke, and then the heavy man was unsealing the room in order to get outside. Rion waited until the smoke was completely gone before unshielding his subjects, and then he strolled out to where Padril stood gulping air and occasionally still choking.

"Not a single cough or gasp in the lot," he observed laconically to the Adept. "Except for you, that is. That's a full four masteries, I believe, sir. Am I mistaken?"

For an instant Padril seemed ready to deny Rion's claim, then fear replaced frustration in his eyes. He seemed to know at last that he dealt with a superior, and his words confirmed the surmise.

"Yes, sir, that *is* a full four masteries," he agreed, now sounding extremely servile. "Excuse me for not having congratulated you at once, the oversight was unforgivable. Allow me to offer you tea to refresh yourself with, and I'll fetch it myself. Just follow me, if you please."

Rion found the man's cringing homage more disgusting than satisfying, but he still followed him out of the building and back toward the eating area. He intended to have something to eat along with the tea, but more importantly meant to do some thinking. He hadn't had the time before, but now. . . .

Now he reclaimed his lunch table, and put the question to himself clearly: if members of the nobility weren't anywhere around there, then where were they? And more to the point, why wasn't *he* there with them? Could Mother have had something to do with his placement, and if so, why would she have done such a thing?

And last but certainly not least: how could he undo whatever was done and finally get to where he really belonged?

FOUR
TAMRISSA DOMON—FIRE MAGIC

The day had become a warm one, but the canopy overhead shielded everyone having lunch from the noonday sun. And there were quite a lot of others having lunch besides me, more than thirty of them. Most of the people were women, just as Soonen, my Adept guide, had claimed, but that was the only difference among the lot of them. Once they'd shown up most of them had spent their time drinking tea, with only one or two drifting over to the practice cubicles. But not to practice, certainly not. I was the one who practiced, while they stared into a cubicle for a while and then walked away.

I sipped at my tea in an effort to calm my annoyance, which now threatened to get out of hand again. It hadn't been much of a problem while I'd been practicing, not with all the strength I'd been expending, but lunch had done a good job of restoring my energies. And being outdoors seemed to help as well. I enjoyed being outdoors, but. . . .

But I was far from being happy. I sipped tea as I looked around again, wondering for the tenth or twentieth time if everyone else there was the same sort of incompetent want-to-be that I suspected Soonen was. My Adept guide had proven to be an arrogant idiot much like Beldara Lant, the

21

woman who shared my aspect and had shared my residence until yesterday. Beldara was convinced she was the best at Fire magic ever to have been born, but she hadn't yet been able to justify the claim with actions.

Soonen claimed to be an Adept, but she'd spent her time calling me useless and helpless, and hadn't even been able to demonstrate the third exercise I was supposed to do. The woman had seemed to be trying deliberately to make me lose control of both my temper and my talent, and I couldn't understand that. If the testing authority didn't want us to qualify for the competition for High practitioner, what were they after instead?

Any possible answer to that would be one designed to make me shiver or tremble, so it wasn't a great disappointment not being able to think of one. Simply knowing I walked a very thin line with various disasters waiting on all sides for a misstep was enough to keep my insides in a permanent twist, at least when I stopped to think about it. What I'd tried to keep in mind instead was the agreement the others at the residence and I had come to: keep moving forward. Nothing about our situation was certain, except for the fact that falling behind would bring immediate disaster, while moving forward at least postponed the time of trouble.

I took a deep breath to ease the fluttering in my middle, and saw Soonen rise from the table she'd shared with two other women. That table had been near one filled mostly with men, but she hadn't even glanced in their direction. Now she made her way toward me, tall and imposing with her arrogant stride, the beginning of a sneer on her plain, undistinguished face.

"If you're through stuffing yourself, it's time you got back to practicing," she said as she stopped beside my table to look down at me. "You don't have forever to make your pitiful attempts at testing, you know, so you'd better get moving."

"If I don't have forever, then I ought to make my pitiful attempt right now," I answered, using my nervousness over the test to counter rising annoyance. "Who did you say I had to speak to about watching me?"

"Gerdol is your examiner," she responded automatically, then shook her head as if to dismiss the entire idea. "But that's ridiculous. You can't possibly be ready after only a single morning's practice. If you think I intend to bother Gerdol for nothing, you have another think coming."

"Either *you* can call him, or I will," I stated, flatly refusing to let her get a rise out of me—at least where she could see it. "If I can't do it, we'll all soon know."

"Yes, yes we will," she said, brightening with the idea of my failure. "And then I'll be rid of you, so it's worth bothering Gerdol after all. I'll be right back."

Her enjoyment and happiness were clear as she made her way toward the table holding mostly men, but by the time she reached it she'd lost a good deal of both. Even though she'd said there were more women than men in our aspect, the only ones who could be examiners were men. That arrangement was an old story, but she acted as if it were brand new—or could be changed by complaining about it. Her complaints had about as much chance to change things as mine would have about my parents trying to sell me into marriage again. Apparently Soonen had never learned that if you don't like the way something is, you have to find a way to change it.

Soonen spoke diffidently to one of the seated men, and after a moment he rose and followed her away from the table. He wasn't a very tall man—a bit shorter than Soonen, in fact—and he had whiskers framing his face. No mustache hid the annoyance in his expression, and he was a bit on the plump side. He followed Soonen at his own deliberate pace, and when he reached my table he frowned down at me.

"I'm given to understand that you've already requested an examiner," he said in a deep, heavy voice. "Can that possibly be true?"

"It can be and is," I answered, hating the way my voice trembled at his obvious disapproval. "I don't blame you for not wanting to take Soonen's word for things, but this time she happens to be right."

Soonen drew her breath in angrily at that, but Gerdol first raised his brows, then chuckled.

"Well, it's been some time since we've had a lady of proper tastes in these precincts," he said, his tone having softened as he looked me over. "Come along, my dear, and do the best you're able. If you find it beyond you to complete the course today, there's always tomorrow or the day after."

He offered his hand to help me rise, and I forced myself to take it as well as to smile my thanks. Jovvi had mentioned how easy it was to use men's weaknesses against them, but I hadn't understood what she meant until just this minute. Soonen complained and apparently made a nuisance of herself, but she would have gotten a lot farther if the men around her wanted to impress her. If a system is designed to exclude you, doesn't it make sense to maneuver members of that system to where they *want* to change it?

That latest line of thought was a bit frightening, but not as much as the testing I was about to undergo. I would have preferred to think about social change, but as soon as Gerdol led me to the first practice cubicle, all my attention centered on what was about to be done. I moved into the cubicle, took a deep breath, then stepped hard on the lever on the floor in front of me. The lever caused a box to fly open and a wide cloud of soil to be thrown into the air, and then it was time to perform.

Reaching for the power had never been very hard, but lately it had developed into a reflex like opening my eyes after hearing a strange sound. It was there almost before I realized it, already having woven my fires into the necessary patterns, sending flame to consume every grain of soil in the air. My fires had to be very hot to accomplish that trick, and when I let them fade again there wasn't even a hint of soil left.

"Well, that was quite impressive, my dear," Adept Gerdol said with pleased indulgence, as if he were speaking to a precocious child. That undoubtedly meant he was able to do the same, and I was about to ask him not to talk down to me when I heard the sound of a bird scolding. I quickly looked up and sure enough, there was the brown, gold, and white chickadee.

I still found it difficult to believe, but all morning while I practiced I'd had the company of that bird. It seemed to have no fear of the fire I used, which was strange enough in itself. Add to that its manner of seeming to support and encourage me when I needed it the most, and you have something that goes beyond strange. Now it seemed to be telling me to keep my mouth closed, a reminder I needed. Lately I'd found that using the power seemed to calm many of my fears and apprehensions, but fortunately or unfortunately, the state of mind didn't stay with me for long.

"Yes, quite impressive," Adept Gerdol was saying as I turned to him. "That's one mastery to your credit, and if you'd like to leave the next until later or tomorrow, I'll join you for a cup of tea."

"I'd be delighted to share tea with you later, Adept Gerdol," I answered in a way that would have made Jovvi proud of me. "Right now, though, I prefer to continue. Once all this testing business is behind me, my mind will be clear enough to concentrate on other things."

"Of course, my dear, I quite understand," Adept Gerdol said as he took my hand and patted it. "We'll continue on as long as you're able, and then we'll have tea."

He led me by the hand to the next cubicle, and I caught a glance of Soonen on the way. The woman had her lip curled into a sneer over the way Gerdol was behaving with my encouragement, which showed she didn't understand the true state of affairs. She'd been the one to give me the idea about trying manipulation when she'd spoken about how men reacted to my "sort," so it was completely accurate to say that she was directly responsible for everything I did.

And that might even include my performance during the tests. I'd finally forced myself to admit that I wanted to *show* the woman, show her what I could do and that I wasn't the helpless little toy she'd claimed.

The second cubicle had a pull cord which released a wide spray of water from a tank overhead. Even as I yanked on the cord I heard a trill of avian support and encouragement.

But by then I had the power flowing through me again,

and the object this time was to burn the water without creating steam. Once again the feat required the use of a woven pattern in my very hot fires, but then that, too, was done.

"Excellent, my dear, truly excellent," Adept Gerdol said heartily with triumphant birdsong as a faint backdrop. "Two masteries one after the other. You'll certainly want to try for the third, and afterward we'll have our tea and discuss the best way to increase your precision."

I turned to the man again with a smile and a nod, but on the inside I was fuming. The oaf expected me to fail at the next exercise, just the way Soonen had almost certainly failed and possibly the way *he* had. The haunted part of my mind feared that they would prove to be right, but the rest of me was too bloody angry to even consider failure. But not too angry to use strong words like "bloody," at least to myself. I'd never said that word out loud, and probably never would.

I walked to the third cubicle surrounded by the most calming birdsong I'd ever heard, so that when I stepped inside I felt less angered and more controlled. The thought came that it would be marvelous to be able to take that bird home and feed it seed and bread until it was too heavy to fly, but that wasn't likely to become possible. The bird wasn't really there to support me, I simply needed to believe it was.

So I held to my beliefs as I looked at the pile of wood thrown one piece on top of another in the middle of the cubicle. The pieces were each about a foot in length and were carved into different shapes, an oval shape with a splotch of blue paint just visible in the pile's middle. The piece with the orange paint splotch which had been there earlier had had to be replaced, and I'd done the replacing myself.

Both Soonen and Adept Gerdol stood waiting silently for me to fail, undoubtedly thinking that I couldn't yet be up to burning one single piece of wood in the pile without at least singeing some of the others. At first I hadn't thought I could do it either, but then I'd tried it—and had discovered I already knew how to keep my flames from burning what they shouldn't. Once or twice I'd had occasion to guard what surrounded my fires, like when Jovvi's sponsor had come to the residence, and the woman's two henchmen had tried to hurt Jovvi and me. I hadn't considered that practice at the time, but apparently it had been nothing else.

"The oval piece of wood, with the blue splotch of paint," I said, naming my target, more than eager to get on with it and have it behind me. When Adept Gerdol murmured his agreement that he saw the piece, I took it as my cue to begin. Yellow-red fire flared all around the oval piece of wood, making me think of winter and logs in the fireplace. But only that one small piece of wood burned (and somewhere far away a part of me marveled that I was able to protect things from my flames as well as burn them—most people never mentioned anything about the protecting part) and then it was all done.

"You've burned it," Adept Gerdol said slowly, now sounding numb. "Without burning any of the other pieces. You've mastered it."

"She couldn't have," Soonen protested, again sounding furious. "There are probably singe marks all over the pieces in places we can't see from here."

"Then go and take a closer look," I offered, turning to regard both of them. "I got rid of every singed piece in the cubicle before lunch, so any you find will prove that I failed."

The two Adepts had gone pale for some reason, but that didn't stop Soonen from pushing past me to get to the wood pile. She began to turn over pieces of wood, after a moment throwing them harder and harder. That spoke more clearly than any words she might have used.

"There aren't any singed pieces, and the third mastery is yours, Dama," Adept Gerdol said, just as if he were a stranger. "Would you care to continue on, or would you prefer to rest for a short while first?"

"Continue on," I answered, wondering why he was acting so strangely. The next three cubicles required an increasingly more delicate touch, but there didn't seem to be much doubt that I'd master that group as well. And my decision to continue on seemed to frighten him even more. He bowed his agreement shakily, then held out a hand to ask me to precede him. So we left Soonen still raging among the pieces of wood, and went to the next cubicle.

That one had wedges of leather rather than lengths of wood, and the following cubicle had strips of cloth. When I'd been practicing the cloth had really made me worry, but then I'd realized that protection was protection. It took the same effort and amount of power to protect cloth as it did to protect wood, even though that didn't seem quite right. It should have been harder to protect cloth, and I had to keep reminding myself that it wasn't.

Especially when I reached the last cubicle, which contained feathers. That one really made me nervous, and by then Soonen was back with us. She wore the oddest expression, something like terrified anger, and Adept Gerdol's expression wasn't much better. The man was obviously nervous and disturbed, and his patronizing had turned to obsequiousness.

"You're supposed to choose the ten feathers I'm to burn," I reminded him, turning in the cubicle's doorway. "Would you like to begin?"

"*Ten* feathers?" he echoed, shaking his head with a frown. "You only need to burn three, Dama. Where could you possibly have gotten the idea of ten?"

"I must have misheard," I said, only glancing at a Soonen who had frozen where she stood. She was the one who had told me ten feathers were required, probably to frighten me into believing I'd never do it. But it hadn't worked out that way, since I'd practiced—and had gotten—ten feathers cleanly burned. Hearing the truth actually relaxed me, so I turned back to the pile of feathers with full confidence underscored by happy birdsong.

Adept Gerdol chose the three most difficult feathers to reach, of course, but once I'd burned the last of them Soonen didn't even suggest there might be singeing. Unprotected feathers don't singe, they burn, a lesson I'd learned well the first time I'd practiced with them. I'd been nervous and unsure of myself then, but now I turned back to the two Adepts with more confidence than I could remember feeling in many years.

"I believe that that's the last of it," I said, speaking only to Adept Gerdol. "If you'll declare the mastery, I'll be able to go and have that tea."

"Of course, Dama, of course I declare the mastery," he assured me quickly while I thought about having something a lot more substantial along with the tea. I'd just finished lunch a short while ago, but I still felt completely hollow. "Allow me the honor of escorting you back to your table and ordering the tea for you."

He offered his arm in a way that looked downright diffident, as though he might possibly be afraid of my turning my fires on *him*. As an Adept he should have had nothing to worry about; after all, it stood to reason that if you were able to protect feathers from burning, you should have no trouble protecting yourself.

But once I'd taken his arm, it came back to me that he— and Soonen—probably weren't able to do that exercise. How they'd gotten to be Adepts without it I had no idea, but I was almost completely certain that that had to be the case. They hadn't been able to attain the masteries but I had, and that must be what they were afraid of. I was stronger than they were, and they hadn't been very nice to me.

I let Adept Gerdol seat me at the table, feeling a small chill creep around my backbone. The fear the two people were showing couldn't be based on the possibility that I might turn out to be offended by their previous behavior. It had to come from reality and past experience, specifically with others who'd proven to be stronger and had also done something to them or to people they knew.

All of which made me uneasy about what sort of situation I would soon be moving into. Tomorrow Soonen would be attacking me with her ability while I performed the same exercises, and I'd have to protect myself as well as gain the masteries. Assuming I was able to do that I would then move to the first of the competitions, and afterward I would have to face someone of my own strength in a direct confrontation.

Someone who might possibly be trying seriously to kill me. My insides lurched at that thought, making it impossible for me to hear what Adept Gerdol was saying to me. My life might well be in danger soon, and I didn't quite know how to handle the idea. In desperation I looked around for my bird friend, needing its support, but it seemed to be gone.

And that, I couldn't help thinking, would prove to be more of an omen than a natural occurrence. . . .

FIVE

VALLANT RO—WATER MAGIC

Vallant sat at the table after having finished his lunch, lost to the pleasure of beautiful birdsong. The woodsy music not only reminded him that he was out of doors, it told him that his bird-supporter was still here. It had kept him company all morning, showing up when he first began to practice.

He looked around then, seeing his Adept guide Wimand sitting a short distance away with two cronies. Vallant was supposed to have waited until after lunch to begin his practice, but he'd been so desperate to get away from Wimand's chattering that he'd taken the first opportunity to begin practicing. Holter hadn't used the first practice cubicle long, which was only to be expected. Despite Wimand's loudly-voiced opinions to the contrary, Holter was every bit as good as Vallant in Water magic.

And that despite the fact that Pagin Holter was a former stableman, a member of the lowest class. Wimand was sure

Holter would quickly reach his limit and thereafter fail, but Vallant knew what was driving the small man he shared a talent with. Holter was the only duplicate talent left in Vallant's residence, and the hurt Holter felt over being rejected by his longtime friends also made him feel like an outsider among everyone else in the residence. Rather than making him give up, the hurt had made Holter completely determined to succeed in the competitions for High practitioner. Vallant had gone through the qualifying sessions with the man, and therefore knew Holter's chances were excellent.

And, in a manner of speaking, a lot better than Vallant's chances. He raised his teacup and took a bracing swallow, but would have needed something as strong as brandy to really feel braced. Vallant had a problem with enclosed spaces, and while the preliminary practice areas were out of doors, the competitions were held in a large, white resin building. A large, white, *windowless* resin building, which made the place feel a lot smaller than everyone else undoubtedly considered it.

But Vallant had to master the various practices, and then *had* to move on to the competitions. He and the others in the residence had agreed that failing to qualify would bring big trouble, even if they didn't yet know what that trouble consisted of. Moving ahead would probably bring trouble as well, but that would be sometime in the future, while failure would bring immediate results.

So Vallant *had* to keep going forward, but the thought of needing to walk into—and stay in—a windowless box for an indeterminate amount of time made his insides twist and a cold sweat break out on his forehead. He'd been able to avoid thinking about it while he practiced this morning, but now even the encouraging birdsong wasn't helping. He *had* to master those practice problems, but if he did. . . .

"You took my advice and had the fish for lunch," a voice said, and Vallant looked up to see that Wimand had come over without his noticing the Adept's approach. "How did you like it?"

"It was excellent," Vallant answered, deciding against

telling the man that any seaport dining parlor could have done better. "Now I'd like to know how I go about earnin' those silver dins you said would be paid when I mastered the practice areas."

"You can't mean you think you're ready to ask for an examiner," Wimand said with a small, incredulous laugh. "I know that your . . . companion has asked Adept Podon to witness his own attempt, but trying to keep up with the man is pointless. He'll certainly fail to establish mastery, and you'll look a good deal better by not joining him in that failure."

"What I expect to do is join him in success," Vallant replied, getting to his feet to look down at Wimand. The man's narrowminded prejudice was something Vallant no longer had the patience for, and therefore no longer intended to put up with. "Podon has made Holter wait for an extra hour, but now that they're gettin' started, I intend to be right behind them."

"You'd do better to insist on going first," Wimand responded with a petulant frown. "If you absolutely must go against my advice about the testing, at least arrange things so that the peasant follows *your* lead, rather than you following his."

"No," Vallant stated shortly, fighting to keep his expression from showing the contempt he felt for Wimand. "We'll do it my way rather than yours. Let's go."

Wimand threw his hands up in exasperated agreement, then led the way toward the first practice cubicle. Holter and his Adept guide Podon were already leaving the cubicle, and the two Adepts exchanged a nod.

"Now, see?" Wimand told Vallant in a low voice. "The peasant has mastered the first practice, leaving you to match him. If you're expecting to surpass him when he reaches the point of failure, I hope you're not overrating your own level of ability."

"I guess we'll be findin' out," Vallant said, forcing himself not to add to the fairly neutral words. "In this cubicle,

I'm to use the vat of ready water to surround those resin circles with water. Isn't that right?''

"First you surround all six forms at once," Wimand clarified, stepping into the cubicle to push the round forms on their movable pedestals together. "As soon as you've done that, I'll separate the six into two groups of three, and then you surround the two groups."

"Then it becomes three groups of two, and finally six individual groups," Vallant put in, to hurry the explanation he had no need of. "All right, here goes."

Vallant used the ready water to surround the six head-sized resin forms, with that bird perched on the top of the cubicle and trilling approvingly all the while. Each time Vallant did what he was supposed to, until all six of the forms were individually surrounded by water. Keeping the globes of water separate had given him some trouble until he'd remembered the sessions exercises he'd done to qualify for this place, and then the problem had been solved.

"Well, at least you haven't been left behind," Wimand said with grudging approval when he'd finished. "Now let's go see how the peasant has done in the second area."

Once again Holter and Podon were leaving as Vallant and Wimand approached, and for the second time the two Adepts exchanged nods. Podon looked . . . faintly nervous but also faintly pleased, which managed to deepen Wimand's frown.

"In case you missed that, the peasant has apparently done it again," he told Vallant accusingly. "I tried to point out how bad an idea this was, but you refused to listen. Assuming Podon isn't giving the man a bit of unmentioned help, you'll certainly regret not having listened to me."

"This second cubicle has those six breadboxes I'm supposed to fill with water," Vallant said, again ignoring Wimand's complaints. "If I do it right, the water will collect in a bowl inside each box, and won't leak out until the bottom of each bowl gets released by the rope pull. I start doin' it in one box, then in two together, three together, and so on until I'm up to fillin' all six boxes at once."

"Yes, that's quite correct," Wimand agreed, sounding

faintly bored. "Now you have only to accomplish it as easily as you discuss it."

It was clear that Wimand didn't expect Vallant to succeed, but Wimand was in for a surprise. Vallant hadn't been expecting to learn something new about his talent, but this particular exercise had taught him that he could *feel* things through the use of that talent. Without knowing how it worked, Vallant had been able to tell the precise size of each box's innards, as well as where each water-catch dish was positioned. The discovery had made the third practice area very much easier rather than harder, which meant that if Holter had discovered the same thing, he was in the midst of gaining his third mastery.

But Vallant still had to earn his second, so he turned his attention to the breadboxes without bread. Putting water into first one, then two, was boring when he could have *started* with doing all six at once, but he didn't say so. He simply did the exercise the way they expected him to, and when Wimand emptied the last dish in the last box, he turned to the Adept.

"It looks like I've matched Holter again," Vallant drawled, distantly wondering why Wimand was beginning to look shaken. "Shall we continue on and see if I can do it a third time?"

"Yes . . . yes, of course you'll continue on," Wimand said, his stuffy superiority apparently forgotten. "Please come this way."

He led off in the direction of the next cubicle, and Vallant raised his brows a bit as he followed. Something was bothering the so-called Adept, and it must have been serious if he hadn't even knocked Holter again. It wasn't far to the next cubicle, only a matter of feet, but even as they approached, Podon turned to give Wimand an unreadable glance.

"Gotta give Dom Holter here congratulations," Podon said to Wimand in an over-hearty voice. "He just got th' third mastery, 'n now he's ready t' start t'morra with practicin' usin' water from th' air."

"Well, Dom Holter, I do congratulate you," Wimand burbled like a young lady being introduced to the gentleman she'd had a longtime, distant crush on. "But I was certain you'd be able to do it, and I said as much to Dom Ro here. Who has only to complete this last exercise before being in the same position."

Some sort of disturbance flashed in Podon's eyes as he made noises to show how impressed he was, but Holter turned to Vallant with a faint grin.

"Go get 'em, man," he said warmly, then walked away toward the tables with Podon trailing eagerly after him. He'd have to discuss what might be going on later with Holter, but right now he had a mastery to earn.

The third cubicle had a curtain across the middle of it, and behind the curtain were different-sized boxes. Vallant had to fill them in the same way he'd filled the previous boxes, only here he wasn't allowed to *see* any of them. He had to discover their sizes through the use of his talent, but he already knew how to do that. So he reached to the vat of ready water with the fingers of his talent, and began to do the exercise.

When he was through, Wimand silently tripped the hidden boxes one after the other. Each one yielded the gush of water it was supposed to, and when the last, smallest box responded properly the Adept turned to Vallant.

"Let me be the first to offer my congratulations, sir," Wimand said in an unsteady voice, his forced smile looking just short of ghastly. "You've achieved the third mastery along with the other gentleman, and now the two of you are ready to begin practice tomorrow on the next level of achievement. May I accompany you back to your table and order you some tea?"

"I think I'll have a sandwich as well," Vallant said with a nod, feeling mellow and pleased. He'd also gotten congratulations from his bird friend, which for some reason were more welcome than Wimand's. And yet a glance around showed that the bird was now gone, disappointing despite being nothing more than expected. Vallant considered the bird his good luck charm, but had to admit he probably wouldn't need any more good luck today.

"And I believe I'll share Holter's table rather than sit alone again," he continued as he followed Wimand back toward the eating area. "Sharin' the success, and all that."

"Yes, yes of course," Wimand agreed instantly, but the man looked more distracted than attentive. Once again Vallant wondered what was wrong, but wasn't certain he ought to ask. Maybe tomorrow . . . after discussing the matter with the others tonight . . . and finding out how Tamrissa had done. . . .

I can still remember how . . . superior I felt back then, cautiously superior but still better than everyone else. The great achievement had been so easy. . . . If I'd known how short a time I'd be feeling like that, I might have enjoyed it more. Well, you'll find out all about it, but only when it becomes time to tell you.

Right now you have to meet our opposite numbers, the people who became our greatest enemies—or so we thought. Nothing worked out the way we expected it would . . . or hoped it would . . . or generally wished it to. And now that I think about it, I suppose their Five could say the same thing. . . .

Six

Bron Kallan—Fire magic

"I hate this, Bron, I really hate it," Nialla complained, leaning up on her elbows in the bed. "I expected you to stay for a while, and here you are getting ready to leave."

"Some of us do have obligations in this life, Nialla," Lord Bron Kallan replied distractedly while checking his long, dark-red hair in Nialla's full-length mirror. "I happen to have an appointment this afternoon, and I don't care to be late for it."

"You don't *dare* be late for it, you mean," Nialla retorted, trying to be as cutting as most of the ladies of her class. "Everyone knows they're making you be in one of their silly little pretend Blendings, the ones they're forming to make Adriari's Blending look good. Adriari's will be the first Seated Blending with more women than men, and we all think it's just marvelous."

"That's because none of you *can* think," Bron retorted with a snort, turning to look directly at her. "The only reason the Advisors have chosen a predominantly female Blending this time is because women are easier to give orders to. Instead of arguing about things they don't like, they simply cry a little and then obey. The Advisors are tired of sharing the running of this empire with a strong Blending, so this time they've chosen a weak one."

"Don't be ridiculous," Nialla returned with a sniff, abruptly changing her position when she discovered how flat her breasts looked in the old one. "No one in their right mind would choose a weak Blending, not when they have to be strong enough to defend us from all those crises the Prophecy always talks about. You're just jealous because you'll be nothing but stage dressing for the performance the Advisors will put on."

"Of course, Nialla, you're correct as always," Bron said smoothly, not about to try to explain the difference between strong in talent and strong in character to the featherhead. Nialla had just one talent, and Bron had already made use of it. "It's been as marvelous as always, and I'll certainly see you again soon."

"*If* I'm free," Nialla put in, her pretty face set in a sulk, getting the last word as she so loved to do. Bron ignored it as he left her bedchamber, but his mood was far from light and forgiving. There were quite a few things Nialla didn't know about, and the uncertainty of one of them had been keeping him in a perpetual temper.

So, after closing her bedchamber door, when he saw the antique piano in her sitting room, he suddenly got an idea. She'd had to wait years to get her hands on that piano, it had cost her a fortune in gold, and it was her pride and joy. But she'd called him stage dressing and pettily jealous, and for that she needed to be punished.

It took only an instant for Bron to embrace the power, and then he directed his flames to the piano's sounding board. He didn't want to burn it to ash, and he also made sure nothing else in the instrument was damaged. He simply worked to fire-harden the wood, which would render it useless as a sounding board. The entire piano would be useless until the board was replaced, but replacing it would destroy the instrument's value as a fully-original antique. Nialla would have the choice of giving up playing the thing as she so loved to do, or losing half the investment she'd made.

Feeling how much his mood had lightened, Bron left Nialla's house and called over his carriage and driver. The man was there and waiting for him, of course, and would have been in the same place even if Bron had been twice as long in coming out. His drivers were either constantly and immediately available or they were dismissed, something they were all well aware of.

It wasn't necessary for Bron to tell the driver where to go next, as he'd already listed his itinerary for the man this morning. That was another thing his drivers had to have, a good memory. He was a busy man, and didn't care to be constantly interrupting his thoughts to give directions.

Once Bron was settled the carriage moved off in the direction of Kambil Arstin's house, where the meeting was being held this week. The Advisors had appointed fools from the lower nobility to work with their group of five and strengthen their talents, and once a week an Advisor's agent held a meeting in one of their homes to discuss the group's progress. It was usually a rather unpleasant time, as agents had a tendency to act as if they were one of the Advisors themselves. Bron hated to be told how badly he was doing because of his laziness, but this week's meeting ought to be different.

He smiled at that thought, knowing the meeting ought to be different for all five of them. It was certainly true that Bron's parents knew how much he hated to be pushed and rushed and so had never distressed him with unreasonable demands, but now he had a special purpose for pushing *himself*. The five of them had decided, privately, of course, that *they* would become the Seated Blending. Adriari and her five were weak in all ways, and their competition would be very public. When Bron's five defeated Adriari's in front of hundreds of people, they would become the ones who were ultimately Seated on the Fivefold Throne.

And there would be nothing the Advisors could do about it. Bron's smile changed to a grin as he pictured the way they would all assure the Advisors how loyal and obedient they would be once Seated. That would mollify and silence all protests from the Advisors, but once their Five was Seated their first official action would be to arrest that pack of fools. Simply dismissing them and sending them home would be a good deal more satisfying, but Delin said they were too dangerous to be treated lightly.

Bron's grin disappeared as his thoughts turned to Delin Moord, high lord and Earth magic practitioner. Delin might have been the one to first suggest that they go against the Advisors' wishes, but Bron couldn't swear to that. For some reason he thought of it as his own idea, one that Delin simply supported. Bron sometimes found himself confused in Delin's presence, but most often he felt flattered. Delin's power and social standing were a bit higher than his own, but it was always clear that Delin admired him. Most certainly as he should.

And Bron was certainly the leader of the group that everyone looked up to. Delin made that clear every time they got together *without* the agent, just as he quietly took over handling things when the agent did happen to be there. Lord Rigos and his high-handed ways tended to upset Bron, and it was a relief to have Delin handle the man for him. Especially since Delin made no effort to *keep* control.

Bron smiled again, pleased that Delin's loss was his gain. Almost every member of the nobility Bron knew was as ambitious as he to gain independent gold and power, but not Delin. He seemed content to let others take the lead, which was probably very wise of him. As unassuming as the man was, he'd never get very far.

But the carriage was moving too slowly, Bron suddenly noticed. A glance at a clock before leaving Nialla's house had shown that Bron was running late as usual, something his driver should have known without being told. He'd certainly have to dismiss the man tonight, no matter that the low-class peasant had worked for him for years. The man deserved to be dismissed, but now he needed to be hurried.

Bron leaned forward to shout at his driver, picturing how upset Lord Rigos would be when Bron walked in late again. . . .

SEVEN
SELENDI VAS—AIR MAGIC

"Selendi, dear, why *are* you rushing around like that?"
Mother asked from where she sat at her precious loom, paying more attention to the weaving than to her own daughter.
"I did remind you of your appointment just when you asked
me to, you know."

"No, Mother, I don't know any such thing," Selendi retorted, throwing the scarves she didn't want to the floor. The
chest was piled high with them, every scarf ever bought except for the one she wanted. "You were supposed to have
reminded me over an hour ago, not ten minutes ago. Since
you know how I hate to be late to appointments, I'm convinced you waited the extra hour on purpose."

"But dear, you were with that marvelous young what's-
his-name, the son of Alette Rumil," Mother protested in that
high voice she used when she felt unjustly accused—and
which never failed to jangle Selendi's nerves even more.
"He's going to be a very important man some day, just like
his father, so how *could* I interrupt?"

"You could have done it easily, and he probably wouldn't
even have noticed," Selendi told her with an angry glance
her mother never saw. "He's as thick in the head as Alette
has always been, and he's only good for one thing. He may

41

well be a very important man one day, but only if he can
perform as he does now, face down in a bed.''

"Don't be crude, dear, it isn't ladylike," Mother corrected
absently, the same thing she always said when she'd driven
Selendi into the foulest of moods. "Alette is simply a bit . . .
easygoing when it comes to understanding things, and her
son obviously takes after her. But he also takes after her in
looks, you'll have to admit. He's one of the handsomest men
I've ever seen."

"You've always been partial to blonds, and if you weren't
sitting there doing manual labor I would have brought him
in to meet you," Selendi said, partially distracted by the fact
that she'd now discarded every scarf in the chest, and still
hadn't found the one she wanted. "What could have happened to it? I know I saw it in here only a few days ago."

"Please don't be disgusting, Selendi," Mother protested,
finally looking up from the ridiculous contraption. "I'm not
doing manual labor, I'm indulging in one of the most popular
current hobbies. I'm sure the boy would understand since his
mother does almost the same thing when she remembers, so
next time do bring him in to meet me. After that I'll handle
the matter myself, but—What *are* you looking for?"

"I want that pale blue scarf of yours," Selendi answered,
turning away from the scattered mess. "It's the only scarf
that goes really well with this dress, and I'm not leaving here
until I find it."

"You should have told me what you were looking for
sooner, dear," Mother said with that defensive reproof she
was so good at producing. "I loaned the scarf to your sister
two days ago, and she hasn't returned it yet."

"Mother, how *could* you?" Selendi demanded, finding
that the last straw. "You should have known I'd want the
thing; you were there when I had the final fitting on this
dress! Now there's nothing decent to go with it and I'll look
like the frump of the ages, all because you never think about
me. If I had the time, I'd cry. My own mother, caring nothing
about me. . . ."

Selendi let her voice trail off, actually almost as wounded
as she'd said she was. Every time Mother gave something to

Leta, it was one less thing to be given to *her*. She didn't know how Mother could treat her like that, but at least her protest had silenced the silly woman with well-earned guilt. And she had to leave right now, otherwise she really would be late.

"But dear, can't you simply change your dress?" Mother began, trying to throw off responsibility the way she always did. "It seems to me—"

"We'll have to continue this discussion later, Mother," Selendi interrupted as she headed out of her mother's bed-chamber. "And you can be sure I'll remember this the next time Emar Rumil comes to visit. Do enjoy your manual labor."

The sound of Mother's indrawn breath of disappointment gave Selendi a good deal of satisfaction, but she hadn't the time to enjoy it now as thoroughly as she would have liked. Her carriage would be waiting outside, so she used thickened air to push the stupid servants out of her way, including the one carrying the tea service. Both service and tea ended up on the floor with a crash, but it didn't matter in the least. Selendi was already past the mess and halfway out the door, so she didn't even get her hem splashed.

Her driver knew the way to Kambil Arstin's house, so she simply had to say where she was going and they were on their way. Her driver was an absolute delight, and not too bad in bed, either. She'd used him a time or two when no one else was available, and the way he'd strutted afterward had amused her. Most peasants knew when they were more than ordinarily privileged, and his strutting would remain amusing as long as he didn't try to put on airs with *her*.

Not that he would, unlike some of the men of her own class. Most of them were absolutely insufferable, even the thickheaded ones like Emar Rumil. Bron Kallan was one like that, and as soon as she tried him in bed she'd probably tell him exactly what she thought of him. Unless he was as good as she'd heard. If he was she'd wait until she tired of him, which wasn't likely to take long. It never took long with any of them, probably because they were so insufferable.

Selendi made herself more comfortable on the carriage

seat, finally having the time to think about where she was going. The rest of the five she'd been forced to join were men, but they seemed to want as much out of life as she did. It was difficult to imagine men being dissatisfied when most of them at least had the chance to do anything they pleased. *Their* mothers were not constantly at them, insisting this or that wasn't ladylike or refined enough. She was beyond being sick of hearing about limits, and had hated it even more when the Advisors' agent had forced her to do what she had no real interest in.

But that made their secret plans all the more delicious. When she and the men defeated that stuck-up Adriari's five to become the Blending that would eventually be Seated, they'd be able to begin their plans for absolute freedom. The Advisors would regret having made them participate in this stupid waste of time called competition that only the peasants took seriously, and *her* parents at least would regret how little they'd cared about her over the years.

Selendi smiled at that thought, wondering what she might do to them first. Her father did something or other in the government, so dismissing him would be easy. And if she told him it was happening because Mother had been so cruel to her. . . . Yes, that should settle Mother's hash nicely. The least she would lose would be her collection of handsome boys, which would certainly make *her* regret that she hadn't been more generous with her most important daughter.

That still left Leta to be gotten even with, which would certainly turn out to be something of a problem. Selendi frowned and shifted in annoyance at the thought of her older sister, whom everyone said took mostly after Father. Leta had no more magical talent than anyone else, but somehow she'd always managed to do exactly what she wanted to. The one time they'd had a serious argument, Selendi had lost.

She still had to take a deep breath at the memory of that, to calm the rage tinged with fear she always felt when thinking about it. They'd both been a lot younger, Selendi barely into her teens with Leta three years older. They'd been arguing about something Selendi couldn't quite remember the details of, but it had been an important something to Leta. She'd usually shrugged over and ignored anything Selendi did, but that time she'd refused to back down. Yes, now she remembered. It had been when Selendi had told the servants to throw away that useless stand of books in the solarium, to make room for the new lounge chair Selendi had just had delivered.

"No, those books will *not* be touched," Leta had announced coolly, sending the servants away. "I haven't finished reading them yet, and I won't want them thrown out even when I *have* finished."

"Then throw away some of the books in your apartment so you can move *these* in," Selendi had countered reasonably, determined to make things work out right. "Or get Father to throw away some of his, and put them in the library. I don't care *what* you do with them, as long as you get them out of *here*."

"Someone should have mentioned to you sooner that you don't own this house," Leta had said with a sound of ridicule that had made Selendi feel completely incensed. "If Father wants the books moved then I'll move them, but you have no say in the matter. Try to confine your selfishness and spoiled-brat behavior to your own life. Mother has to put up with it because she caused it, but I didn't so I don't."

And Leta had started to turn away, arrogantly considering the matter settled. That had brought Selendi up to true fury, and without thinking she'd reached toward Leta with her talent. She'd actually done very little practicing with Air magic until then, but what she'd lacked in finesse she made up in strength. She thickened the air around Leta, just enough to make it unbreathable, knowing Leta's feeble Air magic would never be able to save her.

And Leta's Air magic hadn't. It was Leta herself, obviously holding her breath, who turned back to Selendi and slapped her so hard across the face that Selendi was knocked down. In deep shock she'd half-lain on the floor, her ears ringing and her cheek blazing with pain, and Leta had bent down to take her by the hair and painfully yank her head up.

''It's a shame this must be the first time anyone has ever raised a hand to you,'' Leta had growled softly in a voice that sent shivers through Selendi. ''If you'd been properly punished sooner, I would have been saved the trouble of having to do this. Listen to me, you little slut, and believe what I say: if you ever try to use your ability against me again, I'll kill you. Afterward I'll be hysterical because of the 'accident' and everyone will commiserate and comfort me, and you'll be dead. Don't make the mistake of thinking I'm not serious. If you have to learn the truth the hard way, you'll never learn anything beyond it. And from now on stay completely out of my way.''

She'd shoved Selendi away then and had straightened and left, but it had been quite a while before Selendi had been able to leave herself. Leta had terrified her, and as much like Father as Leta was, Selendi didn't doubt for a moment that Leta had spoken the absolute truth. She'd taken pains to stay away from her sister and her sister's possessions after that, but her hatred of Leta had grown stronger and stronger over the years.

So Selendi had to do *something* to get even with her sister once they were in power, but she didn't know what or how. She couldn't very well face Leta personally, but maybe one or two of the men. . . . Yes, that might work, especially when they needed *her* cooperation to win the Throne. She would cooperate in return for a small favor, one they owed her anyway simply because she was there. She'd have to mention the point after they spoke to that agent, and the loathsome man was gone.

Selendi, once again more pleased with the world, settled back to enjoy the rest of the ride. Being involved with men somewhere other than bed might not be so bad after all, but which ones should she send after Leta? She'd have to think about it for a while, but one of them would have to be Delin Moord. He'd be able to frighten even Leta, if even half of what she'd seen in his eyes the time or two he'd let his mask drop was true. . . .

EIGHT
HOMIN WEIL—WATER MAGIC

Homin crept through the bedchamber, holding his breath to keep it from coming out in great, noisy gasps. His father's new wife Elfini was currently taking her nap, and the last thing Homin wanted to do was waken her. She'd certainly arranged things so that he *would* awaken her, but it was just possible he might get around that. Actually he *had* to get around it, as the time to leave for the meeting was fast approaching. Going through the litany would take much too long, but if Elfini awoke she would certainly insist on it. . . .

"What are you doing in my bedchamber, Homin?" Elfini's voice came suddenly out of the dimness, nearly making Homin's heart stop dead. "This is supposed to be my nap time."

"I—I need my—identification bracelet," Homin croaked unsteadily, his insides tightening with every word. He hadn't even straightened out of his hunched-over posture, and probably wouldn't until he was out of there again. "I—took it off for my—bath, and when I returned from the—bath house it was gone. I—looked everywhere for it—before realizing you must have—accidentally walked away with it. I can't go to the meeting without it, so—"

47

"So you came barging into my bedchamber as if I were one of the maids," Elfini interrupted, her tone very flat. "But now that you *are* here, we can review the lesson. You do remember the lesson, don't you?"

"Elfini, please," he begged in a whisper, unable to look at her where she sat up in the bed. "I'm not my father, and I don't enjoy this sort of thing. I just want my identification bracelet back, and then I can—"

"How dare you try to be impertinent with me, boy?" she interrupted again to demand, her voice much colder than it had been—which he hadn't thought would be possible. "Recite the first of the lessons I taught you, and do it now!"

"Elfini is the mistress of this household," Homin recited at once, too frightened not to. "Elfini is also the mistress of everyone *in* the household. If anyone in her household disobeys or displeases Elfini, she will not hesitate to discipline them. Please, Elfini, I'm going to be late—"

"And you claim to understand what you just babbled out?" Elfini said, scorn dripping from every word. "You insist you disliked your first taste of discipline, but your actions fairly beg for another dose. But I do have to remember how delicate you are. Go to my special wardrobe, and fetch out the light whip."

"Lord Rigos will force me to tell him why I'm late!" Homin blurted out, his desperation almost as great as his fear. "You know how frightened I am of him, and when he turns those eyes on me I simply can't lie. He's already said he'll take stern measures with anyone who tries to disrupt our group, and the anyone includes our families. Lord Rigos is—"

"I know who Lord Rigos is!" Elfini snapped, furious anger now rippling her control. "We've known and hated each other for a number of years now, and he'd just love to interfere with my—Homin, your bracelet is here on my night table. Come and get it and then go to your meeting, but report to me as soon as you return. You're a very naughty boy, and I don't allow naughty boys under my roof."

The flood of relief made Homin stagger, but he caught his balance then forced himself to go closer to where Elfini sat.

Because of the dimness he was just about on top of the night table before he saw the bracelet, and after a nervous glance at his stepmother he snatched it up. He'd almost expected her to grab his wrist when he reached for the bracelet, but that wasn't the way she did things.

"Come directly home after that meeting," she said, her shadowy face and inflexible voice sending shivers through him. "And don't say a word to Lord Rigos beyond what you absolutely must. If he disturbs my household, you'll be the one who pays for it."

"Yes, Elfini," he said as quickly as possible, now backing away from the bed. "I'll be home as soon as the meeting is over, and I won't say a word."

She made a sound that was probably dismissal. In any event that was the way Homin took it. He turned and fled her bedchamber, and didn't slow down until he was through the house and out the front door. His carriage waited outside, so he climbed right in and told the driver to take him to Kambil Arstin's house. Only when the carriage began to move did he make the effort to try to relax.

Sweat beaded his forehead so thickly that he needed to blot it with the handkerchief from his pocket to keep it from rolling down into his eyes. Homin was no stranger to fear, but Elfini was somehow worse than his mother had been. Mother had been the same sort of woman, incredibly strong and a firm believer in discipline, but she'd given most of that sort of attention to Father, who actually craved and needed it. Only occasionally had she felt it necessary to teach Homin his place, and the lessons had been hard but not unduly harsh. Elfini, though. . . .

Elfini apparently wanted to break him, just as if he were strong and virile and defiant. Homin whimpered softly as he hid his eyes behind the handkerchief, at a loss to understand how she could think of him like that even for a moment. He hated and feared discipline and so made every attempt to do exactly as Elfini wished, but she still wasn't satisfied. If only Mother hadn't taken sick and died. . . .

But Mother was gone and Father had been so overcome with grief and loss that he'd married Elfini almost immediately. Homin had the feeling Father partially regretted his haste, but it was much too late now to change things. Father might be rather powerful and even feared in his government bureau, but at home he had no more say over matters than Homin did. Possibly less, now that Homin had been drafted as a member of a competing Blending.

Time and distance were working together to drain the tension from Homin, so he took the handkerchief from his eyes and leaned back in his carriage seat. The drive would be long enough for him to pull himself together, but the day was rather warm and he needed something to help calm him even further. To that end he brought down some moderately cold water from the upper reaches of the sky, applied it to his brow, then sighed in temporary satisfaction.

"Very temporary satisfaction," he muttered, already beginning to dread the meeting with Lord Rigos. No one of their class had any interest in wasting time being part of a pretend Blending for the competitions, not when everyone knew who had been chosen to win this time. But the Advisors needed challenging Blendings from the nobility to make the sham look good, so they sent out agents like Lord Rigos to coerce people into cooperation. He still didn't understand how they'd been chosen, not when people without normal ability were somehow involved.

But he *had* been chosen, along with the other four, and now the other four had embroiled him in some sort of secret plot. Homin had been very tempted to tell Lord Rigos about it and then withdraw completely, but the thought of what he might achieve had stopped him. If their rather silly little plot succeeded somehow, they each would have wealth, power— and a household. He would no longer need to share his father's house, and would never need to see Elfini again. He could look for his own woman, one who would be gentle with him, just as Mother had been. . . .

And he would no longer need to lie, as he had about Lord Rigos. Homin had taken the chance that Elfini would, at the very least, be wary of Lord Rigos, and that part of his desperate, hastily-made plan had worked. She did indeed know the Advisory agent, but hadn't needed to bother threatening Homin into silence. Lord Rigos couldn't have cared less about the five of them, as long as they were all able to make *some* kind of showing in the competitions.

Homin's carriage now passed the fringes of a pretty little park, a taste of the countryside in the middle of the city for those who didn't care to travel out to the real countryside. It would have been wonderful to have his driver turn into that park and drop him off, with orders not to come back or tell anyone where he was. Losing himself would have been marvelous, but he couldn't have stayed lost. As soon as the next mealtime came around he would be forced to return home, where Elfini would be waiting even more angrily than she was now.

And he couldn't face the thought of her discipline, he really couldn't. Faint beads of sweat formed on his brow again at what would be waiting for him when he returned home, but he had no idea how to avoid it. There were days and days yet before he would need to stand with the others in the competitions, so even if he begged Lord Rigos's help he wasn't likely to get it. He'd be over the disciplinary session by the time he was needed, so Lord Rigos would simply sneer and dismiss the matter.

But maybe someone else wouldn't. Homin sat straighter when the thought came, an idea he hadn't considered before. The trouble with Elfini was affecting his practice performances, and the others in the group would be unhappy over that. They'd all agreed that they would work to be at their very best, and then they'd have no trouble winning over Adriari Fant's group. Delin Moord had spoken to each of them individually, supporting and encouraging them, scolding them when they needed it, using his charm to get unanimous agreement.

So maybe Delin would be willing to use his charm on Elfini. Homin had promised not to speak to Lord Rigos, but he hadn't said a word about Delin. And Delin *had* said they were to come to him with any problems they might have. It might work, it just might actually work. . . .

Homin dabbed at his brow one last time before putting his handkerchief away, now actually looking forward to the meeting. Or rather to the time after the meeting, when he would be able to speak to Delin. His membership in the group might turn out to have more benefits than he could have possibly imagined. . . .

NINE

KAMBIL ARSTIN—SPIRIT MAGIC

"Since your guests should be arriving soon, I'll get out of the way, Kambil," his grandmother said, giving him one of her usual warm smiles. "But if you need me for anything, don't hesitate to call. I won't be doing anything important."

"You'll be working on your poetry, and you're the only one in the entire world who doesn't consider that important," Kambil countered with a snort as he took her hand and helped her out of the chair. "It's this meeting that's unimportant, Grami, so don't even think you'll be disturbed. If necessary, *I'll* see to it."

"Don't do anything rash with that Lord Rigos around, love," Grami warned, her smile having disappeared. "He's as nasty and dangerous as his father before him, and the fact that he has no talent to speak of is a point of pride with him. He hates those who do have strong talent because of his jealousy of them, but he'll never admit that."

"I know, Grami," Kambil told her gently, patting her hand before releasing it. "I knew all about him five minutes after we met, and continue to make sure I never turn my back on him. Have you suddenly decided you did a terrible job of training me?''

''No, love, I'm just a worrier,'' she replied, good humor immediately restored. For the millionth time Kambil noticed that she was still a handsome, vital woman, thank any Unknown Aspect that might have had anything to do with the matter. Grami was Father's mother, and had come to live with them after Kambil's mother died in childbirth with the infant who would have been his sister. She'd been the center of his universe forever, and even Father was able to relax and enjoy her presence.

''Yes, you *are* a worrier, and I love you for it,'' Kambil said, walking her halfway to the corridor which led to her wing of the house. ''I'll come to your apartment later, and tell you how things went.''

She patted his arm in agreement before continuing out of the wide sitting-entertainment area, her step firm and brisk but not at all hurried. Grami almost never hurried, not unless *she* considered the matter worth hurrying for. She was different from everyone else he knew, kind of crazy, lots of fun, and someone he loved with everything in him. And she never told him what to do, even when she didn't like what he'd gotten involved in.

''Like this whole affair,'' Kambil muttered, turning back to see that everything in the sitting area was prepared for the arrival of his guests. It might have been *some* comfort if he'd fallen into evil company through his own efforts, but he'd actually had nothing to do with being made a part of this group. He'd been noticed by some Guild man or other and been assessed a strong talent, so when they'd needed someone with Spirit magic to round out a group, he'd been drafted.

And now he was part of another group, and that was only a bit more voluntary than his membership in the first. The others had decided that they wanted to be the new Seated Blending, and had made plans to defeat the Blending chosen by the Advisors. It couldn't possibly turn out to be as easy as his four associates expected, but they were all too emotionally involved with the idea to see anything but the end result they aimed at.

So for his own safety, Kambil had made it clear to all of them that he was with them. He wasn't usually a timid man—rather to the contrary—but heroics were definitely not in order with this group. None of them had the least amount of self-control, and there was no doubt that they would react violently toward anyone or anything trying to stand in their way. Even Homin Weil, who seemed to be afraid of everything including his own shadow. All *that* one needed was a trigger of a particular kind. . . .

Kambil sighed, when he really would have been happier cursing out loud. Because his associates were so far out of balance, *he* had to be constantly in control of himself in case of an emergency. He was just as human as they were and therefore just as likely to lose his temper over something, but now he couldn't afford to. Physically he happened to be larger than all of them, but now he was stuck in the role of gentle giant.

This time Kambil had to take a deep breath before running a hand through his very light brown hair. Unbalance seemed to be catching, because he'd never had this much trouble controlling his temper before. Now all it took was the thought of being in the same room with the others. . . .

"Excuse me, Lord Kambil," a voice said, and he turned to see one of the servants. "Lord Rigos's carriage has just pulled up, and you asked to be informed when it did."

"Yes, thank you," Kambil said, using a final deep breath to pull himself together. "Show Lord Rigos in, and have one of the maids bring the tea immediately."

The servant bowed his agreement and withdrew, leaving Kambil alone again for the moment. But that wasn't likely to last, as Rigos usually arrived only a few minutes before the others were due. Not that most of the others were expected to be on time. Unless the meeting was being held in their own house, Kambil was the only one who appeared when he was supposed to. Rigos knew that as well as he did, but the Advisory agent enjoyed seeing the others squirm when he pretended he'd been waiting for hours.

"Lord Rigos," the servant announced, and Kambil looked up to see the small man stroll into the room. It was unfortunate that he was both ordinarily talented and small in stature, as well as fiercely aware of his dignity. He'd certainly been teased unmercifully as a child, and now used his position to get even with the world. His hair and eyes were very dark, setting off his olive skin and framing his usual expression of cruelty hiding just behind extreme boredom.

"Good afternoon, Lord Kambil," he said in a voice that would never be deep enough to satisfy him. "Obviously it was too much to hope that one or more of your associates would arrive before me."

"If you like, I'll make the effort to do that next week, when we meet at Homin's house for the first time," Kambil said with a friendly, ingenuous grin. "I've never been there, but I have faith that my driver will be able to find the way."

"I'm sure he will," Rigos answered with a very small flash of true amusement. "Unlike the drivers of so many of the others, who all seem to lose their way on a regular basis."

They were discussing last week's meeting at Delin Moord's house, when Kambil had been the only one to arrive on time. Each of the others, when they finally rushed in, insisted in turn that *they* hadn't been late, it was their driver's having gotten lost that caused the delay. When Bron Kallan, the last to arrive, used the same excuse the other two had used before him, the situation had turned pathetically ridiculous.

"Yes, you're truly a jewel among the dross," Rigos murmured as he drifted around the room, looking at the displayed examples of Kambil's father's collection of antique teacups. "I feel so much closer to you than I do to the others, as though you and I were just alike and I might tell you anything. It's my fond hope that you feel something of the same."

Kambil was instantly alert, knowing Rigos felt nothing of

the sort. The agent hated all of them just about equally, with a bit extra thrown in for Kambil because of his added height.

"Well, we do have quite a lot in common," Kambil allowed slowly and thoughtfully, as though he had no idea what Rigos might be after. "Our fathers have almost the same position in society, but you've gone ahead and established your own position. I haven't managed that as yet, so it wouldn't be fair to say we're just the same."

"I'm sure you'll begin to establish your own mark as soon as this competition business is over with," Rigos said, turning to smile at Kambil. He'd enjoyed having his superiority pointed out, just as Kambil had meant him to. "When that happens we'll be even closer, and right now I'd like to confide in you. As a preview of situations which will certainly come to be, if you take my meaning."

The look in Rigos's dark eyes had sharpened, and Kambil suddenly knew exactly what he meant. Rigos was promising him an influential—and well-paid—position, but in return for—what?

"I'd like to feel that you can confide in me under any circumstances," Kambil said, even more carefully than before. "How can I help you?"

"Well, actually, it would not be me you were helping," Rigos replied casually, scratching at one ear as he moved back toward Kambil. "A good friend of mine is also involved with doing things with the groups chosen for the competitions, and she's worried about something. I told her I would think about the situation, and let her know if she was definitely worrying about nothing."

"Ah, there's a lady involved!" Kambil exclaimed with a grin, pretending he believed it. "Now I understand your interest in the matter. Again, how can I help?"

"You can help me to decide if she's imagining things," Rigos answered with a smile that would make a shark uneasy. "You see, she's somehow gotten the idea that some of the groups have plans they're not mentioning, like that they mean to actually try to win the competition. We both know they'd have no chance whatsoever of doing it, but she's still afraid they might try. Are her fears, in your opinion, completely groundless, or is she wise to suspect that something might be going on?''

"I suppose it depends on who the members of the particular groups are, but in general I'd say the poor little thing has let her imagination run away with her.'' Kambil made certain to show a good deal of amusement as he said that, as though he were sharing the joke with Rigos. "You really must remind her that none of us wanted to do this in the first place, so sudden conversions to ambition would be completely out of character. They would have to exert themselves and make an effort, after all, and judging by this group I can't honestly picture anything like that. Can you?''

"Not really,'' Rigos grudged, forced into conceding the point. "When people can't even manage to make a meeting on time—Well, there was always the possibility that someone would be that foolish.''

"If they are, they have my sincere condolences,'' Kambil said, then gestured to the service a maid had brought and left. "Let's have some tea while we wait, and continue our discussion sitting down, like civilized people. I'd still like to know what you mean about my achieving a mark of my own after this competition nonsense is over.''

Kambil let a flash of intense interest and casual greed show briefly in his expression, but not so briefly that Rigos didn't notice it. An innocent man who was uninvolved in plots and plans would certainly pursue the subject, and that should put Rigos even more off-guard—which it did.

"When I referred to your future achievements, I was proposing a trade of favors, so to speak,'' Rigos explained as he reached out to pour himself a cup of tea, no longer paying more than token attention to Kambil's reactions. "You attend quite a lot of receptions that the members of the other groups do, which means that if there's something to be heard, you're most likely to hear it. If you'll do me the favor of passing on anything you might hear, I'll be pleased to return the favor by recommending you for any post which might catch your eye.''

"Now that's what I call an interesting trade of favors,"
Kambil said with a distracted nod, as though he were thinking about the matter. "I'll certainly be glad to pass on anything I might hear, and trust to your generosity when an
interesting post turns up."

"If you happen to hear anything of real value, my generosity will be just about guaranteed," Rigos began, then
abruptly fell silent when a servant appeared.

"Lord Kambil, Lord Delin's carriage is just pulling up,"
he said. "He should be shown in in another moment or two."

"Thank you," Kambil said, then turned to Rigos with a
grin. "Well, that's one silver din I've won from my grandmother. I bet that Delin would be the first to arrive, but she
put her silver on Homin. She thought he would be too afraid
to show up late again, but I know him better than that. He's
also too scatterbrained to plan far enough in advance."

"Unfortunately true," Rigos granted with a nod and another cruel smile, apparently believing the story Kambil had
come up with on the spur of the moment. He didn't want
Rigos to know that he had the servants watching for people's
arrival, or Rigos might begin to wonder what he could be up
to. He'd have to tell the servants to be more discreet in the
future. . . . "And we may have to do something about Lord
Homin," Rigos added. "We do need this group to make
some sort of showing, but right now—"

His words broke off as Lord Delin Moord was announced,
and they both turned to look at the man. Handsome and
charming was too pale a phrase for Delin, communicating
nothing of the personal power he radiated when he entered
a room. The man was better than six feet tall, almost as large
as Kambil, in fact, but somewhat more sleekly built. Women
tended to lust after him at first sight, drooling over his long
black hair and light blue eyes and muscular body, and Delin
was usually only too willing to accommodate them.

"Good afternoon, gentlemen," he said negligently as he
joined them, looking around with amusement. "I was delayed getting started today, but it looks like I'm still the first
one here."

"Yes indeed, Lord Delin, but after what I said to Lord Homin last week, about not having been on time *yet*, you shouldn't be the first," Rigos answered sourly. "I was just mentioning to Lord Kambil that something will have to be done about the situation, before it comes to the attention of my superiors."

"What do you expect to be able to do about Homin short of ejecting him from the group?" Delin asked with continuing amusement. "And if you do that, everyone else including myself will vie to take over his tardiness in order to be the next one ejected. Do you have any idea who I could have been with right now if I hadn't had to come here?"

"Some infinitely enchanting lady, I'm sure," Rigos returned dryly, obviously "feeling" nothing of what Kambil did. Delin was pretending just as hard as Kambil had, and apparently with an equal amount of success. "No, Lord Delin, I won't be ejecting Lord Homin from the group, but I *will* have to do something."

Kambil and Delin exchanged a quick glance as Rigos turned away from them, both of them very much aware that Rigos was deliberately not going into details. It was almost certain that he had something definite in mind, but he didn't seem ready to share the something yet.

Delin helped himself to a cup of tea while Rigos and Kambil chose chairs, and then the newcomer joined them. They sat chatting about nothing of consequence for a number of minutes, and then Selendi Vas was announced.

"Lady Selendi, how gracious of you to grant us your presence," Rigos drawled as she bustled in. "And no more than twenty minutes late."

"I almost didn't come at all," Selendi replied as she looked around, then made directly for the tea service. "The scarf I wanted to wear with this dress was nowhere to be found, so I had to force myself to leave the house without it. If anyone of consequence sees me looking like this, I'll simply die right on the spot."

All three men exchanged wry glances at that, but none of them bothered to tell Selendi that she'd just said they were all completely inconsequential. She would *know* they were wrong and would argue the point, and even seeing her pretty face flushed with anger while she tossed her light brown hair in indignation wasn't worth getting her started. In point of fact Kambil thought she looked lovely in that gray silk dress embroidered with blue, but he didn't say *that* either. Selendi took a compliment as an invitation, and Kambil was in no mood to be swallowed alive.

Once the girl had a cup of tea she chose her own chair among them, and the chatting went on. This time, however, only a few minutes went by before Bron Kallan was announced.

"Sorry to be late, people, but there *is* such a thing as common courtesy," he drawled as he strolled into the room, one hand smoothing his dark red hair. "I tried to leave the sweet little thing earlier, but she simply wouldn't hear of it. What can one do when one is ... so much better than average?"

"One can learn a bit of responsibility," Rigos answered him dryly, not in the least amused. "I've decided to fine tardiness, Lord Bron, but not simply in gold. Your parents will be called before an Advisory board in two days time, and not only will they be required to pay over twenty gold dins, they'll also be made to apologize to the Advisors for not having raised you with a greater sense of responsibility. And it will be made perfectly clear that their embarrassment is entirely *your* doing."

"Why am I being singled out?" Bron demanded, his broad, handsome face flushing with anger. He'd stopped on his way to the tea. "I'm not the only one who's been late, not even today. I can see Homin isn't here yet, so what about *him*?"

"He'll be subject to the same fine and punishment, only in a larger amount," Rigos answered, unimpressed with Bron's aggressive stance. "Originally I intended the procedure only for him, but your cavalier attitude has convinced me to apply it to everyone who shows up late. That means the same goes for you, Lady Selendi, except that your parents will need to produce only ten gold dins.''

''But you can't do that,'' Selendi denied with a headshake, her frown showing a touch of confusion. ''Father will be furious, and Mother will try to give me one of those idiotic lectures. No, I'd hate that, so you simply can't do it.''

''I can and I will,'' Rigos said comfortably, obviously enjoying himself immensely. ''I've already gotten the approval of my superiors, and my associate is now waiting outside in his own carriage, noting down four arrival times. The information will be given to the Advisors even before our meeting is over, and then things will continue as I've described. I wonder if you'll be getting the same spanking and lecture Lady Selendi will, Lord Bron. I mean, a man who's so obviously more than average. . . .''

Rigos let the words trail off in a drawl, either not feeling or ignoring the waves of hatred coming from the husky Bron. Kambil could feel the uncertainty also coming from Bron, as though the red-haired man was uncertain of what his parents' reaction would be. Considering the way they'd indulged him all his life there shouldn't have been a problem, but public humiliation has a way of reaching even the most foolishly indulgent of parents.

And Rigos was obviously not as unimpressed by their talents as he pretended to be. The small man had made it clear that someone else was around who would report to the Advisors, so doing away with *him* would be pointless. It was a clever move, but overlooked one possibility: when irresponsible people get angry, they sometimes act before considering consequences. If Bron lost control and burned Rigos to ash where he sat, it would help Rigos not at all that Bron would certainly be prosecuted for murder.

But Bron, after a glance at Delin, simply continued on to the tea service without another word. Kambil had caught the very slight headshake Delin had given Bron, but Rigos wasn't seated in a position to have seen it. Selendi still glared daggers at the agent while the silence dragged on, but after another moment Delin broke it.

"Forgive me, Rigos, but I'm afraid you're going to have to revamp your policy," he said in his usual smooth and friendly way, self assurance radiating from him. "I was nearly late myself today, and through no fault of my own. If my parents were disturbed and distressed simply because of a random occurrence, I'd be very upset. For that reason you can either rescind your . . . punishment, or I'll be forced to withdraw from this group."

"Forgive *me*, Lord Delin, but I'm afraid you can't withdraw," Rigos countered, vicious delight fairly oozing out of him. "You were told right from the beginning that your participation was required rather than requested, and that hasn't changed."

"On the contrary, you yourself have changed the circumstance," Delin disagreed, still completely unruffled. "The Advisors may require our services, but they cannot require us to put up with humiliation. I'm prepared to argue the point in front of a full assembly of the major Houses, who can override an Advisory decision by unanimous vote. When it's pointed out to them that allowing the Advisors to humiliate *us* today will surely see the same thing happening to *them* tomorrow, I expect we'll see the first unanimous House vote in quite some years."

"Do you really expect to assemble the major Houses on *your* say-so?" Rigos came back. Kambil noticed that the agent *sounded* a good deal more assured than he felt. "In their opinion you're just a boy, and not even heir to your father's estate and position. You'd be wasting your time, and I know it even if you don't."

"Of course I would be wasting my time, but my father would not be in the same position," Delin countered, faint amusement now coloring his words. "Once I explain the situation, Father is certain to insist on doing just as I said, to save himself from the possibility of the loss of an incredible amount of face. Don't you think *your* father would do exactly the same?"

Rigos sat without answering, and Kambil knew that was because Delin was right. Rigos's father *would* do exactly the same thing, because the political situation allowed for nothing else. At the level of power their fathers operated on, even a mild rebuff from the wrong person could mean a loss of standing. Something like this could well ruin a man of great power, and no one who'd accumulated that much power was willing to let it go quite that easily.

"So I'm afraid you're going to have to find another way to turn this group punctual, or you won't have a group to worry about." Delin's words were very gentle, with none of the victory Kambil knew he felt coming through at all. "I suggest you see to the matter now, before it grows beyond the control of *our* efforts."

And ends up in the hands of our fathers, Kambil knew he meant. Rigos also knew it, and after a rather long hesitation he rose to his feet and went to a bell pull. When a servant appeared in response to the summons, Rigos was writing something at the desk which stood to one side of the room. The something was rather short, and after sealing it into an envelope he gave it to the servant along with low-voiced instructions, then returned to his chair.

Nothing more was said on the subject of punishment, but Kambil knew the matter wasn't yet over with. Rigos seethed inwardly as he sipped at his tea, and the smug expressions Bron and Selendi wore weren't helping in the least. Rigos had been bested and now felt humiliated, and Kambil would have put gold on the possibility—no, the virtual certainty—that he would find a way to get even. What Delin had done had been necessary, but it certainly hadn't been wise.

Selendi kept eyeing Bron where he sat sprawled on a couch, but before she could decide to join him there Homin was announced. The man rushed in completely out of breath, obviously having moved too fast for someone with such an excess of weight.

"I know I'm late, but I can explain!" he blurted as soon as he saw Rigos, the fear in his light eyes more than clear. "I somehow managed to misplace my identification bracelet, and had a terrible time finding it again. You told us we weren't to go anywhere without it, so—"

"So perhaps you shouldn't have taken it off to begin with," Rigos interrupted, his tone very cold. "At least this time your excuse is more imaginative, but it's still just an excuse and will be treated as such. You need to be broken of your habit of tardiness, and I will certainly see to it. Find a seat now, so that we may begin."

Homin glanced longingly at the tea service, but he'd been ordered to sit so he found a chair and obeyed. He was also terrified over Rigos's threat, and Kambil could feel him struggling to cope with the terror. Selendi was annoyed and bored, Bron was amused but bored, Homin was terrified, and Rigos was silently furious. The only one Kambil got nothing from was Delin, who no longer even felt that faint sense of victory from having bested Rigos.

And he himself, what did he feel? Kambil tried to analyze his feelings, but his sense of frustration over being trapped with the others was too thick to work through. He was certain there would be trouble no matter what he did to try to stop it, and that realization simply added to the frustration.

So there was nothing for him to do but go along with everyone, hoping a chance to change things would appear. Disaster waited ahead of them in one form or another, caused by any one of half a dozen things done by any of his four "associates." The pit was there, waiting only for someone to propel all of them into it, which could happen at any time.

Which meant he'd have to keep his eyes wide open, and head matters off before they went too far for anyone to pull them back. He just hadn't as yet figured out how he would do that. . . .

TEN
DELIN MOORD—EARTH MAGIC

Delin sat completely relaxed while Homin babbled out his excuse for being late, letting nothing of agitation reach him. He'd spent some time in the beginning raging at blind chance for linking him with this pitiful group, but then he'd finally seen the truth. There were more advantages than disadvantages in being part of *this* Blending, and once he understood that he'd even been able to test them.

To begin with, this group accepted his leadership without argument. Another man, brighter than Bron Kallan, would be harder to convince that *he* was leader rather than Delin, and would also be harder to manipulate. The others tended to avoid arguing with Bron because of the man's uncertain temper, which let Delin run everything without being obvious about it.

It was difficult for most people to believe, but the other members of this group were almost as powerful in their talents as he was. Erratic or objectionable personalities aside, there didn't seem to be anyone else in their class who could match them. That meant there was no one anywhere who might be considered equals, since peasants certainly didn't count.

And Rigos Baril had no idea that that was so. It had been

something of a blow to discover that Rigos—of all people—
had been assigned to bully *his* group into behaving properly.
The two of them had been enemies from boyhood, and if
Rigos had gotten the least hint of what Delin was up to, the
slimy little no-talent would have reported him immediately.
At the moment Delin's father's political position was slightly
better than Rigos's, and exposing Delin's plan would change
that circumstance drastically.

But Rigos saw only the weaknesses of the group, nothing
of their strengths. He was a fool to be so blind, and doubly
a fool for thinking Delin would let him get away with hu-
miliating the others. They would have exploded out of control and ruined Delin's plans, so Delin had had to pretend a
personal objection to Rigos's nonsense. By making it a political issue he'd forced Rigos to back down, which had also
made it unnecessary to kill him.

And Delin didn't want to kill Rigos, at least not yet. He
first wanted the other man publicly humiliated with a serious
loss of status, and then he wanted Rigos to see his father
ruined. Then and only then would Delin kill him, but not
quickly. Ending a life slowly was so exquisitely delicious an
idea, that Delin was prepared to defend Rigos if it became
necessary—until the time arrived to taste that special, long-
anticipated banquet he'd promised himself. . . .

"Now then," Rigos said, drawing Delin's attention back
from the realms of marvelous daydreams. "I have the weekly
reports from your trainers, and we'll go over them one by
one. Some of you are performing adequately, but others. . . ."

Rigos let the words trail off as he glanced around, surely
trying to terrorize as many of the others as possible. But they
were *his* people, *his* special Blending, and if Rigos tried to
go too far Delin would haul him up short.

"Earth magic, Delin Moord," Rigos announced, giving
most of his attention to the report in his hands. "Works fairly
diligently, but tends to be too casual about practice. . . . Advancement through the exercises satisfactory. . . . Attitude:
less than fully eager to cooperate. . . . General progress: average but adequate."

Delin listened to that and the rest with faint amusement. He'd carefully worked out what his image ought to be, and had made sure not to show his trainer anything in the way of unsuitable enthusiasm. It so happened he had practiced rather diligently, but not where his trainer could see it and not to extremes. He didn't *need* all that much practice, after all, not when he was as good as he was.

". . . and so forth and so on," Rigos was finishing up. "I believe it's fairly clear that there aren't many objections to the progress made by our Earth magic practitioner. If that was the worst report I'd be pleased, but unfortunately it's not. The next report is on Selendi Vas, Air magic."

Rigos abruptly had Selendi's full attention, and the girl seemed poised to be indignant. She wasn't at all the sort to put herself out doing something that wasn't her own idea, but for the moment Delin was satisfied to have her that way. He already knew how to get the strongest response out of her when he decided it was needed, and for that reason had spoken to Bron. The man had intended to make her his next conquest, but now would wait—even if invited—until Delin gave him the go-ahead.

"Work habits are a bit sloppy and ill-disciplined," Rigos went on, reading the evaluation with relish. "Practice is almost certainly being ignored, as progress has been somewhat slow. Exercises are sometimes regarded as indignities, but are executed when trainer insists. . . . Attitude is extremely sensitive to all criticism, therefore subject must be treated gently. . . . Overall progress . . . painfully slow."

"Maybe that was written because the trainer didn't get what he kept asking for—and I don't mean teaching results," Selendi blustered, fully indignant but obviously hesitant to show it too strongly. "He's a dull and tedious fool, and usually completely unreasonable. I'm a lot more accomplished than I was to begin with, so that proves he's lying."

"No, Lady Selendi, it only proves how good a job he's done," Rigos corrected, his tone sour. "But you're not the only one at fault, so let's continue. Kambil Arstin, Spirit magic."

Delin glanced at Kambil, the one member of his group

that he wasn't yet entirely sure of. Kambil was certainly a full member of their class, but at times he made Delin uneasy. He wasn't a pliable fool like the others. His only weakness seemed to be a lack of shallowness, and he wasn't filled with burning, unrealized ambition. That last was what disturbed Delin the most, but he had no choice about waiting and seeing.

"Work habits are efficient and based on a full sense of cooperation," Rigos recited with relish, as though deliberately taunting Delin. "Practice is sometimes overlooked in favor of other undertakings, but progress is satisfactory in spite of that. Exercises are being progressed through at too slow a rate, but that seems to stem from excessive caution. Attitude is excellent in this subject, and overall progress is only just under the best to be expected."

"His trainer sounds like he's in love with him," Selendi commented archly, doing a poor job of hiding her jealousy. "Maybe if I tried that with *my* trainer . . ."

"I would suggest, Lady Selendi, that you first try applying yourself to the work," Rigos answered when Kambil just sighed and shook his head. "This is the sort of report I expect to get on all of you in the near future, so kindly keep it well in mind. The next is Bron Kallan, Fire magic."

Bron looked up languidly, but the glance he sent to Delin showed something of his true state of mind. Bron feared Rigos because of the agent's higher social and political position, and was therefore delighted to have Delin to stand behind.

"Work habits are more casual than organized, but something of an effort *is* being made," Rigos read, his voice now neutral. "Practice is done when the subject is reminded about it, but otherwise is ignored. Exercises are being progressed through *too* rapidly, without true mastery being attained. Attitude is generally fair, except when subject is 'fired up' about some matter, and then it approaches an acceptable level. Overall progress is almost acceptable, except for the matter of lack of mastery."

"It looks like I'll have to show him the area where I *am*

a master,'' Bron drawled, uncertain relief in his eyes. "Other than that, though, it didn't sound too bad.''

"It also didn't sound too good,'' Rigos countered, ruthlessly crushing Bron's optimistic outlook. "There's considerable room for improvement, which I expect to see rather soon. And last, as dessert, so to speak, we have Homin Weil, Water magic.''

The extreme relish in Rigos's voice wasn't missed by Homin, who froze where he sat huddled into himself. Impatient intolerance tried to flare up in Delin every time he looked at Homin, but that would have been futile. Homin couldn't help being the fearful lump he was. His presence in the group did most to quiet any suspicions Rigos might have had, and most importantly, Delin had no choice but to use him.

"Work habits are all but nonexistent in this subject,'' Rigos read, making some small effort to appear dispassionate. "Practice is apparently out of the question, for some reason the subject is unable to explain. Exercises are slow and painful attempts that tend to defy advancement for a longer period of time than they should, and the prevailing attitude is a constant expectation of failure. For these reasons, despite the subject's potential, overall progress has been extremely slow when it appeared at all.''

Homin's eyes were now closed, and his overfleshed face had gone pale. He seemed to know that he wasn't destined to escape as lightly as everyone else had, and he was perfectly correct.

"Perhaps you'd care to explain to *me*, Lord Homin, why it is that you're unable to practice,'' Rigos said in a voice chipped from a block of flint. "Your trainer may not be able to understand, but surely the matter can be clarified here and now.''

"I—it's too disruptive to the household to practice,'' Homin muttered, eyes still closed. "I did try, Sir, I really did, but it caused too much—disruption.''

"You drowned someone?'' Rigos inquired politely, his brows somewhat raised. "You flooded your father's library?

You ruined your mother's brand new entertaining room furniture? You turned everyone's underclothes damp? Help me to understand just how disruptive you were, Lord Homin.''

The terrified man simply shook his head in defeat, most likely understanding that nothing he said would do any good. And Delin knew he was correct again, which Rigos promptly proved for the second time.

''Apparently the matter is too trivial for you to be disturbed over it,'' the agent stated, his tone now as flat as his stare was hard. ''You're the worst offender, Lord Homin, but none of your associates is innocent. Each and every one of you needs to improve his or her performances, otherwise forming you into a Blending will be futile. And you're scheduled to soon *be* formed into one, which at this point will also turn your group into a laughingstock. Do you really want to become known as the worst challenging Blending to stand up for the nobility?''

He looked around at all of them then, the look on his face fierce. ''Yes, that's what will happen when you perform in the competitions. Everyone will laugh at your efforts, but that doesn't include the Advisors. You may take my word for the fact that they will *not* be laughing, but they will certainly have something to say to you afterward. And to your families.''

The others promptly began to look almost as upset as Homin, but it was the opening Delin needed. He'd been looking for a reason to speak up, and now he had it.

''And our families are certain to be displeased with us for failing in our duty to the Advisors,'' he said with a weary sigh. ''This is hardly a trivial matter like punctuality, so we'll need to do something about it. Hopefully it will be the right something, and next week's reports will be much improved. We'll certainly discuss the matter as long as necessary once you've left, even if it takes the rest of the afternoon and evening.''

''I knew I could count on you to see the consequences clearly, Lord Delin,'' Rigos purred, delighted to have what he considered a concession of defeat from Delin. ''I'm also taking steps to remedy the problem, but that's for the future when the solution has been approved by my superiors. Right now I'll leave you to your discussions, which will hopefully prove fruitful enough to avoid the necessity of any other action.''

Delin hadn't the faintest idea what Rigos was talking about, but the Advisory agent was definitely threatening them with something. And yet the something could be avoided so it was obviously time to advance to the next part of the plan. When Rigos stood they all did the same, except for Selendi, and exchanged polite bows of goodbye. Rigos left the room slowly, his lack of hurry deliberate, but nothing was said among them even when he was out of sight. Kambil glanced around before sauntering after the small agent, and was gone for a few minutes. Silence reigned until he returned, a relieved expression on his face.

''I personally watched his carriage pull away,'' Kambil announced as he headed for the bar rather than the tea service. ''I also have three servants on watch, just in case he decides to return unexpectedly. Every time that man talks to me, I experience the urge to find a bath house at once.''

''Slimy is much too kind a description of him,'' Delin said with a smile, suddenly feeling considerably better about Kambil. ''But we really do need to discuss our next move, and Bron has told me he's ready to do just that.''

''Yes, I certainly am,'' Bron agreed after glancing at Delin and clearing his throat. ''You all know we've been dragging our feet deliberately to keep them from becoming suspicious, but the time for that is over. They've now *demanded* that we do better, so we'll have to oblige them. But remember to do it slowly and in spurts, not all at once and immediately. They've threatened us into improving, so it ought to please them when we do. Are you going to have a problem with that, Homin?''

The question was obviously because of Homin's expression, which showed his agitation barely calmed. The man apparently had something of a problem, and he pushed himself to his feet and went to the tea service before answering.

"I—normally would have no trouble showing the necessary improvement," he said, paying attention only to his shaking hands, which were engaged in pouring him tea. "My problem goes beyond the normal, however, and I'm—afraid I'll need to—speak with our—general troubleshooter."

Apparently Homin had had to force himself to ask for help, and Delin found himself distantly pleased. One of his people had need of him, and had had the good sense to speak up rather than ruin the plans.

"That means you want to speak to *me*," Delin said, making himself appear flattered. "Certainly, old man, it will be my pleasure to assist you. Let's step to the other side of the room to keep from disturbing the general conversation."

Homin nodded and followed Delin to the far side of the large room, the cup and saucer in the heavy man's hands clattering faintly as he moved. Delin knew that that was due to nervousness rather than to clumsiness, and turned to the other man with a soothing smile.

"Now what can I do for you?" he asked gently. "I'm assuming this has something to do with that odd explanation you gave about not being able to practice."

"Yes, it does," Homin admitted at once, but with a quaver in his voice. "I couldn't tell Lord Rigos, of course, not when I'd been specifically ordered to keep silent around him—"

"Ordered?" Delin interrupted, now having to fight to keep his tone light and easy. How *dare* some outsider give orders to one of his people? Homin wasn't much, but he now belonged body and aspect to Delin.

"Yes, ordered," Homin confirmed with a sigh, his eyes trying to close again. "My father's new wife, Elfini. She insists on being in complete charge of the household and everyone in it, and won't hear of my practicing. She can't control it, you see, so she simply refuses to allow it. The one time I tried she used one of her whips on me, and it was the next day before I could move my back without fainting from the pain."

"I'd heard the rumor about your father's taste in pleasure, but until now I hadn't quite believed it," Delin said after sipping from his own teacup, which he'd carried with him. "Your father is such a strong, uncompromising man in public. . . . But I've also encountered the lady Elfini, so there's no longer any doubt. And she flatly refuses to let you practice?"

"She's now going beyond that," Homin said, visibly fretting all over again. "She took my identification bracelet while I was bathing, and if she and Lord Rigos weren't enemies I'd probably still be begging for its return. And she means to punish me when I return home, simply because she knows how I loathe and fear it. I'll never be able to accomplish anything with her doing things like this, so I wondered if you. . . . I mean, would it be possible for you to . . . speak to her?"

"Speak to her?" Delin echoed, mostly hearing that phrase about Elfini and Rigos being enemies. The possibilities inherent in that situation were fascinating, giving Delin a marvelous idea. "Why, yes, Homin, I'll be glad to go home with you and speak to her. But there's a stop I have to make on the way, so I'm afraid you'll be put to the bother of waiting a short while. Will you mind terribly much?"

"Not at all, Delin, I won't mind at all," Homin babbled, his relief turning him even more pathetic. "I'm sure your charm will change her mind, and I'll be able to become a full member of our group. I don't know how I can thank you. . . ."

"Tut, tut, thanks aren't necessary, old fellow," Delin replied putting an arm around Homin to turn him back toward the others. "We're here to help one another, so that all of us might benefit. Right now we need to rejoin the others, and go into a bit of detail about the proposed changes in our efforts. After that you and I will leave together, eh?"

Homin agreed with loose-lipped gratitude, all but laughing over having Delin on his side. And Delin felt almost as pleased, just for a different reason. Rigos would regret ever having challenged him, and might even live a very long while with that regret. Delin hadn't made up his mind about *that* part of it yet, but there was plenty of time.

Yes, plenty of time to add new wrinkles to old plans. . . .

*Now you've met our opponents, and certainly know them
better than we did to begin with. I remember hearing someone wonder aloud about why it is that people struggle to
make better lives for them and their families, and then
turn around and ruin their children by indulging them too
far or being too hard on them. The man was referring to
the nobility, but I can't see that they have a monopoly on
child-ruining. You don't even need gold and social position to do that, just . . . well, maybe it comes from having
been ruined in some way yourself.*

*But wondering how people got the way they are is the
last thing you think about when you're faced with needing
to deal with them. Their being unbalanced doesn't mean
they're incompetent, and usually they have no qualms of
conscience to keep them from doing anything they please to
you. But I'm sure you already know that, so let's get back
to what happened in what order.*

ELEVEN

Jovvi didn't have long to settle herself in the coach before
it stopped again near a Fire magic symbol. Beside the round
metal disk mounted on a post stood Tamma, who had a
heavy man standing and waiting with her. The man opened
the coach door and helped Tamma inside, all the while radiating such strong fear and uncertainty that Jovvi had to

block him out of her awareness. But as soon as the door was closed the coach continued on, so the distraught man was quickly left behind.

"Let me guess," Jovvi said to Tamma with a happy grin of relief. "You've already tested for some of your masteries, and you've gotten them."

"Every one of the first six," Tamma answered, holding up a small leather pouch. "Six silver dins for six masteries, and full permission to go home even though it's only early afternoon. But the going-home part was for their benefit, I think. Unless I was imagining things, they were so nervous they couldn't wait to get rid of me."

"You weren't imagining things," Jovvi said, losing her good mood. "That man beside you was very frightened, just like the people I was with. I gained all four of the first masteries along with the four silver dins, and suddenly became a different person to them."

"Yes, they went from condescension to fear in six—or four—easy steps," Tamma said, leaning her head back on the coach seat. "Tomorrow may be a different story, but whether it is or not—What can they possibly be so afraid of? Are we suddenly going to turn into some kind of monsters, and they know about it but aren't allowed to warn us? I've learned to dread what I'm not being told about, Jovvi, and this feels like a new version of the same old situation."

"Somehow I don't think it is," Jovvi replied, her brow wrinkling in thought. "The fear was for what we are *now*, not for what we might turn into. And in a way it was a very specific fear, personal to the people involved. I have no idea what details are involved, but it feels—"

Jovvi gestured with one hand, finding it impossible to put her impressions into words. The fear had been both personal and impersonal, and wasn't specifically involving *now*. *Now* seemed to be generating no more than extreme nervousness, but *later*. . . .

"It feels as if we'd better watch even more carefully as we continue to move ahead," Jovvi went on, seeing the way Tamma now listened closely. "I think it's safe to say there's something coming that they know about but we don't, but it's not necessarily bad for *us*. If they knew we were certain to be Seated, for instance, they'd worry about what we might do once we were in power.''

"I hadn't considered that possibility," Tamma said slowly, her brows raised. "Or at least I hadn't considered it seriously. Maybe that's because the worst I would do to any of them is have them fired, and I don't mean in my aspect's way.''

"Very often people expect to see others acting in a manner they themselves would act in," Jovvi said, nodding her agreement with Tamma's intentions. "You and I know we would never cause them any real harm just to get even, but chances are good that in our place they *would* cause harm. Small, spiteful people worry about things like that, so they're punished by their own attitudes. Let's not let that spoil our pleasure over what we've accomplished.''

"You're absolutely right," Tamma agreed with a firm nod, and then she laughed. "Especially when that accomplishment was so easy, at least for me. I'm still somewhat nervous about the next batch of tests where I'll have to do the same thing while protecting myself against attack, but I'm suddenly starting to *believe* I can do it. That makes a big difference, doesn't it? Believing in yourself, I mean.''

"It certainly does," Jovvi told her with a grin, enjoying her bubbling delight. "I've been saying that all along, but it's the kind of thing you have to discover for yourself. Until then, all the saying in the world won't convince you it's true. I just wish Lorand understood that more clearly.''

"Yes, I'm worried about him too," Tamma said with a sigh. "He's such a *nice* person that I wish I could help. . . . But he's gotten past his fear so far, so maybe he'll be able to continue doing it.''

"Forcing yourself to do something and doing that something freely bring two different results," Jovvi said with a headshake, already having considered the point. "Lorand will probably manage now, but what happens when he reaches the real competitions and has to face someone as strong as he is? Even if he hesitates only a moment before reaching for more power, that moment could cause him to lose.''

''But how do you get around something that's frightened you for years?'' Tamma asked, her pretty eyes wide with concern. ''I'm doing it—part way—by remembering I have nothing to lose, but I didn't start out being afraid of dying. If I had . . . would I have been able to get this far?''

''One day soon you'll discover that you're a lot stronger than you've ever been allowed to believe,'' Jovvi told her, automatically soothing Tamma's sudden, extreme agitation. ''That's when you'll understand why you've been able to accomplish what you have—and why you *can* accomplish anything you decide on. Lorand . . . Lorand already knows he's strong, both in character and in ability, and it isn't death he fears. People who worry about burnout usually have a different picture giving them nightmares.''

''Mindlessness,'' Tamma said with a nod, back to being calm again. ''But that's almost the same as being dead, since you have no idea about what's going on around you. It's knowing everything and being helpless to change any of it that gives me the shudders, so maybe Lorand ought to try *my* brand of trouble. I have to admit it's less crippling than his.''

''Maybe we can talk him into taking a temporary loan,'' Jovvi said with as much of a smile as she could manage, then suddenly decided she needed to change the subject of discussion. ''But while we're talking about the others, what do you intend to do about Vallant Ro? He *hates* the way you've been ignoring him, and I have the impression that he might decide to do something about it.''

''He'll find out rather fast that there's nothing he *can* do,'' Tamma replied, abruptly closing herself off against listening calmly and reasonably. ''I had to learn the hard way that he makes me more vulnerable than I am alone, and I don't intend to waste the lesson. He won't ever have the chance to put me in an embarrassing situation with my father again.''

''At the risk of starting a serious argument, I'm going to tell you what the truth is, rather than what you've talked yourself into believing." Jovvi spoke slowly after something of a hesitation, hoping hard that she wasn't making a mistake. "Friends do tell each other the truth, even if both the telling and hearing are painful. Will you forgive me in advance for being blunt?"

Tamma sat staring down at her hands where they twisted together in her lap, but she didn't say anything about not being willing to listen. She might be expecting Jovvi to take her silence as a refusal, but Jovvi preferred to take it in a positive way.

"All right, so you won't forgive me in advance," she said after a moment, fortified with a deep breath. "You may even hate me after this, but I don't hate you so here goes: it wasn't Vallant who embarrassed you in front of your father, and vulnerability isn't what's upsetting you. You're doing this because of jealousy, Tamma, and because you have no idea how a real, beneficial relationship between a man and a woman works. If you like, I'll explain what I mean."

Once again there was just the creak and jangle of the coach's motion to break the silence, so Jovvi took that as an encouraging sign and continued.

"Let's start with the jealousy aspect," she said, noticing the small red spots which had appeared on Tamma's cheeks. "You may not even really know what jealousy is, because you've never associated with a man you liked well enough to be jealous about. If that's the case, let me assure you that finding out you're not the first woman he's involved himself with and immediately hating the idea is nothing unusual. Most women react that way, but some are wise enough to see how foolish they're being."

This time Tamma shifted a bit on the coach seat, a sign that she *was* listening even if she neither looked up nor spoke. And there was a small frown on what Jovvi could see of Tamma's face, an even better sign.

"What you must make yourself understand is how unreasonable it is to expect that a grown man you've just met had no life before your meeting. If that were true you'd probably find you couldn't stand him, because he had either no personality or an unpleasant one. If you want to be the first woman in a man's life, you either have to be born right next to him, or accept a man no one else wants to associate with.''

"How would I go about managing that first option?" Tamma said suddenly with a wry expression, briefly glancing up. "The one about being born next to him, I mean. And I'm *not* jealous of that floozie my father pranced into my house. Any man who ever saw anything in *her* couldn't possibly find anything of interest in *me*."

"That's jealousy," Jovvi stated, but with a grin. "And you have to remember that he didn't find her interesting enough to marry. Maybe she saw other men in addition to him, and that soured his enthusiasm. Men are strange, even the best of them. They'll do everything in their power to continue seeing their favorite courtesan, who probably has anywhere from four to a dozen patrons beside himself. But let his wife try to take even a single lover, and suddenly he wants nothing more to do with her."

"That's probably because they think they own their wives," Tamma said, then gestured away the whole idea. "But maybe that's why I've lost interest. Once you 'belong' to a man he starts to see you as a possession, and I have no intention of being anyone's possession ever again."

"You haven't lost interest, and not all men are like that," Jovvi disagreed again, but gently and without the amusement. "Vallant would probably be one of the exceptions, but I think you're too afraid to find out. If you had let him stand beside you and support you when your father brought that girl to the house, you wouldn't have been embarrassed. But then you would have had to face the start of a serious relationship with Vallant, and you can't cope with something that new and that far beyond your experience. You decided to use anger to free yourself from a terrifying situation, which in this instance *does* make you a coward."

"I told you I was one," she muttered, misery radiating from her slender body, but then she made the effort to square her shoulders. "And since there's no argument about it, I might as well admit that his interest scares me silly. I don't know how to deal with it, Jovvi, even if it made me feel like a carefree child at first. I hadn't realized how . . . complex a relationship with a man can be, so I'm much better off not being involved at all."

"There are times when we have to force ourselves to do the right thing," Jovvi told her, feeling the strength of the girl's resolve with a sinking sensation. "Very often we're wise to back away from something we know we can't handle, but not all the time. In situations like this, where you can gain so much, you have to force yourself to take the chance. And what if he decides not to let you ignore him? He won't hurt you, I know that for a fact, but men can be such in-credible *pests* when they put their mind to it. . . ."

"But Jovvi, I just earned six masteries in Fire magic," Tamma countered reasonably. "Even if he *were* the sort to hurt me, what could he possibly do?"

Jovvi parted her lips to answer that question, then discov-ered that she couldn't, not in just a few words. It took a greater knowledge of normal men than Tamma had, but she did have to give one example.

"Well . . . suppose he decides to do something completely innocuous, like follow you around," Jovvi finally suggested. "He's not threatening you, he's not trying to touch you, and he's not even trying to engage you in conversation. All he's doing is following you around like a puppy, making cow eyes at you any time you glance at him. How are your mas-teries going to help you with *that*?"

"But that wouldn't be fair!" Tamma protested, suddenly turning upset. "If he's not trying to hurt me, how can I defend myself?"

"That's the whole point," Jovvi said slowly and clearly, knowing the girl was still having trouble understanding. "That's the way a normal man might decide to pester, and you won't be able to justify hurting him even to yourself. Or maybe especially to yourself. You have to handle the matter differently, in a much more reasonable way. Why don't you take him aside and tell him the truth?"

"Do you really think that will make him stay away from

me?" Tamma asked in turn, new hope in her eyes. "I hate it when he talks to me the way he did this morning, so sincerely and sounding so wounded. It made me want to comfort him, but I can't afford to do that."

"No, you can't," Jovvi agreed in a mutter, now almost as depressed as Tamma had been a moment ago. "And I said I'd tell you the truth, so I have to keep on with it. If you sit down and talk to him I *don't* think he'll leave you alone, especially not if he sees the way your eyes brighten at the thought of comforting him. He'll know you're just as interested in him as he is in you, and he'll never give up trying to make you admit it."

"As if admitting it would make a relationship easier and more possible," Tamma said, her voice filled with weariness. "Then what am I going to do, Jovvi? If he starts to follow me around, I'll probably have a screaming fit."

"It's possible I may join you in that," Jovvi muttered again, then let the following silence tell Tamma she was out of ideas. She'd never had trouble turning away a man's interest, but then she had a talent Tamma lacked. And she'd never been half in love with the men she turned away, and Tamma certainly was. And now, with Lorand, she was in the process of learning how difficult it was to dismiss certain men from your thoughts. Maybe Tamma would come up with something they could both use.

The rest of the ride went by too quietly, and from all the thinking Jovvi did there should have been the smell of burning wood. Tamma was obviously also thinking, but Jovvi had never seen a more unproductive time. Except, possibly, where their questions about the competitions were involved, and even those were being slowly answered.

When they pulled up to the residence with no sign of the coach the men had used, Jovvi hoped that was because she and Tamma had gotten home first. If not, and she ran into Lorand, there was an excellent chance that she would join Tamma in that screaming fit a lot sooner than either of them had expected. . . .

TWELVE

Lorand was the first to be picked up by the coach, and at first he thought he might be the only passenger. By now he was used to being the last in the group to accomplish whatever they were supposed to be doing, so he half expected the other men—and the women in their own coach—to have returned to the residence hours earlier.

So it surprised him when they began to slow, and he looked out of the lefthand window to see Vallant Ro and Pagin Holter waiting beside the symbol for Water magic. Two strange men stood with them, just as Hestir, his Adept guide, had waited for the coach with *him*. It had been Hestir's idea rather than Lorand's, and even from a distance it seemed that Ro and Holter were no more eager for the company than he had been.

The coach slowed to a complete stop, and Lorand's two residence-mates climbed inside without wasting any time. The two strangers looked as if they meant to wave goodbye, but Ro and Holter ignored them completely as they settled into the seats opposite Lorand. Then the coach was moving again, and both men let out sighs of relief.

''I think I was happier when they were lookin' down at us,'' Ro said to Holter, and then, when the small man nodded emphatically, added to Lorand, ''We earned their masteries, both of us. Before that I was one of their group of 'boys,' and Holter was lower than dirt. Now we're both really important men, and that made me very nervous.''

''I know what you mean,'' Lorand agreed with a sour nod. ''Before I tested I was 'dear boy' to my Adept guide, but afterward I was 'sir.' And I didn't like it nearly as much as I thought I would.''

''Made me feel like more uv a stranger'n anythin' yet,'' Holter put in, a painful expression on his face. ''Din't 'spect 'em t' make me a brother, but a little friendliness wouldn'a hurt. But they wus jest as scared as Ginge an' them others, so we ain't never gonna have friends agin.''

Lorand could feel the pain radiating from the small ex-groom, and groped for something comforting to say as he exchanged a glance with Ro. Holter *needed* friendship the way most people needed food and shelter, but at the same time he seemed to be refusing to accept it. Ro parted his lips to say something, but that was when the coach began to slow again.

Lorand looked out to see Rion standing beside the symbol for Air magic, but no one was with him. Ro saw the same and again they exchanged glances, both clearly wondering and worrying. Was Rion alone because he hadn't attained any masteries? They'd have to find out, but they would also have to be delicate about it.

When the coach stopped Rion got in, a neutral expression on his face. Lorand waited for the man to settle himself beside him, and then he cleared his throat.

''We were wondering how you managed to be waiting alone,'' Lorand said in as light a tone as he could produce. ''The rest of us were forced to put up with the company of our guides, so we'd like to know your secret.''

''There's no secret involved,'' Rion said, sounding distracted and sober. ''I simply told the man to go away, and he did. They may not take you seriously to begin with, but once you pass their foolish little test their attitude changes completely.''

''Yes, Ro and Holter and I were just discussing that,'' Lorand replied with a great deal of relief. ''And Holter said something I was about to disagree with when the coach stopped. You said we would never have friends again, man, but you're forgetting something important. You and me and everyone in our group are now friends, and no one will ever be able to change that. Don't you think that counts for *something*?"

"He's right," Ro agreed quietly when Holter simply looked uncomfortable. "We've all had to say goodbye to our old lives, knowin' we'll probably never be looked at the same again by our family and friends. But in their place we've got each other, and you won't find us turnin' our back on one of our own. If you think you don't belong with us, that's *your* idea, not ours."

"I know you been tryin' t'treat me kindly," Holter said after a brief hesitation, apparently struggling for the right words. "You're all good folk who don't like talkin' down a man jest 'cause he don't use purty words, but you cain't see yer bunch frum th' outside. You all *fit* t'gether, even Mardimil there who din't fit in nuthin' to start with, but me? I don't fit, friend, an' never will. If y'ever hadda choose betwixt Ro an' me, which one would y'choose?"

Lorand started to say he didn't see a reason for choosing, then understood Holter's point. Ro and Holter shared the aspect of Water magic, and if everyone else needed to choose between them, their choice would be obvious. But why would they have to choose? The only place they would need a single representative of each aspect would be—

"Wait a minute," Lorand said, completely sidetracked. "Unless I'm mistaken, you've seen something the rest of us have missed. Are you saying they've kept us together like this because they plan to form five of us into a Blending? But this is a twenty-fifth year, so that has to be absurd. We're here to try for High positions, not—"

Lorand discovered he couldn't say the words, but Ro didn't have that trouble.

"Why *not* as candidates for the Fivefold Throne?" he demanded, revelation widening his eyes. "We don't know how good we are compared to other applicants, but the testin' authority does. If they think we're good enough, who're we to argue? Holter, you're a genius!''

''Definitely more observant than the average man, and also quite astute,'' Mardimil put in, studying Holter quietly. ''The theory seems an excellent one, and may indeed prove correct. In the event that it does, our friend's question becomes more than academic—assuming *we* are the ones who are allowed to choose. Cynicism, however, suggests the choice will belong to those who consider themselves our superiors.''

Everyone looked startled at that, even Holter, but Lorand knew his own expression must be stranger yet. Funny how he'd never seriously thought about being part of one of the challenging Blendings, even though the possibility had always been there.

''I think that covers the question about choosin','' Ro said, after the moment they all seemed to need to adjust to the new situation. ''We could be kiddin' ourselves and find they don't want us after all, but we should be braced in case they do. And we'll have to tell the ladies about this.''

''I hope they haven't already thought of it themselves,'' Lorand said with a small headshake. ''I was starting to believe that women are generally sharper than men, but Holter has helped to restore my self-esteem. Since he's definitely a man, there's still hope for *me*.''

Everyone including Holter chuckled at that, but then the conversation died completely. Mardimil and Holter withdrew back into their brown studies, Ro fell into one of his own, and even Lorand was captured by his thoughts. He'd been concentrating so hard on winning to a Seated High position, that he'd never even considered being part of a challenging Blending. Now that he'd been forced to consider it, he saw the benefits in the changed circumstance immediately.

If winning a Seated High position would let him make a happy, permanent life with Jovvi, how much better would it be if the two of them were part of the winning Blending? Their careers would last no more than twenty-five years, but Lorand was fairly certain that would be time enough to put aside enough gold for a comfortable retirement. He chuckled at that thought, then spent the rest of the ride daydreaming about how wonderful it would be if—*when*!—Jovvi became his alone.

They were only a block or two away from the residence when a coach passed them going in the opposite direction. That said the ladies had gotten back before them, which raised Lorand's spirit even more. He wanted to see Jovvi and tell her how much better their prospects for happiness had become, but when they left their coach and entered the residence, the entire downstairs appeared deserted except for the servants.

"I believe I could use a quick trip to the bath house," Mardimil said, taking Lorand's attention from looking around. "Would anyone mind if I made the time solitary? I promise to be in and out as quickly as possible."

Lorand shrugged and shook his head to show that it was fine with him, and Ro did the same. Holter had already disappeared as usual, so Mardimil nodded in turn and headed directly for the back hall and the bath house.

"I could use a bath myself, but waitin' until he's done won't hurt," Ro said then. "I'll just go to my bedchamber and get a wrap to wear instead of these clothes, and if I take my time he ought to be finished just about when I'm ready to start."

"I could use the same, so if you don't mind I'll join you," Lorand replied. "Unless you're in need of the same solitude? Personally, I could use someone to talk to."

"That makes two of us," Ro agreed, clearly not simply being polite. "Let's meet back down here in that sittin' alcove near the back door, and when Mardimil comes out of the bath house, we'll go in."

Lorand was happy to add his own agreement, so they went upstairs and separated to go into their respective bedchambers. Just for an instant before he opened his door, Lorand fantasized finding Jovvi in his bed, gloriously naked and eagerly waiting for him. Then he opened the door and found the chamber empty, which made him sigh as he walked in and closed the door again. If he didn't get things straightened out with Jovvi soon, he just might find himself daydreaming about her at the wrong time—like when he was supposed to be achieving a mastery, and that couldn't be allowed to happen. Only the best of the best would be chosen to be in a challenging Blending, so that's what Lorand would have to be.

He took his time getting out of his clothes and into a wrap, but he still reached the sitting alcove near the back door first. He had no idea how long he would have to wait for Ro, but before he had time to consider the question the man appeared. And a moment after that Mardimil came in through the back door, wearing a towel wrapped around his middle and carrying his worn clothing. He nodded his thanks for their patience when he saw them, then headed for the front hall and the stairs leading upward. That meant the bath house was now theirs, so they went outside together and walked to it.

The silence he and Ro maintained during the walk and while they undressed felt somewhat strained to Lorand, so he decided to restart the conversation and see how it went. If the strain disappeared, all well and good. If it didn't, he might have to cut short his own bath time.

"Once I'm dressed again, I intend to go looking for Jovvi," Lorand stated with a brief glance over his shoulder, giving most of his attention to entering the bath. "She and I have a—disagreement going on between us, but that's no reason for us to avoid each other. I still don't know why she seems to feel for me what I feel for her, but I'm not about to question the best luck I've had in my entire life."

"You and Jovvi?" Ro blurted as he followed Lorand into the bath. "I had no idea—But what about what was between you and Tamrissa?"

"What made you think there was ever anything between me and Tamrissa?" Lorand asked curiously as he bent his knees so that his whole body would be wet. "The lady is charming and delightful and was wonderful about helping me with part of my problem with Jovvi, but that's all there ever was between us. Is simple friendship what you were talking about?"

"I suppose it was," Ro answered with a grin, just standing there in water up to his chest. "I didn't know it was, but I'm happy to say I know it now. I like you, Coll, and I would have hated to find that I had no choice but to murder you in cold blood. Now murder won't be necessary, so I can get on with plannin' other, more pleasant things."

"Ah, now I understand," Lorand said with his own grin, also understanding about the strain in the silence they'd earlier shared. "You're having a problem with Tamrissa, and you were afraid I'd take advantage of that to make time of my own with her. Well, you can believe it won't be happening, so what do you have in mind for healing the rift between you two?"

"Nothin' yet," Ro admitted, losing his grin and relief together. "I've decided I'm not about to give up tryin' to get through to her, but how I'll do that I can't quite figure out. What I do know, though, is that if I choose the wrong way of handlin' it, life could get really . . . *hot* for me."

Ro submerged after saying that, leaving Lorand momentarily puzzled over what he'd meant. Then he remembered that Tamrissa was a potential High in Fire magic, and quickly began to pity Ro. The worst Jovvi could do to *him* if she decided she didn't want him around was turn off his interest, and that would only be temporary. What Tamrissa could do to Ro was an entirely different story, and Lorand had to duck under the water to wash away the picture of it.

The two men used soap and shampoo first, and only then chose resting areas to relax in for a while. The constantly recycling water was fresh and warm, silently urging soaking, so they let themselves be talked into it. Once they were settled, though, Ro looked over at Lorand with a less hopeless expression.

"You know, our conversation in the coach comin' back here may have given me an idea," he said, using one hand to smooth down his soaking wet hair. "I don't know any more about Blendin's than the next man, but if we're goin' to have any chance at all we have to be as . . . close as possible to each other. That means she'll have to stop actin' the way she's doin', and give me a chance."

"That sounds logical to you and me, but don't forget she's a woman," Lorand warned. "I hate throwing cold water on your idea, but I'd hate seeing you turned into a pile of ash even more. She could decide that business about our being a challenging Blending has nothing to do with how she treats you, and you'd need a *compelling*—and not necessarily logical—counterargument."

"You're right, blast it," Ro muttered, obviously unhappy but just as obviously not depressed. "I'll have to add somethin' else, like . . . like tellin' her animosity will be too distractin'. We'll have to be payin' attention to workin' together, but her thinkin' hate-thoughts and me thinkin' unrequited love-thoughts might ruin it for everybody. She's not the sort who'll hurt others just to get what she wants."

"No, she isn't," Lorand agreed, considering the idea critically. "But you'll first have to get her to believe that the attitudes *will* affect us as a group. It's too bad we don't know more about how this Blending thing works. Both for your problem and for our general one."

"Since anybody tryin' to form a Blendin' on their own faces arrest and summary execution, it's no wonder the details about it are hard to come by." Ro now looked thoughtful, his gaze on Lorand. "What the bunch of us did in that tavern to break up the fight might be illegal, but it can't be anythin' like what a real Blendin' does. Bottom line is we didn't blend, we only worked together."

"And there's no reason to call it a Blending if the members of it don't blend," Lorand agreed, now sharing the thoughtfulness. "But now that you mention it, I wonder why it *is* illegal for people to form their own Blendings. People with ordinary talent can't possibly even come close in strength to the Seated Five, so what's the point?"

"Truthfully, I wish I knew," Ro admitted, his brow furrowed. "Every time we think about or discuss this mess we're in the middle of, we come to a conclusion that answers one question but breeds a dozen more. I can't help thinkin' we're in way over our heads, and no matter how long we tread water we'll come to the point where we're too tired to go on doin' it. If we don't have a good, solid ship to climb up into by then, our only other option will be to drown.''

''I refuse to drown, and even beyond that I'll never let Jovvi drown,'' Lorand stated, not at all surprised at the hardness in his voice. ''I'll never stand by and watch something hurt her, and I'll protect myself in order to be there to protect *her*. If that means we'll have to *build* a ship to climb up into when the time comes, I'm ready to start.''

Ro nodded his agreement with the same hardened expression Lorand knew *he* wore, which undoubtedly meant that Ro had made the same vow relating to Tamrissa. It felt good to know that the other man would stand firm with him, but not much other good was particularly apparent. They would almost certainly have a fight on their hands, but what sort of fight?

And what, if anything, would winning gain them? The answer to that should have been obvious, but was it . . . ?

Thirteen

Rion handed over his worn clothes to a servant with orders to have them washed and ironed at once, then continued on up to his bedchamber. Wearing nothing but a towel about his middle would have made him feel ridiculous at one time, but right now it felt like a statement of freedom and independence. Mother would have thrown a fit if she'd found him walking around one step short of absolute nakedness, and he would have been lectured for an hour on top of it.

But now Mother's likes and dislikes no longer concerned him—although the same couldn't be said for her wants and demands.

After removing the towel and donning a thick cotton wrap instead, Rion walked to a chair and sat heavily. After he'd achieved his masteries and had had tea and a sandwich served to him by Padril, he'd forced the Adept to sit down and answer some very direct questions. Padril had squirmed and sweated and hadn't been entirely forthcoming, but Rion had learned enough to feel deeply disturbed.

To begin with, Padril's superiors would *not* be standing between Rion and his mother. The truth was that Hallina Mardimil had too much gold and power for anyone not of the high nobility to be willing to cross her, and Padril had lied when he'd said they would. He hadn't even known who Rion's mother was, only that there was some sort of to-do over the name on Rion's identification card. When the Adept had learned that it was *the* Hallina Mardimil who was Rion's mother, he'd turned as white as the shirts the applicants wore.

And that had given Rion an odd idea, so he'd pressed until Padril admitted it: the name of Rion's mother had frightened Padril because the man was a member of the lower nobility, just as most of the Adepts were. Each aspect had one or two representatives of the lower orders who were allowed to call themselves Adepts, but all the rest were from the nobility.

And yet there weren't any other members of the nobility around. Rion had pointed that out, and then had demanded to know where they *were* to be found. That was when Padril had hemmed and hawed, and had finally insisted that he knew nothing about the testing facilities for nobles. He himself had gone through the same thing Rion had, and Rion must have simply missed seeing his lesser peers. Or maybe they'd already gone through the testing procedure, and the only ones left had been commoners.

That last suggestion was too much of a real possibility for Rion to argue it, but it still left his final question unanswered. When Rion had put it to Padril, the man had paled again, and then he'd shaken his head.

"Really, sir, how could *I* be expected to know why you alone of your peers have been sent through these facilities?" the man had asked, sweat beginning to bead on his forehead. "I've never been involved in high politics myself, of course, but just like everyone else I've seen it being played at. Someone in your mother's position is bound to have at least one powerful enemy, someone with enough influence to have her son sent to the wrong place in order to embarrass *her*. That's the only possibility I can think of, but it makes a good deal of sense."

It did indeed, Rion had to admit as he leaned his head back in the chair. It also had implications which came close to making Rion ill. If it had made him angry instead he wouldn't have minded, but he seemed to have lost his anger somewhere. Then a knock came at the door, interrupting the mood, so he rose and went to the door. He was prepared to enjoy the relief of any distraction, but couldn't help raising his brows when he saw Tamrissa standing there.

"I—hope I'm not disturbing you," she said, taking in his wrap with a glance and a faint blush. "I only need a moment of your time, and then you may certainly return to your privacy."

"Please believe that the last thing your presence could be is a disturbance," Rion assured her, meaning every word. "Did you wish to speak to me here, or would you prefer to come in?"

He stepped back to allow her access to the chamber if she wished it, and surprisingly she did. She hesitated a very long moment before coming inside, and her expression was determined when she used a gesture to ask him to close the door. He did so with brows raised high, then obeyed her next gesture which motioned him closer.

"I don't want any of the servants to overhear us," she whispered quite low, looking up at him with a delightfully delicate blush on her cheeks. "Jovvi and I need to speak to you men later, preferably after dinner when we can pretend to gather to celebrate over glasses of brandy. We're certain some of the servants are being paid to report everything they hear us say, so we'll have to have a pretend conversation going while we talk about what we need to. You *are* willing to join us in the pretense, aren't you?''

"As it's for the good of the group, I'll certainly participate," Rion responded in a matching whisper, then couldn't help sighing. "But as far as being of use is concerned, I'll probably be more of a hindrance."

"How can you say that?" Tamrissa demanded indignantly in a hiss. "The support you helped Jovvi give me made it possible for me to move forward with everyone else, instead of letting self-doubt bog me down forever. I even achieved my first masteries today—" Her words broke off, and a stricken look replaced the indignation. "Oh, Rion, don't tell me *you* didn't achieve your masteries?"

"But of course I did," Rion said with a smile, deeply touched by her very obvious concern. "That isn't the source of my difficulty, so please don't be unnecessarily disturbed."

"Then what *is* bothering you?" she asked more calmly, obviously noticing that he'd quickly lost the smile. "If it's something I can help with, you have to give me the chance to do it. Very few people have actually been on my side in my life, so I refuse to abandon one who is."

"I sincerely wish it were something you could assist with," he said, finding her fierce determination as delightful as the rest of her. "I have no doubt but that I would be well protected, from anything and everything one could imagine."

"Please, Rion, I'm not your mother," she responded, now looking faintly annoyed. "I won't ever protect you, but I *will* do everything in my power to help you protect yourself. So why don't you tell me about what's bothering you? Sometimes just talking things out makes you feel better about them."

"I doubt that will happen this time, but if you insist," Rion agreed slowly. The truth was that he really didn't want to go back to solitary fretting, not when he might have such pleasant company for a time. "Please take a seat while I consider the best place to begin."

She nodded happily and went to the chair near the one

he'd been using, so he reclaimed his own place and bent forward with forearms on knees and hands clasped tight.

"I've discovered that I'm the only member of the high nobility to go through processing in the facilities we've all so recently shared," he said hesitantly, trying his best not to offend her. "I thought it strange that I came across not a single one of my peers, and now I'm told there are other facilities for the use of my class equals. But I've been sent through these facilities."

"I'm personally very glad you were, but other than that I don't understand," Tamrissa said, sounding disturbed. "If the people of your class are treated differently, why weren't you?"

"The answer to that is the source of my disturbance," he replied with a mirthless smile, still looking down at the carpeting. "There are two possibilities, each one equally repugnant. The first, of course, is that Mother arranged the whole thing to be certain I would be kept isolated from my peers, just as I have been all my life. She would then have been able to come forward and 'rescue' me from an intolerable situation, which she was certain it would be."

"And that, she must have thought, would keep you from trying to break free ever again," Tamrissa said angrily. "It makes sense from her twisted point of view, and I quite believe her capable of it. So what could the second possibility be?"

"It concerns politics, which tends to be a nasty, bloodthirsty game among the nobility," Rion answered. "I don't know everything there is to know about it, not when Mother kept me almost completely cut off from the rest of the world, but I do know how ruthless it can be. It's been suggested that one of Mother's enemies caused me to be separated from my class equals, the object being to embarrass Mother enough to undermine the strength of her position."

"And never mind what happens to *you*, because you're an unimportant pawn?" Tamrissa demanded so indignantly that Rion looked up in surprise. "Well, you're *not* an unimportant pawn, you're our friend, and I really resent someone trying to use you like that. I can see why you're disturbed, but I don't understand why you're letting it get you down. They threw you to the wolves, but instead of being devoured you've become one of the pack. Doesn't that interfere with their plans to *some* extent?''

"I hadn't looked at it that way, but I suppose it does," Rion admitted, again surprised. "And about my becoming a member of the wolf pack. . . . If someone hadn't tried to maneuver me into something they were certain I'd never be able to handle, I'd never have *learned* to handle it. It looks like I ought to be grateful instead, even if the battle to control my movements does escalate.''

"You mean they might fight over you?" Tamrissa asked, back to frowning. "But what would they get out of it?''

"If it's Mother alone, she'll win possession of me again," Rion explained, but without the depression he'd felt before. "If it's an enemy of hers, she'll fight to possess me again to restrengthen her political position, and her enemy will fight to embarrass both me and her and ruin it. So if I simply manage to hold onto my independence and keep moving ahead, both sides should be frustrated. Unless they try something unexpected.''

"If they do, then the rest of us will help you to cope with it," Tamrissa said promptly, refusing to let anxiety get a grip on him. "You keep picturing yourself as all alone, Rion, but you really aren't. Or don't we count as much as members of the nobility would?''

"In one way you count for more," he said gently, reaching over to touch her hand in brief reassurance. "This group had no reason to welcome me into its midst, but the fact that it did anyway is, in my opinion, more a strength than a weakness. But on the other hand you're volunteering to go up against some very powerful people on my behalf, and that makes me frightened for you. They could well destroy you just to get at *me*, and I'd never be able to bear that.''

"If *they* consider us as helpless as you do, we should be able to give them quite a shock," Tamrissa returned with an unsteady smile. "I might have to keep reminding myself that

I'm *not* helpless, but it's been getting easier to do and the others don't have my problem. We'll all stand together against whatever comes, so won't you *please* stop being upset?''

"Only because you ask it, lovely lady," Rion responded, finding it impossible not to laugh gently. "You've restored my sense of perspective as well as my mood, and I only wish I could do as great a favor for you."

"Well, if you mean that, you can," she replied, suddenly blushing a bright red and no longer able to meet his gaze. "I mean, only if you really want to. It's a great imposition, I know, and I can't imagine where I've gotten the nerve to ask in the first place, so if it's really too much of a bother. . . .''

"Tamrissa," he interrupted softly, certain she meant to continue on in the same unintelligible way for the rest of the afternoon. He also took her hand gently in his, and although she stiffened slightly she didn't pull away. "Tamrissa, I don't understand a thing you're saying. I would, as I said, be delighted to return the favor, but first you must tell me what the return favor is supposed to be."

"Oh . . . yes . . . of course," she said after swallowing heavily, her cheeks still flaming. "I haven't actually specified yet, have I? Well, it's really very simple. I'd . . . like you to . . . take me to bed."

And that, from Rion's point of view, was the biggest surprise and shock of the day!

FOURTEEN

"I beg your pardon?" Rion answered blankly, as if I'd spoken in a language he didn't know. "I couldn't have heard what I thought I did . . . could I?"

"Oh, you don't want to, and now I've gotten you upset again," I babbled, more embarrassed than I'd ever been in my life. "I'll just leave, then, and we can both forget I ever said anything about—"

"No, please be calm, it's all right," he soothed in that deep voice of his, one big hand coming gently to my arm to keep me from rising. "Your request just startled me, coming as unexpectedly as it did. I assure you I'm not in the least reluctant, but I do find myself curious. I'd thought your interest had turned to Vallant Ro, so I don't understand why you've put this request to me rather than to him."

"I suppose you *are* entitled to the full truth," I granted him, shifting uncomfortably in the chair. He was really such a handsome man, and was studying me so closely. . . . "Vallant Ro is the reason I'm doing this, so I can't very well ask *his* help. I'd meant to ask Lorand because he's a friend, but then I realized that you're a friend as well. I—don't want Vallant to be interested in me, and something Jovvi said suggested he might lose his attraction if I allow another man to lie with me."

"Are you certain that that was what Jovvi said?" Rion

97

asked, frowning just a little. "If it is, I fail to see the point."

"Well, most men apparently dislike sharing their women," I explained, developing my own frown. "I know Lorand feels that way and Jovvi says it's not unusual, so I'm inclined to believe it. And it also occurred to me that we may just manage to get ourselves out of this competitions mess, and then discover that we need something to do with our lives. Jovvi means to open a residence for courtesans if that happens, and has invited me to remain with her. I thought I would be of more use if . . . I. . . ."

I couldn't quite bring myself to discuss the details of the matter, at least not with Rion. He'd changed so much since the day he'd first come to the residence, and was no longer quite as innocent as I felt.

"How strange that the matter should disturb some men," Rion said, shaking his head and shrugging. "Considering the pleasure involved, it seems mean-spirited to refuse to allow someone the experiencing of it. And how is one to learn all the possibilities of the act, if one refrains from indulging?"

"Is it really all that pleasurable?" I asked without looking at him, fighting to hold down nightmare memories. "Everyone says it is, but my dreams still writhe with the pain of my own experiences. And if it's *supposed* to be pleasurable, why did my husband make it such an abomination for me?"

"Anyone who turns pleasure into torment and pain must surely be very ill," Rion said quickly but gently, reaching out to touch my hand briefly in comfort. "It seems logical to assume that the man received his own pleasure by denying you yours, which almost certainly means he was taught to behave in such a way. The fault, then, would lie with those who taught him such a thing, and also with him for not understanding his lacks and seeking to remedy them. Let's begin our own pleasure right now, and hopefully you'll soon forget the rest."

"Now?" I echoed as my heart began to thump, my head flying up to let me see if he were joking. "But I was thinking about later, in the deep night, when everyone will be asleep . . ."

"And you and I will sneak about like thieves, feeling as

though we did something shameful?'' he countered, this time taking my hand and gently holding it. ''That would be foolish, lovely lady, especially since we have the opportunity at this very moment. Come, let's put your apprehensions to rest once and for all.''

''But it's still light out!'' I blurted as he rose to his feet, using the hand he held to urge me to do the same. ''In daylight . . . I couldn't possibly. . . .''

''Allow me to ease your apprehensions,'' he said softly, and suddenly we were plunged into a dim, gray world where he was no more than an indistinct outline. ''This shield of opaque air can't quite manage blackness at this time of day, but surely it will do? I'm barely able to see you, which should keep your sense of modesty intact. Do you agree?''

He'd removed the shield again by then, so I didn't bother to tell him that it wasn't entirely modesty which moved me. And we certainly did have the time right then, since the episodes with my husband had only seemed endless. In reality they hadn't taken very long at all, and I'd probably be best off going ahead and getting it well behind me. So I nodded to Rion, which made him smile that incredibly attractive smile.

''Marvelous,'' he said, drawing me up by the hand he still held and then kissing the hand. ''Come along, then, and we'll begin at once. Would you prefer to have the shield up before we start to remove your clothing?''

''We?'' I echoed, beginning to follow him toward the bed almost without thinking about it. ''My husband always demanded that I come to him . . . unclothed, except for the times he tore off what I happened to be wearing. But you can't tear *these* clothes, not when I need them for the practice and qualifying area.''

''Lovely lady, I would never be so barbaric as to destroy your clothing,'' he said with obvious disapproval, stopping near the bed. ''When I was a child, some of the other children managed to get me alone and began to try tearing off the brand-new outfit Mother had just presented me with. I had no idea why they were doing it and so was terrified, but I distinctly remember the episode as being painful before I thought to use my magic to force them back away from me. With that in mind, your clothing would stay intact even if they were worthless rags.''

"You really had a terrible time growing up, didn't you?" I said, putting my free hand to his arm in shared compassion. "And now I wonder. . . . My father didn't want my sisters and me forming attachments to any of the boys we associated with at school and at receptions, so any time one of us seemed interested in a particular boy, he paid the boy to get us alone and pretend to attack us. That was to make sure we would be available for the husbands he picked out for us, and that we would still be untouched when we married. Oddly enough, most of the boys took his silver eagerly. I finally found out about it when, during one of the times my husband drank too much, he shared that very amusing story with me.''

"Personally, I find it a good deal less than amusing," he said, a sharp look in his eyes. "But I fail to see what connection your experience had with mine."

"Well, we decided your mother might have arranged to have you sent here with us because she thought you would find it intolerable, and would immediately run back to *her*. Do you think she might have dressed you in a particularly ridiculous outfit that time, and then given those children a chance to attack you? If she knew how vicious they would be, she could have used the opportunity to bind you more closely to her.''

"It never occurred to me before, but I believe you're right," he agreed slowly, his expression hardening. "She's obviously been manipulating me since the day I was born, and with each new thing I learn I find myself more determined to continue on with my present course of action. But speaking of courses of action, let's dismiss thoughts of parental misbehavior and continue on with what's been barely begun.''

He released my hand and lifted me into his arms so abruptly that I squeaked in startlement. But before the fear began to pound and flash I was set down on the far side of the bed, and Rion had released me.

"I have no wish to make this anything but pleasurable for you, dear lady," he said, his expression having softened. "If at any time you wish me to cease what I happen to be doing, you have only to say so. We've both of us been forced to the pleasure of others far too often for this to be done in any other way."

The absolutely determined look in his eyes as he said that should have frightened me, but strangely enough it was more reassuring. I believed Rion in a way I would have had trouble believing almost anyone else. The kind of pain we'd each been given had, for the most part, been different, but it provided a shared bond that neither of us could deny. The smile I gave Rion didn't have to be forced, and he seemed to know it. He showed one of the same kind, sat down on the bed, and then his shield of air was around us again.

"I've also taken the precaution of putting a block of thickened air before the door," he murmured as he moved just a little closer. "We won't be disturbed and you certainly won't be embarrassed, so put all thoughts of distraction from your mind. Now, let's begin by making you more comfortable. You're surely not old enough yet nor . . . overendowed so far as to be corseted?"

"No, not quite yet," I answered with a laugh for the way he'd put it. Only matrons who were beginning to lose their figures—and younger women who spent too much time at table during meals—descended to the shameful expedience of using corsets to alter their appearance. To admit to wearing one was the same as admitting yourself a failure as a woman, and few women had the nerve to do either. "But Rion—how did *you* find out about corsets?"

"A servant we had for a time, when I was a boy," he replied, matching my laugh. "I wondered aloud why some of Mother's friends and acquaintances looked as though they'd been stuffed into dresses and gowns too small for them, and he told me about corsets. But he also warned me not to mention them in Mother's hearing, so that was one lecture I escaped. May I help you to remove your blouse? ''

I felt very shy as I nodded my agreement, but it helped that the gray shadow who was Rion didn't rush through doing it. I was the one who pulled my blouse out of the skirt top, and then we shared the opening of the buttons. I expected the blouse to be removed immediately then, but Rion simply moved closer, opened the blouse just a little to expose only the tops of my breasts, and began to kiss me there.

At first I was quite tense and nervous, but after a few moments of nothing else happening I began to notice how the touch of his lips felt. Feather-light, gentle and warm, an appreciation rather than a demand. . . . Apprehension began to change to a tingling of sorts, one I'd never experienced before.

By then I'd relaxed back against the pillow above my head, finding that enjoyment of this beginning process wasn't difficult. Rion's nearness was slightly disconcerting, so I closed my eyes to stop the automatic cringing my body kept trying to do—and that was when Rion changed the location of his kissing. I gasped when his lips and tongue caressed my left nipple, but was able to keep from crying out. This time no pain followed the caress, the very first time it hadn't.

And things continued on that way. Rion spent an incredibly long time proving to the frightened part of my mind that my responding to his delightful urgings would *not* result in my being immediately hurt. By the time his fingers found the buttons of my skirt I actually almost believed it, and so helped him to remove my skirt, petticoats, stockings, and shoes. My blouse had already been put aside, which meant that he was able to begin to kiss me all over.

Again, quite a bit of time passed, but none of it seemed wasted. Rion's kissing became quite intimate, and although he did absolutely nothing to hurt me, I soon discovered that I neared the end of my ability to endure any more of that kind of attention. Moaning and moving against him feebly was the best I could manage, but strangely enough that proved to be sufficient. He stopped what he was doing, moved above me, and then we were joined together.

Rather than hating and fearing his presence inside me, I discovered that it was just what I wanted. Again my nervousness and anticipation of pain came to nothing, so I was able to eventually join his movement as his murmurings urged me to do. We also shared a kiss, and that made the relief, when it came, much sweeter. Rion's relief came just a short while after my own, and he kissed me one final time before withdrawing and lying on the bed beside me.

We both breathed rather heavily from our exertions, but I recovered first and found something to be curious about. I therefore kindled a very small flame to light the gray dimness a bit, and turned to look at Rion where he lay. He'd discarded his wrap quite some time earlier, and the sight of his bare chest was, surprisingly, not in the least upsetting.

"That was really lovely and I'd like to thank you," I said when his gaze, accompanied by a smile, moved to me. "It seems everyone was right about the pleasure, but . . . Rion, wherever did you learn all that? If your mother kept you so closely tied to her, how were you able to avoid her often enough to gain such expertise?"

"It's hardly expertise," he replied with a pleased laugh, raising one hand to my face—which did *not* cause me to flinch back. "I've only just begun to learn, but I had a marvelous teacher. She's the most . . . compelling person I've ever known, and the more time that passes without my seeing her, the more frantic I become. I've discovered that she'll also need protection from my mother, so I don't dare try to find her until I have gold in my pocket and the power of a sufficiently advanced position in my hand. But then I *will* find her, and she and I won't need to be parted again."

"Well, if I can help in any way, you just let me know," I told him firmly. "No one can deny that we're *really* close friends now, and friends are supposed to help one another. You *will* let me help, won't you?"

"It will be my pleasure and delight," he answered with a grin that made him look especially handsome, and then he glanced at my flame. "Tell me something: isn't that glow supposed to be in the palm of your hand? It seems to me that anytime I've seen someone with Fire magic use a glow like that, it was in their palm. And someone said once that the glow *had* to be in contact with the magic user, but apparently they were mistaken."

"Well . . . maybe not entirely," I said, groping for an explanation that would not upset him. "At school we were taught the same thing, that the glow had to be in the palm of your hand because it was linked directly to the magic user's bodily output. It's a . . . controlled leakage of the user's Fire affinity, and is supposed to go out if you try to separate it from contact with your flesh."

"But yours isn't going out," he observed, happily not looking upset in the least. "Are you doing something else, then?"

"Actually . . . no," I admitted, then decided I might as well tell him all of it. "I discovered accidentally that I *could* disconnect the glow from me without having it go out, but I've never told anyone. None of them could do it, you see, so I thought. . . ."

"That what they didn't know couldn't hurt you," he finished when I didn't, his hand now coming to smooth my hair. "I'm certainly familiar with *that* state of affairs, so please be assured that I'll say nothing about it to anyone. It would seem logical that friends also keep each other's secrets."

"I think that would feel incredibly wonderful," I said, gingerly reaching out to put just my fingertips to *his* face. "Having someone be trustworthy enough to keep your secret, I mean. This is the first time I've ever trusted someone to do that, and I feel glad rather than sorry. But I really must run. I still have to speak to Lorand before dinner, while Jovvi speaks to Pagin Holter and Dom Ro."

"I would suggest that you dress before you run anywhere," Rion said with a chuckle that made me blush. "I, personally, would enjoy the sight of your marvelous body immensely, but the others might become . . . disconcerted."

"Disconcerted," I repeated in a grumble while he continued to chuckle. "I've never heard it called *that* before. . . ."

The two of us were just joking, of course, but as I dressed, part of my mind insisted on thinking about what Vallant Ro's reaction would be to seeing me naked. The rest of me didn't care, of course, not about anything concerning the man, but that one small part . . . now that I knew how pleasurable lying with a man could be . . . it *couldn't* be even better, as Lorand claimed, with someone who meant something special. . . .

Vallant Ro *didn't* mean something special, and I *had* to be determined to keep it like that. . . .

FIFTEEN

Vallant came down to dinner feeling very much like a conspirator, and apparently everyone else felt the same way. Or almost everyone else. Jovvi, the one who had told him about the proposed false party scheduled for after dinner, seemed as natural and pleasant as always. The others, though. . . .

As Vallant took his place at the table—sitting next to Lorand Coll where Beldara Lant had originally been seated, and opposite Jovvi—he glanced around. To Vallant's left, on the opposite side of the table, was Rion Mardimil, who seemed a good deal quieter than usual. Then came Jovvi, who smiled warmly at everyone—including Pagin Holter, who was seated next to her on her other side. Beside Vallant was Lorand Coll, who toyed with his eating utensils while apparently deep in thought.

And at the head of the table between Holter and Coll,

looking glorious in a dinner dress of pink satin, Tamrissa sat looking everywhere but at him. He'd meant to speak to her this afternoon, but when he'd knocked on her door he'd gotten no answer. Jovvi later told him that Tamrissa had gone to speak to Mardimil and Coll just as she had sought out him and Holter, and Vallant hadn't had to ask why it hadn't been Tamrissa who contacted him. She apparently still refused to speak to him or even to acknowledge his existence, and his frustration level was mounting rapidly.

"My goodness, this place feels more like a mourning house than a residence for the victorious," Jovvi suddenly announced as the servants began to bring out their meal. "Am I mistaken in believing that we all achieved our first levels of mastery today? No? Well then, we'll just have to celebrate our success after dinner, if all of you will unbend enough now to simply smile."

Vallant thought she was telling them that maintaining a funereal atmosphere while pretending to have a party just wouldn't do, as even a blind and deaf fool would become suspicious about what they might really be doing. It was an excellent point, and it was quickly proven that he wasn't the only one to pick up on it.

"I suppose I should be smiling," Coll agreed, actually managing something that could be called a small specimen of a smile. "I hadn't expected to gain those masteries quite so soon, which means I thought I'd have more time before needing to face the next level. There are a couple of things waiting that I'd much prefer not to think about."

"But I *have* to think about what comes next in *my* aspect," Tamrissa put in, giving Coll a wan smile. "I'll need to do the same thing I did today, only this time while I defend myself from attack. And don't ask me why I'll be attacked, because I haven't any idea. My supposed Adept guide will be doing the attacking, and although she isn't quite as strong as I am, it was hate at first sight for the both of us."

"But that's exactly why we need to celebrate," Jovvi said, interrupting as Vallant was about to indignantly announce that no one would attack Tamrissa while *he* stood alive and able. Belatedly he realized what a stupid thing that would have been for him to say; Tamrissa would not have welcomed his interference even if they were getting along, and interfering in any event would almost certainly cost her the mastery. But his sudden worry about *her* was almost enough to distract him from his own problems.

"We all have things ahead of us that we'd rather not think about," Jovvi continued, her glance at him suggesting she'd interrupted him on purpose. "That's why we ought to celebrate tonight, so as not to rob ourselves of the victories we've earned. I want to pat myself on the back tonight, and let tomorrow take care of itself for now. Does anyone else feel the same?"

One by one they all roused themselves to agree with her while showing at least a small amount of enthusiasm, so the matter was settled. After dinner they would have a party, and in the meanwhile they began to apply themselves to the food. By the time the second course arrived they were beginning to chat with one another, and the serving of dessert found them all a good deal more relaxed.

Tamrissa had called over one of the servants earlier and had given the man what seemed to be instructions. It seemed odd that it wasn't Warla, Tamrissa's companion and temporary majordomo of the residence, who gave the servants their orders, but Vallant hadn't even seen the girl today. She might be away seeing to personal business, or simply taking a rest from the frantic running-about she'd been doing. But Warla, sweet and helpless little thing that she was, wasn't Vallant's primary concern.

The woman who *was* his primary concern finished her cup of tea, then rose to tell everyone that it was time they began their party. They all dutifully rose in turn and followed after her, but not to the library, where they'd had their first gathering. Tamrissa led them to the back door and outside instead, then gestured to the garden.

"It's such a lovely evening that I thought we might have our party outside," she said, sounding as though the idea had been spur-of-the-moment and hers alone. "I had the servants light the paper lanterns to make everything look more festive, and a table with brandy and glasses, a tea service and cups, and even some honeyed nuts and sweet cakes has been set up. Let's go and enjoy ourselves."

The others all made sounds of approval and agreement, so Vallant added his own sounds of the same sort and walked with everyone to the white-clothed table which had been arranged for them. With everything already brought and prepared there was no need to have servants underfoot, which was the main reason for the party in the first place.

"This garden is almost as lovely at night as it is during the day," Jovvi said in normal tones as she looked around, then she lowered her voice without changing expression. "Lorand, can you tell whether or not there are any listeners lurking in the shadows where the lanternlight doesn't reach? That one servant standing near the house won't be able to hear what we say, but I want to be certain he's the only one out here."

"I hadn't realized I'd be able to tell," Coll responded just as softly, but with a surprised expression he quickly wiped away. "But you're right and I *can* distinguish plant and animal life from human, and there's none of it out here but us."

"I'm glad to have you confirm my own opinion," Jovvi told him with one of her beautiful smiles. "I felt nothing in the sense of a human being out there, but it *is* possible for some people to hide from my perceptions. Blanking your mind completely and simply listening can do it. . . . But that isn't what we've gathered here for. While we each supply ourselves with a glass of brandy, I'll tell you that I've confirmed the guess that we don't have any time to waste. If we're going to be part of the competitions, we have to qualify for them as quickly as possible."

"What makes you think so?" Coll asked as the group drifted toward the table holding the drinkables. "We all agreed that we have to keep moving forward, but why the sudden rush?"

"My Adept guide admitted that the competitions are almost on us," Jovvi said, picking up the bottle of brandy to play hostess. "When I mentioned that everyone at the lower level had to qualify by week's end or not at all, and that meant the competitions were only a few days away, she corrected me by saying, 'Well, more than just a few.' The correction was reluctant so I'm sure it wasn't deliberate misdirection, but please note she didn't even say something like 'two weeks.' She said 'more than a few' *days*, which could even mean less than a week."

"It looks like it's a good thing we all got our first level masteries today, then," Tamrissa put in after a moment, during which time a heavy silence had begun to form. "I'm not looking forward to having Soonen, my Adept guide, attack me, but I'm certain she isn't nearly as strong as I am. And neither is that male Adept who witnessed my masteries, which reminds me about something else which should be mentioned. Were the rest of you also treated differently after you achieved the masteries than you were before them?"

"Yes, I was, and I didn't like it," Coll answered, also smiling his thanks to Jovvi for filling his brandy glass. "The man nearly got down on all fours to offer his back as a seat, and that reminds *me* about something. Tamrissa said her Adept guide was a good deal weaker than her, and so was mine. If that goes for everyone else's guides as well, why in the world are those people allowed to call themselves Adepts? I can't quite believe that we're the strongest talents ever to come by."

"But of course we're not," Mardimil said with a small laugh after sipping at his brandy. "Those people are allowed to call themselves Adepts because most of them are members of the lower nobility. They were undoubtedly given the positions as repayment for political debts to their families, and they're the strongest representatives those families were able to supply. All those stronger than them are either members of other families, or uninterested in wasting their time in such a way."

"But—that's stupid," Vallant couldn't help protesting, even though the idea of political favors was nothing new to him. "*Givin'* somebody a job they should have to qualify for makes the whole system rotten, especially since we almost died gettin' to where we are. Where do those fools get off *handin'* out things like Adept positions while everybody else has to fight just to stay alive?"

"Not *everybody* else," Jovvi corrected, smiling as she lowered her voice even more. Vallant hadn't actually started to shout, but without the reminder he might have. "Obviously most members of the nobility are excused from having to go through what we did, but that shouldn't surprise any of us. The testing authority is made up of people from the nobility, so they've obviously been running things to suit themselves."

"Which, as Ro said, is stupid as well as unfair," Coll told her, clearly as annoyed as Vallant. "Everyone claims to understand that natural selection usually produces the strongest and smartest members of a species, even if it's as far from kind as you can get. By excusing their own people from having to compete or be brushed aside they can only have weakened the nobility, which they ought to be bright enough to understand. But if all this is true, what are *you* doing here, Mardimil?"

"That was my question as well," Mardimil replied wryly, speaking to all of them. "The answer seems to be one of two possibilities, which are one, my mother caused me to be here in order to convince me how horrible the world is away from her side, or two, an enemy of hers arranged my presence, thinking possibly to see me fail, but in any event to embarrass her. Whichever the cause, my presence is no accident."

"I'd be willin' to put money on *that*," Vallant agreed, his sense of outrage suddenly turning to come forth on Mardimil's behalf. "Personally I'm glad you're here, but that's one dirty way to treat somebody who's supposed to be one of your own."

"It doesn't surprise me either," Coll said with a grim nod. "It takes intelligence and compassion to show a sense of honor, and those testing people obviously have neither. But how does that affect what we were discussing this afternoon, about us being chosen as members of a challenging Blending, I mean?"

"What's this?" Jovvi and Tamrissa said almost together, just using different words. "What makes you think we'll be chosen as members of a challenging Blending?" Jovvi finished for both of them.

"Well, that was one of the things we meant to tell you right away," Coll said ruefully, his glance around making Vallant feel as though he and the other men had been keeping secrets. "Holter there was the first to notice that except for Water magic, our residence holds only one representative of each of the five aspects. And if you add to that the fact that when two of our group didn't qualify as quickly as the rest of us they were moved out, you have at the very least an extremely strong possibility."

The ladies exchanged a glance without saying anything, both of them looking faintly stunned, and then Jovvi raised her brows.

"That *would* explain why we're suddenly being treated so deferentially," she suggested, her tone nevertheless sounding faintly skeptical. "Something still doesn't feel *quite* right, though, but I can't seem to put my finger on it. Well, hopefully it will come to me later, but right now I have a question: why *two* representatives of Water magic?"

"Probably because Holter and I have been runnin' neck and neck until now," Vallant put in when Holter refused with a headshake to voice his own theories. "They must be waitin' to see which of us will do better, and then they'll choose that one."

"So we really do have to be as good as possible to qualify," Tamrissa said, but to the group in general rather than to him. "Sometimes I get the feeling that being *too* good will ruin our chances rather than help them, but that's ridiculous. If they're putting together challenging Blendings, they'll want the best of the best.''

"They *should* want that," Jovvi agreed, "but sometimes I get the same feeling. We'll have to try to find out, but let's not be obvious about it. If the opening to ask a useful question doesn't come up naturally in casual conversation, don't anyone *bring* it up. I can't get past the feeling that we're walking a tightrope here, and one misstep is all it will take to plunge us into the abyss. It's possible I'm just being a silly woman about all this. . . .''

She let her words trail off as she glanced around, making the statement a question that any or all of them were free to answer. No one accepted the offer, though, so Vallant put in his own copper's worth.

"If you're bein' a silly woman, then I'm bein' the same," he admitted heavily, doing no more than looking down at the brandy he held. "I keep gettin' a feelin' very much like yours, which takes the . . . pleasurable excitement from the possibility of bein' put in a challengin' Blendin'. If they've been handin' out Adept positions to people who don't deserve them, what about the Seated Blendin' itself?''

"I'd say that was another matter entirely," Coll protested while everyone else made sounds which showed their disturbance over the idea. "The general public has no idea about what goes on in these testing facilities, so they can get away with just about anything they please. The major competitions are another matter entirely, which people travel for days to come to see. With anything that public, they *have* to play it straight.''

"I'm inclined to agree," Mardimil said thoughtfully. "I've never seen a challenge involving the Blending, of course, but I did attend one against the Seated High in Water magic. The competition took place in front of a very large audience, and there was no doubt about the outcome. The challenger seemed very strong, but the Seated High proved stronger.''

"So we may have a chance after all," Tamrissa said, her brows raised in partial disbelief just as Jovvi's had been. "I think what we have to decide now is whether or not to go for it. Please, Dom Holter, tell us your opinion. You're the only one of us who seems to have done any real thinking about this.''

''Yeah, I done some thinkin' on it, ma'am, but I don't see as how it helps much,'' Holter answered slowly, obviously reluctant to speak but unable to refuse Tamrissa. ''It waren't me who made the real point, but Dom Mardimil there. He said like as not we ain't gonna get th' choice, just have it made *fer* us. That sounds like a purty fair guess t'me, so I'll jest go along with 'er.''

''A statement which gives us all something to think about,'' Jovvi suggested in a distracted way. ''It might be best if we pretend to be partying for a while, and return to serious conversation after we've had the chance to consider what we've heard. Does anyone think we ought not to?''

No one spoke up to disagree with the suggestion, so the fairly tight group simply dissolved a bit as people moved a step or two away to drink their brandy and do some thinking. Vallant finally took a sip from his own glass, but just a sip to bolster his courage. The time had come to speak to Tamrissa, and he wasn't about to play the coward and let it slip past.

The object of his intentions stood alone just a few feet away, clearly doing the thinking Jovvi had mentioned. Vallant moved slowly and calmly until he stood beside her, his back to most of the others.

''Before you dismiss me again, you'd better add *this* to your thinkin','' he said very softly. ''If we do get chosen to be a challengin' Blendin', we'll all have to work together in order to win. If you keep tryin' to pretend I'm not even alive, you could be the reason we lose.''

''You're forgetting about Dom Holter,'' she said, still not looking at him but surprising him by responding without hesitation. ''He could be the one chosen to represent Water magic, and then there won't be a problem.''

Vallant blinked, not having seriously considered that even

for a moment. The outlook was no reflection on Holter and his abilities, simply an awareness of Vallant's own.

"But what if he isn't chosen instead of me?" Vallant pursued almost at once. "I happen to like Holter and respect what he can do, but I'm the better practitioner. Once I prove that everyone will be forced to acknowledge it, so I repeat: Are you goin' to keep on blamin' me for somethin' I'm not guilty of and make us lose, or will you listen to reason and bring us closer to winnin'?"

She hesitated a brief moment, still gazing at the lantern-lit garden, and then she showed a very odd smile.

"Isn't it strange how our chances of winning have suddenly come to depend on my listening to *you*," she said, a very faint tremor in her voice. "It so happens I don't believe that, Dom Ro, so please find someone else to tell your tall stories to. This incredulous little girl simply isn't interested."

"But why *not*?" Vallant demanded, fighting to keep his voice soft and his temper from flaring out of control. "You know I'm not guilty of anythin', so why can't we go back to the way things were before two vindictive people forced their way in here and between us?"

"Because the . . . 'way things were' should never have happened," she replied in a whisper, now looking down at the brandy glass in her hands. "I've . . . thought about the whole thing, and I realize now that I was wrong to lead you on. The truth is I'm . . . involved with a large number of other men, so becoming involved with you as well would simply be unfair. I know you dislike the idea of . . . sharing a woman, so it would be best if we forgot the entire thing. Please excuse me now."

With that she hurried away from him, and Vallant was too openmouthed with confusion and startlement to even consider following. She'd been "leading him on?" How? By making him all but drag her out for a simple walk in the garden? And was he really supposed to believe that *she* was involved with a "large number" of other men? He almost wished she was, and with men who would give her pleasure rather than pain. She'd had enough hurt in her life to justify any change for the better.

But *he* wanted to be the one to give her that pleasure, along with excellent reasons for letting him be the only man to do it. He'd been raised to understand that the decision should always be the woman's choice, and it was his place to influence her choice only with superior ability, not with superior strength. He'd never minded rising to the challenge, so to speak, one of the things which had made him so popular with the ladies.

So where could she have gotten the idea that he disliked having to share a woman? It was true he had no intentions of sharing Tamrissa once he made her his wife, but if she needed something like that to make her really happy. . . . He would do his best to make it unnecessary, but if his best wasn't good enough and her happiness depended on it. . . . Damn it, where *had* she gotten those ridiculous ideas?

Vallant took a calming sip of brandy, trying to rid himself of the feeling that he stood alone on the deck of a sinking ship without a single bit of dry land in sight. He would even have settled for a log canoe if it were seaworthy, and would refrain from spinning him around in dizzying circles. He'd managed to get Tamrissa to talk to him, but the conversation had ended with her being "honest" and "fair" with him. The whole thing was ridiculous, but what was he supposed to do now?

Frustration returned to Vallant with the question, and it was only worsened by seeing Coll in what looked like a pleasant conversation with Jovvi. He wanted to have the same with Tamrissa, but the maddening woman had gone to the refreshment table, and was apparently replacing her glass of brandy with a cup of tea. What *could* he say to her . . . ?

And then an idea came, one that wasn't very nice but which still made Vallant grin slightly. So Tamrissa was involved with a "large number" of other men, was she? Only a real innocent would say something like that and expect to be believed, but she was the one who'd opened the door. If he pretended to be hurt by having been "led on" by her, he could then insist that the only way she might make it right was to give *him* what she was giving all those other men.

Vallant chuckled just a little as he watched Tamrissa, knowing he would never actually force her into his bed. His aim would be to get her to admit she was spinning yarns, and then they could go on from there. But if she refused to admit it and became determined to prove she spoke the truth, there was only one thing he would accept as proof. The choice would be hers, but then it would be his turn to exercise some ability. . . .

Vallant quickly added some details to his plan, then began to walk toward Tamrissa to start it. She stood gulping her tea, something she'd certainly want to do again once he began to speak to her, but he was only halfway there when an interruption came. One of the house servants appeared on the path, and cleared his throat loudly for attention.

"Please excuse the interruption, gentles," he said when he got that attention. "I must announce that there's a caller at the door."

Everyone but Pagin Holter seemed to freeze in place, and that included Vallant. They hadn't yet been told who the caller was for, but each of them stood clenched in the fist of dread. Someone was about to be given trouble again, but which of them? That was the question: which . . . ?

SIXTEEN

Delin Moord spent a bit longer listening to Bron tell everyone just how much their abilities should "improve" by the following week, and then he encouraged the meeting to end. They all had other demands on their time, demands which couldn't be ignored without making people suspicious. If their group was to be seen as having no intentions concerning winning the competition, they couldn't afford to spend too much time discussing the matter.

And Delin had something fairly important to take care of. Homin needed help with his father's new wife, and Homin was going to get it. Nothing could be allowed to interfere with the purpose of the group, which was what interfering with one of its members really accomplished. . . .

"I'm ready, Delin," Homin said, bringing Delin out of his thoughts. "Shall we travel together in one carriage, letting the other one follow?"

"Yes, and we'll use mine," Delin said, seeing that Bron and Selendi were already at the front door, being shown out by Kambil. "But let's not advertise your predicament. If anyone asks, we're merely going to the local entertainment district for some tea and private conversation."

Homin nodded jerkily, as though he would find it possible to disobey even a suggestion, then trailed along behind Delin to the door. Delin used warmth when he thanked Kambil for the hospitality of his house, deliberately reminding himself that Kambil *had* acted for the good of the group. He still didn't really like the man, but that was unimportant beside the fact that Kambil was now one of *his*.

Delin went to his carriage, using the time while Homin scurried to tell his driver to follow to give his own driver instructions. When Homin finally joined him, puffing a bit from having hurried, they were immediately off.

"You do remember, I hope, that I have a stop to make before we continue on to your house," Delin said as Homin settled himself on the seat opposite. He hadn't dared to sit *next* to Delin, of course, which showed there was *some* hope for him. "It shouldn't take *too* long, but when a lady is involved a gentleman should never rush."

"Oh, I quite understand," Homin assured him, nevertheless paling a bit. "You'll need to mention to Elfini that the delay was on your behalf, and hopefully she'll be reasonable about it."

"I'm certain she'll be reasonable," Delin assured him, smiling as he made himself more comfortable. "For some reason the ladies look upon me rather favorably, and I expect Elfini to be no different."

Homin made a sound that was more hopeful agreement than certainty, then remained silent. Which was quite useful, as Delin had plans to make.

It didn't take long for them to reach their local entertainment district, an area of perhaps two blocks in the center of their residential district. Going into the city proper for a simple afternoon or evening out would have been too bothersome for people like them, who lived a fair distance out, so entertainment districts had been approved and built. There were dining parlors for full meals, tea rooms for snacks, theaters for plays and auditoriums for music recitals.

There were also gambling parlors and pleasure parlors, but those were devoted to people with more sophisticated tastes than the ordinary. They were located behind the small number of exclusive shops the district also boasted, and one had to be brought to them by someone who was already a member. Delin had meant to go there after the meeting, but now his plans had changed. And he wouldn't have vouched for Homin in any event. Those places had certain standards, and people like Homin simply didn't measure up.

His carriage took them instead to one of the tea rooms, one which also offered discreet apartments on its upper floors for brief or longterm rentals. Delin was one of those few who kept a permanent second home there, one no one else knew about. The ladies he brought to the apartment assumed he'd rented it for the afternoon or evening, and Delin had never disabused them of the notion.

"You'll sit and take tea while I tend to my previous commitment," Delin said to Homin as they left the carriage. "Your driver can put your carriage next to mine in the accommodation across the street, and we'll send a boy for them when we're ready to leave."

Homin nodded and turned to gesture his driver after Delin's, and then the two of them entered the tea room. Soft, pleasant music was being played by a small group to one side of the room, and Delin saw Homin seated with tea ordered before he left him. He wouldn't have wanted Homin to come searching for him under normal circumstances; today the idea was completely unacceptable.

Once out of sight of the patrons of the tea room, Delin took the stairs to his apartment two at a time. He first had to change out of his fashionable clothes into something less noticeable, and then he would leave again by the private entrance in back. His interview with Elfini would go a good deal more smoothly if Homin was nowhere about.

The stables across the street from the back of the tea room was as private as the apartments, and Delin kept a horse there to be used when a carriage simply wouldn't do. He saddled the horse himself as was the custom there, with only the half-blind old caretaker left on the premises. The boys who cleaned the stalls and exercised the horses were long gone, which effectively meant no one was there to see him leave.

Delin had never been to Homin's father's house, but he'd made it his business to learn where everyone of the slightest importance lived. When you have great plans for your life you never know when some bit of information will come in handy, so Delin had simply collected every fact available to him. The ride wasn't a long one, and Delin made sure to avoid the front drive. Going through the woods separating that house from the estate next door was a much better idea, and also let him leave his horse tethered in those woods.

It was a good five minute walk from the woods to the house itself, but happily there were no gardeners about to see him cross the back lawn to the gardens, go through the gardens and past the bath house, and then reach the house. There was also a few minutes worth of looking through windows to locate Elfini without being seen, but this wasn't the first time Delin had done something like this. If necessary he would climb a trellis to reach the second floor, but checking the back rooms of the ground floor first only made sense.

And the effort proved to be a worthwhile expenditure of time. Elfini sat in a large room reading a book, and Delin would have wagered that she'd decorated the private sanctum herself. The walls were covered with paintings showing men and women being severely punished, and in each instance the one doing the punishing was female. There were also various wooden frames standing about the room, waiting for a victim to be strapped to them in either upright or bent over positions.

"Obscene, all of it," Delin muttered as he looked in through a pane of the terrace doors. It was the reason he'd been so certain that Elfini's room would be at the back of the house: obscene places like that always were. Those involved in the obscenity refused to understand how wrong they were, but that didn't change the fact that they were. Normal people understood that it was a *man's* place to do the punishing, a woman's place to receive it. He'd put girls on some of those very same frames in the pleasure parlor, and knowing that *these* were meant for men turned his stomach.

So he lost no more time opening the terrace door quietly and stepping inside. Now he could see the full array of whips and switches and straps displayed on the right hand wall of the room, along with chains and rods and half a dozen instruments of pain which might have been of original design. Elfini sat three-quarters turned away from him and so failed to notice his presence at first, but suddenly she looked up and saw him.

"Well, *this* is a surprise," she said, putting her book aside and rising to face him. "We've never actually met, Lord Delin, but I do recognize you. Are you here to . . . make my acquaintance in private?"

"It so happens I am, Lady Elfini," Delin responded, finding it impossible not to grin at her choice of words. "And this meeting *will* be private, won't it?"

"Without the least shadow of a doubt," Elfini agreed with the coldest smile Delin had ever seen on a woman. "I haven't lived here all that long, but the staff is already completely trained. You may remove your clothing while I prepare to greet you properly."

By then she'd already opened and slipped out of the wrap she wore, exposing another obscenity. The tight, red silk trousers and shirt she sported were cut in the style of *men's* clothing, with nothing of proper skirts to be seen. Delin felt outraged, but managed to keep his tone even.

"Lady, you mistake me," he said, causing her to stop after only a step or two in the direction of the wall holding her toys. "I've come here to speak on Homin's behalf, not my own. Homin tells me that you've forbidden him to practice his aspect talent, and that you also intend to distract him even further by including him in your . . . pastime despite his unwillingness. Is this true?"

"Homin has earned himself an even more thorough . . . inclusion by speaking out of turn," she said, all trace of the least amusement now gone from her. "And he was supposed to come directly home and present himself to me, which means he has even more to answer for. Unless you mean to offer yourself in his place, Lord Delin, you may now leave. Before I decide you've earned punishment of your very own."

The glitter in her otherwise lifeless eyes said she'd enjoy deciding that, which added quite a lot to Delin's outrage.

The woman had no idea of what her true place in life was meant to be, and Delin looked forward to teaching it to her.

"You are, without doubt, the stupidest woman I've ever met," he said with his most charming smile and an amused chuckle. "Not only have you threatened the well-being of Homin—who is now one of mine—but you've also attempted to threaten *me*. Do you really believe I'd let *anyone* stand in the way of my destiny, let alone an unnatural slut like you?"

"Now you *will* be punished," she said with the glitter in her eyes sharpened, partially by insult and partially by anticipation. "After that you may attempt to brush me out of your way—once you're able to move without pain again."

"Why wait?" Delin asked, for the second time keeping her from turning and walking to the display wall. But this time he used his ability to do it, a much more potent force than mere words.

"What do you think you're doing, you fool?" she spat, glaring at him. "I have Earth magic too, so how long do you think you can keep me paralyzed? Release me at once, or it will certainly go harder for you."

"Oh, I'm quite hard already, thank you, and I'll hold you as long as I please," he responded, beginning to walk toward her. "I have your leg and arm muscles locked tight, but please do feel free to try to escape the hold."

As he reached her she grunted, the only outward sign of her inner struggle for freedom. The day might come that an ordinary talent would find it possible to match a talent like his, but it wasn't likely to happen in his lifetime—or hers.

"And so it becomes clear who the master here is," Delin said, using one hand to smooth back her already perfectly smooth hair. "Now to demonstrate that truth, in a manner just as undeniable as paralysis."

"No," she snarled as he lifted her in his arms, a thin and bony woman who would normally be not at all to his taste. "You wouldn't dare to force yourself on *me*, you wouldn't *dare*!"

"To hear you, one would think you were a person of importance,'' Delin commented as he carried her toward one of the wooden frames. "You weren't of any importance even before your father was forced to resign his place with the Advisors, and now that he's dead by his own hand you're worth even less. Allow me to show you I believe what I say.''

He put her down by the wooden frame, made her bend over it, then opened those obscene trousers of hers and let them fall to pool about her ankles. She wore nothing underneath them, of course, which meant there was nothing to hinder his enjoyment of her. The enjoyment was hardly mutual, though, not in the way *he* used her, but her screams of shock accompanied by babbled threats were really quite entertaining. Delin was thoroughly satisfied when he stepped back and adjusted his clothing, then let her straighten up.

"You filthy animal, I'll see you destroyed for this," she managed to get out, pain and shock still holding her as strongly as his talent. "Doing that to a woman is perversion, and your father won't even *try* to save you. I'll—''

"You'll do nothing at all," he interrupted her ragged indictment, almost able to feel her inner frenzy. If she had been unstable before, now she was doubly so. "But you certainly can't be trusted to stay in your proper place without assistance, so here it is.''

He released her muscles then, but not before seizing hold of her heart. She gasped and whitened when he bore down slowly on the organ, and actually tried to reach her wall of toys. In order to use one of them on him, no doubt, having no idea that he would never allow such a thing. It wasn't *her* place to discipline a man, but it was certainly his to do so with her.

The stupid woman tripped over the trousers caught around her ankles and fell, but the pain of landing on the floor was probably unnoticed amid the rest. Her breath came in gasps as she fought the pain being given to her heart, and she writhed on the floor mewling with fear as she tried to escape. But for her there *was* no escape, and Delin felt his manhood begin to harden again at the thought that he *would* kill her.

He'd never killed anyone but a peasant before, and was startled to discover how much more exciting *this* was.

But he didn't have an infinite amount of time, so he couldn't allow the pleasure to continue until he reached climax. That would have to wait for another time with another . . . helper, so he increased the pressure on her heart just a bit. The woman tried to scream as the organ abruptly ceased functioning, not yet realizing that she was already dead.

Delin found it impossible to wipe the smile from his face, so marvelous had his mood become. For another moment he stared down at the woman who had given him such pleasure, then he gathered himself to leave. But first he straightened the woman's obscene trousers, and fought them back into their proper place on her. Once the authorities saw how she was dressed, their investigation would be quickly terminated.

Then Delin left the same way he'd come, and once he reached his horse he let himself whistle a merry tune all the way back to the stables.

SEVENTEEN

Homin was nearly frantic before Delin reappeared. He knew that Delin had gone to meet with one of his lovers and so he couldn't follow to see what was keeping the man. But that didn't stop him from visiting the tea house's sanitary facilities more often than tea-drinking normally called for. It became more and more clear that if Delin didn't return rather soon, all the charm in the world would not save Homin from Elfini's wrath.

And then, finally, Delin was striding toward him across the floor, a big grin on his very handsome face. Homin lurched to his feet at once, more than ready to leave, but Delin chuckled and gestured at him to sit down again.

"Just five minutes more of patience, Homin, as a favor to me," Delin said as he fell heavily into the second chair at the table. "She's positively exhausted me, and I really must have at least one cup of tea before I perish."

"But Elfini will be furious," Homin whispered as he sank back down, watching Delin gesture to a serving girl. "The angrier she gets the worse it will be for me, and that no matter how charming she finds *you*. Please, Delin, I'm begging . . ."

"Now, *that*, Homin, is your entire problem," Delin said as he relaxed back in his chair. "If something is happening that you don't like, don't *beg* for it to stop, demand it. As you're supposed to be a man, it's time you began to act like one."

Homin slumped in his chair, wishing it were possible to close his eyes and hide in a world of soft, comforting black. If he tried to do as Delin suggested and demand that they leave right now, Delin would undoubtedly become so angry that he would refuse to accompany Homin after all. And as far as refusing to allow Elfini to do as she pleased. . . . How was he supposed to refuse someone so much stronger? If he tried she would hurt him even more, so what option did he have other than to simply accept what she gave . . . ?

"Ah, thank you, my dear," Delin said, and Homin looked up to see that the serving girl had brought Delin's tea. The girl smiled at Delin and swung her hips as she waited to be paid, something she hadn't done with Homin. She'd all but demanded the payment as well as a tip, showing the method worked well enough for *her*. But for Homin to use it, that was quite out of the question. . . .

"Four minutes to go, Homin old fellow," Delin said once he'd paid the girl and had begun to stir sugar into his tea. And he hadn't even noticed the way the girl had been flaunting herself at him. It must be wonderful to be as handsome and self-assured as Delin, but Homin found it completely impossible to picture himself living such a life. Even if he thought it might be possible, he'd have no idea how to begin.

So he just sat there and watched Delin drink tea while he felt his insides tightening more and more. By the big clock on the far wall behind Delin eleven minutes passed, and then Delin lifted his cup and gestured with it.

"Four minutes exactly, and I'm down to the last swallow," he announced, then finished the tea with a satisfied "Ah! Now a quick trip to the comfort facilities, and we're on our way."

Homin couldn't bear the idea of waiting again, so he went with Delin and also used the facilities. This time Delin was through first, and when Homin emerged from the privacy room Delin shook a finger at him with a grin.

"Time is passing, old fellow, and you're the one causing the delay," he said in a mock-serious tone. "But I've sent the boy for our carriages, so the time shouldn't be entirely wasted. Come along now, and we'll complete this mission of mercy."

Homin followed Delin outside, and the carriages really were pulling up to be boarded. Delin told him to ride in his own carriage and lead the way, as he had no really clear idea where Homin lived. Homin realized that that was true so he agreed immediately, although he would have felt much better if Delin were right there beside him. It was always possible that for some unknown reason Delin would desert him at the last moment, and he would have to face Elfini alone.

But Delin didn't desert him, even though Homin's stomach was in knots by the time he reached home. Delin's carriage followed up the drive directly behind his own, and a moment later they were both climbing out in front of the house.

"I love these older houses," Delin commented as Homin hurried up to him, his examination of the house slow and leisurely. "Father would never live in something that hadn't been built to his own specifications, but I prefer smaller places like this. They're so much cozier. . . . Shall we go in?''

''Of course,'' Homin said quickly, biting his tongue before he pointed out that it was Delin who had been simply standing there, not him. Delin's request had suggested the opposite, but it wasn't something to argue about *now*. Elfini was waiting, and every extra minute added to her wait would mean more pain for Homin.

A servant opened the door as they reached it, and once Homin had stepped into the entrance hall he was reminded that Lady Elfini awaited him in her private sanctum. Homin nodded spasmodically even as he swallowed hard, but Delin didn't look at all disturbed. He ambled along behind Homin without a care in the world, but that was because he'd soon be leaving again. Homin had nowhere else to go, and the knowledge terrified him.

The door to Elfini's sanctum stood closed as usual, but he knocked as he was supposed to, waited the required half minute, then turned the knob and entered. Delin had caught up to him by then, and entered right behind him.

''You'll regret having made me wait, Homin,'' Elfini said in the coldest tones he'd ever heard, her eyes filled with that malicious glitter that frightened him so much. ''And were you given permission to bring home one of your little friends with you?''

''Elfini, I'd like to present Lord Delin Moord,'' Homin began with a quaver, but when he turned toward Delin the rest of the words died in his throat. Delin stood staring at Elfini with his mouth open, his skin as pale as milk and his eyes filled with shock. Not only was all the charm Homin had been counting on gone, but Delin looked as though he might faint!

Delin knew that Homin was saying something to him, but nothing came through the ringing in his ears that echoed and reechoed in his head. She was alive, the woman was alive, but that was impossible! He'd killed her and looked at her dead body, so she couldn't possibly be alive!

His right hand groped until it found the doorjamb, and only just in time to keep his knees from buckling and sending him down to the floor. This was a nightmare and it couldn't be happening, not when it was so important, not again. . . .

Again. That word brought a clutch of illness to Delin's middle, as he'd been certain he'd outgrown the condition. As a child he'd fantasized all the time, and some of the fantasies had seemed absolutely real. He'd go about his business thinking he'd done something, and then it would turn out that he hadn't done it after all. On those occasions where his dereliction had come to his father's attention, Delin had been sternly punished for failing to obey and then lying about it. But he hadn't failed to obey and hadn't lied, at least not knowingly. . . .

And now it looked as though the condition had returned, at the worst time it possibly could. This matter of the competitions would be his one and only chance to make his mark, and if he failed he would be trapped in obscurity forever. Forever in Father's house, a concept too horrible to contemplate without shuddering.

"Delin, are you all right?" Homin asked anxiously, hovering only a step away as though ready to catch him if he fell. "Do you need to sit down? Perhaps a cup of tea would help. . . ."

"Have the servants put him in his carriage and send him home," the woman said impatiently, cutting into Homin's expressions of concern. "I've had to wait too long already, and refuse to wait any longer. Unless you've brought him here to share what I have for you, and then you may drag him inside instead."

The amusement in the slut's voice was intolerable, and it actually helped Delin to pull himself together. He straightened away from the doorjamb as his blood began to flow properly through his veins again, and he looked directly at Elfini.

"Homin, have one of the servants pack you some clothing," he ordered without taking his eyes from the slut. "If you stay here you'll be useless to the group, so I'm taking you home with me.''

"How dare you try to interfere with my household?'' the female demanded coldly, but too late to stop Homin's scurrying away. "When he returns you'll tell him you've changed your mind, and then you'll leave. If you don't, my husband will have a private talk with your father.''

"What good do you expect *that* to do?'' Delin countered with a snort of ridicule, absolutely certain about his position in a circumstance like that. "All I'd have to do is tell Father that your husband spends his leisure getting his bottom spanked by his wife, and Father won't even let him in the house. Not to mention that he'll probably decide to ruin your husband's career. Father loathes this sort of perversion even more than I do.''

"Get out,'' the female snarled, her left hand curled into a claw. "Take the sniveling little coward with you if you must, but get out of my house!''

"At your pleasure, Dama,'' Delin said with a sarcastic bow, then he turned and walked completely out of the room. The slut stormed after him to slam the door closed, but her frustrated anger wasn't nearly as pleasing as it should have been. Once again he'd had to use the threat of getting his father involved in order to make things go the way they were supposed to, and his hatred for having to do that grew greater each time he did.

But until he made his mark nothing would change, so he'd have to do anything and everything to protect his group. And in the real world, not in some delusion that his mind dreamed up for him. And yet how odd it was, that the chamber looked exactly as it had in the illusion, all the way down to the specialized devices on the wall with the whips. How that could be he had no idea, unless he'd actually come to the house, looked in through the window, and then fantasized the rest. But that would make him a crippled coward who couldn't even admit his failures to himself, so it couldn't possibly be true.

Delin paced up and down the hall, his thoughts black and

ugly and hating, until Homin finally reappeared. The fat fool was being followed by a servant carrying a small trunk, which explained what had taken so long. Without saying anything Delin turned and stalked off toward the front door, letting Homin and the servant catch up as best they might. And he would insist that Homin use his own carriage, to keep the jittering fool away from *him* as much as possible.

As he sat in his carriage waiting for Homin to get his trunk stowed and his overweight body settled, Delin made two decisions. The first was to tell Father immediately what Homin's situation with Elfini was, which would certainly set in motion Homin's father's ruination. The man was powerful, but not nearly as powerful as Father, and if he were engrossed with imminent ruination he *couldn't* obey Elfini and make trouble for the group.

That idea made Delin feel a good deal better, and helped to convince him that his second decision was just as necessary as the first. Tonight, after retiring to his apartment, he would sneak out and return to kill Elfini, this time in reality rather than illusion. He *had* to do it now, there was nothing else possible, not when making his mark was at stake. Nothing could stand in the way of that, nor would it be allowed to. His group meant his future, and he *would* defend it with everything he had. It was time to really act, it was *time*. . . .

EIGHTEEN

"Good morning, Lord Bron," Deever said as he was shown in, his sharp gaze flickering everywhere. "All ready to begin the day's practice?"

"Since these practice sessions last only a few hours, why can't they be done in the afternoon?" Bron demanded as usual, finding that his body had no interest in rising from the couch he sprawled on. It was much too early for anyone really civilized to be up and about, but his instructor had no more compassion for him than he'd ever had.

"You're hardly the only group member I instruct in a day," Deever returned, also as usual, acting like high nobility rather than the only-just-barely-acceptable lower born that he was. "Since someone has to be first, you've been chosen to be that someone. Shall we begin?"

Bron muttered under his breath as he made the supreme effort of struggling to his feet, but then he noticed the clock. Deever was always right on time, but this morning he seemed to have missed.

"Well, Deever, it seems there are times when even you oversleep," Bron gloated as he pointed to the clock. "Less than half an hour, but late is late."

"It wasn't sleep that kept me, it was the news," Deever said, raising supercilious brows. "You can't mean you haven't heard?"

"Heard what?" Bron demanded, annoyance quickly returning. "If there's news, you should have said so immediately."

"It's difficult to understand how anyone could have *missed* hearing," Deever replied, still looking around the sitting room rather than at Bron. "Lady Elfini Weil was murdered last night, and they suspect one of the household staff—or a common tramp—to have done it."

Bron knew his jaw had dropped, but that news was too incredible to react any other way. Lord Aston Weil was *powerful*, and if anyone's family should have been safe, it was his. Anger came as Bron realized his own household staff must already know all about it, but no one had bothered to tell *him*.

"How could anyone who valued his own life have killed her?" Bron asked, determined to get the details now. "And how can they suspect 'one of the staff or a tramp' in general? Doesn't knowing which aspect was used narrow it down a little?"

"That seems to be the major problem, and is one of the things making everyone discuss the situation," Deever said, finally bringing his gaze to Bron. "She wasn't murdered by the use of one of the aspects, she was hacked to pieces with some bladed weapon. It was incredibly gory, I hear, and so bad that some people actually threw up at seeing the body."

"Just as I probably would," Bron muttered after feeling his face pale. "I've never even *heard* of anyone being killed like that. . . . It must have been done by some talentless freak, but. . . . How do you hack someone to pieces and keep it quiet? Surely the woman screamed at least a little before she died, so why didn't someone—like Lord Aston, for instance—hurry in to help her?"

"That's another odd aspect of the matter," Deever said, and now he studied a point beyond Bron's right shoulder. "There's no official word on that part of it, but rumor has it that Lord Aston was hanging unconscious in a wooden whipping frame while she was being murdered. It isn't something to mention everywhere just in case it turns out to be untrue, but there have been . . . interesting rumors about Lord

Aston before. This one matches those others perfectly.''

"What a mess!" Bron said with a headshake, then another thought occurred to him. "But what does Homin say? I nearly forgot that that's his family, and he's a member of my group. He should know what happened, because he was right there."

"It seems Lord Homin *wasn't* there," Deever informed him, now looking openly satisfied. "The Advisors were concerned because he *is* one of your group, but it so happens he left the house yesterday afternoon for an extended stay with Lord Delin Moord. No one yet knows why that was done, but the fact of the matter cannot be denied."

"That's too bad," Bron said with a fatalistic shrug. "For a moment I was able to hope that *he* would turn out to be the murderer, and then he would have to be replaced in the group. He's the worst among us, and if he doesn't improve we'll—all look like fools in the competitions."

Bron stumbled just a little over the end of his speech, remembering only at the last instant that he wasn't to say anything about *winning*. No one was meant to know they intended to try, and happily Deever didn't seem to have noticed the near slip.

"*Your* training results could bear some improvement as well, Lord Bron," Deever said, safe behind the authority given him by the Advisors. "Shall we visit the training cubicle now? I must be off to my next student as close to on time as possible."

Bron would have enjoyed giving the dolt a piece of his mind, but Deever was backed by too many influential people. And as understanding as his father had been all Bron's life, the one thing that would turn him to thoughts of severity and unreason was Bron's trying the patience of the Advisors. His father's own position would be put at risk then, so the old man refused to even entertain the idea. Or continue to support Bron if *he* entertained it.

So Bron had no choice but to clamp his jaw closed and lead the way out of the sitting room toward the back garden, where the practice cubicle had been installed. The idiotic old man who was his father would be sorry when Bron's group was Seated as the reigning Blending, but by then it would be too late. Bron would remember how he'd been treated, and would repay exactly as he'd gotten.

The cubicle, which had been placed to the far left side of the garden and away from the house, was made of clear resin. It was also much too small to accommodate the presence of a decent chair, and a small shed installed beside it contained all sorts of paraphernalia that was meant to be used inside the cubicle. Right now there was only a box fitted out with a foot pedal, a fixture Bron had grown so tired of that he was delightedly relieved it had become time to advance.

"Please remember what's necessary here, Lord Bron," Deever began to lecture as they reached the cubicle. "The patterns you've been taught to weave since childhood are what's necessary, so let's try not to forget again to use them."

Once again Bron had to grit his teeth, this time because Deever was such a fool. All children of their class were taught to weave with their talent as soon as they became capable of doing it, and it was unreasonable to expect an adult to constantly remember a child's game. So he'd forgotten to weave his fires once or twice; there was no need to make him seem so feebleminded that he'd always forget.

But it was now time to get rid of this device for good and all, so Bron stomped down on the pedal. The lid of the box flew open and a cloud of soil was thrown into the air, a cloud that didn't stay aloft long. But Bron was ready, so he reached out with his *woven* fires and burned all that soil the way he wanted to burn Deever and his superior Lord Rigos. It felt marvelous, magnificent, and then it was all done.

"Well, how gratifying," Deever said, his brows high with surprise. "You've actually burned nearly every grain of soil. A few small grains escaped you, but they're nothing to be concerned about. Congratulations, Lord Bron, on achieving your first mastery."

"And tomorrow I intend to achieve the second," Bron said loftily, chest swelling with well-earned pride. "I'm tired of being called lazy and incompetent, so I'm going to *show* all of you.''

"I'm delighted to hear that, Lord Bron, so let's get to practicing the next exercise as soon as the servants set up the equipment. We haven't much time, you know, so we dare not waste any.''

"You talk as if the competitions are to begin after this week's end,'' Bron scoffed, annoyed that he wasn't yet to be allowed to return to bed. "There's a lot more time than that, so why must we engage in this ridiculous rush?''

"The competitions may not be that close, but the forming of Blendings is set to begin only a few days past next week's end. The longer it takes for your group to be ready to be formed into a Blending, the less practice time you'll have *as* a Blending. We'd prefer not to have any of our groups look overly foolish when they come forward to compete, but all we can do is warn you. If you fail to heed that warning, you'll be the ones who must live with the ridicule of your peers afterward.''

Deever was now pretending not to study him, but in truth was watching very closely. That threat of ridicule was meant to reach him and galvanize him into action, so he would have to pretend that it had. What had really reached Bron, however, was the knowledge of how close they were to being formed into a Blending. They *would* need all the practice they could get if they were to win, so there was nothing else for it.

"You're quite right, Deever,'' Bron said as he squared his shoulders. "Time *is* running short, so let's have the servants out here to arrange the next mechanism. I intend to finish today with *two* masteries.''

"I bow to your wisdom, Lord Bron, and will fetch the servants myself,'' Deever said with a nod of his head rather than a bow. "I'll return in a moment.''

Bron watched the powerless fool walk away back toward the house, knowing the man wore a smirk now that Bron couldn't see it. Deever thought he was so good despite his family's lacks, but even his talent couldn't be all that much if he was training rather than doing. No, Bron was his superior in all ways, and when *his* Blending won the competition Deever's smirk would be wiped from his face for good and all.

NINETEEN

"Forgive me for being tardy, Lady Selendi, but I'm afraid everyone is tardy this morning," Pracer said as he strode into the conservatory where Selendi sat taking tea. "You've surely heard the news?"

"About Lady Elfini?" Selendi said, putting her cup aside and leaning forward. "Every servant in the house is chattering about it, and my mother has gone to visit one of her friends, who lives only a short distance away from the Weil estate. If *she* doesn't get all the details no one will, but what have *you* heard?"

"That poor Lady Elfini was hacked to death by a deranged Guild member," Pracer said as he took a chair and began to pour his own cup of tea. "People are remembering that no one liked the idea of having a Guild for the talentless, but the Advisors have always insisted on protecting them. No matter how this turns out, the Advisors will have some answering to do."

"We heard that the deranged lunatic tied Lord Aston to a wall and whipped him almost to death," Selendi said, more interested in discussing the good parts. People who went on about the Guild were so *boring....* "Lord Aston may or may not be able to identify the murderer, depending on whether or not the monster wore a mask.''

"The deed itself was so arrogant, that the deviant most likely spurned the idea of a mask,'' Pracer said after sipping at his tea. "Can you imagine, chopping someone up into little pieces right in front of her husband, and then taking the time to almost kill *him* as well? Deranged simply doesn't cover it, not without adding arrogant as well, and that describes most of the Guild's members.''

"How many Guild members do you know?'' Selendi asked, partially distracted. "Only a few of them come from noble families, and I've never met even one.''

"Well, I've never met any of them either, but everyone knows the truth,'' Pracer admitted reluctantly. "The Guild is full of abnormal deviants, and shouldn't be allowed to continue in existence.''

"Oh, Pracer, that's just your father talking,'' Selendi said with an impatient shake of her head. "Why you have to parrot his ridiculous ideas I don't know, but it's terribly tiring. Do you hear *me* parroting *my* father's opinions? My father is much more important than yours, so if *I* don't do it *you* have absolutely no excuse.''

"I don't need an excuse,'' Pracer said, sitting back as he showed a small, vindictive smile. "I'm a man and will be taking over from my father one day, and must therefore carry on the proper tradition. You're just a girl and no one will ever listen to you in any event, so it doesn't matter in the least what you say. Shall we get to the practicing now?''

"Certainly,'' Selendi agreed coldly, thoroughly insulted. She began to rise from her chair, but then a thought came to her. "Just a minute. If Lady Elfini and Lord Aston were attacked by someone without any talent, why didn't they use their own talent to protect themselves? Even ordinary ability can overcome someone without any at all, so how did that . . . talentless deviant get away with it?''

Pracer suddenly looked stricken rather than handsome and cool, bringing Selendi a good deal of satisfaction. She'd wanted to get even for that comment he'd made about how unimportant she was, and now it looked like she had.

"Why . . . they were probably . . . taken unawares, that's it, they were taken unawares," Pracer suddenly suggested, his expression clearing. "Yes, the monster crept up on them while they weren't looking, and then it was too late to stop him."

"But you said Lady Elfini was hacked to death while Lord Aston watched," Selendi pointed out at once. "That means he should have been able to do something, and yet he didn't."

"Maybe *he* was beaten first," Pracer returned, then nodded his approval of the idea. "Yes, he was beaten first after being crept up on, and then, when Lady Elfini heard his screams and came running, she was taken from behind as well. It's all quite simple once one thinks about it."

"Simple is the word," Selendi retorted with a sniff. "If Lord Aston was awake enough to scream, he was certainly awake enough to also use his talent. If he couldn't use his talent he also couldn't scream, so Lady Elfini would have had no *reason* to come running in. That means it probably wasn't someone without talent after all, but someone with more talent than the two of them. That means you'd better watch out, in case it turns out that *I'm* the murderer."

"If you ever murdered someone, it would be someone male and it would be in bed," Pracer said with a sudden grin, finally abandoning his ridiculous stance and air of superiority. "I apologize profoundly for upsetting you, my sweet, and hope my foolishness won't keep us from ending your practice time in the usual way."

"That all depends on how good a weekly report I can look forward to," Selendi said, keeping him from taking her hand by standing up. "I didn't like the last one at all, especially when it was read out loud by Lord Rigos in front of everyone. Next week's report will be much better—won't it?"

"I promise it will be as good as I can make it without actually lying," Pracer said, his tone begging for understanding as he also stood. "Lying about your progress is the one thing I can't do, sweetling, at least not very much. They *will* eventually find out when you reach the competitions, and then they'll have my privates as well as my head. Please be reasonable, because I'm also doing it for *your* good.''

"Raela's father said that same exact thing all those years ago just before he spanked her so hard she couldn't sit down for the rest of the day," Selendi pointed out, again keeping him from taking her hand by moving it back out of reach. "He also forbade her to associate with the rest of the girls in our group, so we were never able to visit that marvelous house again. I don't like things done for my own good, not unless *I* decide they need doing.''

"But you did decide," Pracer said, now sounding like a merchant trying to sell her cotton at the price of silk. "You said you'd die if you made a fool of yourself in front of everyone, but that's exactly what will happen if I lie about your progress. You won't be able to match the others in your group when you're formed into a Blending, and everyone will be able to tell that the fault is yours.''

Selendi still didn't know how that would be possible, but even the chance of it gave her pause. She *would* die if she ended up looking foolish in front of everyone, but even more importantly she hated the thought of being outdone by those oafish men in her group. And she suddenly remembered that they were all supposed to start showing some progress, and now she had the excuse to do just that.

"Oh, all right, I'll work at your silly exercises," she grudged, taking the opportunity to make him believe she did *him* the favor. "But you'd better be really good afterward, or I'll start inviting other men over for post-practice relaxation.''

"I promise to be absolutely marvelous for you," he answered with a grin, then stood aside with a small bow. "After you, sweetling, who nevertheless remains a lady who *cannot* be matched.''

Selendi knew he wasn't referring to her talent with Air magic, so she let a pleased little smile curve her lips as she led the way out to the side garden. A small resin building had been established there, one that was capable of being sealed completely. The three servants assigned to be her subjects were already there, of course, waiting outside and whispering among themselves. Selendi knew what they had to be whispering about, but refused to return to the subject of the grisly murder. She really did want to have Pracer after the practice, and hearing him sound off again would just ruin the mood.

When the servants saw them coming they entered the small building, and a moment later Selendi led Pracer inside after them. The lamps behind their clear resin windows had already been lit, and the servants had lined up in a straight row. Selendi found a place on the comfortable couch she'd had installed while Pracer sealed the building, and by the time he sat down beside her she was ready to start.

"I'm about to pull the rope that will release the smoke," Pracer warned, reaching to the rope hanging above the couch. "All right, here we go."

Selendi had no idea how they managed to fill tanks with smoke, but understanding the method wasn't necessary to countering the presence of the smoke. She'd already wrapped herself and the three nervous servants in bubbles of air, this time making sure the bubbles didn't leak. The servants had suffered while she was in the midst of pretending to be less able than she really was, but the time for that was over.

"All right, now the subject at the end will move apart from the others," Pracer said, gesturing to the servant on the right side of the line. "Make sure you keep your sphere intact while you divide it in two."

Selendi felt annoyed at the way he spoke to her, sounding as though he spoke to a backward child instead. But he always did that during practice, acting the full ten years and more older than her that he was, so she forced herself to ignore it and complete the separation. No more than the faintest trace of smoke popped in before she sealed both sides of the separation, but Pracer didn't seem to notice.

"That was marvelous, Lady Selendi, just marvelous!" he enthused, turning his head to give her a beautiful smile.

"One more successful separation, and you'll have earned *two* masteries."

Selendi hadn't realized she would get anything *directly* from doing that exercise, so it came as a very pleasant surprise to hear that she already had one mastery. But one wasn't enough; she wanted both, and wasn't above exerting herself a bit in order to get it.

This time it was the servant on the left side of the line who moved, and Selendi concentrated on separating the air bubble a second time. She could see how it would be possible to keep every bit of smoke out of the pockets of air, but it was also a great deal more trouble. So she let that faint trace of smoke in again instead, and again Pracer missed it.

"Lady Selendi, you've done it!" Pracer exulted, turning to her to give her a radiant smile through the smoke that filled the room but not their individual bubbles. "Two masteries one after the other! Next week my report will *glow*, and you have my word on that."

He got up then and went to unseal the door, and Selendi was so delighted that she forgot what she was in the midst of and released the protection around the servants before the door was open. The heavy smoke immediately began to make them cough, and as soon as the door was open they rushed outside. Selendi joined Pracer at the door, both of them waiting for the smoke to clear out completely, and once it had Pracer closed the door again, then turned to her with a grin.

"What a wonderful idea that was to bring a couch into the practice building," he murmured, slowly pulling her close to his chest. "Now we not only have privacy but comfort, two things we ought to begin using at once."

His mouth lowered quickly to hers while his hand went behind her, and a moment later he was quickly raising her skirts in back in order to reach her body. She held to him tightly as she moaned out her need for him to hurry, but with his mouth over hers it just came out as a noise. And then he *had* reached all the way under her skirts to touch her, and the feel of his hands on her flesh drove her wild.

But rather than taking her immediately to the couch, he made her stand there with him while he used his fingers to stroke her desire to absolute frenzy. She didn't need that encouragement and he knew it, but he seemed to enjoy forcing her to wait. She *didn't* enjoy it, but she always forgot what he was like until it was too late. Next time she would remember, though, and next time she would find someone else to be with.

Someone she hadn't already had. That thought made her even hotter, and she moaned again as she struggled against being kept from the couch. She wanted every man she hadn't already had, *had* to have them or she would die. No man who attracted her could be allowed to refuse, or then she wouldn't *have* him. They were all hers, every man she'd ever lain with, but they weren't enough.

But she'd come closer to having enough once she and the others were Seated on the Fivefold Throne. Then no one would ever be able to refuse her anything, which was only the way things were meant to be. . . .

TWENTY

Kambil was sitting quietly and drinking a cup of tea when Oshin arrived, more than an hour late. But the instructor still maintained the same sedate pace as always, possibly because of his size. Oshin's greatest pleasure was a long, leisurely meal, and he indulged his pleasure as often as possible.

"I was wondering whether you'd heard the news, and now that I see you I'm certain you have," Oshin said by way of greeting, lowering himself into a chair opposite Kambil's.

"You would never believe the rumors that are afloat out there."

"Yes I would, because I've probably heard every one of them this morning," Kambil countered with a sigh as he watched Oshin pour himself a cup of tea. "One version had everyone in the Weil household murdered in their beds, and another version had each body mutilated by perversions of all five of the aspects. The only point each of the stories agreed on was that Lady Elfini was definitely one of the dead. You don't happen to know the actual details, do you?"

"It so happens I do, and that's the reason I'm this late," Oshin replied after taking a long swallow of his tea. "After hearing the wild tales being repeated by my household staff, I knew I'd never regain any semblance of balance until I learned the truth. And I do happen to know quite a large number of people, so I stopped at the Weil estate to see if any of them were there as investigators. It turned out I knew two of them, and they asked me to stay for a while to help calm the house's staff."

"So that they might be more easily questioned," Kambil said with a nod as he leaned forward. "So what did happen? Or have you promised not to discuss that?"

"No, my friends are very practical people," Oshin said with a mirthless smile. "They know there's no hope of keeping any of the story quiet now, so they don't even mean to try. As briefly as possible, the facts seem to be this: Homin returned yesterday afternoon accompanied by Delin, packed a bag, then left again with Delin to stay at *his* place. Elfini was annoyed even before that, but when the two young men left she was absolutely livid. Her mood worsened the later in the day it got, and by the time Aston arrived home—later than expected—it wasn't even safe to breathe in her vicinity. She stormed out of her 'sanctum,' ordered Aston to follow her, then stormed back in."

"And of course Lord Aston obeyed," Kambil said wearily. "I was once introduced to the man, and couldn't believe the difference between his public face and his private feelings. Very frankly I couldn't bear to stay near him for long."

"Yes, that sort of . . . mismatched emotions is very difficult for one of us to stand," Oshin said, sending a brief flow of compassion. "Love is pain and self-hatred is acceptance, and both are pleasure. I'm very glad to say I don't understand it, and hope I never do. At any rate Aston was a fool and went with Elfini willingly, and she apparently took out all her anger on him. The servants heard him screaming for a very long time, and then there was nothing but silence."

"Did she kill him?" Kambil asked with brows high, then slowly shook his head. "No, I would guess that she didn't, not after she'd worked off most of her outrage. She was a woman who always needed to be in complete control, and whipping Lord Aston within an inch of his life would have returned that control to her."

"That's a very astute summation," Oshin said with a nod of approval. "Aston was stretched out face down on a whipping rack to one side of the room, and apparently Elfini left him there unconscious. She went to the dining room and ate alone, then returned to her sanctum. That was the last time anyone saw her alive."

"Except for whoever killed her," Kambil pointed out. "One of the stories said a masked intruder broke in, and Lord Aston might have seen him. Is there any truth in that?"

"Unfortunately, no," Oshin said, his sigh rather deep. "Aston apparently remained unconscious all night, and wasn't even lucid when a physician called by the guard finally managed to rouse him. Elfini had gone much too far, and he was badly hurt. He might have died as well if one of the staff hadn't gotten up his nerve to knock on the door of the sanctum this morning. Elfini always took an early breakfast at precisely the same time every day, and when she didn't appear the staff was worried."

"And when the servant got no answer, he probably just walked right in," Kambil said, leaning back in his chair again. "It would have been out of character for Lady Elfini to lock a door in her own house. I wonder if the servant went searching because he was worried about *her*, about his lord and master—or about his job."

"You seem rather cynical this morning, but I suppose disappointment does produce cynicism," Oshin said, studying him with calm blue eyes. "And you *are* disappointed, but I'm afraid I don't understand why. Would you care to explain?"

"It's . . . idealistic foolishness," Kambil apologized with a vague wave of his hand. "I know we're all human rather than perfection incarnate and that ordinary humans have problems, but this—I can't bring myself to believe that someone in *my* world would do such a thing. Was she really . . . chopped into pieces?"

"She was killed with some edged weapon and was cut up rather badly, but not chopped up in any manner," Oshin said, compassion flowing from him again. "The investigators are calling it 'thorough' rather than 'enraged' or 'insane' or anything like that. It's perfectly possible that some vagrant broke in with the idea of forcing Elfini to tell him where the gold and silver was hidden. She thought she could handle him herself and therefore made no effort to ring for help, but she was mistaken, He realized he would get nothing out of her, so he simply killed her."

"And that way it wasn't done by anyone from *our* world," Kambil said, trying not to send too much depression at Oshin. "We'll all be able to go back to our comfortable little niches without needing to suspect our neighbor of being a monster, but I wonder how true that explanation is. Could it *really* have been a vagrant, who is hopefully miles away from here by now?"

"I hope fervently that the answer to both parts of that is yes," Oshin said, faintly echoing Kambil's depression. "I think my friends mean to recommend adopting the conclusion in the report they give to the Advisors, and if the recommendation is taken, that will be the end of it."

"We *hope* that will be the end of it," Kambil corrected, then he stirred in his chair. "I suppose you'd like to get to the practice now. I'll do my best, of course, but don't expect anything extraordinary in the way of results—at least as far as a good performance is concerned."

"I think we can afford to let you pass one day without practicing," Oshin said, waving him back into his chair. "Our aspect has to be the most heavily touched by a tragedy like this, so take the day to regain your balance. And if you think more conversation on a different topic would help, I'll be glad to stay for a while."

"I'd be very grateful for that," Kambil said, working to produce a normal smile while he shoved all his previous emotions aside. "There's a question I've been wanting to ask, but the opportunity never seemed to arise. Would you mind if I asked it now?"

"Since we may never again have the leisure for casual conversation, you might as well," Oshin agreed with a better smile than Kambil's. "If it turns out to be too personal or too embarrassing, I'll simply refuse to answer."

"It's not really anything like that," Kambil said, letting Oshin's amusement touch him. "It's just that I noticed right from the first how really strong and capable you are with Spirit magic. That led me to wonder why you're instructing me and the others, rather than being part of a group yourself. . . . Or *does* that come under the heading of too personal or embarrassing?"

"Actually it's neither," Oshin said, refilling his cup after having drained it. "I thought you knew, but since you obviously don't I'll have to explain. Not everyone is able to become a member of a Blending, and it has nothing to do with strength. There are other factors involved, and one of the most rigid is age. Haven't you noticed that you and the other members of your group are approximately the same age?"

"Well, I noticed we were all from the same generation," Kambil answered slowly with a frown. "Is that the same thing, or am I missing the point?"

"The point is that people of the same age have a much greater chance of successfully Blending," Oshin said, now reaching for one of the small cakes displayed on a plate near the tea service. "Widely mixed age groups have the smallest chance, and those beyond the age of thirty or so have no chance at all unless they've Blended before that. Your group and the others are all expected to manage it, so it's nothing for you to really worry about.''

"I think my worry-compartment is too full at the moment to add anything else," Kambil told him ruefully. "Tomorrow or the next day will probably be another story, but right now I intend to take your advice. I'm going to put everything unpleasant out of my mind, and enjoy my day off. Do you expect to turn the rest of your students loose as well?''

''Probably not,'' Oshin said, using one of the linen napkins to wipe crumbs from his chin. ''You heard about what happened so quickly because you live right in the neighborhood, so to speak, as do the rest of the members of your group. My other students live progressively farther away, so I ought to reach them before the news does. Which tells me I really should be on my way now.''

Kambil knew Oshin really had decided to leave, so he saw the older man to the door and then stood and watched his carriage drive away. He felt a lot better now, thanks to Oshin's conversation, but was glad he hadn't had to practice. He might not have been able to control the results properly, and that was very important now. Bron had repeated that to him at least three times the day before, so he couldn't have forgotten even if he'd wanted to.

But there were things he did have to make himself forget, so he went back into the house and directly to his apartment. His life could very well depend on how good a job he did, since the results would affect the performance of his talent. And considering the other members of the group, he'd better do a very good job indeed. . . .

Delin was finally able to return to his apartment once Homin was gone. The furor had continued for hours after the guardsmen had first appeared with their news. Homin had been sound asleep in one of the guest apartments, and it took a while for the servants to rouse him and bring him down to speak to the guardsmen. Delin had already come down to find out what the commotion was about, and so had been there to witness Homin hearing the news and promptly fainting.

They'd had to send for a physician then, but Delin could have told them that Homin was all right. The man's muscles had all tensed at once when he'd seen the guardsmen, probably thinking that Elfini had sent them to drag him home. When he learned that Elfini would never bother him again, his relief had undoubtedly been so great that he'd fainted.

Delin walked to a chair and sat, the smile on his face wide and finally out in the open. Homin should have thanked *him* for the relief he'd felt, since it had been his efforts which had caused it. He'd left the house last night after everyone was asleep, returned to the Weil estate, and then had done what he'd had to. His group was now safe, and before Homin had left, the pudgy man had whispered that he meant to practice for the rest of the day—as soon as all the investigators and guardsmen were gone. He had to be at home to make sure his father was properly cared for, but aside from that he would spend his time practicing.

Which was just what Delin wanted him to do. Their progress as a group was the most important thing right now, so nothing could be allowed to stand in their way. There was just one regret. . . .

Delin lost his smile when he thought about that, and frustration rose up to choke him with anger. He remembered leaving his own house, remembered reaching the terrace doors of Elfini's "sanctum" again, and remembered starting to go in. But from that moment until he found himself leaving the estate again, nothing but blankness filled his memory. He'd finally managed to do what he hadn't been able to do earlier—the blood on his clothing and on the long knife he'd held testified to that—but he couldn't remember the act itself. He'd suffered brief periods of blackout before in his life, but never at such an inconvenient time!

It was necessary to take a deep breath to calm himself, and much of the frustration remained even afterward. He really wanted to remember the most glorious moment of his life, and maybe after some time had passed he'd be able to.

In the meanwhile he'd removed every trace of blood from his clothing, and had buried the knife on the Weil estate in a place only he would be able to return to.

After all, he'd probably need the weapon again, and the second time he'd *certainly* remember. . . .

TWENTY-ONE

"Who has the visitor at the door come to see?" Jovvi asked the servant who'd come out to the garden. By rights I should have been the one to ask, since it was still my house; but I'd somehow gotten the idea that if I didn't bring myself to the world's attention by speaking, the visitor would turn out to be someone other than my father. And to make matters even worse, Vallant Ro had seemed about to approach me again. I wasn't *quite* up to the point where I would rather face my father than speak to the tall, blond ex–sea captain, but I had the sinking feeling that that point was not very far away.

"The caller at the door and his companions have asked for Dom Coll," the servant answered, looking around at the men. It became clear then that he didn't know which of them Lorand was, and that's why he'd made a general announcement. He was one of the extra servants put on by the testing authority to keep the residence running smoothly, and I didn't know his name either.

Everyone but Lorand relaxed at hearing the answer, and for a brief moment that included me. But then I realized that I was still in danger of needing to deal with Vallant Ro again, so I made the fastest decision of my life. Putting my teacup back down on the table took only an instant, and then I hurried over to a still-hesitating Lorand before Vallant Ro could cut off my escape.

"It might not be that former friend of yours again," I said softly to Lorand, looking up at his expressionless face. "But in case it is, why don't I go with you again?"

"You wouldn't mind?" he asked at once, partial relief filling his dark and pretty eyes. "I know Hat needs my help, but I can't give it to him yet—and I really hate having to admit it."

"What makes his refusal to accept reality something *you* have to feel guilty about?" I asked, honestly curious. "Did you do anything to cause him to be like that? Are you responsible for his having failed the test?"

"The answer to both questions is no, but it also isn't quite that simple," he replied, gesturing vaguely with one hand. "Hat is my friend, and you owe help to a friend if you're in a position to give it. I know he'd do the same for me."

"Somehow I doubt that, but I don't know the man as well as you do," I granted him, then gestured toward the house. "Well, shall we go to see if it really is him?"

Lorand's nod was a bit on the reluctant side, but he still began to move toward the house with me. He also still held his brandy glass, so I took it from him gently, gave it to the servant stationed near the house, and asked the man to put it on the table. Lorand was a big man and obviously very capable, but in this instance I had the definite feeling that he needed protection as well as support. The idea of *me* protecting a man his size was laughable, but somehow that laughter felt extremely good.

The servant who had announced the "callers" led the way back through the house to the front door, which had been closed again with the visitors still on the outside. That made me wonder about what they must be like, but I didn't have to wonder long. The servant opened the door to reveal Lorand's friend Hat—looking more disreputable than the first time—flanked by two husky men who simply looked dangerous.

"That's him," Hat said at once, pointing a trembling finger at Lorand. "He's the one who's responsible, so talk to *him*."

"Responsible for what?" Lorand asked in confusion. "Hat, what's going on?"

"Guess that shows he knows 'im," one of the husky men said, obviously speaking to the other, then he continued to Hat, "But you ain't off th' hook yet, shorty, so don't try t'disappear thinkin' I won't be lookin'. Now you c'n tell the man how much he owes us."

"What does he mean, how much I owe him?" Lorand demanded of a Hat who seemed to be groping for words— and who also seemed to be looking for a chance to run. "What did you tell these men?"

"Just the truth," Hat finally responded, sounding both defensive and aggressive as he wiped his mouth on the back of one grime-covered hand. "Those tests for High are fixed so that only one applicant is accepted at a time, so we agreed that that one would be you. In return you're supposed to be responsible for any . . . debts I incur while I wait for *my* chance, and now you have to pay up. I owe these men two gold dins, but you might as well make it three. I'll need something to live on for the few days before I go to pass the test myself."

"That's your idea of the truth?" I asked in outrage as Lorand just stared at the man openmouthed. "At least your claims are more logical this time, but they're still just as ridiculous. When are you going to grow up enough to admit that you didn't delay taking the test, you failed it? And even if they gave people second chances normally, you'd still be too late. Everyone able to qualify for the competitions has already done so, and after this week's end no one will even be allowed to try. All the testing is over for the year, and won't start again until after the competitions."

"No, that isn't true!" the small man shouted hoarsely, a wild look now in his eyes. "I'm going to test again in just a few days, and this time I'll pass! You don't know anything about it, slut, so why don't you just go back to codding Lorand the way you're supposed to, and the rest of the time keep your mouth shut!''

"Hat!" Lorand barked while my cheeks flamed red over the disgusting man's language. "You know better than to talk to a lady like that, and Tamrissa is a lady! She also happens to be one of the successful applicants in this house, so you'd *better* watch your mouth. Since you obviously can't read or can't see what her identification says, I'll mention that her aspect is Fire.''

The two husky men paled and took a step back, which probably meant they *couldn't* read. Hat looked nervous as he tried to focus on my identification card, but he still seemed to be too full of alcohol to manage the feat. He shook his head a little, possibly to clear it, then looked at Lorand again with the belligerence back stronger than ever.

"What difference does it make *what* her aspect is?" he demanded. "She isn't allowed to do anything to me, so I won't let her get away with lying. And I won't let *you* get away with it either. You said you'd give me money, so I want those three gold dins *now*.''

"I said I'd help you all I could *when* I could," Lorand corrected, his voice now stiffer than it had been. "I never agreed to pay your gambling debts, and it *isn't* my fault that you failed the test. Telling yourself fairy tales won't change the truth of the world, Hat, and you'd know that if you ever let yourself sober up. Right now all I have is silver, and barely enough for my own needs. If I start to win during the preliminary competitions that will change, but until then I guess I can spare one silver din—''

"Charity!" Hat snarled, then he spat. "*That* for your charity, when you *know* how much you owe me! Keep your codding charity, I don't want it or need it! In a couple of days *I'll* be qualifying for all those competitions, and then *you* can come crawling to *me*! But he's still the one who owes you that gold, Meerk, so get it from *him* or forget about it. I made a deal in good faith, and *I* mean to stick to it!''

With that he turned and pushed between the two big men, then stalked away up the drive. He ignored the hired carriage standing near the steps, and the two men he'd been with watched him go with frowns on their faces. Then they turned back to Lorand, and Meerk, the one who'd done the previous talking, nodded.

"Just when's all this gold comin' t'ya?" he asked, inspecting Lorand with his gaze. "I ain't gonna wait long, so you better come up with it real fast like."

"Why are you making it sound as if I'm the one who owes it to you?" Lorand asked with his own frown. "Hat's apparently been drunk ever since he failed the test, which hasn't helped him to accept the truth. I told him I'd give him as much of a hand as I could and that still goes, but—"

"Look, jobby, I don't care *what* th' truth is," Meerk interrupted, his dark, dull eyes unmoving from Lorand's face. "That chump who just left owes me gold, an' if I can't get it from him then I'll get it from *you*. If I don't, then maybe you won't be in any *shape* t'be in them competitions, get what I mean? You think about it, an' I'll be back."

The two men stopped staring at Lorand darkly and turned to leave, heading for the waiting carriage. The way they'd acted had disturbed me, but Lorand's behavior disturbed me more.

"Why didn't you tell them not to be absurd?" I asked as he began to close the door, the expression on his face distantly troubled. "*You* don't owe them a thing, so there's no reason for them to come back here. And if that's the way a friend is supposed to behave, I'm glad I never had any."

"Hat's not normally like this, and the trouble he's in is worse than anything he's been in before," Lorand answered, sounding distant and disturbed. "But he's still a friend, and I don't believe in abandoning friends when they're in trouble. If I don't pay off his debt those two might kill him, since it's perfectly obvious that *he'll* never be able to pay it off. I'll just have to . . . make sure I do win the gold."

"Lorand, what world are you living in?" I couldn't help asking, well beyond exasperation. "You claim you don't be-

lieve in abandoning a friend in trouble, but you're doing all
this for someone who *brought* you trouble, then walked away
leaving you to cope with it alone. And no matter what those
two said, they won't kill the idiot. At worst they'll beat him
up and then force him to take a job, so what you're really
saving him from is having to pay for his stupidity with a
little pain and a lot of sweat. If you don't believe that pain
teaches a very thorough lesson about what not to do again,
just ask *me* about it.''

"I know you're right, Tamrissa, but there's nothing I can
do to change matters," he said with a sigh as he patted my
hand. "Hat *isn't* behaving the way a friend should, but that
doesn't give me the right to be just as uncaring. I have to
help him if I can, but at this point it's more for my own
benefit than his. I don't want to forget how a friend is supposed to behave.''

"I think I understand now why there are so many nasty
people in this world," I replied with my own sigh. "Being
nice lets too many people take advantage of you. Well, all I
can do at this point is say that if *I* win any gold in the
preliminary competitions, I'll help you pay them off.''

"Now *that's* what I call being a friend," he said with a
laugh, then his smile softened as he gently touched my face.
"Thank you, friend Tamrissa, for disapproving of what I'm
doing but supporting me anyway. In turn I'll try not to need
your help, but it still feels good to know the offer is there.
Shall we go back to the others now?''

"We might as well," I agreed, returning his smile as I
took his arm. "And you're right: *being* a friend does feel
awfully good, no matter *how* dumb your friend's behavior
is. I'll have to remember that.''

"I don't think I've ever been insulted so nicely before,"
he said, laughing again as we retraced our steps to the back
of the house. "But if a friend isn't entitled to insult you, who
else is?''

We discussed that point as we walked outside, but Lor-
and's laughter wasn't fooling me. He was still upset about
what had happened, and there was nothing I could do to

make things better for him. I was beginning to learn that it was possible to give people pain in ways that weren't physical, but had no idea how to cope with it. People tend to defend themselves from physical pain, but with the emotional kind. . . .

The refreshment table held Lorand's brandy glass and my teacup, so we each retrieved our possessions before Lorand went off to tell Jovvi about what had happened. I stood and sipped my cooled tea, simply glad it was over, then abruptly discovered that *that* conclusion was extremely premature. Vallant Ro was once again heading straight for me, and this time there was no possibility of escape.

I finished the tea in my cup in a single gulp, then turned to pour myself more. It was the oddest thing, but after the time I'd spent in Rion's bedchamber I now found taking Lorand's arm and holding it tightly not in the least difficult. But for some reason facing Vallant Ro was harder, and speaking to him seemed one step below torture. I would have run to hide if I could have, but something told me he'd simply follow.

"Tamrissa, I'd like to speak to you for another moment," he said from behind me while I spooned sugar into my tea. "I promise not to intrude long, but something has been disturbin' me and I'd like to discuss it with you."

"I think I know just how you feel," I muttered, paying very little attention to what I did with the tea, then abruptly decided on surrender. If I simply stood there and let him have his say, the torture would hopefully soon be over.

"All right, I'll listen," I said in a tone loud enough for him to hear as I took my tea and turned to face him. "Just please make it brief."

"As best I can," he agreed with a small bow. I couldn't help noticing again how marvelous he looked in his practice clothes, how broad-shouldered and slim-hipped. My cheeks warmed as I found myself trying to remember how he looked without them, his platinum hair falling loose about his shoulders and those light blue eyes staring directly at me. . . .

"Tamrissa, are you all right?" he asked, bringing me back

to reality with a jerk. "I somehow had the feelin' you didn't hear what I said."

"I'm . . . sorry, I was just . . . distracted for a moment," I apologized, trying not to die of embarrassment. "Please go on, and I promise I'll hear you this time."

"I just said I've been doin' some thinkin' about what *you* said," he obliged, faint puzzlement in those beautiful blue eyes. "You told me about all those men you're involved with and so didn't want to lead me on, but I'm afraid it's too late. You already *have* led me on, and now I find myself feelin' . . . hurt."

"Hurt?" I echoed, now even more appalled. "But I didn't mean to hurt you, truly I didn't! Let me apologize again, because I really—"

"Please," he interrupted solemnly, holding up one big hand. "I realize you didn't hurt me deliberately, but that doesn't change how I feel. I've been standin' there picturin' you . . . sharin' yourself with all those men, but when it comes to me you just want . . . brevity. Treatment like that says that in your opinion I'm not even good enough to talk to."

"Oh, I really didn't mean anything like *that*," I babbled, silently cursing that stupid idea I'd had. "I was actually trying to show *concern*, not—"

"Concern?" he interrupted again, taking the teacup and saucer out of my hands before I managed to spill the tea all over both of us. He'd put his brandy glass down somewhere, so he had no trouble holding the teacup and saucer.

"It doesn't seem to me like concern when you're willin' to walk about on Coll's arm, but don't even want to *talk* when it comes to me." He looked so serious and so really upset that I wanted to hold him close and comfort him— right after I cut out my tongue. "I understand how betrayed you must have felt when your daddy lied to you about me, but it *was* a lie and we both know it. Does that mean I'm not fit to breathe the same air as everybody else?"

I wanted to tell him that it meant nothing of the sort, but if I agreed to forget the incident he'd want to go back to the way things had been between us. I was beginning to very much want the same thing, but he really did make me too vulnerable where my father was concerned. He was a point of attack my parents would not hesitate to use against me, and I simply couldn't let that happen.

"Your silence says I got it just right after all," he told me heavily after a moment, those eyes now infinitely sad. "I was goin' to suggest somethin' that would make things . . . less than right but at least fair, but now I suppose we'd better forget it. I'll just get out of your way, and won't be botherin' you again. . . ."

He looked so forlorn as he began to turn away that I simply couldn't bear it. I finally had to admit that he'd never actually done anything to harm me, but circumstance had had me treating him as shabbily as Hat was treating Lorand. I'd been hurt too often myself to casually do the same to someone else who was innocent, so I had to make whatever amends were possible.

"Wait," I said before he'd taken even two steps away. "I . . . don't want you to believe what isn't true, so I'll . . . agree to your suggestion about how to make things fair. As *you* said we might have to work together, and working around something like this is just too hard."

"Don't you want to hear the suggestion before agreein' to it?" he asked after turning back to me, an odd look now in his eyes. "It might be somethin' you'd find objectionable, even though it would only be fair. I don't want to think I'm forcin' you into somethin' you don't really want to do. . . ."

"You're not," I assured him as forcefully as I could, looking up into those incredible eyes. "I *want* to do this for you, I really do! Just tell me what it is, and I'll do it."

"Well, if you're sure," he gave in with a sigh that looked rather odd. "And it does make me feel a lot better to hear you agree. Now all we have to decide is when to do it, but I don't want to rush you. How about in two days' time, which will make it week's end night?"

"Yes, that would be fine," I agreed, relieved that I would have two whole days to get ready to— "But you still haven't told me what it is that we'll be doing, not to mention where. Were you thinking about out here in the garden if it doesn't rain?''

''No, to tell the truth I *wasn't* thinkin' about usin' the garden,'' he said, scratching his ear as he tried to swallow some sort off amusement. ''Actually it came to me that if you were lyin' with so many other men, it would only be fair if you lay with me as well. Now that you've agreed I don't feel so much less than them, but this garden isn't the proper place. I'll come to your apartment, and maybe you'll even let me stay the night.''

After saying that he gazed at me in the blandest way I'd ever seen, pretending that I wasn't gaping at him with my jaw down to the ground. And that I wasn't blushing so furiously it was a wonder the nearest trees hadn't caught fire. My thoughts were in the most chaotic whirl it's possible to experience, but after a moment a very definite thought broke through.

''You tricked me!'' I hissed, knowing it beyond all shadow of doubt. ''You deliberately told me stories and tricked me! I've never heard of anything so vile, so—so—''

''Excuse me, but I offered to tell you my suggestion before askin' you to agree,'' he interrupted for the third time, the look in his eyes having hardened. ''You were the one who insisted on agreein' before you heard anythin' about it, so you have nothin' to complain about. We have a date, Tamakins, and I'm really lookin' forward to it.''

He grinned at the way I began to sputter, caused by trying to say seven things at once. I hated him for tricking me like that, but I realized with a sinking feeling that he was right. I *had* insisted on agreeing to terms I didn't yet know, and he *had* offered to tell me first. That meant I was trapped unless I found it possible to go back on my word, something I'd never been able to do. Not being able to trust the word of those around me, I'd sworn to myself that *my* word would always be good. . . .

''What a relief it is to get this problem out of the way,'' the monster said, trying to sound innocent despite his continuing grin. "The worry was interferin' with my sleep, but I'll certainly get my rest tonight. And tomorrow night, so that I don't disappoint you on our date."

He was really enjoying himself, and then I saw him notice that he still held my cup of tea. Rather than return it, though, he raised the cup to his lips just where my lips had been. Those eyes were on me as he took a deep, sensual sip, all but commanding me to remember what it had been like when those lips had really touched mine. In spite of myself I began to feel what he so obviously wanted me to, and then—

And then he made a strangled sound and turned away to spit the mouthful of tea into the grass. I couldn't imagine what was wrong—until I remembered that I'd lost count of the number of teaspoons of sugar I'd put into the cup. I'd been distracted by *his* presence, which made the entire episode one of poetic justice.

"I hope there was so much sugar in there that it poisoned you!" I snapped as he stood there trying to get the cloying sweetness out of his mouth. "And I may have agreed to lie with you, but I said absolutely nothing about speaking to you. Don't bother addressing me again, Dom Ro, as you and I have already exchanged our last words!"

And with that I hurried back to the house, needing to be alone in my bedchamber. I hated Vallant Ro for tricking me like that—but now could think of nothing but the approach of week's end night. . . .

TWENTY-TWO

Rion felt positively lighthearted as the carriage took him and the others back to the new testing area for the second day. Yesterday had not only seen him gaining his first set of masteries, but it had also brought Tamrissa Domon to his bedchamber with her totally unexpected request. The time with her had been very sweet and pleasantly fulfilling in an odd way, considering that he felt no more than warm friendship for the girl. Her constant support of him had prompted him to agree to something he'd had no actual burning desire for, but he'd granted the request as a favor.

And afterward he'd been extremely glad he had. As despicable as his own personal situation was, Tamrissa's was clearly a good deal worse. He'd almost felt her waiting for him to give her pain, and only after they parted had she seemed willing to believe there would, in truth, be none. She was such a harmless, soft, little thing; how any man could bring anguish to her was completely beyond him.

Rion shifted on the carriage seat, taking the opportunity to glance at Vallant Ro. Ro seemed distracted this morning, but not broodingly so. It seemed more a matter of . . . day-dreaming, with an occasional sigh thrown in. Last night he'd obviously had words with Tamrissa, but it hadn't been anguish that he'd given her. Furious anger was what it had

160

looked like to Rion, and although he hadn't been able to hear what was said, he'd seen the pained look on Ro's face after Tamrissa had stormed off.

Which most likely meant things hadn't quite gone the way Ro had wanted them to. Rion chuckled to himself, feeling a bit sorry for Ro. The soft, harmless woman *he'd* held in his arms had become a growling, claw-covered tigress where Ro was concerned. Rion freely admitted that he'd rather have Tamrissa defending him than attacking him, a position Ro couldn't seem to find a way into.

After Tamrissa had left, Jovvi had casually spoken to the rest of them about not being too quick to follow her example. They had to establish a picture of people who enjoyed spending time in each other's company, or any future meetings and discussions they held would be noticed by the servants who were reporting to the testing authority. Even Holter had agreed to the request, so they'd stood around having unimportant conversations—until one of the regular house servants had approached Rion.

"Excuse the intrusion, Dom Mardimil, but there's a young lady at the servants' entrance asking to see you," the man had murmured. "If you'd care to follow me I'll take you to her, otherwise I'll send her on her way."

For an instant Rion had been terrified that Mother had returned, but once the servant began to speak he'd been able to relax. Mother would never have used the servants' entrance even if she'd known where to find it, and the servant had definitely said *young* lady. He'd immediately wondered who that could possibly be—

And then he'd known who it *had* to be. With pulse pounding he'd told the servant to lead the way, and then he'd followed the man into and through the house to a side door off a narrow hall near the servants' quarters. The servant indicated the door and then quickly disappeared, leaving Rion to open it to find just the one he'd hoped it would be: Naran Whist.

"Dear lady, how did you find me here?" Rion had asked as his entire body began to tingle at the sight of her. "But

I'm being just as rude as that servant was. Please come inside.''

"My lord, forgive me, but I haven't the time," she begged off with the loveliest smile, looking up at him with those incredible eyes. "I asked some discreet questions among . . . acquaintances I have, and in that way discovered which residence you were in. I hope you'll excuse my intrusion, but I'm leaving the place I currently live and couldn't bear the thought of you coming there and not finding me. Here.''

She pressed a folded envelope into his hands, but Rion couldn't take his eyes from her in order to examine it. She wore a dark gray hooded cloak, the hood framing her darkhaired loveliness. Beneath the cloak he was able to glimpse a red gown trimmed in gold, but one that seemed . . . scantier than what Tamrissa and Jovvi wore. The gown emphasized Naran's charms, and Rion would have enjoyed seeing more of it.

"I've written down where I'll be by this week's end night,'' she went on, slowly withdrawing her hands from his. "If you've changed your mind about coming to see me I'll understand perfectly, but if you haven't . . . I wanted you to know where I would be.''

"Since I haven't changed my mind, I'm very grateful for the information," Rion said with his own smile, wishing it were still her hand in his grasp rather than the envelope. "Are you certain you can't come in even for a little while?''

"Unfortunately I have a . . . an appointment which I'm already late for,'' she said, sadness and regret clear in her expression. "It isn't far from here, so I was able to stop on the way. Now I must go, but—I'll dream about seeing you again.''

That last was said with such shy delight that Rion yearned to take her in his arms, but a breath later she had disappeared into the night. His first thought was to follow and at least see her to her carriage, but then he remembered the men Mother's agent had watching him. If they had the least idea that he was involved with Naran, they would quickly report the fact. Then Mother would have Naran thrown out of the city of Gan Garee—or maybe even worse.

For that reason Rion quickly closed the door, to keep from being seen by accident. There seemed to be a thick hedge just beyond the wide path to the door, so his meeting with Naran might have gone unnoticed. If it hadn't and Mother did indeed find out, Rion didn't know what he would do. But his immediate rage at the thought gave him something of a hint, so he would hope that it never came to that.

Rather than return to the garden, Rion first found the excellent servant who had been so marvelously discreet, privately tipped the man one of the four silver dins he'd earned that day, and then he returned to his bedchamber. He wanted to look at the contents of the envelope he'd been given, but without an audience. He tore the envelope open and pulled out two sheets of paper.

The first sheet had nothing but an address, which Rion recognized as being somewhere in the middle of the city. It told him exactly where Naran would be by this week's end night, so he turned curiously to the second page. If they were directions on how to reach the address, he didn't really need them.

But they weren't directions. It was recognizably the same gracefully delicate hand which had written the address, but this was a letter. Rion had never gotten a letter before, most especially not from a woman, and the scent of lilacs reached him as he began to read.

"*My dear sir,*" it began, for all the world like a greeting from a merchant one had patronized before.

Please don't think me forward, but I felt I had to make some attempt to say what knowing you has meant to me. I'm certain you will quickly grow tired of me, and you need have no fear that I will try to hold you longer, but until then I live for the few brief moments we're able to be together. You fill my dreams each night and my thoughts each day, and I live for the time you will find it possible to come to me again. Until the day, I remain,

> *Yours devotedly,*
> *Naran Whist*

"Mine devotedly," Rion had echoed aloud, never having heard such a marvelous phrase. It was the way he felt as well, but he would certainly have to speak sternly to that young lady. To even *suggest* that he would tire of so beautiful and marvelous a woman—! That would never happen, but seeing her as soon as possible must. Somehow he would avoid the men watching him, and then—

"Rion, this is where you get out," Lorand said, bringing him back to reality with a jerk. He hadn't even noticed that the coach had stopped, so deeply into his thoughts had he been. He nodded and got out of the coach, then walked through the resin wall to find a reception committee of one. Padril jumped up from a nearby table, and it was clear that the so-called Adept had been waiting for him.

"Good morning, sir," he said as he came toward Rion, a strange smile framed by his ring beard. "Will you have some tea before you begin?"

"Yes, I believe I will," Rion said, making no effort to stop in order to talk to the man. He was on the way to the table he had begun to think of as his, ignoring Padril's side-scrabbling effort to keep up as he spoke.

"Then do please join me at my table, the one you passed," Padril urged, gesturing back toward the entrance. "The tea was only just brought, so it's perfectly fresh. And the table position will allow you the privacy which is so much your due."

That last was probably said because quite a number of people sat about while talking and drinking tea, but Rion wasn't in the least tempted by the idea. It sounded too much like something Mother would have said, and his own table stood empty and unclaimed.

"I prefer to be in the thick of things, with truly fresh tea," Rion answered, ringing a bell for a servant before sitting at his table. "You, however, may return to your privacy, and I'll summon you when I'm prepared to begin."

"You're denying me permission to join you?" Padril whined, sounding more disturbed than puzzled. "But I don't understand, sir. Why would you do that?"

"I've never been able to bear spastic behavior at this time of the morning," Rion replied without looking at the man. A cup of tea was already being brought to him, and that was a much more interesting sight. "Now please go away and do your fidgeting and spasming somewhere else."

Padril apparently had no reply to that, but he continued to hover for a moment as the tea was put in front of Rion. When Rion gave all his attention to the tea and none to the Adept, Padril at last accepted the fact that he'd been dismissed. He walked away with dragging steps, and Rion finally had the privacy that had been mentioned earlier.

Which let him sit back and look around after sipping at his tea. The crowd spread out among the tables looked no different from the one of the day before, except for the people at the table where Padril had taken his lunch yesterday. Everyone else's conversation looked desultory and bored, but the people who were presumably Padril's associates seemed to be engaged in an intensely serious conversation. They appeared to be as unhappy as Padril had been, and briefly Rion wondered why.

But the question held very little true interest for him, as Rion was in the process of shaping his determination into a vehicle for success. Yesterday he'd earned enough silver to pay for his keep, and today he would earn enough to take Naran to the best dining parlor in the city for dinner. He very much wanted to give her the world, but would have to begin with very small parts of it.

This time he deliberately kept himself from falling too deeply into his thoughts, and considered instead the test which was before him. Rather than keep his subjects supplied with air, this time Rion would have to take their air away. The biggest benefit to that arrangement was the fact that Padril would need to declare the masteries a good deal more quickly than he had yesterday—otherwise they would run out of subjects rather quickly. That thought made him chuckle as he finished his tea, then he rose to his feet and turned to gesture to Padril.

The Adept still appeared to be hovering even though he'd

seated himself, and at Rion's summons he lurched to his feet
and lumbered over. The man really was much too overweight
for the low position he held in life, and was also rather wasteful. The tea on his table looked as untouched as it had been
on Rion's arrival, but it was some distance away so Rion
might have been mistaken. It was also completely unimportant, so Rion put it from his mind as Padril reached him.

"I'm ready to begin," he announced unnecessarily. "You
may lead the way to the testing building."

The Adept seemed to shrink in on himself as he heard
that, and his steps turned plodding as he obeyed. But as they
passed the table filled with his friends, friends who had
started out laughing at Rion just as Padril had, one of them
rose and came over to join them.

"I . . . believe I'll come along and watch the witnessing,"
the man announced to Padril, sounding oddly hesitant. "I
trust you don't mind, Padril?"

"No, Arnot, not at all," Padril responded, not quite sounding hearty and welcoming. "This is Dom Mardimil, who will
surely soon be Master Mardimil. Sir, this is Adept Arnot."

Rion nodded curtly, annoyed that *he* hadn't been asked if
the intrusion was acceptable. It also annoyed him to be addressed as "dom" rather than "lord," but the point wasn't
one he cared to press at the moment. And soon his proper
title would be "master," something he hadn't realized and
actually preferred. "Lord" he'd been born with, but "master" he would have to earn.

Both men led the way to the second small practice building, and when Rion walked in he noticed the difference from
the first building at once. None of the practice rooms was
capable of being sealed, and some even had windows. Considering the fact that applicants were the ones who were expected to do the sealing, that was perfectly understandable.

Padril went to summon the subjects Rion would work
with, and he returned with six people who seemed to have
been drugged. They moved as though walking in a dream,
stopped immediately when ordered to do so, and stood staring off into other worlds with what appeared to be limitless

patience and unconcern. Rion understood why they would be drugged—otherwise their terror would be completely disruptive—but he discovered that he didn't care for the practice. The chill white of the resin walls grew colder with their presence, and Rion would have shivered if he made a practice of allowing himself to do such things.

"I believe we're ready to begin," Padril said as he closed the door to the small room, now, for some reason, sounding determined. "Please start any time you wish."

The man Arnot hadn't said another word, but he and Padril now stood together. Not long ago Rion would not even have noticed that, but now he noticed and also wondered. These people had proven they weren't to be trusted, and having two Adepts in the room seemed suspicious. Rion decided to keep a wary eye on them, as they were almost certainly here for their own benefit rather than his.

But his main concern was getting through this test, so he turned his attention to the six subjects. The four men and two women stood grouped together the way they'd been left, and Rion was surprised to find himself hesitating. He hadn't found it difficult to take the air from those two ruffians who had invaded the residence with that odious woman, but these six people weren't menacing women he cared for. How could he, in all good conscience, take the very breath of life from them . . . ?

Rion suddenly felt very alone in that room, being the sole person who stood by himself. Not long ago being alone was the most familiar thing in the world, but now he'd learned what it was to have the support and companionship of friends. He hated being without anyone on his side when he had to do something he disapproved of—and then, abruptly, he noticed he wasn't quite as alone as he'd thought. A small spider had come down on a thread to hang above his right shoulder, just a bit below eye level. Normally Rion would have moved away from the thing in disgust, but now. . . .

But now the spider was his only companion, and its companionship let him turn to the six subjects again. He didn't like what had to be done but his approval hadn't been asked for, so he'd better get on with it and put the distasteful time behind him.

Reaching for the power was unnecessary, as Rion seemed filled with it the instant he wanted it. This was something new and it startled him, but not so much that he forgot what he was about. He formed a large sphere around the six subjects, and the next instant they were all gasping for breath.

"Nicely done, sir," Padril said, for some reason now sounding almost as greasily insulting as he had to begin with. "It took longer than I'd expected for you to get started, but it was certainly done well. You must hold them like that for a full minute, and when you release them I'll order them to their second positions."

Rion had just as good a sense of time as anyone else, but that single minute seemed longer than any other he had ever lived through. The subjects choked and clawed at their throats while he held them airless, but when the minute was up and he released them they went back to their waking dream state. They breathed deeply for some seconds, but other than that they showed no signs of knowing how close they'd come to death.

Padril let the subjects return to breathing freely for a while, and then he ordered them to split into two groups of three. They moved immediately into the commanded arrangement, and it was time to do the same thing to them again. Rion glanced at the spider, delighted that it was still there with him, then he formed two spheres from which he took the air.

"Ah, much more lively this time, sir," Padril said while the subjects choked again and Rion waited for another endless minute to be up. "This will be your second upper level mastery, but in a manner of speaking you have to admit that it's actually easier than first level. Yesterday you had to keep *yourself* supplied with air along with the subjects."

Rion wasn't prepared to admit anything Padril wanted him to, even though the Adept was absolutely correct—in a way. Talentwise it was certainly easier to take air from people than to keep them supplied with it, but personal standardswise. . . .

When the minute was up Rion released the subjects, and

again Padril waited before arranging them in three groups of two. Rion waited even longer to give the pallor on their emotionless faces a chance to fade a bit more, and then he took their air for the third time. The small spider seemed to be commiserating with his deep disturbance, exactly the kind of support he needed right now.

"We'll give the subjects an extra pair of minutes to recover this time," Padril said when Rion released them at the end of the required delay. "Being without air for even so short a time weakens the subjects, and we wouldn't want any of them to die, would we? I hope you don't mind waiting, sir."

Rion didn't answer the man, but Padril didn't seem to be expecting an answer. The Adept's recovered superior amusement was even more noticeable now, and his friend Arnot was clearly sharing it. But he had only one segment to go before he attained all four upper level masteries, so Rion didn't understand the change in their attitudes. Why had they started out fearful and unsure, but now had done a complete about-face?

The puzzle wasn't one that Rion was able to solve during the intermission, not when the time allowed was so short. Padril announced that it was time to resume much sooner than Rion would have liked, and argument simply wasn't possible. The exercise was best over and behind him anyway, so there wasn't even any sense in arguing.

Rion took a deep breath as he prepared to smother the six subjects again, only this time individually. Six spheres of airlessness were required to do the job properly, so he reached out—and ran into some sort of resistance. The necessary volumes of air slid through the fingers of his ability, avoiding his attempt to touch them. That had never *ever* happened before, and for a moment Rion was stunned.

But just for a moment. It took that long to realize that Padril and Arnot simply stood there to his left and behind him, neither of them commenting on how long he was taking to perform the exercise. Since most of their original nastiness had returned they ought to be snickering at the very least, but an instant-quick glance over his shoulder let Rion see they weren't. In point of fact they were both staring at the six subjects intensely, and the concentration in their expressions was anything but amused.

Rion felt like snarling, and his spider companion seemed just as disturbed. If Padril and Arnot weren't blocking Rion's efforts with their ability, he would eat that entire building without salt. They meant to keep him from the fourth mastery and in turn also from the competitions, and they were most likely under orders to do so. No wonder Padril had been so frightened yesterday and Arnot disturbed this morning. They knew how much strength he had, and had worried about opposing him.

But now they considered themselves entirely safe, because they'd seen him hesitate over taking away the breath of life from the subjects. Many people weren't able to do it at all, Padril had told him yesterday when he'd first arrived, and the two Adepts now considered him almost as helpless as one of that sort. They would point to his many hesitations, tell him his failure was due to a hidden fear of harming the subjects, something he could be expected to believe. It would also be expected to keep him from trying for the mastery again, but trying a second time would *not* be necessary.

Taking his spider friend's continued presence as active support, Rion deliberately opened himself to more of the power than he'd ever used before. For a timeless moment there was a silent rushing sound in his ears, but certainly not caused by anything in the ordinary world. Along with the sound came an influx of strength, and the oddest feeling that his body would soon begin to glow. The entire experience was heady and faintly dizzying, as though he'd been drinking a bit too heavily, but then all those strange reactions went away and Rion was back to the way he'd been.

Except for now being able to wield substantially more power. He hadn't been sure his ability would support the added strength, but he'd been too angry to consider any consequences other than success. And now that he'd found his success, it was time to teach two "Adepts" a lesson.

Rather than reach to the subjects again, Rion reached first toward Padril and Arnot. The men were too deeply immersed in their tampering to notice at first, but they certainly noticed when Rion surrounded them with their own sphere, then took away *their* air. After that he surrounded the six subjects just the way he was supposed to, and as they began to choke for the fourth time, Rion spoke without turning.

"One last minute, and then the final mastery will be mine as well," he commented, knowing Padril and Arnot were able to hear him. "That certainly isn't very long, so I'll think about extending the period while I wait for the time to pass."

The Adepts weren't able to speak, of course, but Rion could feel the way they fought against his strength in an effort to escape. They weren't all *that* weak, which meant perspiration broke out on his brow from their efforts to resist, but once again success was his. He held all seven spheres intact and airless for the full required minute, and only then did he allow them freedom.

Rion had already turned to look at the Adepts, neither of whom was a pretty sight. Arnot stood with his shoulders braced against the wall, and Padril had gone to his knees, both with their teeth bared in their efforts to break free. Their abrupt release came like the unexpected snapping of a rope, causing Arnot to slide down the wall and Padril to go to all fours. Both men were pale and immediately began to gasp in air, giving Rion the opportunity to speak first.

"You now have my thanks for having tried to interfere with my advancement," he told them coldly, noticing that they seemed to tremble from something other than the results of their ordeal. "If anything like this is ever tried with me again, no one will enjoy my immediate anger. Now let me hear you declare my fourth and final mastery."

"Con—gratulations, sir—on achieving—the level of—master," Padril quickly obliged, panting even in the midst of the words. He also studied the floor rather than look up at Rion, and being able to breathe hadn't lessened his pallor. "Please—forgive us, sir, we were—under orders to—do as we—did. But you—triumphed anyway, and—in a moment

I'll—fetch your silver dins—and master's bracelet.''

"Bring it to my table, where you'll find me resting from my exertions," Rion ordered, then he turned and walked out of the room. He'd first searched for his spider friend, having some vague idea about taking it outside where it might have a better chance to survive, but the spider had disappeared. Which was rather a lucky thing, as Rion was badly in need of the time to do some thinking.

The bright morning sunshine came as a surprise when Rion stepped outside, since he felt as if he'd spent hours—if not the entire day—in the practice building. He also felt as if he hadn't eaten in almost that long, so he rang a bell for service before sitting at his table. The servant who quickly appeared took his order for food as well as fresh tea, and then Rion was able to lean back for a while—

—and ask himself why the testing authority would try to hamper his efforts to move onward. That theory Holter had come up with, about the members of their residence having been arranged into a potential Blending—if the authority really did want them to compete as a Blending, why make such a strong effort to disqualify one of them?

The suggestion that it had been done because the authority wanted no one but the strongest and best to compete would probably be what they would claim, but Rion didn't believe it. Despite the solid reasoning behind such a stance, something about it rang untrue. Their aim wasn't to disqualify the unfit but to disqualify everyone possible, which explained why every ruling Blending for the last hundred years had come from the nobility. The testing authority had eliminated all real competition before the final confrontation came about.

"Excuse me, sir," a voice interrupted his thoughts, and he looked up to see a trembling Padril standing there clutching something. "I have your eight silver dins and your master's bracelet."

The servant was also coming with his food and tea, so Rion put out a hand to Padril.

"Give me the dins, and then explain about this bracelet

thing," he ordered the Adept, making sure his tone was as cold as it had been. "And make sure your explanation leaves nothing out."

"Yes, sir," Padril responded at once, still looking gray from his ordeal. He handed over the dins and watched while the servant put the food and drink in front of Rion, but only glanced at one of the empty chairs at the table. He hadn't been invited to sit, and obviously knew better than to try it anyway.

"The master's bracelet takes the place of the applicant's identification card," Padril began as soon as the servant left. "It marks the wearer as a full participant, firmly beyond the level of applicant. There's really nothing more to the matter, since it's only a higher-status indicator."

"And how many of those testing previously earned their higher status despite interference?" Rion put bluntly after sipping at his tea. "Some of them? Most of them? *All* of them?"

"Please, sir, you must understand how late in the year it is," Padril whined, all but squirming in agitation where he stood. "It's been our experience that those applicants with so short a time for practice rarely do anything more than get in the way of those who have an actual chance to attain the various positions. 'Helping' them to drop out does a service to both them and us."

"Allow me to say that I don't think much of your 'service,' " Rion told him dryly, then waved a hand at him. "Go away now and allow me to eat in peace, but don't go too far. I have questions about what happens next, and I'll expect you to be available to answer them before I leave."

"Yes, sir, I'll be right over there," Padril responded, indicating the table with the rest of his cronies. "Just raise your hand when you want me, and I'll return immediately."

When Rion nodded absently he scuttled away, looking as if he'd just narrowly escaped death. In a manner of speaking he had, for Rion knew that if he and Arnot had made the mistake of attacking him directly rather than just trying to block him, the end result of his efforts would have been a good deal less pleasant for them. He'd been victimized for enough of his life; from now on he meant to make up for that.

Rion picked up his sandwich and began to eat it, but his thoughts were on things other than food. He would have to be sure to discuss his suspicions with the others, to warn them that everything might not be as open and aboveboard as some of them believed. And then he'd be able to plan his visit to Naran, which he now had the silver to pay for. Naran . . . one day soon he would have gold to spend on her, and *no* one would be allowed to stand in his way, *no* one. . . .

TWENTY-THREE

Lorand felt like a personal servant by the time he left the coach. First he'd had to wake up Mardimil when the coach reached his stop, and then he'd had to do the same for Ro. Both men had been deeply into their thoughts, but Ro had also seemed to be brooding. Holter had only been partially distracted, but enough so that Lorand had felt that he rode alone in the coach.

And it wasn't as if he didn't have his own things to brood about, he thought morosely as he left the coach. He'd wanted to talk to Jovvi again, and after the celebration broke up last night he'd managed to make it happen. He'd drawn her aside after everyone else had left, and had smiled down at her.

"So far things aren't going too badly for me," he'd said, trying to recapture the wonderful mood they'd shared when they first met. "Before you know it I'll have gold and a really good chance to win in the competitions, and then we can start to plan our life together. Or, if you'd rather not wait, we can start the planning right now.''

"I really do like you, Lorand Coll," she'd answered with a smile, putting one soft and shapely hand to his face in a gentle caress. "I knew at once that you would turn out to be someone who was important to me, and I'm not often wrong about things like that." Then her smile had faded, and the hand was gone from his face. "But right now I think it's time I went to bed."

Lorand wanted to ask if he could join her there, but suddenly the suggestion seemed out of place.

"Jovvi, what's wrong?" he asked instead, wishing he could take her in his arms. "Have I done something to offend you?"

"It isn't you," she replied with a headshake. "Or at least it isn't you alone. How can we plan on anything at all, when we don't even know what tomorrow will bring? A very large part of my childhood was filled with that kind of uncertainty, and I thought I'd fixed things so it would never happen again. Now it's happening anyway, and every day it gets worse."

"All the more reason for us to stay as close as possible," Lorand had told her, taking her hand despite the presence of the servant stationed near the house. "If we can't count on anything else, at least we can count on each other."

"Can we?" she'd asked, making no effort to pull her hand away but still looking at him oddly. "I've spent a lot of time worrying about you, Lorand, because I have a small, distant understanding of your problem. So far you've been able to force yourself to move ahead with the rest of us, but what if tomorrow comes and you find that you can't do it again? How strongly will I be able to count on you if you aren't here?"

Lorand hadn't been able to answer that question, and after a moment he'd released her hand in defeat. He'd expected her to go back to the house immediately, but after an instant's hesitation she'd put her arms around his neck and kissed him. There was nothing of passion in the kiss, he knew that at once; it felt more as if she were reluctantly kissing him goodbye. Lorand returned the kiss with silent desperation, and a moment later she was hurrying back to the house.

And now, walking toward the resin walls surrounding the practice area, Lorand still couldn't argue with what she'd said. It had been nothing but the truth, and even a sleepless night of tossing and turning hadn't done anything to change that. You can't count on someone who can't even count on himself, even if the someone is too thickheaded to keep that fact clearly in mind.

"Good morning, sir," a voice said, and Lorand blinked back to his surroundings to see that Hestir, his Adept guide, stood waiting for him. "I look forward to watching you practice this morning, and then perhaps I'll get some idea about when you mean to test for your next masteries."

Lorand was about to say that it would probably be a while before he was ready for the next tests, but the words were never spoken. He'd caught a glimpse of someone over near the first set of practice cubicles, and when he looked directly at the someone he felt jolted.

"That's Eskin Drowd," he all but blurted, beginning to move closer to the cubicles to be certain of that. "But what's he doing *here*? The last time I saw him he was having all sorts of trouble qualifying."

"Apparently he got past his troubles," Hestir remarked, having followed along. "He reported here first thing this morning, and after his guide showed him around he went right to work practicing. He seems to realize that he's the last of his group, and means to make up for lost time."

At that point Drowd glanced over his shoulder, then looked again more directly, just as Lorand had done. When he saw that it really was Lorand whom he stared at, the well-remembered sneer appeared in his eyes and on his face. *You forgot all about me*, the sneer said without words, *but I've caught up now and I won't fall behind again. This time it will be* you *eating* my *dust—just wait and see if it isn't.*

And then Drowd turned back to his practicing, complete determination clear in every line of his body. He'd been bested for a while by a "mudfoot," but he'd sworn to Lorand that he meànt to change that. Lorand would have no choice but to stand there and watch that sneering Drowd move past him, and then Drowd would be put back into the residence and Lorand would be out. After that he'd probably never see Jovvi again. . . .

"I won't be practicing this morning," Lorand heard himself saying to Hestir. "I know what's necessary, so I've decided to go straight to the testing. Let's begin right now."

"But . . . now?" Hestir blurted, suddenly looking shaken. "I was certain you would decide to wait until this afternoon. . . . Well, if that's your decision, so be it. I'll fetch you a cup of tea to drink while I get another Adept to join me in the witnessing. This stage requires two witnesses, you know—"

"Thank you, but I don't want any tea," Lorand interrupted, knowing he didn't dare give himself time to stop and think. "I'll go with you to find that other Adept, and then we'll get straight to it."

"If you insist," Hestir agreed after a brief hesitation, now looking considerably less calm and pleased. "My associates are over there."

He gestured toward a table filled with men drinking tea and talking, then began to lead the way over to them. The Adept also seemed to be thinking about something, but Lorand chased too many of his own thoughts to wonder about Hestir's. He was committed to taking the test now, and backing out simply wasn't possible. No matter how many doubts and fears he had plaguing him, he *had* to succeed.

"Morin, a moment of your time, please," Hestir said when they reached the table. After a brief hesitation, an average-looking man with brown hair and eyes rose and came over to join them, and Hestir gestured toward Lorand.

"Dom Coll here has just informed me that he wishes to

take the next tests immediately," Hestir said, his voice coming out with an odd, flat inflection. "He's in such a rush he even refused a relaxing cup of tea, so I'll require your assistance with the witnessing."

"Of course, Hestir," Morin replied in that same odd tone, and then he looked at Lorand and produced one of the coldest smiles Lorand had ever seen. "It will be my pleasure, Dom Coll, since there are very few successes in this area to witness. The exercises are so difficult that far more people fail than pass, but I'm certain you'll be one of the few rather than one of the many."

"Of course he will," Hestir agreed heartily while Lorand felt a definite sinking feeling in his middle. "Dom Coll understands that it's simply a matter of using sufficient strength to get the job done. Let's go over there now, shall we?"

The restoration of Hestir's jovial good mood worked to weaken Lorand's determination even more, since both of the Adepts had chosen to say exactly the wrong thing in an effort to bolster his confidence. If that many people failed to pass the tests, then they had to require a *lot* of strength, just as Hestir had stressed. That meant—

Lorand's fretting came to a sudden halt as suspicion flared like a torch of pitch. Both Adepts *had* said exactly the wrong thing, and right after Hestir had seemed so disturbed by Lorand's decision to test. It didn't make sense for them to want to discourage him, but they couldn't be doing anything else—while pretending to be on *his* side.

Anger grew in Lorand as he followed after the men, burning high and hot for two reasons. The first was that the Adepts seemed to know all about his problem, and the second was that they were trying to use that knowledge against him. It grated on his sense of pride that they obviously considered him too backward to notice what they were doing, too much of a "mudfoot" to discover their little trick.

And then Lorand wondered if that was the only trick they had in store for him. Thinking back to his first conversation with Hestir, Lorand now remembered the Adept saying he needed "a" witness to his attempts at mastery, not two witnesses. Hestir could have meant a witness in addition to himself, but Lorand didn't believe that. The two were definitely up to something, and now Lorand had to discover what that was.

"All right, my friend, we're here," Hestir said, and Lorand looked up to discover that they'd reached the proper cubicle. Inside was a vat of thick black liquid, a liquid that came from beneath the ground and was therefore in the province of Earth magic.

"All you have to do, Dom Coll, is explode this liquid in the same way you exploded the pile of soil yesterday," Hestir explained as he and Morin ranged themselves to either side of the resin doorway in front of Lorand. "It does happen to be more difficult, but I have confidence in your level of strength."

Lorand kept his face straight as he stepped into the cubicle, but inside himself he fought to hold his temper. These two were trying to make him fail, so that Jovvi would move completely beyond his reach and Drowd would be able to laugh in ridicule. But Lorand wasn't going to let either of those things happen, not if he could possibly help it. Death would be better and easier to take. . . .

Even as he looked at the vat holding the thick black liquid, Lorand's ability was already spreading toward it as well. Merging with the power had always been an incredibly vital experience for him, and if not for his fears about burnout it would have been the best thing in Lorand's life. When he touched the black liquid with his ability, he was able to feel the individual drops that the whole was made of, their viscosity and texture, their weight and natural movement.

And all of that told him what he would have to do to scatter it the way he'd scattered the soil, to send it fountaining up in a proper explosion. It *would* take more strength than it had taken to explode the soil, but Lorand was already using that much strength and more. All he had to do was work out the proper addition to the necessary weaving. . . .

"Have you changed your mind, Dom Coll?" Hestir's voice came from behind him, so bland that Lorand's anger tried to rise again. "If you have, we quite understand. But if you haven't, please begin right now."

"As you wish," Lorand answered with his own blandness, making no effort to turn. "Right now it is."

And then he exploded the liquid, sending it splashing up and around with no more warning than that. But he'd first woven a very fine net of soil in front of himself, to keep the liquid from splashing *him* along with everything else. From the immediate shouts of surprise and disgust erupting behind him, Lorand was forced to guess that the two Adepts hadn't thought to do the same. They must have moved to stand in the cubicle's doorway, possibly believing there was no danger in doing that. . . .

"Hestir, weren't you and Morin standing behind the resin walls?" Lorand asked once he'd turned, now fighting to put concern in his voice rather than breaking down and laughing out loud. Hestir was spattered all over his left side and Morin had the same all over the right, showing they hadn't moved out of the doorway quite fast enough. It couldn't have happened to two nicer people, but it would be unwise to make that opinion visible to the two.

"It's a shame your clothing had to get stained, but you were absolutely right," Lorand burbled on as he left the cubicle, pretending he couldn't see how angry the Adepts were. "That wasn't as hard as I thought it would be, so I'm ready to tackle the next exercise. But I would advise you men to get those stains out of your clothes right now, before they damage the underlying dyes beyond repair."

"We appreciate the advice, Dom Coll, but unfortunately Morin and I haven't the time to play with stains right now," Hestir replied through his teeth, having removed the black liquid from nowhere but his face and hand. "We'll see to the matter later, after we've witnessed however many masteries you gain."

Lorand shrugged and nodded before leading the way toward the next cubicle, but his thoughts were grimly amused. The two men claimed that they didn't have time to remove the stains, but Lorand would have bet his chance in the competitions on the virtual certainty that they *couldn't* remove them. The black liquid really was difficult to work with, and it wasn't hard to believe that men who had been *appointed* Adepts just weren't up to it.

His good humor lasted only the few steps necessary to reach the next cubicle. A large wooden device had been built in there, a thing which resembled a strange farm wagon. Inside the device was a bar of metal. Lorand was supposed to use his ability to take apart the bar of metal, but the metal was steel rather than iron. Lorand had never tried to take apart steel before, but he already knew it wouldn't be easy.

"This should be a simple task for you, Dom Coll," Hestir's voice came from behind Lorand, once again vastly amused. "You did so well taking apart the iron that I'm surprised to see you hesitate. Taking apart steel requires nothing more than the use of additional power."

Being prodded like that brought back Lorand's anger, which in turn let him pose a silent question: just how much strength *did* it take to cause steel to crumble? The bottom-line truth was that Lorand didn't know, so it made sense to find out before deciding he couldn't do it. And it would take quite a lot to make him admit *that*, with Hestir and Morin poised and ready to laugh.

So Lorand reached out to the wooden device and found the bar of steel inside it. The bar seemed to be the main brace for other metal mechanisms inside the wagon, but that part was unimportant. It was the slim steel bar itself that he examined, and despite its general appearance of solidity he discovered pits and weakness lines that couldn't be found with eyesight alone. Iron was grainy, but steel had all those pits. . . .

Without stopping to think about it, Lorand poured every ounce of the power he wielded into deepening the pits he'd found. An effort like that couldn't be sustained long, but it didn't have to be. Suddenly various parts of the wooden device collapsed or sprang out of line, and Lorand was able to turn a sweat-covered face to the two frowning Adepts.

"I think that makes two additional masteries," he said,

doing nothing to hide how hard he'd worked. "Is this the end of it, or is there more?"

"There's one more exercise which you haven't seen as yet, sir," Hestir replied, now looking more disturbed than angry. "If you'll follow us, I'll explain the problem once we reach the proper cubicle."

Lorand didn't like the sound of that, but he had no choice about complying. He followed the two men toward an odd-looking cubicle some distance away from the others, wondering why Hestir now looked disturbed. So far the Adepts hadn't done anything but try to shake his confidence in himself, but maybe that was about to change. With only one more exercise to go through, it would be their last chance.

When they reached the separate cubicle, Lorand was able to see why it had looked so strange. It was at least four times bigger than any of the other cubicles, had a small white resin building attached at the back, and it was completely empty. The white resin building had a door leading directly into the cubicle, and oddly enough there was a barred gate across the front of the clear-walled cubicle. Lorand had also caught a glimpse of a portion of the area behind the white resin building before they'd reached the cubicle, and that was the strangest part. It looked like there was a grassy area back there, surrounded by some sort of high metal fence . . .

"Please step inside, sir," Hestir said when they stood in front of the cubicle, Morin on the other side of the doorway. Lorand had no choice but to comply, and this time the others made no effort to follow him. The sound of a click came, and when Lorand turned he saw that the barred door had been closed with both Adepts outside.

"Don't be alarmed, this is simply part of the procedure," Hestir said quickly, no trace of amusement in the man's voice. "There could well be danger for us if you fail, so we're allowed to remain out here."

"Danger for *you*?" Lorand echoed, frowning as he watched Morin walk to a large lever at the far side of the cubicle. "What danger are you talking about, and what about me? I'm here on the inside."

"That's the—ah—required place for an applicant," Hestir replied, and this time Lorand knew the man was lying. "It won't be for long, I assure you. . . ."

Hestir's words trailed off as Morin threw the lever, and a sound behind him made Lorand turn. The sound came from the slow opening of the door in the small resin building, and Lorand suddenly became aware of the fact that there was something alive in the building.

"This is a variation of the third exercise, the one with the rats," Hestir's voice came as Lorand tried to identify the living thing inside the building. "In this instance, however, you're simply to bring the beast out and up to you, then return it to its lair."

By then Lorand's blood had begun to run cold. He'd identified what the building held, and it was a puma! There had been some pumas in the hills beyond the farms of his county and once he'd even sensed one in the distance, but to be *this* close. . . .

"You can't seriously expect me to use Persuasion on an animal like *that*," Lorand protested, his insides twisting. "If it doesn't respond, I'll be killed!"

"That motivation is considered sufficient for those who qualify for this exercise," Hestir said, his tone beginning to sound more confident. "I would suggest that you take control of the beast now, before it emerges on its own. Once it begins to move voluntarily, controlling it will prove to be much more difficult."

As if controlling it now was easy! Lorand felt like laughing, but with hysteria rather than amusement. He had to get the puma under control, or it would certainly maul him. He could sense the way it had begun to stir, obviously getting ready to emerge. *Now or never, Lorand, boy. . . .*

Lorand's hands would have been trembling if he'd tried to use them, and even the fingers of his ability were the least bit unsteady. But he still reached out to the puma with his talent, intending to judge what level of strength would be required to handle it. At the same time he clung to the bravado he'd generated a moment before, telling himself that except for being larger, the puma was no different than the rat. . . .

"They say that a big beast's volition is very much like that of a man," Hestir commented while Lorand carefully sent his ability toward the big cat. "It's the beast's feral nature that makes it so, therefore I advise caution."

The words reached Lorand only distantly, as most of his attention was on the process of beginning to touch the puma. He was just a breath away from it, so he stretched his ability that extra breath of distance—and ran smack into some kind of barrier! Something was between him and the big cat, keeping him from even trying to exercise control!

"Better hurry," Hestir said, and the choppy, breathless way the man spoke made Lorand glance back. The two Adepts stood directly behind the barred door, and the intense expressions on their faces said they were using their own ability. Obviously that meant the barrier had been erected by *them*, to keep him from gaining the final mastery—and possibly even to keep him from surviving.

Fear flared all through Lorand, but he didn't have the time to pay attention to all the different levels and sides of it. Once again "maybe I'll burn out" had changed to "I'll certainly die," and the stronger fear was able to overcome the older and slightly weaker one. Before doubt had a chance to creep in, Lorand opened himself to more of the power—a good deal more.

Warm, tingling lightning immediately began to race through him, bringing assurance and physical strength and alertness. He'd need all that and more to do everything he had to, but now he felt that nothing was beyond him. The influx of power had also brought confidence, so he took immediate advantage of it.

Reaching out to the two so-called Adepts was effortless, so much so that their straining to hold the barrier in place was completely obvious. It was clear now that they were no more than strong Middles, and all their attention was on maintaining the merging of their talents. Ordinarily Lorand would have been certain it would be impossible to touch them, but now he had no doubts the other way.

So he reached to their bowels and bladders and closed a strong grip around each of the organs, then began to squeeze. Certain bodily reactions had the ability to break through the strongest air of concentration, and those were two of the best. Lorand felt the two men falter in their merge as they automatically tried to keep from soiling themselves, and that was all the opening he needed. His ability kicked down the weakened barrier, and reached for the puma behind it.

And not a moment too soon. The big cat was already beginning to step through the opened doorway, a feral eagerness filling it. It didn't mind that it wasn't yet lunchtime, it would be glad to make a meal exception in Lorand's case. It snarled when it felt him beginning to search out its muscle and nerve connections and then it tried to attack, but by then its movements were no longer under its own control. Lorand felt the sweat breaking out all over him from the need to use that much strength, but he didn't lose his grip on the struggling animal.

Instead he began to direct its movements, forcing it to walk stiffly toward him. The rat he'd done the same thing with had hated and feared being treated like that, but its inner raging had been nothing compared to the puma's. Lorand knew instant death awaited the least slip in control; for that reason his attention was glued to the procedure, to make certain there *were* no slips.

Walking the puma back to its building was almost harder than bringing it to a point just in front of him, but Lorand managed to do both. Once the big cat was inside he turned to look at the two Adepts, both of whom were staring white-faced through the bars.

"Close that door," Lorand gritted out between his teeth, unable to release the puma until that was done. When Morin hesitated, Lorand managed to add, "If I find I'm about to die, I swear I'll take you two with me."

That, at least, prodded Morin into motion, and he hurried over to the lever and moved it back to its original position. That made the door begin to close, but its movement was much too slow. By the time Lorand was able to release the puma, exhausted was too mild a word for the way he felt.

"Now get this gate open," he growled at Hestir, in no mood to play any more games. "This makes a full three masteries, and I want to hear you acknowledge it."

"Of course, sir, of course," Hestir babbled, releasing the latch on the gate before stumbling back a few steps. "The masteries are yours, along with your new designation. I'll fetch your dins and bracelet immediately, while you refresh yourself at a table."

"What bracelet?" Lorand asked as he stepped out of the cubicle, momentarily distracted from what he'd meant to say.

"It's your master's bracelet, which shows you to be a full participant rather than just an applicant," Hestir answered as fast as possible, the look in his eyes one of terror. "Please, sir, about what was done. . . . I'd like to explain—"

"Don't bother," Lorand interrupted, the growl still clear in his voice. "I don't care why you two did what you did, the action isn't one I mean to forgive. Go and get what you owe me, but don't try to talk to me when you bring it."

"Yes, sir," Hestir quavered with a gulp, then he hurried off in the direction Morin had already taken. Lorand followed more slowly, and was able to ring a bell for a servant before he collapsed into a chair. When Hestir returned, Lorand might not be *able* to speak, so he'd made sure speaking would be unnecessary.

The servant came quickly to take his order, which included enough solid food to fill the mile-deep hollow Lorand felt in his middle. Eating and relaxing would restore him to a great extent, but after that he'd also need some sleep. Tomorrow would be soon enough to demand explanations, when he'd have enough strength to stand and listen to them.

Lorand had the odd feeling that he was being stared at, and when he raised his head to look around he discovered he was right. Eskin Drowd stood near one of the practice cubicles, and his stare was filled with amusement and ridicule. At a guess Drowd thought Lorand had failed, and was taking the opportunity to laugh at him.

And that would be the second best thing about the day, Lorand realized as he sat up a bit straighter. He'd gained the masteries that he needed, and now Drowd would see him step up another level above him. The look on the man's face would be worth seeing and remembering, but right after that and his meal he would go directly back to the residence. As soon as he got the sleep he needed, he'd have to find out what was going on. . . .

TWENTY-FOUR

For the first time in a long while Jovvi felt utterly depressed. She'd said her goodbye to Lorand last night when she hadn't really planned to say anything at all, and then she'd gone to her bedchamber and cried. Telling herself Lorand was just another man wasn't working at all any longer, but there was nothing to be done about it. She simply couldn't bring herself to depend on his being there if she needed him, and that was the one fault she found it impossible to overlook.

So she would have been happier to pass the ride in depressed silence, but Tamma's presence refused to allow that. One minute the girl was projecting excited anticipation at the top of her emotional lungs, and the next it was outraged annoyance tinged with faint apprehension being projected. Jovvi couldn't have ignored that combination even if there hadn't been so much strength behind it, so after a few moments she admitted defeat with a sigh.

"All right, Tamma, tell me what's bothering you," she

said wearily, drawing the girl's attention. "If you don't, we'll probably both explode."

"Oh, Jovvi, I'm sorry," she answered, blushing a bit with fluster. "I didn't realize you'd—But of course you would, so—I'll try to stop."

"You'll try to stop feeling completely scattered and almost irrational?" Jovvi actually smiled at the thought, Tamma's regret and concern for her coming through just as clearly as the rest. "I appreciate your wanting to try, but if you ever found a way to do it, you'd probably be able to take the Fivefold Throne by yourself. Tell me what's causing the storm."

"One of my plans came back to bite me," Tamma admitted reluctantly after a short hesitation, now looking down at her hands. "Specifically the one to discourage Vallant Ro."

"Oh, dear," Jovvi said, then curiosity began to move aside her depression. "I knew it would be difficult to get anywhere with that man. What did you try?"

"Well, I remembered a comment you made about his probably not liking women who lay with other men," she replied with a vague gesture. "I decided that that would be the most likely thing to discourage him, so I lay with Rion and then I told the beast Ro that I had too many gentlemen friends now, and apologized for leading him on. But then—"

"Wait!" Jovvi finally managed to get out through her shock, one hand up to halt Tamma's flow of words. "I think I'd better take this one point at a time. You wanted to tell Vallant that you had a lot of gentlemen friends, so you lay with Rion. I seem to be having trouble understanding why that was necessary, since you can't call him a large number, only one. What's the difference between a complete lie and an almost complete one?"

"The difference. . . ." Tamma echoed, looking more perplexed than embarrassed. "I suppose you could say the difference is mostly in me. If it had been a complete lie, I never would have been able to say it. It was hard enough saying it after the experience with Rion, but *that* bit of truth let me lie about the rest. And besides . . . if this thing about the competitions comes to nothing and you end up opening a residence for courtesans after all . . . I want to be able to contribute actively, not just watch everyone else do the work.''

"I see," Jovvi said, which wasn't quite true. And her brows were still raised so high they might never come down, which was partly due to being impressed. "To be honest, Tamma, I never expected you to accomplish quite so large a change in yourself. The effort must have been enormous, and I admire you for having been able to do it. I take it you benefitted from lying with Rion?''

"Oh, yes," Tamma answered with a smile that made her look even younger and more innocent. "He promised to give me nothing but pleasure, and he kept the promise. I was so nervous and even frightened, but he just kept on being gentle until I didn't want him to be gentle anymore. That was when he gave me the pleasure.''

"Yes, that's the way it's supposed to work," Jovvi said, intrigued in spite of herself. A man like Rion, with almost no experience of his own, shouldn't have been able to produce that much enthusiasm in a woman like Tamma. When your experiences have been nothing but painful, even ordinary clumsiness can bring back hurtful memories and ruin the pleasure. If Tamma had felt nothing *but* pleasure, then Rion's performance must have been almost extraordinary.

"Well, that's the way it did work with Rion, but after that nothing went right," Tamma said glumly, all exuberance suddenly gone. "I told Vallant the lie as best I could, and for a little while he seemed to believe me. Then he came over and told me how hurt he felt at being led on by me, and a moment later I found myself insisting that he tell me what I might do to make him feel less . . . despised and left out. I even promised to do it without first hearing what it was.''

"Oh, dear," Jovvi said again, now fighting to keep from laughing. "Even in general it's a bad idea to promise to do something without knowing what the something is, but with a man like Vallant. . . . I think I already know what he asked for.''

"Everyone in the world but me would have known," Tamma said, self-disgust tingeing the glumness. "When he thanked me for agreeing to lie with him, I suddenly understood that he'd been planning that outcome all along. I was absolutely furious, and I told him that I might have to lie with him, but I certainly didn't have to talk to him."

"And then you stormed back into the house," Jovvi said with a nod. "I wondered what had happened this time, and now I know. It explains why you're so annoyed, but there's one emotion you've been projecting that you haven't discussed yet. You may be furious over being tricked, but you're also . . . anticipating the time, aren't you?"

Jovvi had tried to put the question very gently, but Tamma still flinched on the inside.

"I've—come to the conclusion that lying with Rion might have been a mistake," Tamma muttered, back to looking down at her hands. "As long as I thought of a man's use as painful, I had a—a—barrier of sorts to protect me from Vallant. Now . . . all I can think about is how marvelous it will be with him, and I don't want it to be marvelous. If it is. . . ."

"If it is, you'll find it painful in the extreme to keep from becoming involved with him," Jovvi said, at least understanding *that* part of it perfectly. "So what are you going to do? Tell him that his having tricked you means you don't have to keep your part of the bargain?"

"It was a promise, not a bargain, and he offered to tell me what he wanted before I gave my word to do it," Tamma responded, the glumness having deepened. "I was the one who insisted on giving my word first, so now I have to keep it. In one way I hate the idea, but in another. . . ."

This time Jovvi simply nodded, the point much too familiar to need discussing. She'd always remember the time she'd shared with Lorand, and that was a good part of the trouble. If only she were able to forget, she might find it possible to believe that she'd turned her back on a man no different from any of the others she'd known. . . .

The rest of the ride went by in silence, and once again Tamma was the first to get out. Jovvi simply readied herself until the coach reached her own stop, and then she got out and entered the practice area. There were more people present than there'd been yesterday morning, but all of them were sitting at tables and drinking tea. No one seemed to be watching the practice buildings, waiting for people to come out so that they might take their turn, and somehow that wasn't surprising.

"Good morning, Dama Hafford," Jovvi heard as Genovir, her Adept guide, suddenly appeared beside her. The tall woman was apparently trying to smile, but the result looked far from natural. "I hope you had a pleasant, restful time after leaving here yesterday."

"I certainly did," Jovvi replied with her own smile, then she looked around. "I don't see Adept Algus. He does have to join us for the testing, doesn't he?"

"You're already prepared to continue?" Genovir said, still maintaining that forced smile despite the—lurching distress—Jovvi was momentarily able to feel in her. "We expected you to practice a bit first. . . . I'll fetch Algus at once. Please feel free to sit and have tea while I do so."

Genovir turned and hurried away, leaving Jovvi with the impression that the larger woman's balance was on the verge of coming apart. Under other circumstances that would seem curious, but with the testing authority involved the reaction felt more suspicious. Those people were up to something, and the something wasn't likely to be to her benefit.

Jovvi considered taking the suggestion about tea, but old habits made her decide to sit down and simply wait. As a child she'd learned better than to eat or drink near people who couldn't be trusted, especially not when those people had access to what she would be eating or drinking. She remembered that very pretty young boy who had roamed the same part of the city that Jovvi and her brothers had. The three of them had watched the boy accept food and drink from a smiling stranger, and afterward they'd never seen the boy again. . . .

After a few minutes Genovir reappeared with Algus, both of them coming from the second small practice building. Their pace was less hurried than Genovir's departure had been, but there was a definite . . . *determination* to the tall, thin man's stride. Jovvi wondered about that, but as soon as the two reached the place she sat, it was no longer necessary to wonder.

"Well, good morning, Dama Hafford," Algus said in an attempt to sound jolly. "Genovir tells me you're ready to try for the next masteries, which is fine. But I must insist that you pause for a cup of tea first, which will help to relax you. It would distress me to see you faint from your efforts."

"That's very kind of you, sir, but unnecessary," Jovvi said as she rose, interrupting Algus in the process of reaching for a bell rope. "Since I haven't fainted yet and have no intention of doing so in the future, I must insist that we get on with the testing. Once I've achieved the masteries, I'll take a cup of tea as my reward."

Algus turned back to her and seemed about to speak, but his touching her lightly with his ability first stopped that. He had to have realized that Jovvi wasn't about to change her mind, and so gave up on the argument.

"Very well, Dama," he conceded, immediately covering his flash of frustrated annoyance. "Please come with us."

He and Genovir began to lead the way back to the second practice building, and Jovvi followed with less satisfaction than her victory would have given someone else. She'd gotten around whatever they'd had in mind with the tea, but the set of their shoulders told her there was more plotting ahead. Jovvi would have been delighted to find she was imagining things, but unfortunately it wasn't very likely that she was.

The second practice building was just like the first, divided into smaller rooms for the purpose of privacy. The only difference was the lack of windows in the room Genovir led her into. Wall lamps did the job of keeping the gloom at bay.

"Algus will be right here with the subjects you'll be working with," Genovir said, just as though Jovvi had no idea where the man had gone. The taller woman gave the appearance of being calm, but on the inside her nervousness was barely under control. Jovvi smiled and nodded to acknowledge what she'd been told, but her insides were almost as unsteady. The two Adepts were definitely up to something, but she had no idea what to be on guard against.

It really wasn't long at all before Algus appeared with the six subjects, this time the mix consisting of four men and two women. The men were generally larger than the previous male subjects had been, but with all of them drugged in the same way, that didn't matter. The—*deadness* of the six people was more disturbing than usual, though, so when a spider slid down its thread to hang beside Jovvi to the right, she appreciated the company. Spiders were beautifully tranquil on the inside, and it was nice to have one to keep her from being all alone.

"I'm sure you already know what's necessary, Dama, but I'll review the matter anyway," Algus said as the six subjects drifted to the far side of the room. "These subjects will start out calm, and your task will be to enrage them. They'll begin by standing together, then will shift through the various stages until each stands alone. For these final masteries you must be standing in the middle of the room, just as you were for the previous ones."

Jovvi agreed with a sigh and walked to the middle of the room as Algus closed the door, hating to desert her brand new companion but having no choice. The spider would be left behind while she went to the—

Suddenly Jovvi was very alert. There had been no need to tell her where to stand—unless the point was more important than it seemed. A glance at Algus showed her nothing, and it was too bad there was no time to think about it. . . .

"All right, now we'll begin," Algus said from where he stood near the door, behind her, then continued to the subjects, "Hear one who is authorized to command you. This woman is your friend, and she means you no harm."

The six subjects, properly cued, all began to smile, not the slightest bit of anger in any of them. Jovvi had already reached out to them, wondering if the trap lay in some difference between them and ordinary subjects, but that didn't seem to be the case. So she reached to their calm peacefulness, and a moment later they were shaking fists and moving angrily in place.

"Enough," Algus said after a very long minute, and the subjects calmed immediately. "Nicely done, Dama, very nicely done indeed. All right, you people, division one."

The subjects obeyed the second command as well and drifted into two groups of three, restored to serenity. Their movement took them a good distance apart, but not quite on opposite sides of the room. As soon as they stopped it was Jovvi's turn again, so she swallowed her distaste and reached out to them with her ability. Calming and easing people was completely natural and right, but *enraging* them . . . !

"Enough," Algus finally commanded after an even longer minute, calming the rage of the six subjects. Some of them had seemed ready to move in Jovvi's direction, which had disturbed her quite a lot. "Now you have two additional masteries, Dama. Let's move on to the third. You people, division two."

The six subjects drifted into three groups of two, and now they were in a triangle around Jovvi. For some reason their complete calm disturbed her, but she couldn't quite pinpoint why. And then there was another spider—or the same one—sliding down a thread right next to her again, which was somewhat surprising. It hadn't seemed there were that many spiders in the building, but obviously she'd been mistaken. She would have enjoyed being able to think about that along with what the Adept might be up to, but Algus could well decide to call any hesitation a failure. With that in mind she reached to the subjects again, and once more set them raging.

"Enough," Algus said in a *shorter* time than before, an odd satisfaction in his tone. "That makes three additional masteries, Dama, with only one more to go. If you like, I'll permit a pause now for a cup of tea."

"Thank you, no," Jovvi declined without turning to look at him, having no intention of deserting her spider companion again. And the spider *was* her companion, its steadiness holding her steady as well. ''I would prefer to have the testing over and done with first.''

''As you wish,'' Algus agreed, his now-roiling emotions too mixed to be easily interpreted. ''We'll conclude this, then. You people, division three.''

The subjects in the three groups separated to where each of them stood alone, and now they surrounded her even more completely. Jovvi *really* wanted the whole thing over and behind her, so she reached to the six individuals and set them raging. Once again this part of the exercise was easier than the previous part, except for the waiting. The six people raged furiously all around her, needing the command from Algus before turning calm again.

It took the first advance of the four male subjects to make Jovvi understand that the command from Algus was more than overdue. The four male subjects, with the two females not far behind, were in the process of beginning to attack her, and if Algus were going to turn them off he would have done so already. That must be the plan, then, to let the subjects attack her and later claim it was caused by *her* lack of control. That brought Jovvi her own anger, along with the determination not to let Algus and Genovir get away with it.

So she reached to the subjects again, intending to calm them herself—and found something blocking her. For an instant Jovvi had no idea what could be causing the block, but then it became obvious. A glance over her shoulder showed that Algus and Genovir were in the midst of some great effort with their own abilities, so that was the answer. *They* were the ones keeping her from reaching the subjects, a doing they'd obviously planned right from the beginning.

And now that Jovvi knew their plan, she certainly wished she didn't. The six subjects were so furious they were ready to cause serious harm, and they were all around her. They'd already advanced to a point where the diameter of their circle was half of what it had originally been, and another minute would see them even closer. If anything was going to be done about it, it had to be done *now*.

Swallowing against the fear trying to rise up inside her,

Jovvi opened herself to more of the power. The inrush was exhilarating and strengthening, flowing over and erasing her faint uneasiness over the necessity. The power she already wielded was more than she'd ever handled before, but if she were going to break out of the trap, she needed even more.

And now she had it, so she reached first to the two so-called Adepts. Their struggle to maintain the double block was now completely clear, showing how little of the power they were actually able to use. But breaking through the block was out of the question, so Jovvi did the only other thing she could: she sent the fear of enclosed spaces to the pair, forcing it through their individually inadequate personal defenses.

Genovir moaned as Algus gasped, and the block disappeared only just in time. The four large male subjects were only two steps away from Jovvi when she finally managed to calm them, doing the same for the women at the same time. The combined effort against eight people had covered Jovvi with sweat and started her faintly trembling, but she'd still accomplished what had needed to be done. And her spider companion was still perfectly calm, as though knowing she could be relied on to take care of the problem. But the problem had more than one side. . . .

Including continuing to hold the fear in Algus and Genovir. Once the six subjects were back to being calm, Jovvi was able to turn and look at the two who had plotted against her. They were in the midst of a mewling, panting struggle to get the door open, each one trying to push away the other so that he or she could be first to get outside. That meant neither of them was able to accomplish it, so the induced fear grew stronger by the minute.

Jovvi stood and watched them for a moment, feeling a great lack of understanding. She'd expected the two to fight her once they dropped the block, but their only attempt to resist had been so weak she'd almost missed it. And now they were completely under her control despite her weariness, which shouldn't be so. Was she mistaken, or were they really no stronger than Middle practitioners? Well, there were other answers she wanted more, so that particular question would have to wait.

"All right, calm down," she said after releasing her hold. "Genovir, let Algus open the door and then both of you can get out."

Genovir, still very confused, hesitated at Jovvi's order. That let Algus finally get the door open, and the two stumbled out quickly and hurried along the central hall to the front entrance. After turning and sending the emotion of gratitude to the tiny spider which still hung at the end of its thread, Jovvi followed behind the two "Adepts." She, of course, stopped when they did, a good half dozen paces along the walk.

"That, I think, makes four full masteries," Jovvi said, drawing a frightened stare from Algus. "First I want to hear you declare it, and then I want an explanation for your behavior."

"Yes, Dama, four full masteries," Algus mumbled, making no effort to stand straighter. "I do hereby declare it, and will fetch your bracelet and silver immediately. It will only take a moment . . ."

"Stop," Jovvi said quietly as the man began to turn away, seeing that he obeyed immediately. "You'll explain about that bracelet comment in a moment, but first I want another answer. You two deliberately tried to make me fail the test—not to mention trying to get me injured or killed—and I want to know why. What did I do to make you behave like that?"

"It—wasn't you, Dama, nor was it really us," Genovir babbled out when Algus hesitated. "It's standard practice to do that to late qualifiers, to weed out those who can only just squeak past. Letting them go on wastes the time of our superiors, and it's much too late in the year for time-wasting. Please—don't be angry. We really do apologize."

Both of them stared at Jovvi by then, underscoring the continuing fear that filled them. They seemed to be telling the truth—at least, the truth as they knew it—and the explanation had provided the answer to another question as well.

"So that's why you began to bow and scrape yesterday,"

Jovvi said, looking back and forth between them. "You were trying to cover yourselves in case I somehow proved to be stronger than the both of you. Submission posturing, to keep me from eating you alive in anger—*after* I noticed how much pleasure you were getting from doing your . . . *duty*. And that tea you tried to force on me. . . . It would have had something in it to make your job even easier, right?"

The two didn't answer, but the way they avoided her gaze was answer enough. They'd meant to drug her, and that would have been the end of her being an applicant.

"We'll just put that matter aside for another time," Jovvi said after a moment, words calculated to do nothing to ease the fear the Adepts felt. "Now you can tell me what that bracelet thing means."

"It's—it's to be worn in place of your identification card," Algus stuttered out, his relief on the faint side. "You've now reached the level of master, so you're no longer an applicant. The master's bracelet will show your new, higher status, that of full participant. Congratulations, Dama, on rising so high."

There was now hope in the man's voice and mind, hope based on the possibility that his news would put Jovvi's attention on something other than him. The whole thing was so clear that the man might as well have discussed it aloud, but since *he* seemed unaware of it, Jovvi decided against mentioning it.

"I'm going to sit down and have some refreshment now," Jovvi said after a pause that would have been longer if she hadn't been so tired. "Bring my bracelet and dins to the table, and then we'll see if there isn't more to discuss."

Algus paled before nodding vigorously and then hurrying away, a deeply frightened Genovir right behind him. Jovvi wasted no time watching the two escape, not when she needed food and drink so badly. Instead she headed for the eating area and an empty table, where she'd be able to refresh herself—and worry—in peace. The others . . . what if one or more of them actually drank the tea they'd be offered? They would certainly end up being disqualified, and it might even turn out to be Lorand. . . .

And if it was, what in the whole wide world would she do?

TWENTY-FIVE

Vallant's ride to the practice areas wasn't a pleasant one. He stared out of the window beside his right arm, seeing nothing of the passing scenery. Instead his thoughts kept going over and over the conclusion he'd come to last night, a conclusion he hadn't *expected* to come to. But expected or not the idea had come, and the more he thought about it, the more certain it became.

Last night had started out really amusing, with Tamrissa the Innocent falling right into his trap. Her expression had been priceless when she finally realized what she'd promised to do, but it had also been touchingly vulnerable. He'd waited for her to turn speechless with embarrassment, intending then to tell her he'd only been joking—or wishfully thinking—but that hadn't happened. Instead, fury had flashed from her beautiful eyes, and after promising never to speak to him again, she'd stormed back into the house.

Vallant's first reaction to that had been faint hurt, to see that she really believed he'd force her into his bed. At first he tried to tell himself she had no reason to believe otherwise, but that wasn't true. He'd not only done nothing to hurt her, he'd gone out of his way to be more than ordinarily gentle.

But she'd still immediately treated him like a lower life form, like someone she had no interest whatsoever in associating with. He'd spent his time apologizing for something that hadn't been his fault to begin with, and she'd spent her time trying to avoid him. He'd decided he couldn't bear the thought of being without her, and she'd decided she wanted nothing to do with him. By the time he'd gotten back to his bedchamber, it had come to him that he'd done everything but crawl for the woman.

And since that was something he'd never do for *anyone*, it was obvious he'd reached the end of the line in his quest for Dama Domon's attention. Quest . . . Vallant had laughed at himself bitterly over that one. It had been more of a pitiful display of begging than a quest, since that was what chasing after an uninterested woman *always* was. Which meant that it was more than time it came to an end.

Vallant stared out of the coach window and remembered the terrible disappointment he'd felt at that thought, but there was no arguing with the conclusion. Tamrissa wanted nothing to do with him, so it was time to bow to her decision and walk away like a gentleman of dignity. It wasn't what he really wanted to do, but it was the only option left open to him.

Brooding over that inescapable decision took up all of the coach ride, and even caused him to miss Mardimil's departure. The first thing he noticed when Coll called his name was that Holter was in the process of getting out, which meant he had to do the same. The practice area looked no different from yesterday, but as soon as he and Holter walked through the wall opening, Wimand, his Adept guide, hurried toward them, followed closely by Holter's Adept guide Podon.

"Good morning, Dom Ro, good morning," the thin Adept greeted him, forced warmth in his melodious voice. "I trust you rested well since we parted yesterday?"

Vallant hadn't had much sleep the night before, so he ignored Podon's burbling the same question to Holter to say shortly, "It was a wonderful time. Now let's get on with it."

"Of course, Dom Ro, we'll begin as quickly as possible," Wimand replied, his enthusiasm fading for an instant before being dragged back in place. "We must wait for two more Adepts to become available to witness your and Dom Holter's masteries, so we might as well have tea during the wait. We already have a pot and cups right over here. . . ."

"No," Vallant said, a refusal Holter clearly joined him in. "I'm not in the mood for waitin', with or without tea. You and Podon can witness our efforts together instead of separately the way you did yesterday, since we'll be performin' one at a time. So let's get this thing goin' *now*."

Vallant knew that any delay would send him back into brooding distraction, and that could mean a delay in passing the tests. Since this was probably the last time he'd be comfortable during a test—in other words, outdoors—his mood wanted the time behind him. Being faced with struggle would satisfy him a good deal more, so that was the point he had to reach. Struggle . . . and maybe a failure that would end all of his problems for once and all. . . .

Wimand spent some time in feeble argument with Podon backing him up, but Vallant and Holter had formed a united front. Neither of them would hear of a delay, and today it was Vallant's turn to go first. The Adepts were clearly unhappy about that, especially since they didn't seem able to refuse. It was completely obvious that they *wanted* to refuse, but instead Wimand drew himself up.

"I can see that you gentlemen have made up your minds," he decided aloud, his tone definitely sour. "Continuing on without the others is irregular, but as long as there *are* two of us to do the witnessing. . . . Very well, we *will* begin."

Vallant wasn't at his sharpest or most attentive, but it was still impossible to miss the . . . vindictive intent behind Wimand's words. The Adept sounded as if he had plans that would not be to Vallant's benefit, but that was all right. Vallant would welcome a skirmish right now, preferably one that was physical. If abilities became involved instead, that would also be acceptable.

Wimand and Podon led the way to the first of the testing cubicles, but not before Wimand insisted that Holter wait at a table some distance off.

"To be certain that no one is able to later raise a charge of collusion on the part of you two gentlemen," the Adept explained with a faintly amused smile. "Having to achieve the same masteries a second time is *such* a bore."

Holter shrugged to show that he didn't mind waiting at the table, so Vallant also allowed the matter to pass without argument. Simply going along would get them out of there sooner, a result Vallant was quickly coming to want rather badly.

The first cubicle held resin spheres the size of a man's head sitting on posts, but unlike the original first cubicle there was no vat filled with water. Vallant would have to take water from the air to surround the forms with, which *was* harder than using standing water.

"At least you needn't worry that anyone will think you used water from the vats in the other cubicles," Wimand remarked from behind Vallant. "The resin walls don't let people reach through with their ability, so that's one concern behind you. Just please be certain that you don't run afoul of the other, more important one."

"And what concern would *that* be?" Vallant asked, turning to look at the man. Podon stood more behind the first Adept than beside him, which, with Wimand's prejudices in mind, wasn't very surprising.

"Why, the concern behind the reason that *these* exercises are so much more difficult," Wimand replied, a sleek nastiness underlying the words. "It's not only harder to take the necessary water from the air, it's also more dangerous. The extra effort needed to do it sometimes causes a practitioner to also surround *himself* with water. If he then loses his head to fear, he can end up drowning himself. It *has* been known to happen, and on far more than one or two occasions."

"Oh, yes, I remember hearin' somethin' about that now,"

Vallant drawled, not about to let Wimand think his scare tactics had a chance to work. "That's a nasty way to die, but I don't ever expect it to happen to *me*. Are we ready to begin?"

"Yes, of course," Wimand muttered in answer, the sleekness having disappeared. "You may begin when you wish."

Vallant nodded his thanks and turned back to the targets, almost disappointed that that was all the plotting Wimand seemed to have in mind. Apparently the Adept had hoped to frighten Vallant enough to ruin his try for the masteries, which simply showed how blind it was possible for a man to be.

The exercise was just like the first time in that Vallant had to first surround the six forms with water while they were all together, then when they were in two groups, then three groups, then individually. Podon was the one who shifted the positions of the forms, of course, a fact Vallant noticed but ignored. Gathering the necessary moisture from the air took concentration, but it wasn't long before the exercise was completed.

"Well, you now have your first mastery, Dom Ro," Wimand said then, making an obvious effort to sound hearty. "Let's continue on to the next cubicle."

"I think you're forgettin' about Holter," Vallant said as the Adept began to move away. "It's now his turn to earn the mastery."

"No, I'm afraid it *isn't* his turn yet," Wimand denied with a smile as he looked back at Vallant. "Other applicants aren't given a rest between exercises, so it would be unfair to allow *you* to have one. Please follow me, Dom Ro."

There was nothing Vallant could say to that without sounding as if he were trying to cheat, so he followed Wimand as requested. Yesterday Holter had started first with Vallant following, but there hadn't been any pauses between the exercises. And, considering the smugness Wimand now showed, it was too bad argument *wasn't* possible.

The second cubicle held six breadboxes, which Vallant had to fill with water. First one box was to be filled, then two together, then three together and so on, until all six boxes were filled at once. Each box held a catch bowl, and if the exercise was properly done the water would come out when the bottom of the box was released. Once again Vallant had to concentrate on what he was doing, but other than that the exercise wasn't difficult.

"And that's mastery number two," Wimand said, but the lightheartedness of his tone was surprising. Vallant turned to look at the man, and was startled to see that two strangers had joined Wimand and Podon.

"How amusing that your mastery has been witnessed by four Adepts rather than two," Wimand continued, his expression bland. "Dom Ro, I would like to present Adept Rilin and Adept Kinge, whose presence will make it possible for Dom Holter to begin at once. Adept Rilin will accompany *me*, and Adept Kinge will go with Adept Podon."

It would have been more accurate to say that the man Kinge had already gone with Podon. The second newcomer hadn't even nodded to acknowledge the introduction before turning away, and Rilin was no different. He simply stared hard-eyed at Vallant as if he were some lower life form, which brought Vallant's head up as his jaw muscles tightened. Tamrissa had looked at him in almost the same way, and Vallant was sick of that particular reaction.

"We can go to the third cubicle now," Wimand announced, still sounding much too smugly satisfied. That had to mean something had changed to make the situation more pleasant for him, and the only change was the presence of Rilin. Vallant took that as his cue to start being more alert, but otherwise followed the two Adepts silently.

"Now, here the boxes are hidden behind that curtain," Wimand said once Vallant was in the cubicle, possibly trying to suggest that Vallant was too dim to remember on his own. "The boxes are of different sizes, so you must use your ability to discover their dimensions as well as to fill them. Just as in the last cubicle, you'll begin by filling one, then two at the same time, and so forth. You may start when you feel yourself ready."

"That's mighty kind of you," Vallant murmured in answer without turning. Yes, the man was definitely up to something, but it still wasn't clear what that might be. Could Wimand be trying to get him angry, which sometimes resulted in a loss of control? It was possible. . . .

But Vallant didn't have the time to worry about that now. The third and final mastery had to be earned, so he reached out with his talent to discover the dimensions of the first box. It was very much on the small side, which meant it had to be filled very carefully. He did that, and Wimand's tripping the box's release showed rather quickly that he'd done it properly.

Vallant had filled three boxes successfully and was beginning to probe the size and shape of the fourth when it happened. He suddenly found himself surrounded by water, and for an instant believed he'd had that accident Wimand had mentioned and had done it himself. But his automatic attempt to return the water to the air didn't work, which immediately told him the true state of affairs.

A glance over his shoulder showed Vallant that Wimand and Rilin were using their own talents rather intensely, which meant that the two so-called Adepts were responsible for the water around him. It was also a fairly safe guess that Rilin was a good deal stronger than his associate, and that was why Wimand had been so smugly pleased. He would have had trouble doing this to Vallant with no one but Podon helping, but with Rilin's assistance. . . .

All of which was really interesting, but still did nothing to free Vallant from the globe of water. He'd held his breath at the first appearance of the water out of habit, a reflex related to how experienced and strong a swimmer he was; that in itself, however, wasn't going to save him. He had to force the water away completely, but with two men holding it firmly in place he simply couldn't break free.

At least not with the amount of power he now wielded. Vallant realized that even as the strain increased on his lungs, and his mind grew aware of the fact that he was trapped *inside* the small globe of water. Panic threatened to rise up and overwhelm him, but if it did he was dead. He *had* to find a diversion, so he quickly opened himself to more of the power.

The immediate inflow of golden strength surprised him, as the inflow also seemed to include a bit more oxygen for his straining lungs. But even more it seemed to spread throughout his body, bracing him to wield the additional power and clarifying his wildly roiling thoughts. The way to escape the trap came to him instantly, so he quickly put the plan to work.

In the upper reaches of the sky, water is closer to being ice than a liquid. Vallant reached down two large globs of that ice, and applied each glob to the private parts of the two men trying to drown him. Their screams could be heard even through the water around his head, and then the water was no longer there. Vallant stood and breathed deeply while he listened to the unfiltered screams, grimly satisfied. Cold, beyond a certain point, becomes true pain, and if these two didn't deserve the pain then no one did. He let them experience it for a full minute, and then he withdrew the ice a very small bit.

"Gentlemen, your screams are disturbin' me," he said then, keeping his voice reasonably low. "They're also disturbin' all those other people, so I suggest you turn and assure them that you're perfectly all right."

The two so-called Adepts glanced at him with fear in their eyes, then turned to do as he'd said. People from the eating area had crowded up when the screams first began, but once Wimand called to them that everything was fine, they shook their heads and returned to their tables.

"Nicely done," Vallant said in the same soft tones. "Now we can discuss the fact that you're still able to feel that ice, and the additional fact that you can't force it away from your . . . dignity. Each of you has been tryin', and you've discovered you're simply not up to it."

The two men exchanged desperate glances, understanding without being told that linking against him again was impossible. They were beyond the point where they could surprise him, and only greater strength than *he* wielded could break his hold.

"Now we're goin' to continue with this exercise," Vallant said, giving them a pleasant smile. "The ice will stay where it is until I've achieved this final mastery, and then we can all forget about it. Do you agree?"

The two men nodded raggedly, so Vallant turned back to what he'd been doing. It didn't take long to finish filling all the hidden boxes, and when Wimand tripped the lever there were six matching streams of water produced.

"C-congratulations, D-Dom Ro," Wimand said immediately through chattering teeth. "The s-second level m-masteries are all yours, s-so *please* . . . !"

Rilin's gaze was also begging, but Vallant still felt reluctant to release them. Experiencing pity for people who had deliberately attacked him wasn't one of his failings, but it *was* time to end that farce. So he released his hold on the ice, letting the two men reach it themselves, and a moment later they both sighed with relief.

"Now I'd like to know what happens next," Vallant said after giving the two an additional moment to pull themselves together. "Aside from your fetchin' six dins for me. How soon do I get to the first of the competitions?"

"You'll be notified about that, sir," Wimand replied after taking a deep breath, now firmly back to being obsequious. "I'll fetch your dins immediately, along with your master's bracelet."

"What's that about a bracelet?" Vallant asked, trying to divert himself from a mixture of disappointment and relief. He'd thought he wanted to get on with the time when he had to enter that enclosed building, but now that the occasion had turned indefinite, he felt it a lot easier to breathe.

"Your status has changed from applicant to full participant, sir," Wimand told him in explanation, all but bowing. "You've reached the level of master, so a master's bracelet will replace your applicant's card. Congratulations again on achieving that much higher status, and would you care to sit and take tea while I get your bracelet and dins?"

Rilin had turned and walked away while Wimand spoke, leaving Vallant with the impression that he would not be back. That was fine with Vallant, since he had one further thing to say to Wimand.

"Yes, I believe I *will* take tea while I'm waitin'," he said, then moved closer to Wimand and lowered his voice. "I don't know why you and your brother slime did what you did to me, but I also don't care why. I'm simply advisin' you to make sure that the same thing doesn't happen to Holter. I'll be watchin' while I have that tea, and if it does I'll feel obliged to help the man. Do we understand each other?"

"Perfectly, sir," Wimand said with a gulp, then hurried off—in the direction of the two—*Adepts*—with Holter. Vallant nodded to himself in satisfaction as he walked toward a table, looking forward to the tea, something to eat—and a chance to firm up his decision to have nothing more to do with Dama Tamrissa Domon.

TWENTY-SIX

When the coach stopped at my practice area I got out, and Jovvi was so deep in thought that I didn't want to disturb her even to say goodbye. Our discussion had helped me quite a bit in that it usually helps to share your problems with someone else. But in another way it hadn't helped at all, because now I couldn't decide what to do.

I stopped on the walk leading to the practice area, trying to pull myself together before going in. Talking things out with Jovvi had made me realize something I hadn't admitted to myself before: a very large part of me *wanted* to be with Vallant Ro. Looking at him made me feel things I'd never felt when looking at any other man, and even the thought of simply strolling with him in the garden sent me into a minor flutter.

But I'd decided against associating with Vallant Ro, and right or wrong the decision had still been made. That meant the man had had no *right* to keep bothering me, not to mention trapping me into a very disturbing promise. Maybe I *had* insisted on making the promise; that didn't mean Vallant Ro wasn't wrong to let it happen in the first place.

Anger rose in me again at that thought, covering over the possibility that I'd been wrong to say I'd never speak to him again. Putting the entire blame on him had seemed unfair because I *had* encouraged him to a large extent, but the anger wiped out that feeling as well. It usually isn't wise to let yourself walk around being angry, especially when the use of magic is involved, but this wasn't a usual situation. If the anger kept me from being distracted by conflicting wants and desires, it seemed wiser to simply go with it.

So I took a deep breath to settle the anger down to a dull roar, and then walked through the opening into the practice area. Today I was supposed to perform those exercises while Soonen attacked me with her own magic, and for the first time since I'd learned about it I didn't dread the coming experience. I was in the process of learning that anger sometimes turns fear into indignation, and it couldn't have happened at a better time.

"Well, well, so you actually showed up," a woman's voice said, and then Soonen stopped not far from me. "I thought sure you would remember what we'll be doing today and decide to stay in bed."

"That's your biggest problem, Soonen," I countered, the coals of my anger glowing hot. "You *don't* think, you just flap your big mouth. I happen to be more than eager to get started, so let's get to it right now."

"What a surprise," the big woman scoffed, looking at me

as if I were some sort of insect. "You're in such a hurry to get started because you're afraid your nerve will break, and then you'll show everyone what a sniveling little coward you really are. If you had real nerve, you'd sit down first and have a leisurely cup of tea."

I was an instant away from saying I'd have *two* cups of tea, but then rationality came to my rescue. If I sat down for any length of time at all, all those conflicting wants and desires plaguing me in the coach would come right back. I couldn't let myself be distracted like that, so only one answer to Soonen's challenge was possible.

"You want me to sit down for a while to give *you* the chance to work up the nerve to face me?" I asked with a mocking smile. "Really, Soonen, the extra time won't do you any good at all, so we'll skip the tea. Go and find Adept Gerdol, and tell him we're ready to begin."

The flashing look in Soonen's eyes was a combination of frustration and fear, and then she'd turned away from me to stalk off toward the front of the eating area. She'd also gone faintly red at my accusation, which had been a considerable surprise.

I'd only been trying to insult and refuse the woman without being put on the defensive, but it looked like I might have struck the nail squarely on the head. Soonen *did* seem to be afraid to face me, which meant I couldn't understand why she'd tried to antagonize me. Hadn't she realized that that would only make things worse between us?

No logical answer came for that question, so I shelved it for the moment and drifted after Soonen. The woman seemed to be heading for the table where Gerdol had sat yesterday, and sure enough the man was there with his friends. When Soonen spoke to him, her face looking drawn, he seemed startled and upset. They then exchanged a few words, after which Gerdol rose and joined Soonen in coming back to me.

"Well, good morning, Dama Domon," Gerdol said heartily as he approached, his mustacheless whiskers rising with his smile. "I certainly hope you had a pleasant evening and rest—but of course you must have. You're just as lovely as ever.''

"Thank you," I said with my own forced smile, fighting to keep my anger from taking over. "You're very kind . . . as usual. Now I'd like to begin the testing."

"Without first sharing a fortifying cup of tea?" he asked with brows raised, making it sound as though the practice was unheard of. "Surely you'll join me for a brief time, Dama, while Adept Soonen serves the both of us. . . ."

"That's a really tempting offer, sir, but I must decline," I said when his words trailed off on a coaxing note. I'd *never* be able to stand his greasy compliments without exploding. . . . "I've come for no other reason than to gain the next masteries, and now I'd like to get to it."

Gerdol and Soonen exchanged a glance, and strangely enough Soonen showed nothing of relief over not having to serve me. I'd been expecting her to be delighted, and the fact that she wasn't became another puzzling item for the file of unanswered questions I'd begun to build.

"Very well, Dama, your wish is our command," Gerdol finally allowed with a sickly smile, giving me the impression that he'd had no choice but to respond in that way. "Please follow us to the first of the cubicles."

The two Adepts didn't speak as they led the way, but I had the definite impression they wanted to. It would have been nice to know what was going on, but I was almost getting used to *their* way of doing things. When they reached the first cubicle Gerdol stopped, but Soonen continued around to the other side of it. The far side, like the near, had an opening in the clear resin wall with a free-standing curtain-wall three or four feet behind the opening.

"This exercise will be the same as it was yesterday, with one exception," Gerdol said to me when I reached him. "You must burn every grain of sand in the gout thrown up by the device, but at the same time you must protect yourself from attack by Adept Soonen. Soonen is rather stronger than most around here, and for your sake I truly hope you *are* prepared for this. If not. . . ."

He let his words trail off in an obvious attempt to frighten me, but obvious or not, the attempt began to work. I could see Soonen clearly where she stood, and her arrogance seemed to have returned completely. I glanced away from her in my own obvious attempt to hide hesitation—and suddenly felt shocked. Down by the third cubicle, staring straight at me—It was Beldara Lant!

For a moment I had trouble understanding why Beldara would be here, and then I realized that she must have managed to qualify on the very last day. I hadn't seen her since the testing authority had taken her things and Eskin Drowd's out of the house, probably expecting that neither of the two would qualify. But apparently Beldara had fooled them, and now she was here to try qualifying for the competitions.

And to stand there smirking her imagined superiority in *my* direction. Beldara had been raised to believe that she was the best at Fire magic ever to be born, and even coming out of her small town into the real world hadn't brought her to a more reasonable attitude. Now she stood there, delaying her own practice, waiting for me to fail the way she'd always said I would.

The anger I'd begun with had cooled to uselessness, but seeing Beldara and her Soonenlike arrogance brought it back to full, roaring life. Both of those women tried to claim superiority with words rather than deeds, but I'd already stopped letting mere words defeat me.

"I'm ready," I said to Gerdol in what was almost a snap as I drew myself up. "Tell Soonen to begin any time she feels up to it."

Gerdol's brows drew down as he gestured to Soonen, but his unhappiness and Soonen's slight hesitation were no longer my concern. I'd reached for the power and had drawn it into myself, and abruptly found myself weaving *two* patterns of fire. The first would burn every bit of soil Gerdol now prepared to make the device throw into the air, and the second would keep Soonen's efforts away from me. Distantly I realized that the second pattern was the same one I used to keep from burning anything but what I was supposed to, and that it was woven power rather than woven fire. But that didn't matter to me now, not when there were masteries to achieve.

Gerdol used the lever to make the device throw soil into the air, and that, of course, was when Soonen struck. Even as my hottest fires consumed the soil completely, I was able to feel Soonen trying to set my clothes and hair alight. The way she clenched her fists said she tried really hard, but it just wasn't possible for her to go around or through my protection.

"How was that?" I asked Gerdol when the soil was completely gone, pretending to ignore Soonen's continuing efforts. "Worth another mastery, wouldn't you say?"

"Yes, certainly, Dama," Gerdol quickly agreed, apparently finding himself shaken by my stare. I still retained active contact with the power, of course, and felt as if I could face down the entire world. "You've achieved the first of your second-level masteries without a doubt. Let's continue to the next."

Gerdol now seemed to be in a rush to get on with it, and that was perfectly all right with me. As I moved after him and out of the cubicle entrance, Soonen's attack was immediately cut off. With even a single resin wall between us, it would have to be.

We didn't have to wait long for Soonen to stalk to the other side of the second cubicle, and it looked as if her temper had gotten the best of her. If determination were clothing, Soonen probably would have been muffled to the eyebrows. As soon as Gerdol released the spray of water I was to burn to a point beyond steam, her attack resumed—slightly stronger than before. This time I happened to notice the actual level of her efforts, and decided not to consider her an Adept ever again. She was a fairly strong Middle talent, but that was a far cry from the operating level of a High.

"And now we have two new masteries," I said to Gerdol once all the water was gone without a trace, smiling faintly at the way I'd called myself a High talent without blushing at the boastfulness of the claim. When I finally released my hold on the power I'd be absolutely exhausted, but for now I meant to enjoy the experience of life without fear or nervousness.

"Two, yes," Gerdol muttered, his glance at Soonen putting a look of frustrated fear on his face. "You—ah—haven't mentioned anything about the difficulty of being under attack. I hadn't realized you would do so well with hiding your efforts to resist it."

"You think I'm hiding my efforts well?" I asked with a very pleased smile, ignoring his roundabout attempt to get some details on the matter. "How nice of you to say that, Adept Gerdol. And now we're ready for the third exercise, aren't we?"

"Yes, surely," the man muttered, then edged carefully behind me before leading the way. Soonen's attack was now causing sparks to strike against my protection, but causing sparks was the most she could do against it. Flame was completely disallowed, and that no matter how red in the face she got.

As we approached the third cubicle, I smiled faintly to see the fury in Beldara Lant's eyes. She'd obviously seen me complete the first two exercises, and now clearly hated the fact that I hadn't failed.

"You'll have to move aside, young lady," Gerdol said to her with impatience in his voice. "The dama is in the midst of achieving masteries, and that takes precedence over a beginner's practice."

"It so happens *I'm* ready to achieve masteries, too," Beldara announced indignantly, humiliation burning hot in her cheeks. "Let that little do-nothing step aside and wait for *me* to show you how it's *supposed* to be done."

"Don't be a fool, girl!" Gerdol snapped as Beldara turned back to the cubicle's interior—only to stop and stare at Soonen. "This lady has already achieved the first-level masteries you're only beginning to practice, and now she's in the midst of second-level. Do you really want Adept Soonen to attack *you* the way she's been doing with Dama Domon?"

"But . . . I haven't seen any evidence of attack," Beldara

returned, trying for belligerence but achieving disturbance instead. ''If that other one is supposed to attack her, she isn't doing a very good job of it. This one probably paid her not to, and that's why you think she's so good. Yes, that's probably it, she paid—''

''Beldara,'' I interrupted her babbling, feeling my anger begin to climb again. ''I'm not going to stand here and listen to your idiotic accusations. If you think Soonen's been paid off, volunteer to take her place. But I do have to warn you: if *you* attack, I'll probably find it impossible not to respond in kind.''

Her eyes widened at that, her startled surprise over my new attitude more than clear. I'd never answered her challenge so directly before, and sudden lack of confidence made her wilt visibly.

''It's . . . not my place to expose your shoddy little tricks,'' she muttered as her gaze fell, the faintness of her tone belying the belligerence of her words. ''They'll find you out without me, and then—''

At that point she simply stopped talking and hurried away, obviously tired of making a fool of herself. Gerdol's expression said it was about time, and my power-enhanced attitude simply agreed with him. At another time and place I might have felt sorry for Beldara, but right now the only thing concerning me was achieving the rest of the masteries.

That third cubicle held wooden blocks carved into different shapes, and I burned the one Gerdol chose without harming any of the blocks around it. I had to divide my protective shield in order to do it, but that didn't seem to affect the strength of the shield. It remained just as strong as it was originally, and that held true through the next two cubicles as well. First a strip of leather and then one of cloth burned without a problem, and the fact that Soonen was just about foaming at the mouth hadn't increased the strength of her attacks.

When we finally reached the last cubicle, the awareness of exhaustion was a good deal sharper in my mind. When I released the power I'd probably fall, but achieving all the second-level masteries would even be worth getting bruised. Gerdol was now supposed to choose three feathers, and once I burned each of them cleanly I'd be able to rest and restore my strength.

"I think I'll choose . . . the red, the pink, and the purple," Gerdol said, pointing out the three widely spaced feathers in the sprawling stack. "You may begin whenever you wish, my dear, but you do seem a bit—fatigued. Perhaps you'd care for some tea before completing this last exercise. I'd be more than happy to permit it."

"Thank you, no," I answered, distantly disturbed over that "my dear." And he was offering me tea again, as though he knew I'd be too tired to start over if I stopped now. Suspicion tried to flare in my mind, but I was even too tired for that. Instead I wiped at the sweat on my forehead with the backs of two fingers, then turned my attention to the designated feathers.

Sparks flew from my shield again while I burned the first two feathers, but before I could get to the third there was a sudden, shocking difference in the attack. I nearly staggered at the strength of it, and even worse, my shield trembled under the onslaught. I couldn't imagine how Soonen had managed to find so much more strength, but then I caught a glimpse of Gerdol, who stood to my left. He stood in the same attitude of straining that Soonen did, which meant he'd now joined her attack.

That would have been the perfect point for my anger to return, but it couldn't seem to get past rapidly growing fear. I knew it was beyond me to sustain the shield for long against this strong an attack, and when the shield fell I would certainly burn. Soonen's frustration had gone on too long for her to be satisfied with burning no more than my clothes and hair, so my life was definitely on the line. If I faltered in protecting myself, I was as good as dead.

Panic tried to grow from the fear, and it took almost all I had to prevent that. I had to think rather than panic, but the one thought that came was a risky one. If I drew in more of the power I should be able to maintain the shield, but I wasn't sure I had the strength left to handle more power. If I didn't I would be just as dead as a burnout, instead of simply burning up.

And that realization seemed to steady me. I had nothing at all to lose by trying for more power, since life would no longer be worth living if I couldn't continue to advance to the competitions. With that in mind I opened myself wide, welcoming the golden strength pouring in rather than fearing it. It filled me completely with new vitality, calmed all my worries, and brought another idea that almost made me chuckle.

Soonen and Gerdol were attacking both in front and in back, so to speak. Their attempts to burn me to ash surrounded me completely, but somehow I was now able to perceive a . . . *level* they weren't operating on. I'd never before been aware of that level, but now I could perceive it clearly—and knew I could use it. It would take my ability *around* the attacks somehow, and if I liked I could even attack in return.

But mounting my own attack didn't seem wise, not when it would cause a delay in my achieving the final mastery. It would do more good to hit the two so-called Adepts in a way that would hurt them in a different manner, and I knew just the thing. So I turned my attention back to the final feather, burned it cleanly, then slumped against the side of the cubicle and turned a weary smile on Gerdol.

"Done at last, and just in time," I told him weakly, pretending I saw nothing of his efforts to destroy my shield. "I really need to sit down now, Adept Gerdol, and will appreciate your arm in assistance—as soon as you declare the final mastery."

Gerdol turned white and the attack faltered, showing he'd probably pulled out of the joint effort. A moment later Soonen's efforts stopped as well, and a glance in her direction showed me she'd collapsed into a seated slump against the back curtain-wall. They'd put everything they had into their final effort, and it had turned out not to be enough.

"C-congratulations, Dama, congratulations," Gerdol stuttered, his face still white with fear. "You've now achieved the level of master, and as soon as I seat you at a table I'll fetch your master's bracelet and silver dins. Here, take my arm."

Gerdol fussed over me nervously until he got me into a chair at the nearest available table, and only when he hurried off after ringing for a servant did I release my hold on the power. The world swirled dizzyingly for a moment then, but despite utter exhaustion I didn't faint. I needed desperately to eat, drink, and rest—but other than that I seemed perfectly all right.

I gasped out, "Food and tea, quickly!" to the servant who came up to me, and once he rushed off I simply sat there and waited. It would have been nice if I'd had two strong arms around me to hold me up in the chair, but—

My mind clanged to a halt with the shock of that thought, especially since I knew exactly whose arms I'd been thinking about. It was Vallant Ro I wanted, Vallant Ro I'd wanted all along. I no longer had the strength to deny that, no matter *how* frightening the idea was. Constantly getting angry at him had been an escape reflex, to keep myself free and un-involved.

But now I no longer seemed to *want* to be free, at least where he was concerned. I kept dreaming about being in his bed tomorrow night, and each of those dreams, both sleeping and awake, were filled with desire. I really, *really* wanted his arms around me, and tomorrow night I would have them.

Rather than having to fight a shiver of fear, I found myself smiling in anticipation. Even my attitudes seemed to be changing, and I wondered if that was due to the power as well. I didn't see how it could be, but the question wasn't important enough to be disturbing. I simply sat back and smiled, and waited for Gerdol to return with my dins. And a master's bracelet, which I'd have to remember to question him about.

And tonight . . . tonight I just might tell Vallant Ro how much I looked forward to being fair. . . .

TWENTY-SEVEN

Homin was right there to greet Lord Rigos when the Advisory agent arrived. For once Homin felt less than completely terrified. The relatively peaceful and quiet days he'd passed in his own home had done wonders, so now it was just Rigos himself who caused Homin's fear. The small man seemed to have one or two character traits in common with the late Elfini, a circumstance which made Homin's hands tremble even as he forced a smile.

"Ah, good day to you, Lord Homin," Rigos said as he strolled past the servant holding the door without looking at the man. "Hosting our weekly meeting has given you the benefit of being precisely on time, but I do hope the intrusion won't disturb your father. How *is* Lord Aston, by the way?"

"Actually, he isn't here," Homin answered while hurrying after Rigos, who was in the process of walking toward the main reception room. "He's gone to the lake house to recover from his ordeal in peace, and so far has sent word only to tell me that he arrived safely."

Rigos nodded casually at that as he kept going, bringing Homin the hope that the subject of his father would be dropped. Lord Aston Weil was not only in need of physical healing, he was also in jeopardy of losing his social and professional positions. Too many people now knew what his relationship with his wife had been, a knowledge which could well ruin his political position for all time.

Homin's father had explained that he needed to be out of touch until he was physically fit again, and then he'd shocked Homin by crying while saying a temporary goodbye. He and his father had never been all *that* close, and the only time they'd cried together was when Mother had died. The same hadn't happened over Elfini's death, and in fact they'd never even spoken about her.

"And how are *you* bearing up in the aftermath of the tragedy?" Rigos asked as he reached the tea table, pausing to glance at Homin. "I now understand your previous comments about being unable to practice, by the way. I hadn't realized that Lady Elfini would be so foolish as to interfere in an Advisory matter, but apparently she overestimated her husband's political strength. You really should have told me, and I would have taken care of the problem."

"I . . . couldn't tell anyone about it," Homin said, immediate and intense apology in his tone. "I had no way of knowing it would make any difference to you, and couldn't imagine what you might do in any event."

"What I would have done was have you moved at once to the residence you and the others of your group will soon share," Rigos replied, turning with a cup of tea in his hands to stare expressionlessly at Homin. "Don't you understand *yet* how important this matter is to us? If it were possible to replace you, it would have already been done. Your government needs you, Lord Homin, and what we need we protect."

"Yes, of course, I should have realized," Homin murmured as Rigos carried his cup of tea to a chair. What he actually realized was how serious the government really was about that competition business, and how angry they would be when he and his group disobeyed them and won. The thought was enough to make Homin wish he were with another, more docile group, but the wish lasted only a brief time. He still needed to be out and on his own, and then his father's wives would no longer concern him. Others might think his father had learned to moderate his desires, but Homin knew better. And then he really heard something else Rigos had said.

"Excuse me, sir, but what was that about a residence the group is going to be moved to?" Homin asked while returning to his own chair and cup of tea. "I thought we were told we all had to remain in our own homes."

"That applied only to the time of the preliminary process," Rigos answered after tasting his tea, bringing that intense gaze of his back to Homin. "I'll go into details about it once the others are here, and that way I won't need to repeat myself. Until they arrive we can talk about other things, like the tragedy so recently past. Have the authorities found the culprit yet?"

"No, not yet," Homin answered with a sigh, resigning himself to discussing the matter he would most prefer to forget. "It took a short while before the investigators were completely convinced that I had nothing to do with the murder, but happily Delin's father's household staff works around the clock. I was somewhat upset when I reached the house so Delin told them to keep an eye on me, and they did. One or another servant looked in on me constantly even when I was asleep, and they were able to tell that to the investigators."

"How lucky for all of us that that's so," Rigos murmured with one of his frigid smiles. "The Advisors would have been furious if they'd had to interfere with the investigation. Everyone knows about the murder by now, of course, and it doesn't matter if most people think Lady Elfini simply got what she deserved. They can't allow *any* member of the nobility to be murdered without something being done about it, and that goes double for a member of the high nobility."

"Yes, the investigators made me sit down and give them a list of everyone who had ever known Elfini," Homin agreed, remembering how frightened and cornered he'd felt at the demand. "I wasn't able to give them more than two or three names, but my father supplied dozens. As a matter of fact—"

"As a matter of fact, what?" Rigos prompted when Homin's words broke off in mid sentence, the agent's dark eyes intense. Homin had begun to tremble as he silently cursed his big mouth, but there was no getting out of it.

"As a matter of fact . . . *your* name was . . . on his list," Homin answered slowly from a dry mouth. "Father said you and she had had . . . words once, but that was some time ago. And you weren't the only one, so please don't think—"

"No, no, it's quite all right," Rigos interrupted with one hand raised, his gaze now hooded and his face expressionless. "I'd been wondering if they knew about that incident, and now I know they do. The fact that they haven't spoken to me about it undoubtedly means they've dismissed it as the unimportant spat it really was."

Homin quickly and eagerly nodded his agreement, and then fell prudently silent. The fact that the investigators hadn't spoken to Rigos really meant nothing, and Homin was certain Rigos knew it. But at least *he* wasn't the one who had supplied Rigos's name, thank any Superior Aspect there was. . . .

The silence was in the process of growing intense and painful when a happy interruption occurred. Kambil and Bron were shown in together, and while those two were helping themselves to tea, Delin and Selendi arrived together. Homin had known that would happen, but the surprise pulled Rigos out of his brown study.

"I'm impressed," Rigos said, looking from one to the other of the new arrivals. "All of you are precisely on time, and without needing a life-threatening situation."

"Actually, most of us have decided that we're bored and want this matter over and done with," Delin said for the group with a charming smile. "The best way to accomplish that is to keep the distractions to a minimum, so Kambil and I volunteered to help the others keep to the schedule. I hope you don't mind?"

"On the contrary," Rigos assured him, his frigid smile now somehow colder. "I feel I owe you two a vote of thanks, and will therefore include your selfless actions in my report. As soon as you're all seated, we'll be able to begin."

That ended the conversation for the moment, but didn't produce the hurry Rigos might have wanted. Homin watched his peers examining the room while they waited for their turn at the tea urn, or at least some of them did the examining. Kambil had simply taken one glance around, and then had given all his attention to pouring tea. Delin seemed too pleased with what Rigos had said to bother with even that single glance, but the second two made up for the first.

Bron and Selendi wore an identical expression as they slowly looked around, and that expression wasn't one of approval. The reception room was just as Homin's mother had decorated it, since Elfini hadn't yet gotten around to changing it. The old fashioned but very comfortable furniture and accessories had brought looks of ridicule to Selendi and Bron, which shockingly made Homin angry. It wasn't cost or bad taste which had kept his father from modernizing the room, it was sentiment—and yet those two dared to look down on what was really his mother's memory. Homin was completely unused to being angry, but in *this* case—

"And now we can begin," Rigos said, pulling Homin out of distraction to see that everyone had chosen a seat. "Last week's report was a satisfying improvement over previous ones, but this week's is even better. Allow me to congratulate all of you on having achieved your second-level masteries."

Murmurs and comments blended into a soft gabble at that, and Rigos smiled his winter smile.

"Yes, that does include Lord Homin, something you all seem to be asking," he said with his version of amusement. "The excuse of not being able to practice was apparently no excuse after all, as Lord Homin quickly caught up to the rest of you once he had the opportunity to work at it."

"Actually, we expected nothing less," Delin said with a broad smile for Homin, taking some of the sting from Rigos's ridicule. "We've all made a pact to do our utmost to keep ourselves from looking ridiculous during the competitions, and gentlemen never break a pact with other gentlemen. Besides, we all know how much it will please our families."

"Yes, your families *have* been asked to be attentive to your efforts," Rigos drawled, now sending his ridicule to all of them. "With all talk of decisions and pacts aside, that point still remains. I suggest you keep it firmly in mind over the next several days."

No one responded to that, and Homin could see how pleased the silence made Rigos. The agent obviously believed it was fear of parental displeasure which had finally moved them all to proper behavior, and that was precisely what they all wished him to believe. Selendi looked sullen, Bron resentful, Delin annoyed, and Kambil bland, and that seemed to please Rigos as well.

"You now have two scheduled events before you," Rigos went on once he'd had his enjoyment. "The first comes on the evening of the first rest day after week's end, and is a reception being given in the palace. All competing groups will attend, ours as well as theirs, and I'm sure I don't need to tell you who 'theirs' is."

"You don't mean the peasants?" Selendi asked with an expression of shock. "But that's disgusting! Isn't it bad enough we have to lower ourselves to compete with them? Asking us to *associate* with them is completely unreasonable."

"You won't be there to associate, but to study," Rigos answered, giving her a withering look and then one of dismissal before turning his main attention to Kambil and Delin. "Your Blending will face one or more of the Blendings *they* form, and after the reception you'll be given even more information about them. The information will mean more to you if you can attach faces as well as names to it."

"What do you mean, we'll be facing one or more of their groups?" Delin asked, leaning forward with concentration. "We've been told nothing about this, so it's about time we were."

"That's one of the reasons we're gathered here today," Rigos replied comfortably, his attitude saying that Delin should have known that without being told. "There will be five noble groups and five peasant groups competing for the Throne, and the first round of competitions will pair one noble group and one peasant group. The winning group of each pair will face another winning group in the second round, and if all the peasants—or your own group—haven't lost in the first round, you'll need to face a second group of them."

"But of course they'll all lose in the first round," Bron said with a snort of ridicule. "They're peasants, aren't they, which means they don't stand a chance against us. That also means we'll only have to face a single group of the rabble, so why will we have to learn about *all* of them? Why not just the group we'll be facing?"

"There are two reasons for what you consider a waste of time, Lord Bron," Rigos responded, now using that ridicule on a new target. "The first is that we won't know for certain which group you'll be facing until the pairing is approved by the board appointed to oversee the competitions. Our suggestions have usually been accepted in the past, but not always. If someone on the board decides to change them, you have to be ready."

Homin could see the way Bron's jaw clenched, but the big man didn't respond to Rigos's taunting. And then, with a great deal of surprise, the reason for that came to Homin: Bron feared Rigos almost as much as he did! It was a revelation to think that the flamboyant, undisciplined man was no better than Homin in that respect, which definitely made it something to remember.

"And what's the second reason?" Kambil asked quietly when no one else did. "I, for one, am grateful for the help that's been given me, and I intend to continue being grateful—especially for necessary information."

"I would expect no less from you, Lord Kambil," Rigos said with a small inclination of his head. "With that in view, the second reason is that peasant groups *have* won in the first round, usually against groups like the one yours was just a short time ago. If one of the groups of your peers grows indifferently lax, it will certainly happen again."

"So it's to our own benefit to learn as much about the peasants as we can," Delin said, pretending to speak to Rigos while actually speaking to Homin and the others. "Since that's the case, I think you can depend on me at least to do all the studying necessary.''

Homin nodded with most of the others to show he joined them in agreeing, but Bron still seemed annoyed.

"In my opinion it's a waste of time to worry about them, but I won't stop anyone who enjoys wasting his time." Bron glanced at Delin then, and Homin had the impression that Delin was part of Bron's annoyance. "What else is there that we need to know?"

"You might want the details of the second scheduled event," Rigos suggested, the disdain in his expression showing his opinion of Bron. "That will come at the beginning of the new week, when you'll all be moved into a single residence. You'll need to be together once you've been formed into a Blending, and that's the only way to accomplish it."

"It better not be small, or dirty, or without decent servants," Selendi told him sourly while everyone else made a sound of surprise. "And it better not be old and ugly, or I just won't go. If any of my friends ever saw me in a house that was old and ugly, my social life would be over."

"I'm sure your social life will survive with flying colors," Delin said to her quickly before Rigos was able to voice his very obvious exasperation. "We all have to make sacrifices, remember, but I'm sure this won't be one of yours. The Advisors need our participation too badly to put us into a hovel—isn't that true, Rigos?"

"Of course it is," Rigos confirmed with vast annoyance. "Anyone with a mind would have known that without being told. We'll expect you to have your clothes and possessions packed and ready to go first thing in the morning, and if you aren't ready that will be *your* loss. The reception will begin somewhat early, so be sure you're ready for that as well. And now it's time for me to go, but first I'd like a private word with Lord Kambil. A lady has asked me to pass on her . . . greetings."

His smile was coldly amused as he rose and headed for the door, making no effort to see if Kambil actually followed.

But Homin realized he didn't have to look, since Kambil followed the agent out of the room without hesitation. Kambil was big enough to break Rigos in half, and politically powerful enough to get no more than a slap on the wrist if he ever did. Rigos surely knew that, but he still demanded Kambil's attention—and got it.

That was one of the things power did for you, Homin mused as he watched the door close behind the two men. It was a frightening thing to consider, but if their plans were successful *he* might one day have that much power . . . or even almost that much . . . and then he would be safe from *everyone*. . . .

TWENTY-EIGHT

Delin watched Kambil walk out behind Rigos, and made sure to keep nothing but a pleasant smile on his face. Inside himself was another matter, however, where suspicion had suddenly sprouted. Kambil might be one of *his* people, but that still didn't mean he liked or trusted the man.

"I wonder what that's all about," Bron said, still watching the door Delin had turned away from. "And I hadn't realized those two were such good friends."

"It might be a good idea to ask Kambil when he returns," Delin said, giving the thickheaded Bron the prompting the man always seemed to need. "For myself, I'm going to get another cup of tea."

Bron grunted his agreement with the suggestion as Delin

rose, but he didn't seem very happy about doing it. Something was obviously bothering Bron, but at least he had the good sense not to mention whatever it was while Rigos was still in the house. For all they knew, the agent might be simply standing and listening at the door, with Kambil out there in the hall just to fool them. Kambil would be unable to call out and warn them; if he tried it, Rigos would be instantly certain that they were up to something.

All of which convinced Delin that the time had come to rid them all permanently of Rigos's presence. As he poured tea into his cup, Delin frowned, wishing it were possible to save Rigos for a more lingering and painful ending. That was something he'd been looking forward to, but now he had to admit that waiting would simply be too dangerous. Rigos already knew them far too well, and if he discovered the least hint of what they were up to, he would inform on them at once.

And as it happened, Delin knew exactly how to get rid of Rigos without any of the group getting involved. His frown turned to a smile as he remembered how easily the plan had come to him, appearing complete and fully detailed when he awoke two days ago. If that didn't show that his destiny was for greatness, nothing else would. A problem arose, but the true leader of the group already had an answer to take care of it.

"How long are they going to be out there?" Selendi demanded as she stood and flounced over to refill her own teacup. "I mean, just how long does it take to give a man a message from a girl?"

"Some girls send messages on more than a single subject," Bron told her with a laugh. "I know you have no idea what those other subjects are, my sweet, but don't let that worry you. No one expects you to."

"As if _you_ would know about other subjects," Selendi returned, faint color in her cheeks as she glared at Bron. "The only thing _you_ know about is—"

Her words broke off as the door opened again, just a heartbeat before Delin would have broken up the squabble. Kambil came back in, closing the door again behind him.

"He's gone," Kambil announced as he headed back for his seat and teacup. "I walked him to his carriage, watched him pull away, then told one of the servants to let us know immediately if he happens to come back."

"And he gave you your message?" Bron asked him without the cueing Delin was ready to perform. "It seems strange that you two should be close enough for something like that."

"There was no message, Bron," Kambil replied with faint surprise, as though he'd expected everyone to know the truth. "He wanted to thank me privately for that 'report' I sent him last week. Don't you remember that I told all of you what I was doing?"

"Oh, yes, that business about repeating things said by members of other groups at parties," Delin interrupted, only now remembering about it. "So you made things up and he liked them, did he?"

"But I didn't make things up," Kambil corrected with faint amusement in his eyes. "I may have . . . reworded some of what I heard, but every bit of it was really said—in one way or another. I even included quotes from Bron and Selendi."

"What?" Bron exploded, rising from his chair. "You told that—that—*deficient* something about *me*?"

"You *and* Selendi," Kambil corrected again, apparently completely undisturbed by Bron's anger. "I said I heard you musing aloud a time or two about what you would do if our group ever actually won the Throne—but Delin, Homin, and I were too bored to speculate about something that would never happen. Selendi, though, thought your ideas were marvelous, and went on to discuss how many servants she would have and how many new gowns if she were one of the Five on the Throne. Rigos told me he found that part of it amusing."

"But not suspicious, which it would have been if he hadn't said anything about us at all," Delin explained to a still-angry Bron, trying to settle the man down. "Rigos couldn't have been surprised to hear you have ambition, Bron, but without the support of the rest of us your ambition is nothing to worry about.''

"It *better* be that way," Bron growled, glaring another moment at Kambil before switching his stare to Delin. "And you and I have something to discuss. I'm the leader of this group, and I didn't like the way you made it look as if you and Kambil were. Maybe Selendi needs help to get to a meeting on time, but I don't need *anyone* nursemaiding me."

"Bron, that was just more misdirection," Delin told the fool, pretending to be wearily repentant. "I'm sorry if what I said disturbed you, but I *was* trying to keep Rigos from realizing that you're our leader. Would you like me to apologize more fully?"

"No . . . no," Bron decided, his anger having drained out to leave his head in its usual empty state. "Now that I understand what you were doing, you don't have to apologize. Just warn me in advance next time. . . . And now we can get to discussing these other things Rigos wants us to do. I happen to have made plans for the time we're supposed to be at that reception, so I say we 'forget' to go."

"But we can't do that," *Homin* blurted, startling everyone, apparently including himself. "I mean, we'll be facing some of those people in the competitions. If we don't learn all we can about them, we might *lose*. Once we're seated on the Throne, we'll be able to have any girls we want."

"I agree with Homin," Kambil said with a smile of encouragement for the fat little man, while Bron developed a stubborn look. "We do need to see who we'll be up against, and maybe even do a bit more. If we can get one or two from each group to tell us about any problems their groupmates might have, it will give us even more of an advantage. And if any of them happen to be pretty girls, Bron, we'll certainly need your help."

"Yes, I suppose you would," Bron grudged, finally coming around to reason. "All right, here's what we'll do: we'll go to that stupid reception, talk to those peasants as though we considered them actual people, and I'll handle any attractive females there might be. We find out everything we can, and that way we won't have any surprises during the competitions. Is all that clear?''

Everyone nodded without comment, just as though the plan were Bron's and he'd only just unveiled it. Delin found it ludicrous to think that a supposedly grown man had no idea he was being led around, but apparently *everything* about Bron was ludicrous.

''Now we're up to this business about moving into a residence together,'' Bron said after a short pause. ''That happens to be something I approve of, since we'll then be out from under our fathers' thumbs. As long as we don't get in the way of each other's private lives, things should work out nicely.''

''And as long as the place is decent,'' Selendi apparently felt compelled to add again. ''I simply refuse to live in a shack, and I expect the rest of you to back me up on this. Unless one of you *wants* to live in a shack.''

She looked at each of them in turn, and to Delin's amusement they each solemnly assured her that they did *not* want to live in a shack. That seemed to satisfy the emptyheaded girl, so Delin was able to get on with truly important things.

''Bron, don't you think we all ought to keep practicing while we're waiting to be formed into a Blending?'' he said, giving the idiot another prod. ''And I, at least, would like to congratulate Homin on catching up to the rest of us so quickly despite the tragedy in his life. We're proud of you, Homin, and doubly proud that you're one of us.''

Homin reddened and began to stutter through a thank you for what Delin had said, but Bron managed to ruin the mood by adding, ''As long as he *continues* to keep up. I can't see that he'll be terribly important to the Blending, but one weakness can weaken us all. That's why I want all of you to continue practicing, and if you have any problems, make an appointment to see me. We'll see each other again at the reception, and now let's all go home.''

Homin tried to tell them that they were welcome to stay for a while and visit, but everyone seemed to feel as smothered by that old house with its tasteless furnishings as Delin did. They all claimed prior commitments and escaped, and in just a few minutes Delin was in his carriage and on his way back home.

But not to stay there. He smiled as he thought about the first step in his plans, which was to go and dig up the knife which had done such a thorough job on Elfini. Then he would remove every trace of himself from the thing, every drop of sweat and every hint of bodily oil. The third step would take him secretly to Rigos's house, where physical traces of the man would be everywhere. It had never before occurred to Delin that those traces might be transferred to the cleansed knife, but with Earth magic it was more than possible. Then he would rebury the knife, somewhere on Rigos's property.

Then would come the fourth step, which would be the "accidental" meeting with Atri Folgar, a girl pretty enough to make you forget that her father was one of the Advisors' top investigators—and that she was bright as well as pretty. Delin usually chatted and flirted with her, but this time his chatting would casually mention how strange his group's "protector" Rigos was. It would turn out that Delin had heard someone say something about Rigos and Elfini, a passing comment that had made him believe Rigos was more closely involved with Elfini than anyone had realized. Then Delin would make a delicately rude comment about the tastes of some men before changing the subject.

Which ought to make Atri mention the conversation to her father. That part of the ploy was dangerous, but not overly so. Since a weapon had been used to commit the murder rather than ability, no one should suspect a man with High ability. Rigos was the one who would come under suspicion, enough of it for the investigators to bring in a Middle talent strong enough to locate hidden, finished metal. The buried knife stood out sharply to Delin's least probe, so even a Middle talent ought to be able to find it.

"It's a good thing they didn't try that before now," Delin muttered very softly to himself with a chuckle. No one had thought to search the grounds surrounding the victim's own house, not when the murderer *must* have taken the weapon away with him. When they found it on Rigos's property there would still be traces of Elfini's blood on it, something the physician who had examined the body would be able to confirm. That, along with Rigos's own traces, would settle *his* hash, and Delin's group would no longer have to worry about premature discovery.

"And his trial ought to be quite entertaining," Delin murmured to the passing scenery. "He'll be arrested at once, of course, but the trial might well be delayed until the new Five are enthroned. If so, I'll enjoy the time even more."

Delin chuckled again, picturing Rigos's father disassociating himself rather than trying to help Rigos. With the victim a member of the high nobility, *no* one would get away with no more than a slap on the wrist for committing the crime. But even if Rigos *were* to get away with it, Delin would be far from disappointed. The man would still be ruined, which meant no one would notice if he suddenly disappeared.

Yes, Delin thought, *and then I could have my cake as well as eat it.* His mind went off to picture the joy he would find in killing Rigos slowly and painfully, and the smile remained on his face for quite some time.

TWENTY-NINE

Vallant came to the dinner table pretty much with everyone else, except for Tamrissa Domon. He'd been there earlier in the day when Tamrissa and Jovvi had returned in their coach, with Tamrissa sound asleep. Jovvi had had one of the servants carry Tamrissa to her bedchamber, and Vallant had firmly squashed the automatic thought that *he* would have enjoyed carrying the girl. He now wanted no more to do with Tamrissa than she wanted with him, and he was glad that she'd slept away the entire day—as had some of the others.

And now she was late coming down to dinner, almost as late as Pagin Holter. The small man had been there for lunch, actually joining the table conversation without being prodded into it, and afterward had even spent a short time chatting with Lorand Coll. That was the last Vallant had seen of him, and when Tamrissa hurried into the room, he was the last of them still missing.

"I'm sorry for being late, everyone," Tamrissa said with an embarrassed smile meant for all of them as she took her place at the table. "I managed to exhaust myself during those tests, and it was hard to get up even after sleeping all day. Has anyone sent a servant to see what's keeping Dom Holter?"

Jovvi seemed about to answer, but Warla's sudden appearance kept the words from being spoken. The shy girl seemed to be just as nervous as always, and she cleared her throat to announce her presence, just as though everyone hadn't already seen her come in.

"Excuse me, ladies and gentlemen, but you have a visitor," the girl quavered once it was clear that she had everyone's attention. "Lady Eltrina Razas would like a few minutes of your time."

"Thank you, child," Eltrina Razas said, making an entrance befitting what she obviously thought was her proper station and due. Vallant didn't like the woman, and wouldn't have trusted her behind his back under any circumstances.

"Yes, my dear people, I come with news," Eltrina continued, beaming around at them. "First let me congratulate all of you on achieving your second-level masteries, which your bracelets proudly announce. And you have my thanks for settling another week's finances."

The woman grinned at the "joke" she'd make, but Vallant wasn't the only one who did no more than smile politely. They'd gotten the silver they'd been promised, but the gold was still nowhere in sight.

"Now to the news that I think will please you," the woman went on, apparently ignoring the lack of enthusiasm over her attempt at humor. "Tomorrow morning you'll all be going to the first of the competitions, where victory will mean the gold you were promised. Doesn't that sound good?"

This time she got more of a reaction from everyone, especially since Vallant felt as though she'd read his mind. Fear struck him at the thought of his having to enter that small, windowless building, but Vallant pushed it away to worry about later.

"Yes, I thought you'd enjoy hearing that," Eltrina said once the exclamations had died down, her smile having grown sleek. "You might also be interested in learning that those of you who win will get something in addition to the gold. The day after tomorrow there will be a reception at the palace for all successful candidates, and if you qualify you'll be attending it."

The reaction to that news was more of a shocked silence,

which Vallant was forced to admit he participated in. In general the idea of nobility left him vastly unimpressed, but the Five's palace was another matter entirely. Ordinary people had to be satisfied with seeing it from the outside—and at a distance—but *they'd* just been given personal invitations . . . assuming they won.

"That's very exciting news, Lady Eltrina," Tamrissa said, and there *was* a sparkle of excitement in her beautiful eyes. "I'm sure we'll all do our best, but I wish you'd waited for Dom Holter to join us before telling us about it. He'll be disappointed that he missed hearing it directly from you."

"That's another point we need to discuss," Eltrina said, hidden amusement of some sort clear to Vallant as he looked at her. "Dom Holter was moved to another residence this afternoon, one that would have been running at a financial loss without another participant in residence. I'm sure you'll all miss him, but if he's successful in the first competition, most of you will see him at the reception. Are there any questions?"

Vallant had to fight to keep himself from looking at the others, and he could see that Coll, the only one in his direct line-of-sight, appeared to be having the same problem. If Holter no longer shared their residence, there was now only a single representative of each of the five aspects. That had to mean they'd been chosen to be a challenging Blending, even if Eltrina wasn't yet ready to tell them about it.

"There don't seem to be any questions," Eltrina said brightly after looking around at them. "That means I can now leave you to enjoy your meal, but don't worry if a question occurs to you later. I'll also be at the reception, and those of you who attend can ask me then. Good night, all."

The woman turned and left the room after giving them an airy wave of her hand, but for a moment no one seemed able to speak or move. Vallant knew exactly how they felt, and it was a definite relief when Jovvi sighed and leaned back in her chair.

"Well, that was clear enough," she said, looking at each of them to see that they understood what "that" was: the virtual certainty that they would soon be made into a Blending. "We seem to have only one more challenge before us, which will be the competition tomorrow. Anyone who doesn't win doesn't get to go to the reception."

Or join the Blending, was the unspoken addition. By then the servants had entered with their food, so no one did any more than nod. Not that anyone needed to do more, Vallant admitted silently. Or point out the fact that he, at least, might not make it after all.

"Excuse me, Dom Ro, but I wonder if I might have a few minutes of your time after dinner?" Vallant heard the words which dragged him back to the present, and for an instant thought it was Jovvi who had spoken them. When he realized that it was Tamrissa instead, his insides tightened into a painful spring. Most likely the woman wanted to tell him again how distasteful she felt sharing his bed would be, or possibly she meant to tell him again that only cowards refused to see how far they could go in life. He was in the mood for neither thing, and so shook his head as he gave his attention to the food.

"I'm sorry, Dama Domon, but I intend to go right to bed after dinner," he replied in the most neutral tone he was capable of, making sure not to look at her. "Tomorrow will be a difficult day for some of us, so I'm afraid the conversation will have to be saved for another time."

Nothing of words came in the way of a response or argument, and a glance at the girl while reaching for a roll showed Vallant what seemed to be disappointment on her face. He'd obviously taken away her chance to make him feel even worse than he did, but that was just too bad. She could try again tomorrow night—assuming he still rated a place in the residence.

Which, considering where the competition would be held, wasn't very likely. And he'd been the fool who'd *wanted* to get to the first competition because it suited his mood. Well, there was no arguing that it certainly did suit his mood *now*. . . .

*   *   *

Eltrina Razas let the servant help her into her carriage, the smile on her face showing just how pleased she was with the way things were going. She'd even managed to form *six* groups of potential challenging Blendings, so if any of the members of the first five happened to become unavailable, it would be possible to replace him or her.

But the peasant Holter would *not* be returned to this residence if that beautiful man Ro happened to fail in his attempts to keep up. Holter had actually begun to settle in as a full member of the group, proving how little taste those lowborn commoners had for encouraging such a thing. The man was a peasant even to them, after all. . . . But Holter was gone, leaving Ro and his problem—and his ever-growing feud with the Domon female. Her spies had told her that they'd even stopped speaking, and as she lingered in the hall she herself had heard, just a moment ago, the way the man had refused to grant the girl even a handful of minutes of his time.

Eltrina's smile widened as her carriage began to move. Her plans had been easily adapted. These people would never make an effective Blending, and when they failed she would exercise her authority and take first choice from among them. She'd been too busy to notice earlier how really beautiful a man Ro was, with those broad shoulders, that handsome face, and that delicious platinum-blond hair. But she'd noticed tonight, and once his bright and mighty prospects turned to powdered dust, he'd be more than anxious to give her the pleasure she desired.

And while she enjoyed herself completing her plans, Lord Ollon, her superior in the testing authority and current lover, would have his tragic accident. It was already mostly arranged—although there had been an unforeseen and annoying delay—and afterward Eltrina would go from second in command to being completely in charge. Her political position and power would more than triple, and finally, at long last, she would be in charge of her own destiny.

After something tragic happened to her husband as well, she added silently without the amusement. The tiresome pig had been bothering her even more than usual, and she didn't yet dare refuse him. He wasn't above tossing her aside if he grew displeased, and after she'd given him so much. Well, *that* debt would soon be repaid, the first of quite a few. . . .

Eltrina felt a surge of impatience, but used the sight of the beautifully calm night to help push it away. Everything was going perfectly, and that despite the efforts of a great many fools. That group looking for applicants who fit the description of the Chosen Five in the Prophecies, for instance. She'd had to let them paw through her notes and records in order to get rid of them, but she hadn't let them see the private reports she'd had assembled. Just about everyone in her residences fit the Prophecy in one way or another, but only if you knew everything about them.

So Eltrina hadn't let the searchers know everything. They would have intruded with their ridiculous investigation and ruined all her plans, and she refused to allow *anyone* to do that, especially not for nonsensical gibberish. People who believed in the collection of fairy tales called the Prophecy were fools, and Eltrina had never suffered fools gladly. After the reception she would tell her people about forming challenging Blendings without the interference of idiots, and then. . . .

And then Eltrina would have what she'd ached for for so long. Freedom, and power, and all the wonderful things that went with them . . . She leaned her head back and closed her eyes, actually tasting what would so soon be hers. . . .

THIRTY

Rion was delighted to see the Razas woman leave, and that despite the welcome news she brought. He'd been picturing himself turning up on Naran's doorstep with no more than a few silver dins in his hand, feeling and looking like a beggar. Now . . . now he would have gold, assuming he could find a way to avoid being followed. Maybe he would do best to take Tamrissa up on her offer to help. . . .

"I had a surprise today," Lorand Coll said suddenly, breaking a silence which had continued since their food had first been brought. "Holter's having been moved out reminded me, even though Holter will be missed and *he* wasn't. Eskin Drowd showed up in the testing area today."

"So he finally qualified," Rion said, finding it impossible to keep the distaste out of his voice. "I hope you had the good sense to bury him in the ground, or Encouraged a tree to grow up around him."

"I can't say I wasn't tempted," Coll agreed sourly. "Even after 'eating my dust' for so many days, as one Adept put it, Drowd was still sneering with imagined superiority when he saw me. I could also see that he was waiting for me to fail, so I decided I couldn't let that happen. If I hadn't been too tired afterward to think of it, I would have thanked him for helping me to succeed."

"I had almost the same help, and from a similar source," Tamrissa put in with a grimace, apparently having pulled herself out of disappointment of some sort. "Beldara Lant has also qualified, and she got me so angry that I invited *her* to attack me in place of Soonen. But I also promised to respond if she did, which I hadn't done with Soonen. At least not to begin with. Afterward, I think Beldara was glad she hadn't accepted my challenge."

" 'At least not to begin with,' " Jovvi echoed, looking at Tamrissa with a frown. "Does that mean you did respond eventually? And did that have anything to do with why you were so exhausted that you were asleep as soon as they helped you into the coach?"

"Yes to both," Tamrissa agreed. "I certainly did respond during the last exercise, but only because Soonen suddenly had the help of Adept Gerdol in attacking me." Rion started at hearing that, and apparently so did everyone else at the table. "For some reason they both tried to burn me to ash, but I couldn't return the favor without missing out on my last mastery. So I drew in more power than I'd ever used before, and worked *around* their attack to complete the exercise. Pretending I didn't even notice their efforts scared the starch out of them, but it used up so much of my strength that once I finished eating a *really* large meal, all I wanted to do was sleep."

"Now isn't that an odd coincidence," Jovvi commented, looking around as she said it. "I had almost the same experience, and apparently so did everyone else. Genovir and Algus tried to gang up on me, but I was able to overcome them and gain the mastery. Afterward it became perfectly clear why they were so deferential yesterday after I gained the first-level masteries. They knew they would try to interfere with me during the second-level testing, and wanted to give me a reason to go easy with them if I ended up victorious."

"Subservient behavior in front of a superior," Coll agreed with a nod. "That's what works with lower animals, so now we know what they think of us—if there was any doubt before."

"But they were also frightened because they weren't certain it would work,'' Rion pointed out. "They claimed they were under orders and did the same with every applicant, but for some reason I didn't believe them. My personal guess is that they do it only with those whom they consider unacceptably strong.''

"How can someone in *our* position be 'unacceptably strong?' '' Ro suddenly demanded, his previous dark mood still obviously with him. "Those bastards could have killed me, or at least come close enough to it to break my nerve. After that my decidin' to stick it out would be meaningless. When it finally came down to it, I'd be—''

Ro's words broke off as he realized what he was saying, and Rion joined everyone else in exchanging disturbed glances. With the servants around they were all being careful of what they said, but even with circumlocution Ro had made an important point after Rion's own. If the testing authority wanted the strongest and best for the challenging Blendings, why were they trying to weaken some of those who *were* best? The obvious answer was that they didn't want any common challengers who were *too* strong, not when those commoners would be facing members of the nobility.

"I think, under other circumstances, I would find my appetite gone now,'' Jovvi commented, staring down at the food in her plate. "Confusion often does that to me, and right now I'm *very* confused because of what we were told only a short while ago. We have to *win* the competition tomorrow, or we don't get to go to the reception the day after.''

That was another excellent point, and Rion joined the others in considering it silently. Being too strong had brought down attack on their heads, but now they'd been told they had to be stronger than everyone else. And there was no doubt that they were being urged to win. The Razas woman's voice and attitude had made that clear, and yet. . . . What *were* they supposed to do?

"You know, it's really strange,'' Tamrissa said suddenly, drawing everyone's attention. "I've just now remembered one of my late husband's more odious games. He would give all the servants a few hours off, and once they were gone he would chase me from room to room all over the house. The longer I kept running the happier he was, and when I finally dropped from exhaustion he would . . . have the rest of his entertainment. It took me a while to realize that I didn't *have* to keep going to exhaustion, I could simply pick a time to *pretend* to be exhausted and he never knew the difference. After all, I was only being measured against my own strength. . . . I'm sorry, I don't know *why* I brought that up. . . ."

Rion joined Jovvi and Coll in assuring her it was quite all right to mention something without relevance to the conversation, but that was just as much of a lie as Tamrissa's apology. The girl had had an excellent thought, and had found a way to mention it to the rest of them without alerting any servant who might be listening.

The fact had slipped Rion's mind, but that first competition would be on the order of a footrace. Each participant would be striving to be best, but against time and situation rather than directly against each other. And in a footrace, it was possible to win by a single body length as easily as by ten or twenty yards. If they pretended that that was the best they could do, who would be able to prove otherwise? And then a thought of his own occurred to him.

"If we're sharing personal incidents, I have one of my own I'd like to share," he said, keeping his voice diffident but looking around pointedly at each of the others. "Once, when I was a boy, Mother began to invite people over who had sons of their own who were approximately my age. I thought at the time that she did it to provide me with playmates, but during each visit she insisted on having some sort of contest among all the children. Once it was a race, and once it was a test of strength, and once it was even a comparison of book learning."

"So you were constantly being required to perform," Jovvi said with a sympathetic nod. "Did she expect you to win at everything?"

"Yes, and most of the time I did, but being able to brag wasn't her entire reason for doing it," Rion said. "She held the contests to see how well I would do against some criterion of her own, using the other little boys as nothing more than yardsticks. She didn't care about *their* performances, only mine, which took me awhile to realize. At the time I was too busy wondering why the other boys hated me when I won."

Again there were murmurings of commiseration, but the expressions of understanding in everyone's eyes told Rion they'd gotten his point. Depending on how strong the other competition entrants were, the whole point of the exercise might be to assess the strength of Rion and the others. If the thing was legitimate, they would face other possible members of Blendings; if it wasn't, the testing authority would have dross there just to make it all *look* good. But they would have to wait to find out which it would be.

The rest of the meal passed in relative silence, and once it was over Vallant Ro was the first to leave, with Jovvi right behind him. Ro had seemed to be struggling with some sort of strong emotion while Tamrissa told them about the way she'd been attacked, but the man hadn't said anything to her afterward. It was possible his struggle had had nothing to do with Tamrissa, but that was something Rion had no time to worry about. If he were going to ask Tamrissa's help with his own problem, it had to be now.

"I wonder, dear lady, if you have recovered sufficiently to share a brief nightcap with me in the library," he said when it seemed that Tamrissa was ready to take her own leave. "I have something I'd like to discuss with you, and you as well, Coll, if you're willing."

Rion didn't know precisely why he'd included Coll in the invitation, but it might have had something to do with how miserable and alone the man looked. Coll had helped him on more than one occasion, so now it wasn't possible to exclude the man while asking for Tamrissa's help.

"Well, all right, but just for a short while," Tamrissa agreed after a moment, looking really weary. "I needed to get this food into me, but I need more sleep just as much."

"Well, I don't have anything better to do with my time," Coll said with a shrug as he threw his napkin aside and rose.

"No offense, Mardimil, I'm just in a terrible mood. What I should have said was, if we're not here for each other, who can we expect to be here for us?"

"No offense taken, Coll," Rion said as he rose as well, actually meaning the words. "And we *do* have to be here for each other, so becoming insulted over nothing would be stupid. Here, dear lady, take my arm."

Tamrissa had gotten to her feet before he reached her, and the girl looked more distracted than unsteady. She did, however, take the offer of his arm, and they made a small, slow procession to the library. Once there he tried to seat her, but she shook her head with a small smile.

"Thank you, Rion, but I need to stand up for a while," she said, patting his arm before releasing it. "Now, what sort of problem do you have that I might be able to help with?"

"By tomorrow night I expect to have gold," Rion stated, seeing that Coll paid attention as well. "With that in mind I intend to meet—someone, but my mother is having me followed. Do you have any idea how I can avoid those followers without letting them know I've done it?"

"Well, we *should* be able to figure out *something*," Tamrissa replied, suddenly more caught up. Coll stood with raised brows, but didn't seem ready to comment. "The best idea would be to have them think they *are* following you, while it's really someone else in your place. That way they won't go searching, and won't be on the alert the next time you want to do the same."

"The suggestion is excellent," Rion said with his own brows high. "What I can't seem to picture, however, is how I might accomplish it. It's a virtual certainty that Mother's people have at least one house servant in their employ, which means I'm under almost constant observation."

"Yes, you probably are, so we'll have to take you *out* of the house," Tamrissa returned, her mind clearly in the midst of deep calculation. "There's a lovely dining parlor not far from here, one I went to a few times before I married. If we decide to visit it tomorrow night, your shadows will certainly follow."

"And I'm to slip away from there?" Rion asked, feeling confused. "Leaving you completely unescorted and departing on foot? Unless I'm mistaken, even if I were willing to do that it would never work. As soon as I disappeared they would begin to search for me."

"Of course they would, so you won't disappear," Tamrissa countered with a glorious smile. "You and I will leave the house together in plain view—a short while after Lorand leaves by himself. Lorand will go to the dining parlor, arrange for the rental of a horse from the nearby stables, and then he'll wait in the entryway of the dining parlor, which happens to be fashionably dim. When we walk in he'll take your place, and you'll slip out the back while the watchers have their attention on *him*. If he's willing to do it, that is."

Both of them turned to look at Coll then, Rion ready to plead with the man. But Coll's face wore a look of surprised anticipation, and then he grinned.

"It sounds like fun," he said, and the words actually rang true. "My friends and I occasionally did this sort of thing when we were too young for our parents to be willing to let us come and go as we pleased. You and I are approximately the same size, Mardimil, and even our hair color is close enough to pass at a distance. If we wear the same clothes the way we're doing now, it should work like a charm."

"And you really don't mind?" Rion asked, looking from one to the other of them. "I've never had *anyone* willing to do things for me without being paid, and certainly nothing like this. How can I ever thank you?"

"Some day *we'll* need a favor, and you're the first one we'll ask," Coll assured him with a much more gentle smile. "Isn't that right, Tamrissa?"

"Certainly," Tamrissa agreed, but her impish grin reminded Rion that she'd already gotten a favor from him. "Besides, I needed something like this to take my mind off my own troubles, and somehow I think Lorand feels the same. By asking us to help, you're doing *us* the favor."

When Coll nodded his agreement, Rion would have enjoyed finding the words to express how he felt. An experience like this was priceless, but also seemed beyond verbalizing. So he took Tamrissa's hand and kissed it instead, then exchanged a handshake with Coll before turning and hurrying out of the room. Rion hadn't cried in quite a long time, but certainly felt like doing so now.

But when he reached his bedchamber, he found himself ready to laugh instead. Tomorrow night he would see Naran again, and not for a moment or two and not as a beggar with hat in hand. It would be wonderful, marvelous, and now he didn't know if he'd be able to stand the wait. . . .

THIRTY-ONE

Jovvi stared at Tamma for a while once the coach began to move the next morning, trying to decide whether or not to say anything to the girl. Her own problem wasn't quite as pressing as it had felt last night, when she'd gone directly to her bedchamber after dinner to avoid needing to speak to Lorand. But Lorand hadn't *tried* to speak to her, either last night at dinner or this morning at breakfast. He still looked at her in the same way when he thought she wasn't likely to notice, but he hadn't tried again to get her to change her mind.

Which was both a good thing and a bad one. Jovvi sighed as she silently admitted that she didn't really want to lose Lorand, but the uncertainty surrounding him was impossible for her inner self to overlook. She both wanted him and didn't want him, but at least *he* wasn't adding to the turmoil she suffered with. That made it only a little easier to bear, but Jovvi was prepared to be grateful for small favors.

"Is everything all right?" Tamma said suddenly, startling Jovvi. "I don't mean to pry, but that sigh sounded like one of mine."

"Actually, I was going to ask *you* the same question," Jovvi replied, finding something of a smile. "I can tell that you're disturbed again, but it's not the same disturbance you felt yesterday."

"I'll say it isn't," Tamma agreed glumly, then she looked up at Jovvi with her head to one side. "I seem to have changed my mind about Dom Ro again, and it occurred to me that there may be something seriously wrong with me. All this, 'yes I want him, no I don't want him' back and forth can't possibly be normal, but wouldn't you tell me if I were seriously ill?"

"Yes, I would, and no, you're not," Jovvi said with a laugh she couldn't possibly have held back. "Women may not have a *lot* of rights in this world, but changing our minds does happen to be one of them. And in your situation, vacillating back and forth couldn't be more normal. But does this mean you've now decided you want Vallant?"

"Yesterday morning, after the testing, I decided I did," she agreed, back to being glum. "It was probably a residual of all that power affecting me, but I made up my mind to at least try. That's why I asked to speak to him last night after dinner, but now it looks like *he's* changed *his* mind."

"Infringing unfairly on one of *our* prerogatives," Jovvi sympathized, feeling Tamma's disappointment very clearly. "So what have you decided to do now? Forget about him after all?"

"I should, but I can't seem to force myself to be that rational," Tamma complained, most of her disturbance now aimed at herself. "I mean, how am I supposed to change a man's mind once he's made it up? I wouldn't know where to begin, but something won't let me drop the whole thing. He was so cold when he refused even to talk to me, but somehow I could feel pain behind the coldness."

"And you aren't capable of ignoring someone in pain," Jovvi said gently, nodding her understanding. "I won't try to tell you what to do, but I have a suggestion you might consider: think about this whole thing before you decide on a course of action. If you're interested in nothing but easing a man in pain, getting him to change his mind again would be wrong. You have to be just as interested in a relationship as he is, otherwise you'll simply end up hurting him more."

"That sounds like the best idea I've heard in quite a while," Tamma said ruefully. "That means I'm going to take your advice, so that takes care of *my* disturbance. Now what about yours?"

"Oh, mostly it's the same old thing," Jovvi forced herself to say, feeling the way her mind instantly closed in on itself. "I *have* walked away from Lorand, but I can't stop thinking or worrying about him. Take this morning, for instance. I'm almost certain that we'll be facing no more than an attempted measurement of our strength, but what if that guess is wrong? What will happen if Lorand finds it necessary to really stretch his ability—and can't? Even if that doesn't happen today, it could happen tomorrow, and I can't bear to picture it."

"So *don't* picture it," Tamma responded, sounding as if Jovvi had missed the most obvious solution to her problem. "If there's nothing you can do to change something, what good does worrying about it do? Either you have to *find* a way to change the thing, the way I did with my parents, or you have to simply give up and accept whatever comes. I never thought I'd be saying this to *you*, Jovvi, but which route would you *rather* take?"

Tamma's tone had been more diffident and apologetic than the words suggested, which helped to keep Jovvi's indignation from being overwhelming. That was the sort of thing *she* was used to saying to Tamma, not something she needed to be told herself. Of course those were the two best options, but—

"But what could I possibly do to change things?" she complained aloud, feeling as though she and Tamma had switched places. "If it was easy—or even often possible—

to help someone get around the fear of burnout, people would be doing it all the time. Holding his hand during testing wouldn't work even if I were able to do it, so what else is there?''

"I have no idea," Tamma answered with a small shrug, looking and sounding sympathetic. "If it were my problem I'd be frantic, so feel free to be the same."

"But being frantic doesn't solve anything, and I seem to be out of the habit," Jovvi said with another sigh, fighting an urge toward depression. "I guess I'll have to take my own advice and think about this, but in the meanwhile I owe you congratulations. You've grown to the point of discovering that other people's problems are usually easier to solve than your own."

"And you do have to understand their problems before you can do anything about them," Tamma commented, now looking thoughtful. "That's a good point to keep in mind, and definitely something else to think about. But for right now I did want to ask—You agree with Rion, then, about what this first competition will be? Just an opportunity to measure exactly how strong each of us is?"

"It seems to be the most logical guess," Jovvi agreed, tacitly joining Tamma in putting aside their personal problems. "I was specifically told that I would not be competing against anyone directly, only against their efforts. And they obviously want us trying our best, otherwise they would hardly be dangling that carrot."

"The invitation to the reception," Tamma said with a nod of understanding. "I wasn't joking about how excited the idea of it made me feel, but that was last night. This morning I'm afraid I'll do something horrible to embarrass myself if I go, so maybe I'd be best off staying home."

"You could always come down with some 'female problem,'" Jovvi pointed out with something of a smile. "That's another of our rights, but it doesn't say whether or not you've decided to try winning the competition. Personally, I'd like the option of whether or not to go to be mine."

"Yes, so would I," Tamma replied, instantly brightening.

"And that 'female trouble' thing is another good idea. So it looks like I *will* be trying to win the competition, but not by too much of a lead. It won't be easy to manage to *just* win, and I suppose that's why I was thinking about not even trying. I was really tired yesterday and not at all interested in making the effort, and something of that carried over to this morning. But now I feel back to my usual self, so I'll see what I can do."

"I suspect that deliberately holding back will be harder for *me* to hide," Jovvi said, having already thought about it. "With Spirit magic, you have access to a good deal of information about the people around you. If someone is frightened, or uninterested—or holding back—you can usually tell, so I'm going to have to project false emotions as well as gauge my response. I don't expect it to be much fun, but there's no doubt about its being necessary."

"I wonder if they'll have someone there at *my* competition who can tell things like that," Tamma said, now sounding worried. "I wouldn't put it past them, and I don't know if I can fool someone like that."

"That's a good question," Jovvi said with a frown she could feel, then took a moment to think about it before finally shaking her head. "No, chances are there *won't* be anyone there with Spirit magic. We're not expected to know that they might be trying to get rid of—or at least handicap—anyone capable of besting their noble participants, so it's unlikely that they'd bother to check on whether or not we're pretending about anything. They very well might have one of their strongest aspect participants there to measure us against, but not anything more."

"I just thought of something else," Tamma said, sudden disturbance straightening her in the seat. "We've been talking and thinking about a footrace, which seems to be a phrase used by all of our guides. But what if we're actually required to perform one at a time, and *we* don't get to go last? How will we know how much strength to use?"

"I hate to say it, but you've done it again," Jovvi replied, quickly sharing Tamma's disturbance. "I have no idea how we'd tell, but we'd better think of something fast. We're already more than halfway there.''

Tamma nodded with immediate distraction, so Jovvi immersed herself in her own thoughts. That footrace concept probably *was* a deliberate attempt at misdirection, leading them to expect one circumstance when an entirely different one awaited. Just how *would* it be possible to judge . . . ?

By the time the coach began to slow for its first stop, Jovvi had to admit defeat. Nothing in the way of an idea had come to her, and looking at Tamma brought nothing but a shake of Tamma's head.

"If there's an answer, it seems to be avoiding me," Tamma said dispiritedly. "Your expression tells me it's doing the same with you, but that's only faintly comforting. I'm about to get out, and I still don't know what to do."

"Personally, I intend to hope that we're wrong," Jovvi said with a wan smile. "I don't expect the hoping to do any good, but doing *something* is always better than doing nothing."

"A lot of help *you* turned out to be," Tamma said, but her wry smile took the sting out of the words. "I gave up on hoping a long time ago, so I can't even do that much. Well, it's too late for that anyway. In just a few more minutes I'll know, so all I can do is wish us both good luck."

Jovvi returned the wish and then Tamma was gone, out of the coach and walking toward the Fire magic practice area. The coach started to move again, but the distance to Jovvi's own area wasn't long enough to be of any practical use. When the coach stopped again near the symbol for Spirit magic, she still hadn't been visited with inspiration.

But that didn't mean she could just sit there, so she got out after taking a deep breath and headed for the practice area. It wasn't particularly early so Jovvi expected to see a good number of people at the tables, but the sight of the *crowd* stopped her in her tracks. There was more than twice the usual number of people present, and Genovir came from behind one group of them to glide over to where Jovvi stood.

"Quite a turnout, isn't it?" Genovir said with a smile,

glancing back at all the people. "Usually there's very little interest left in watching low level competitions at this time of the year, but this year, of course, is different. Would you like some tea before we go to the competitions building? There's time yet before the event is scheduled to begin."

"No, I think I've had enough tea this morning," Jovvi replied with a faint grimace. "Later will probably be another story, but—What did you mean about this year being different. What's different about it?"

"Why, the fact that it's a twenty-fifth year, dear," Genovir responded with a wide-eyed innocence that was completely false. She'd *wanted* Jovvi to ask about the comment, so Jovvi had obliged her. She also knew what reaction Genovir wanted to elicit, so Jovvi obliged her again.

"My goodness, I forgot all about that!" Jovvi exclaimed, showing what was hopefully a better version of innocence. "That means I'll have to try even harder now, doesn't it?"

"Just do your best, dear, and it's sure to impress everyone," Genovir counseled, hiding behind an air of gentle and benevolent amusement. "If you don't want any tea, we can start for the building now."

Jovvi nodded and followed after the larger woman, wondering if she was really supposed to have forgotten so soon about what had happened yesterday. Apparently *Genovir* considered the matter forgotten, or she wouldn't have had the nerve to show herself today. Well, however it was supposed to go, Jovvi opened herself even more widely to her talent. It was hardly likely that the crowds contained many people who would be on *her* side, and Jovvi would need as much help against the other sort as she could get.

But then all thoughts of enemies disappeared behind a brand new experience, that of being aware of the people around her *in depth*. The emotions and reactions of those in the crowd were so clear that Jovvi felt she could reach out and touch them. But not in the partial way she'd used until now, something the drugged subjects in the exercises had almost made her believe was all there was. This . . . this was new and different, filled with a potential that was downright exciting.

"Don't be shy or frightened, dear," Genovir said suddenly, and Jovvi realized she'd stopped following the so-called Adept and had come to a complete halt. "But if you've changed your mind about the tea, I understand perfectly."

"Yes, I'm sure you do," Jovvi murmured in answer, knowing now how eager Genovir was to see her fail in some way. The woman both hated and feared Jovvi, but a blind arrogance that was an integral part of Genovir's character made her believe that Jovvi couldn't possibly see past her facade. Genovir would do her best to ruin Jovvi's standing, and at the moment the way to do that seemed to be doing nothing at all.

"No, I haven't changed my mind about the tea," Jovvi continued, giving the woman a sweet, grateful smile. "Please go on, and this time I promise to keep up."

"As you like," Genovir agreed with a small shrug and a smile of her own before turning and continuing on. She still seemed convinced that Jovvi was afraid of what the coming competition would bring, and there was the very definite suggestion that she was supposed to soothe the fear. But Genovir was deliberately refraining from doing that, which did nothing to confirm Jovvi's guesswork about what the competition was for.

But Genovir wasn't very bright, Jovvi reminded herself as she followed the woman through the crowd. Part of Genovir's mindless arrogance was the certain knowledge that no one would dare to harm her, not unless it happened to be by accident or reflex. She seemed to think that what Jovvi had done yesterday against her and Algus had been just such a reflex, and couldn't possibly happen again. It wasn't likely that Algus thought the same, which was probably why Algus was nowhere to be seen.

Then the awareness of Genovir slipped away as Jovvi became aware of the crowd instead. She'd wondered if all those people had been ordered to be there as decorations for a carefully set scene, but that didn't seem to be the case. Most of them were there completely voluntarily, with something about betting behind their thoughts. But not betting that they meant to do today, with the upcoming competition. To them, this was more of a time of research and investigation. . . .

Jovvi smiled faintly as she passed through the last of the crowd and onto the path which led to the large resin building she hadn't yet been in. Those people in the crowd who were visitors were all of the nobility, and they obviously knew things that ordinary people didn't. Like the fact that at least one someone would be rated today, a someone who would be involved in other, more important things later. But Genovir's attitude still made everything uncertain. Was she withholding reassurance because she'd been told to do so, or because of vindictiveness? It made a considerable difference. . . .

Genovir reached the large resin building and went through the open doorway without hesitation, simply glancing back to make sure that Jovvi still followed. Jovvi did, and when she also stepped inside it was to see one large, open floor without partitions or rooms. Six people stood in a loose group on the far side, people who were drugged and therefore meant to be subjects. Perhaps ten feet closer to the door was a thick white line painted on the floor, and no one but the subjects stood beyond that line.

Before it, though, were other groups of people. Jovvi knew at once that the vast majority of them were people who had Spirit magic, and some of them stood about chatting in the bright lamplight. Others stood there feeling extremely bored, while the members of the smallest group of all—two people—were definitely nervous.

"Ah, there you are, Genovir, and this must be Dama Hafford." The voice belonged to a man who had approached them, a tall and thin man in his mid-thirties. "I am Adept Lomad, Dama Hafford, the one in charge of this competition. If you will kindly follow me, I'll show you to your proper place."

"Certainly," Jovvi agreed with a smile for the man's gracious bow, saying nothing about his claim of being an Adept. It had been immediately clear that Lomad was no more than a moderate Middle in strength, which meant he had to be a member of the nobility. As Jovvi followed him, she suddenly realized that these people were doing more than feeding their egos by calling themselves Adepts. They were also hiding the fact that they were used to being addressed by other titles, like lord and lady. Apparently the nobility wasn't so oblivious to public opinion that they carelessly flaunted just how much of the competition process they actually controlled.

"There are ten participants competing today, and you, of course, are one of them," Lomad said, slowing to walk beside Jovvi rather than in front of her. "Everyone is now here, so we'll be starting in just a little while. Please have a seat among the other participants, and the rules of the competition will be explained to you shortly."

By then they'd reached a place to the right where nine other people sat, with a tenth chair still unoccupied. Jovvi took that chair as Lomad had requested, finding herself mostly ignored by the seven people who were extremely bored. The remaining two were the two who were nervous, both of them men. They'd looked at Jovvi in a calculating way, but for the most part dismissed her presence. They were male and she was female, so they saw her as nothing of a threat.

For her own part, Jovvi had made a discovery. The two men were, along with her, the only potential Highs in the building. She sensed a . . . depth of ability in the two that was missing in everyone else, and she probably wouldn't have been able to reach through to them if they'd opened to the power. But they hadn't opened themselves, undoubtedly because the competition hadn't yet started, and they were as conditioned as everyone else against using their ability when they weren't specifically supposed to.

Jovvi moved about just a little to settle herself in the rather uncomfortable wooden chair, finally appreciating just how uncontrolled she was in comparison to everyone else. It should have been beyond her to open to the power almost as soon as she arrived, but she hadn't had the constant formal schooling that even the poorest children in their society were given. She'd had some before her father died, but after that she'd mostly spent her time on the streets. The lessons of her childhood, repeated many times every day in the class-room, had faded after a while to vaguely recalled memories.

And that seemed to have given Jovvi a definite edge. If there was ever a time to be completely aware of what went on around you, this was it. Those two potential Highs, though, had handicapped themselves by refraining from us-ing their very potent power. For the first time Jovvi began to understand how Tamma had lived through two years of a brutal marriage without once using her ability to defend her-self. The conditioning instilled in school was so strong that people could overcome it only by going insane.

Or by being told they were allowed to use their ability. Jovvi could vaguely remember that one exception, the power placed in the hands of those "in authority." That was why those with strength enough survived that very first test, being "allowed" as it were, to use whatever they had. But what about those who couldn't make that exception to the condi-tioning? Had potential Highs died because their minds were unable to accept the fact that it was perfectly all right for them to perform?

That thought made Jovvi shiver, and so did the one that followed immediately after. Conditioning like that didn't happen by accident, and didn't have to when there was such a thing as a nobility. There were a large number of people who called themselves lord or lady, but compared to the number of people in the general population, they were very much in the minority. And it had to be remembered that the children of the nobility didn't attend schools with their low-class age-peers. Did that mean those noble children weren't conditioned at all, or simply conditioned in some other way?

That newest question disturbed Jovvi even more, but there was no time now to think about it and consider ramifications. The building had been filling with observers during the time Jovvi was lost in her thoughts, and now there seemed to be very little room left. The rumbling mumble of muted conversation also filled every part of the large room, at least until Lomad stepped out of the crowd and across the line to hold up both of his hands.

"Friends, please give me your attention," he called, and one after the other the muted conversations stopped until there was silence. "Thank you, my friends, and welcome to one of the last basic competitions of this year. Today we have ten participants, and they're seated right over there."

Some few people in the audience applauded politely, but most just turned to stare. Jovvi shared the discomfort felt by the two nervous men, but not from simply being looked at. As a courtesan, Jovvi had never minded being inspected by men; after all, that was one of the things she'd been there for. But a moment earlier she'd glanced across the room, and had seen a familiar face.

The man who had been there when she'd taken that very first test; he was here again now, but seemed to be staying as far from her as he could while still being in the same room. He'd also moved out of sight behind others when he'd seen her looking in his direction, just as though he didn't want her to know he was there. But hadn't he said something about intending to see her again? Why, then, would he try to hide . . . ?

"As many of you know, this basic competition is very simple," Lomad continued when the polite applause ended. "The six subjects will be cued to exhibit five different emotions, with only one pair sharing the same emotion at any one time. Our participants will be given a list of those emotions in a set order, and will need to change each subject from the emotion he or she exhibits to the next emotion on the list."

A burble of comments erupted at that, and at least Lomad had enough ability to tell that the outburst was caused by confusion.

"Perhaps I'd better explain in more detail," he said, and the noise died down again. "The five emotions being used are fear, love, hatred, amusement, and anger, in just that or-

der. What our participants must do is take the subject showing amusement, for example, and change the emotion to
anger. The one showing fear has to be changed to love, and
the one showing anger has to be changed to fear. Each of
the six subjects must be put through all five of the listed
emotions in the listed order, but not all five at the same time.
Whichever emotion the subject starts with, the next one on
the list is what he or she must be made to feel next.''

This time the murmuring had overtones of being impressed, and the two nervous men grew even more nervous.
Jovvi felt tempted to join them in that as well, since the
exercise would be the most complicated thing she'd ever
tried. Five *different* emotions ranged through six people, and
the differences would have to be maintained even while they
shifted position. And to add to it, a large clock was being
prepared not far from where they sat. At least it looked like
a clock; Jovvi couldn't be completely sure, as its face was
turned away from them and toward the audience.

"And, of course, each participant's efforts will be timed,''
Lomad added, causing one of the two nervous men to moan
low. "At their level we expect all of them to be able to
perform the exercise, but just how quickly they do it will be
another matter entirely. We'll begin as soon as I've given
the participants the order in which they'll compete.''

Lomad left his position in front of the audience to walk
toward the place where Jovvi and the others sat, but Jovvi
felt nothing of the urge to stiffen with anticipation which
held the two nervous men. She'd already formed the basis
of a guess, one she would have bet gold on. *Her* name would
be first on the list, followed immediately by the two other
potential Highs. Their scores alone would be of interest to
the watching nobility, and the other seven people probably
weren't even going to compete. They'd try to hide that from
her and the two men, of course, but Jovvi didn't yet know
how they'd do it.

"All right, people, please pay attention,'' Lomad said
when he reached them, pulling a piece of paper out of one
pocket of his coat. "I'm going to speak a name and then a

number. That will tell you when it's *your* turn to compete, so please don't forget the number.''

He began to read his list then, and Jovvi smiled sourly when she learned she would have won her bet. Her name was first, and from their reactions, the two nervous men were listed right after her. They didn't seem to understand why her name came first, but Jovvi did. She was supposed to perform at her absolute best in an effort to outdo the men who had made no secret of their low opinion of her, and her effort was meant to spur *them* on to keep from the humiliation of being beaten by a woman. Very neat and tidy, but it still meant that she would have to go first.

Which she hadn't wanted to do. Jovvi forced herself to examine the problem calmly while Lomad finished reading off his list and then turned to speak privately to someone. Going first meant she couldn't know how strong the two men were, and therefore she would also not know what was needed to *just* win. There had to be *something* to give her a hint. . . .

The urge to be frantic was in the midst of trying to overwhelm Jovvi when she realized that the answer was staring her in the face—or, to be exact, *not* staring her in the face. That clock, the one which had been set up where only the audience could see it. . . . If it was a special clock, one meant to be reset for each participant, then the outcome was obvious. No one would know how well he or she actually did until the testing people announced the results, and those results could be anything they wanted them to be. It would even be possible for them to say that all three of the real participants had tied for first place—if they'd already chosen all three participants for membership in various challenging Blendings.

Jovvi took a deep breath in an effort to calm her rampaging thoughts. Most of the ''answer'' she'd gotten was sheer speculation, and fairly wild speculation at that. Taking guesswork as fact was dangerous, most especially in a situation like that. If she was proved wrong, she could find herself out of the residence and out of luck. But something told her that showing her full strength to people who were watching carefully was more dangerous still, so she had to take the chance. Maybe the worst that would happen would be her exclusion from the reception at the palace. . . .

"All right, Dama Hafford, please come with me," Lomad said suddenly, dragging Jovvi back to her surroundings. "You *are* first, you know."

"Yes, I do know," Jovvi muttered in answer, wishing it were possible to find somewhere to hide. Instead, she rose and followed Lomad, who took her to the white line painted on the floor.

"Please remember that you must remain behind this line at all times," Lomad told her. "Those who cross it are disqualified, but I'm certain that that won't happen to *you*. Once the subjects are cued, you may begin as soon as you feel able to do so. Do you remember the order of the emotions to be used?"

"Fear, love, hatred, amusement, anger," Jovvi answered after glancing over her shoulder. The clock *was* a special one, meant to be stopped and started at specific times, and that helped her to make up her mind. She *would* take the chance of losing, and hope with all her might that she wasn't outsmarting herself.

"Yes, that's completely correct," Lomad told her with an approving smile, and Jovvi had to remind herself that he meant her recitation of the list of emotions. Everything else was still pure speculation, and would remain like that until the results of the competition were made known.

Jovvi set herself solidly behind the line while Lomad moved behind her, and then someone was cueing the six subjects. The immediate and varied range of induced emotions would have knocked Jovvi over not long ago, but now she simply found herself aware of them. To her further surprise she also discovered that she could begin the exercise almost at once, but the caution of her plan kept her from being that foolish. She had to remember not to be *too* strong, and responding too quickly was part of that.

So she waited through a slow count of seven, then began

to change the emotions of the subjects in the prescribed way. She could have done all six of them exactly at the same time, but a tiny lag in reaction time seemed wiser. Once each of the subjects had gone through the entire range, Lomad stepped out in front of her again while the audience applauded.

"All right, my dear, you're finished now," he said with a smile as he took her hands in his. "You've done marvelously well, and should be very proud of yourself."

"Just how well did I do?" Jovvi asked, immediately pretending to be really tired. "I'll need to sit down for a while, but first I'd like to know."

The way her hands were held had kept her from turning to see the clock, and by the time Lomad released her it was too late. Turning showed Jovvi a clock which had already been reset, and Lomad chuckled as he put an arm around her shoulders and headed her toward the door.

"I'm afraid you'll have to wait until the competition is over before you find out how well you did," he said as he handed her over to another man. "That won't be for quite some time yet, so you'd be wisest if you went back to your residence to wait. You'll be much more comfortable there, and there are no penalties for not being here for the announcement. Have a cup of tea while your carriage is being summoned, and we'll certainly meet again at the next competition."

And then he was gone, heading back to the white line and the next participant while the strange man helped Jovvi to the door and out. So that was how they kept the real participants from knowing what was happening, she thought as she let herself be helped along. One by one they were sent home, and then the rest of the "participants" would be free to leave as well.

Jovvi's escort sat her at a table and ordered tea for her, then presumably left to send someone for her carriage. Her being ejected from the competition building was really quite encouraging, something that let her enjoy the tea when it came. She wasn't nearly as exhausted as she'd pretended to be, but that wasn't to say her strength hadn't been drained. Real or not, that competition was *hard*, and Jovvi didn't mind the idea of going home at all.

Two things arrived together: the last of the tea in her cup, and the man who had gone to see about her carriage. The speed in getting her vehicle back made Jovvi feel even better, so much so that she assured the man she could make it outside alone. He stood and watched her head for the way out, but his presence disappeared from Jovvi's awareness almost immediately. Her main worry now was how the others would do, hopefully neither too well nor too badly. If there were only some way she could get word to them . . . assuming, of course, that it wasn't already too late. . . .

Jovvi paid very little attention to her surroundings as she approached the carriage and began to climb inside, but seeing people already in the seats took her attention away from worrying. She also paused in entering the carriage, but that did very little good. Someone appeared behind her without warning, lifted her and thrust her inside, then followed to close the door and block it.

"Oh, do sit down and behave yourself, child," a female voice said as Jovvi began to struggle. The coach had also begun to move, which left the practice area behind. "We have a long trip ahead of us, but at the end of it you and I will settle up."

Jovvi looked up from the floor of the coach where she'd been pushed, her blood beginning to run cold. There were two men present, Ark and Bar, and sitting there with a triumphant smile on her face was none other than Allestine, the woman who had been her sponsor and who had sworn to take her back to her former life as a courtesan!

THIRTY-TWO

Rion spent his breakfast time floating through a dream of going to see Naran with gold in his hand, which meant the others barely registered with him beyond being presences. Once the coach arrived, though, he was forced to notice how slowly Coll and Ro moved, suggesting they might be reluctant to face what he looked forward to so eagerly. Insensitivity to the feelings of others was something Rion had never worried about, which probably meant he was often guilty of the oversight. If he were going to grow into a human being worthy of having friends and knowing a woman like Naran, it was time to change that.

"We should all do very well this morning," Rion said after he'd taken his seat beside Coll and across from Ro, trying to sound open and encouraging. "No matter what that competition consists of, we'll certainly be able to handle it . . . handily."

He tried to chuckle at his little joke, but discovered how difficult it is to chuckle alone. Coll looked out of the right-hand window and Ro did the same with the left, and Rion almost felt that he was alone in the coach. He also felt at a loss about what to say next, but inspiration suddenly visited.

"All right, so you *don't* think I'll win my competition," he said with a sigh, leaning back and putting a hand over his eyes. "Well, you're probably right and I'm just fooling myself by trying to believe otherwise."

"Rion, there's no reason you *shouldn't* win your competition," Coll said at once, responding the way Rion had hoped he would. "I'm the one who probably won't win, and that will be that."

"If anybody's goin' to mess this up, *I'm* the one," Ro said next, sounding extremely depressed. "It hurts to get this far before bein' thrown out, but that's what's bound to happen."

"Would they really throw one or more of us out after all but forming us into a Blending?" Rion asked after dropping his hand, and not only to keep them talking. They were suddenly discussing a very important point, one Rion hadn't fully considered. "As I mentioned last night at dinner, this 'competition' could very well be nothing more than their effort to find out what sort of strength we possess. In that event, their objective will be measuring rather than disqualifying."

"But if we don't win, we don't get to go to the reception at the palace," Coll protested. "Doesn't that *have* to mean the competition is important?"

"No, I think Mardimil is right," Ro contributed slowly, nevertheless looking more animated. "Until now it was clear that failin' to pass meant bein' booted out, but now if we don't win we don't get to go to a party. I haven't been seein' that part of it, and now I'm wonderin' why they want us to try so hard. If there's still a chance of us gettin' thrown out, why wouldn't they say *that* instead?"

"They would use the party instead only if they *know* we'll be going up against their noble groups, and want to find out just how good we are." Coll's agreement was laced with anger, his gaze moving back and forth between Rion and Ro. "If that's the case, I don't see any reason to give them what they want. If it means surviving a confrontation with the nobles, I'm willing to give up a chance to see the palace."

"But what about the gold?" Rion protested even as Ro nodded his concurrence. "If I hold back and don't win the competition, I also won't win the gold. I can't bear the

thought of going to Naran with hat in hand like a beggar. . . ."

"Rion has met a lady, and means to see her tonight," Coll
explained quickly to a puzzled Ro. "Tamrissa and I have
agreed to help him avoid the notice of the people his mother
has following him. . . . You've made a good point, Rion, but
there's another one to consider which may be even better: if
those people learn enough about your ability to let someone
do you harm, won't that ultimately be worse for Naran?"

"And here's somethin' I learned the hard way," Ro
added. "If a lady loves you for your gold, it isn't you she
loves. If she wants to be with you even without gold, you've
found somethin' beyond price. Keepin' yourself safe for
someone like that is more important than supplyin' what she
never asked for in the first place. Or *did* she ask?"

"No, actually, she never did," Rion said, delighted to
have an experienced man like Ro confirm the wisdom of his
attraction. "*I'm* the one who wants to have gold for her, but
you may be right. Putting myself at a disadvantage to get it
doesn't make much sense."

"You know, we've just decided to lose the competition,
but that might not be as easy as it sounds," Coll mused,
again looking between the other two men. "I had to stretch
myself to gain those masteries, so I can't pretend to have no
strength at all. I was thinking I'd just hang back behind the
strongest of those we'll be competing against, but how do I
tell who that is or how strong he is?"

"And what happens if we don't all perform at the same
time?" Ro put in, now looking as disturbed as Coll. "I was
picturin' us doin' the thing like the footrace they mentioned,
but that doesn't have to be. They could have us perform one
at a time, and the only ones we'd know about would be those
who went ahead of us."

"And if one of us happens to be first, he'll have a real
problem," Rion added, closing the circle. "I can judge the
approximate strength of others of my aspect once they begin
to use their ability, but how am I to tell before that? If any
of us falls too badly below the level we've risen to, they'll
know we're holding back."

"And that just *might* get us tossed out," Ro said with a nod. "So we'll just have to decide how much to hold down what we can do, and stick to that level no matter what happens around us. If we don't make it *too* low, nobody should notice. At least not that part of it."

The last of Ro's words were muttered, and Rion didn't understand what they meant. Coll did seem to understand, though, and he leaned toward Ro looking earnest.

"You can't let them use your problem against you," Coll stated, sounding just as earnest. "I discovered during the mastery tests that they seem to know *my* problem, and getting mad over that helped me to get around the problem itself. Can't you do something like that for yourself?"

"You don't think I've tried?" Ro asked wearily, looking at Coll bleakly. "Gettin' mad does help a little, but I keep picturin' that small, windowless resin buildin', and I get sick instead. As soon as I walk inside there won't be any air to breathe, especially when the walls start closin' in. I'll choke and then I'll panic, and then I'll run out without competin' at all."

"It's too bad you don't have Air magic like Rion," Coll said, now apparently sharing Ro's depression. "I can't imagine what your problem feels like, but being able to bring in extra air would probably help a *little*."

"Maybe it isn't extra *air* that Ro needs," Rion mused, suddenly getting an idea. "You seem to do all right in these coaches, Ro, and you also seem to have no problem in the bath house, which is definitely windowless. Have you ever tried to add more *moisture* to the air in enclosed places? Resin tends to dry the air of the places it encloses, I've noticed, so—"

"So maybe that's it!" Coll enthused, interrupting Rion with a gentle clap on the back. "Rion's come up with the answer, and now you can compete."

"I suppose it's worth a try," Ro said, not nearly as enthusiastic as Coll, but then he smiled. "Thanks for tryin' for me, Mardimil. Even if it doesn't work, it feels good knowin' there's somebody on *my* side."

"And if it does work, you're set," Coll said, also giving

Rion a smile. "That means we'll all be set . . . except for the girls! Damnation! Why didn't we talk about this last night? Now there's no way to tell them."

"Hopefully they're thinkin' the same about us," Ro soothed, but Rion felt that his worry had suddenly taken a new direction. "Jovvi doesn't let much get past her, so they ought to be just fine."

"Ought to be," Coll echoed, in no way an agreement. "Let's hope they are, and also agree to have group meetings every night. If we don't stick together, they'll get us for sure."

Ro made a sound that might have been support for the idea, but Rion made his response much more positive. If anything happened to Tamrissa and Jovvi because the men were too distracted by personal concerns to plan properly, Rion knew he would find it impossible to forgive himself. It would hardly be his fault alone, but it would certainly feel that way.

They lapsed back into silence after that, and this time Rion made no attempt to break it. His disappointment over the gold was rather deep, but he did still have some silver. It might be enough for a modest dinner, and possibly even enough for a small gift for Naran. He spent some time wondering what would really please her, and before he knew it the coach was slowing for his stop.

"Well, here's hoping we all find the proper way to fail," Rion said softly as they came to a full halt. "In any event, good luck, my friends."

The others fervently returned the sentiment, and then Rion was on the walk and the coach was continuing on. There was no reason to stand there and watch it, so Rion strode to the entrance to the practice area and inside. The number of people present had grown considerably, and when Rion paused to look around at them, Padril suddenly appeared to his left.

"I was sent to await your arrival, sir," Padril said at his most obsequious, even offering a bow. "The other participants have already arrived, and the competition will soon begin. Would you care to stop for a cup of tea, or go immediately to the competitions building?''

''I have no interest in tea,'' Rion answered, making no effort to pretend friendliness toward the man. ''Lead me to the building.''

Padril bowed again and began to move through the crowds, and Rion followed after taking a final glance around. For some reason it disturbed him that many of the people there were certainly of the nobility, although no one Rion had ever met. There had been no sign of his class peers until now, but the competition seemed to have brought them out. A low level event like this one promised to be shouldn't have held enough interest to do that, and for that reason Rion felt disturbed.

But there was nothing he might do about the matter even if it proved sinister, so he simply followed Padril into the large resin building. Most of the floor was open from wall to wall, but a heavy tan curtain had been draped across the back section of it. Others were entering at the same time to join one or another group already inside, but Padril ignored them all to lead Rion to a man standing alone near a group of seated people. Those in the seats wore master's bracelets like Rion's, and the man standing alone smiled as they approached.

''Sir, this is Adept Worlen, who is in charge of the competition,'' Padril said rather quickly, obviously eager to be finished and away. ''He will see to you now, and I wish you luck.''

With that the overfed fool scurried away, and Rion was glad to see the back of him. He knew precisely what sort of luck Padril wished him, and he returned the sentiment exactly.

''Well, Mardimil, glad to see you made it,'' Worlen said with that lower-nobility charm Rion usually found extremely grating. ''Come and take a seat with the other competitors, as we'll be beginning shortly.''

No other response than sitting was called for, so Rion made none. Worlen didn't seem to notice, though, as he was much too busy watching the spectators enter. Rion himself looked at his fellow competitors, one of whom was a lady, instead. She and two of the men seemed very much ill at ease, while the remaining four men appeared more bored than nervous. Something felt odd about that, but Rion didn't have the time to wonder what. He still hadn't decided just how strong he should be, and that had to be taken care of first.

A number of minutes went by while Rion thought, but the process was far from productive. He was finally forced to admit that he needed to know what was involved in the competition before any lucid decisions might be made, and that was when Worlen stood himself in front of the curtain and raised his arms.

"Friends, please give me your attention," he called. "We're about to begin, so please find your places."

There was a final amount of shuffling and throat-clearing and coughs, and then there was silence. Worlen smiled, obviously enjoying the audience's interest.

"This, as most of you know, is a low-level competition in Air magic," Worlen lectured. "We have eight participants today, and each of them will test their ability against the ticking of that clock."

The man pointed then, and Rion turned in his seat to see the back of what appeared to be a sporting event clock. Both human and horse races used the device, but it was positioned so that only the audience might see it, not the participants.

"What they will need to do is as follows," Worlen continued, pulling aside the tan curtain. "There are ten bell devices arranged around this area, some closer together, some farther apart, some high, some low. That small steel ball sitting up on the starting 'tower' toward the back must be maneuvered around to ring each of the ten bells, but the participant won't be permitted to simply grasp the ball in thickened air and move it that way. The ball has to be 'guided' into position to ring each bell—otherwise the bell simply won't ring. Here's a demonstration to show what I mean."

A young lady hurried over to where the small and shiny ball lay atop a wooden tower about five feet high. To the tower's left, rising perhaps an inch from the floor, was a small, flat-topped device. Rion watched as the young lady took the steel ball in her hand, then she walked to the flat-topped device, bent, and struck it with the ball. The device made a thick clicking sound, and then the young lady stood and tried to *drop* the ball on the device. Despite what should have been a straight-line approach, the ball veered off at the last moment and missed the device altogether.

"So you see," Worlen said as the girl retrieved the ball and returned it to its tower. "Only 'guiding' will let the ball ring the bell, and ten rings are required. Let's begin now with our first participant."

Rion had convinced himself that he would be first, and so found himself surprised when the young woman was approached. Worlen had to charm her out of her chair as she tried to protest, and then had to walk her back to a rather thick white line painted on the floor. The so-called Adept spoke softly to the girl for a moment, and then he left her to begin her effort.

The girl was extremely nervous, but when she opened herself to the power it became clear that she was far from untalented. Rion watched her form a cylinder of air then tip the ball into it, which brought the ball down at a steep angle to strike the flat-topped device at the bottom of the incline. This time a bell sounded, but then the girl just stood there, looking around at the other bell locations in bewilderment.

"That's all right, my dear, consider it part of the demonstration," Worlen said with a chuckle as he returned to her. "You've just discovered that you can't go from bell to bell in order, not when they're set at varying heights. You struck the lowest bell first, which means that you would have to grasp the ball in order to raise it again. Since grasping it is against the rules, you'll have to start again and choose your landings in advance."

The girl nodded miserably and began to study the various bell positions, obviously too upset to notice that the clock hadn't been started as yet. But Rion had noticed, and something else as well: all of the other participants were watching the girl with their eyes alone. Not one of them touched the least amount of power, which struck Rion as being extremely strange. No one had said they shouldn't, and no one had remarked on the fact that Rion *was* touching it. He was obviously missing something, but what that could be he had no idea.

This time the clock was started when the girl began the exercise again, and this time she completed it. Her guiding cylinders took the ball from bell to bell in wide sweeps, but always with the downward curve working to her benefit. When the final bell was struck the girl seemed ready to collapse, but Worlen was right there to take both her hands in his.

"Congratulations, my dear, that was wonderfully done," Worlen enthused while the audience applauded. Then his voice lowered as he spoke to her more privately, finally releasing her hands only after a full minute. When the girl turned she looked up at the clock, but her disappointed expression showed that there was no longer anything to see. Rion wasn't surprised at *that*, but the speed used in getting the girl out of the building was startling.

"She really did very well indeed," Rion heard, and looked back to see Worlen. The man had let someone else accompany the girl, and now had returned to the rest of them. "Those of you who follow her will really have to stretch yourselves, otherwise you'll find yourselves outdone by a woman. And the first one to stretch will be Rion Mardimil."

Rion was tired of having these people forget his title, but this wasn't the time to make an issue of it. There were more important things going on, not to mention questions to be asked.

"Just what *was* the young lady's time?" he put to Worlen as he stood, looking down at the man. "And why was she made to leave so quickly?"

"Her time—and your own—will be given to you once the competition is completely over," Worlen responded smoothly, looking toward the others as well while he spoke. "Until then you are to make no attempt to learn this information, and you're to leave the building as soon as you're told you may do so. Someone will be sent to the winner's residence with the good news and a purse containing his— or her—gold. Have I made myself clear?"

Rion thought it was quite clear that they were up to some trick, but rather than say so he simply smiled. The others nodded uneasily, and it was Worlen's turn to smile.

"Good," he said in approval. "Now, Mardimil, if you please. . . ."

His arm swept toward the thick white line, so Rion walked over to it and looked at the arrangement of bells. Each stood on its own small tower in different places around the rough circle, each tower a different height. When Rion opened himself fully to the power, he was able to detect a strange . . . *feeling* of sorts around each tower. He had no idea what caused the feeling, but suspected it was produced by whatever made the steel ball miss the bell without a guiding cylinder.

And just how strong that cylinder should be was another question. The girl had caused the air they were made of to be almost completely rigid, but that might not be necessary— or particularly desirable. Rion suddenly remembered he was supposed to lose the competition, and since he couldn't really argue the decision he decided he might as well get it over with.

The steel ball had been returned to the top of the highest tower, and lifting it a breath off its resting place showed Rion just how heavy it was. He could have constructed one single cylinder to curve around to each bell, and then would have only needed to nudge the ball on its way again after it rang a bell. But the girl had constructed her cylinder sections one at a time, so he had to do the same and more slowly. Happily, he had a general idea about how long it had taken her.

Rion heard the clock being set in motion the moment he nudged the steel ball from its first resting place, and that helped to remind him to take his time. He discovered that the steel ball needed constant attention even as it rolled along its guiding cylinder; added momentum somehow seemed to add to its already-considerable weight, and without strict watchfulness it could burst through the cylinder wall at the bottom of the slide, either before or after it rang the bell. Losing the ball midway would probably also have lost the competition most easily, but Rion's pride refused to allow him to do that. Going more slowly than the girl would have to suffice.

When the final bell rang, Worlen came over to shake Rion's hand with enthusiastic congratulations. The man also babbled meaningless questions at him, so by the time Rion was able to turn it was too late to see what the clock had read. Nevertheless he was certain his time had been longer than the girl's, so he made no argument when some stranger insisted Rion follow him outside.

The eating area wasn't completely emptied by any means, but it was mostly the usual low-born hangers-on who were left. The girl who had performed first sat alone at a table gulping tea, and Rion considered joining her. His thoughts must have been too obvious, though, as his guide spoke up before Rion made up his mind.

"Participants in a competition aren't permitted to fraternize," the man said in a very flat voice. "When ordinary people see casual mixing, they too often decide that there's been collusion and that the competition was fixed. The authority wants nothing of trouble of that sort, so you must take a table by yourself."

"Yes, by all means, let's be certain there's no collusion," Rion returned dryly, choosing a table and sitting. "You may ring for a servant for me, and then see about sending for my coach. As I'm supposed to return to the residence, that would be the first logical step in accomplishing it."

"A servant is already on his way," the man replied, gesturing with a nod in the direction of the kitchens. "Someone else is already arranging for your coach, so I'll simply stand here and keep you company."

Rion shrugged in an effort to show that he didn't care one

way or another, but after ordering tea and a sweet cake from the servant he sat back to think. The man standing so casually not far from the girl's table must be *her* guard, just as the man near Rion was his. And guards the two certainly were, although the reason for their presence was far from clear. What did they expect Rion to do to the girl, or she to him, that each of them had to be guarded . . . ?

And then Rion saw how foolish he was being. Unless he was mistaken, these people were afraid of what he and the girl would *say* to each other, not do. But that led to another question, such as what sort of thing the authority didn't want discussed. There were no real secrets to impart, after all. . . .

Or were there? What would he and the girl learn if they were to compare notes? The answer to that was impossible to guess, but just as impossible to dismiss. It was something he would have to discuss with the others when they all returned to the residence, but right now Rion had to fight to keep from turning his head to stare at the girl.

They would probably end up deciding they needed to speak to members of other residences, but how would they do that when they had no idea where those other residences were?

THIRTY-THREE

Lorand wished Ro luck when the man left the coach, and a few minutes later it was his own destination that the coach stopped at. In the interim Lorand had wondered why he felt so lighthearted, but the answer was rather obvious. This was the first time he would approach a test with the knowledge that he had to lose rather than win, and the freedom of that realization almost had him laughing and singing.

At least until he was out of the coach and walking toward the entrance to the practice area. He'd very much wanted to talk to Jovvi again, but telling her he meant to do his absolute best wouldn't have changed the reason she'd withdrawn from him, and now he couldn't even say *that* much honestly. A man who was determined to win in the end would be very unhappy over needing to lose at *any* time, but Lorand wasn't in the least unhappy. That said something about himself, and would have said even more to Jovvi.

So Lorand walked through the entrance feeling guilty for feeling relieved, a combination odd enough to be very uncomfortable. The sight of all the extra people in the eating area helped to distract him a bit from that, and Hestir's approach did the rest of the job.

"Good morning, Dom Coll, it's good to see you again," Hestir said with a great deal of obsequious respect, actually bowing. "Would you care to pause for a cup of tea before joining everyone else in the competitions building?"

"I don't need any tea this morning," Lorand answered shortly, and for the first time truthfully. He *didn't* need any stimulants or excuses designed to waste time, but even more he didn't intend to chat with Hestir as though the man had done nothing unusual yesterday.

"Then it's my honor to lead you to the building," Hestir said, looking and sounding as if "terror" would have been a better word than "honor." "Please follow me."

The man turned and walked off at a pace that should have been dignified, but the fact that Hestir would have preferred running was much too obvious. It turned his stride choppy, and Lorand followed a bit more easily while wondering why Hestir's terror didn't bother him. It had to be because of the man's actions, which proved that Lorand wasn't as forgiving as he'd considered himself. Being feared should have bothered Lorand, but in Hestir's case it didn't.

Much of the crowd was heading toward the building as well, and Lorand walked inside to find that it was already fairly well filled. Hestir led the way through the throng toward the back of the building, where a man stood in front of a curtain, talking to a woman who seemed to have just arrived. As Hestir approached, the man directed the woman to a seat among others who were just a few steps away, and then he turned to the newest newcomers.

"Sir, this is Adept Lidim," Hestir said over his shoulder to Lorand with a gesture toward the man. "Adept Lidim is in charge of the competition, and—"

"And this must be Dom Coll," Lidim interrupted with barely a glance for his brother Adept. "That's all, Hestir. You may return to your other duties now."

Hestir wasted no time in obeying that command, bowing briefly before disappearing back into the crowd. Lorand wanted to watch him go just to be sure he *was* gone, but Lidim put a distracting hand to his shoulder.

"Listen to me, now, Dom Coll," he said, sounding brisk and very efficient. "We'll be starting very soon, and you need to know how things will work. Participants will be called up one at a time to tackle the exercise, which I'll explain to the audience and yourselves once we begin. Each participant's performance will be timed, but you and the others aren't to know how anyone else has done. That goes for your own time as well, and once you've completed the exercise you'll leave the building and return to your residence. The winner will be notified—and given his or her gold—as soon as all the results are tabulated. Any questions?''

"One," Lorand responded, unsure about whether or not he liked this man's abrupt manner. "I can see the clock standing right there, in front of those seated people. What happens if I turn away from the exercise too soon and *do* manage to find out my own time? Will I be executed, or simply banished forever from the realm?''

"Very droll, Dom Coll," Lidim replied with the faintest smile Lorand had ever seen. "Neither thing will happen, of course, as I expect every contestant to be properly circumspect. Now, if you will take a seat with the others, I'll be able to begin."

It was no surprise when Lidim gestured to the people seated behind the clock, since they were the only ones in the room who were unable to see what the clock would show. Lorand gave up trying to rattle Lidim and shrugged his agreement, then made his way over to the last remaining empty chair. In addition to the woman and himself there were seven other people, but only one man looked as nervous as the woman. The rest seemed . . . almost bored, but Lorand decided he must be mistaken. Even he wasn't bored, and *he* meant to lose.

"Attention, everyone, give me your attention, please," Lidim called out almost as soon as Lorand was seated, holding up one hand as he spoke. "We're ready to begin, so if everyone will settle down, I'll explain what this exercise consists of."

The crowd shifted so that everyone faced the area Lidim stood in front of, and once silence settled over them Lidim gestured. Two men came forward to remove the curtain blocking sight of the area, and once they were gone Lidim gestured again, this time behind himself.

"The large cube that you see there is the main basis of

this contest,'' he said as a murmur went through the crowd.
''The cube is made up of various layers, each of which is a
different sort of material. The competitors will each be provided with a cube, the various components arranged in different orders, and their job will be to disassemble the thing
layer by layer until it's gone. They'll need to discern what
each of the materials is, of course, and remove the entire
layer at once. And now for our first competitor.''

The girl drew in her breath a bit sharply when Lidim put
out his hand to her, but she still rose and went to join him
where he stood. Lidim positioned her behind a thick white
line painted on the floor, spoke to her briefly and quietly,
then left her alone. The girl took a deep breath as she examined the four-foot-square cube where it rested on a low
platform, and then she began the exercise.

Lorand watched her take apart the first layer of the cube,
which was made of heavy leather. The leather came apart
and crumbled to nothing at all at once, and her effort impressed Lorand to the point of raising his brows. The girl
was *strong*, much more so than the so-called Adepts around
her, and Lorand couldn't help wondering what it would take
to be better than her. Not that he wasn't glad he wouldn't
have to be, of course. Trying to pull in enough power to top
someone else was a good way to destroy yourself.

The layer of leather had been painted a splotchy orange
and tan, making it look like some cheap and gaudy cloth.
The girl had had no more trouble telling that it was leather
than Lorand had, but she paused briefly before tackling the
next layer, which showed itself as green and purple diago-
nals. It turned out to be copper and quickly went the way of
the leather, but Lorand took careful note of the girl's pause.
No matter how quickly he figured out what something was,
he'd have to remember to pause just the way she was doing.

The girl went through half a dozen layers in the same way,
and every time she dissolved one the cube dropped a short
distance to the platform, showing that all six sides were being
taken apart at the same time. The cube also shrank, of course,
until it disappeared with the very last layer. A smattering of

polite applause broke out then, and Lidim walked over to the
girl and spoke to her softly again. Lorand noticed the way
she deliberately kept her back turned to the clock until someone came over to join her and Lidim, and then she followed
the newcomer away without hesitation.

"And now we're ready for our second competitor," Lidim
announced, gesturing to the man who had been sitting next
to the girl. "It's too bad for him that the young lady did
such a marvelous job, and now he's in the position of needing to do better or lose to her. But I'm sure he'll try his best,
and will be able to say that honestly if he does happen to
lose."

A ripple of amusement went through the crowd as the man
stood himself where the girl had been. Lorand saw the stiff-
ness of the man's stance and the way he'd squared his shoulders. Those two things, among others, speaking of how
determined the man was to keep himself from embarrassment. Lorand knew just how he felt, but also knew *he* would
not be standing like that. No matter how distasteful the matter would now be, Lorand was still determined to lose.

Lidim spoke to the man softly for a moment, then left him
alone to begin the exercise. A second cube had been brought
in and wrestled to the low platform, and its top layer was
orange and red and yellow, like a fire gone flat and crazy.
The man at the white line studied it a brief moment, then
dissolved the layer of camouflaged wood.

Lorand couldn't help but notice that the man's pause
wasn't to confirm an immediate impression, but to figure out
what the substance was in the first place. He was neither as
fast nor as strong as the girl had been, which worked out
fairly well for Lorand. Now no one should question the matter when *he* lost as well. The man was trying harder and
harder to match the girl, but his desperation showed that he
knew he wasn't making it.

From an outside point of view, everything went perfectly
well until the man was two layers from finishing the cube.
During the time the man worked, his increasing frustration
and distress said he knew the girl had done significantly bet-

ter. That awareness had worsened the man's performance rather than bettering it, of course, and finally it caused disaster.

After pausing to assess the fifth layer, the man attempted to dissolve it. Lorand knew it was a mild steel painted a lead gray, but the color must have misled the man trying to take it apart. The steel shuddered and pitted here and there, but didn't even come close to dissolving completely.

"No, that can't be right!" the man protested at once, his voice wild as he looked to where Lidim stood watching. "People are holding the layer together and blocking my work, trying to make me look like a fool! Stop the clock and make them pull back, and then I'll be able to continue."

"No one is blocking you, and stopping the clock in the middle of a performance isn't permitted," Lidim told him, loudly enough for everyone to hear. "You merely mistook the composition of the material, but if you hurry you can correct the error and possibly still win."

"Now *you're* trying to make me look like a fool!" the man shouted, clearly losing even more control of himself. "I can't win now, not when *she* didn't hesitate at all! Your trying to convince me otherwise says that *you're* the one behind the plot! Well, your friends may get away with it, but you certainly won't!"

And with that the man sent his ability toward Lidim, obviously intending to take the man apart the way he'd done with the first four layers of the cube. People shouted and screamed all over the room, but Lorand had already put his own talent between Lidim and the man who had cracked under the pressure. The attack had been a very strong possibility from the moment the man began to shout, and Lorand had been ready.

The man screamed when he couldn't reach the cringing so-called Adept with his ability, but he wasn't permitted to take more than a single step in Lidim's direction. Lorand became aware of a large number of people linked together who touched the man at the same time, and then the man collapsed. They'd probably touched the part of the man's mind controlling sleep, and had forced him into the state. It had taken a *very* large number of people with Earth magic, simply because the man *was* that strong. Not as strong as the girl or Lorand, but definitely a potential High.

And a potential High who was probably no longer in the running for any sort of position. The man's mind had collapsed under the pressure, and it would take the efforts of a very capable physician to see him well again. Lorand thought about that as people carried the man out, compassion for the poor pawn strong inside him. That could have happened to anyone put through what the testing authority considered "qualifying," and it was the man's bad luck that he had turned out to be the anyone.

"I'd like to thank whoever added their strength to mine in shielding me from that madman," Lidim suddenly announced, still looking shaken. "I didn't require the assistance, of course, but I'd like to personally thank whoever was thoughtful enough to try. Would that person please acknowledge the considerate gesture?"

Lorand joined everyone else in looking around curiously, not about to admit that he was the one who'd done it. Lidim had lied about not needing the help, since he hadn't tried to erect even a feeble barrier. Someone with decent strength would have been able to recognize Lorand's efforts as soon as he began to do the exercise, but with Lidim involved, Lorand had nothing to worry about.

"Well, my attempted benefactor is apparently too modest to claim his due in recognition," Lidim said after a moment or two of no one coming forward. "I'll simply repeat my thanks, then, and we'll continue with the competition."

People began to settle down again with that, and Lidim gestured to Lorand to show whose turn it was. Lorand stood and came forward while a new cube was brought in to take the place of the uncompleted one, and Lidim stepped closer.

"You aren't permitted to move over the white line, Dom Coll," he said rather quickly, obviously eager to return to where he'd been standing. "And I hope *you* understand that there's really no plot involved here. Just a competition, which anyone is free not to compete in.''

''Thank you, Adept Lidim, and I certainly do understand,'' Lorand assured him, trying to speak warmly. ''If I do happen to fail, it won't be anyone's fault but my own. You have my word that I won't be attacking you.''

Lidim simply nodded and hurried away, so it was time for Lorand to pay attention to the exercise. The top layer of his cube was a dark blue with larger and smaller green and white spots, making the thing look rotten with mold. The coloring didn't change the fact that the material was a hard baked clay, though, so Lorand set to work.

The exercise turned out to be a lot of fun, and Lorand had to constantly remind himself not to hurry to see what the next layer would be. He dissolved the cube one layer at a time, reflecting that they should have required that all the layers be done at once, and found himself surprised and a bit disappointed when the cube abruptly disappeared completely. There was scattered applause, and then Lidim was beside him again.

''Wonderfully done, Dom Coll, really marvelously done,'' Lidim said, sounding as if he simply repeated memorized words that he didn't mean at all. ''You'll be free to leave in a moment, and here's the man to accompany you now. If you like, you may have some tea while your coach is being sent for.''

Lorand nodded and followed the man who had come to lead him out, not even glancing at the clock which had probably already been reset. He was rather anxious to get back to the residence, but would definitely have that cup of tea while waiting for the coach. And at the same time he would try to figure out why he was no longer as happy as he'd been. His relief had disappeared somewhere, and Lorand couldn't quite tell what it had been replaced with.

There were a number of empty tables available in the eating area, and Lorand chose one after looking around. The girl who had performed first in the competition was nowhere in sight, which probably meant she'd already left. The man accompanying Lorand also looked around, then excused himself after saying he'd be back when Lorand's coach arrived. Lorand nodded absently at that, because the servant he'd rung for was approaching.

After ordering tea and anything in cake that happened to have a cream filling, Lorand sat back and began to try to figure out what was wrong with him. He'd just reached the point of understanding that the competition had been some kind of disappointment to him, when someone sat down at his table. Thinking it was Hestir, Lorand looked up ready to order the man away. The words floated off, however, when he saw that it *wasn't* Hestir.

"That's right, friend, don't say nothin'," the man cautioned, his large friend standing closer to Lorand than to him. "I told you I'd be back, an' now that yer done with that there competition thing, I'll have m'gold."

It took a moment for Lorand to make himself believe that the man Hat owed money to had had the nerve to show up *here*. He obviously had good enough connections to find out about the competition today, and also the fact that there would be a large number of strangers about. That had clearly let him saunter in and hang around with no one demanding to know what he was doing here, and now he thought he had Lorand cornered.

"The competition isn't over yet, so no gold has been paid out," Lorand told the man mildly, finally remembering that his name was Meerk. "But even if it had been paid, none of it would be going to you. I'm willing to lend *Hat* the money, and what he does with it is *his* business."

"Look, you, don't you try coddin' me around," Meerk growled, coming across even rougher and meaner in the daylight. "That friend a yours is gone, crawled into th' woodwork somewheres, an' I ain't got the time 'r patience t'dig 'im out. You come up with th' gold right now, 'r you'll get what I woulda give that little drunk. You get me?"

"Oh, I understand you perfectly," Lorand said, suddenly fighting to hold a flame-hot temper. He'd just remembered he wasn't going to be getting any gold, not after deliberately losing the competition, and he didn't believe the man. Hat hadn't simply disappeared, the lowlife could well have done something to him, and that meant Lorand had to do something of his own.

"And since I understand you perfectly," Lorand continued, "let's see if I can make *you* understand *me*. Do you have any real idea of what sort of competition is being held today?"

"Why would I give a damn?" the man began, gesturing aside the question impatiently. "All I wanna know is—"

The words disappeared as the man choked, his friend staggering and choking in the same way. They'd both gone pale, of course, and Lorand smiled faintly.

"This was—and still is—a competition for potential High practitioners in Earth magic," he said, leaning back at ease in his chair. "The reason you can't breathe very well is because I'm strangling you two from the inside, where the strain marks can't be seen. If I don't release the hold you'll die, and all the officials here will do is get rid of your bodies and say nothing. Do you doubt that?"

Meerk shook his head spasmodically while the other fell to his knees, no longer able to stand. They both thought they were dying, but even as angry as Lorand was, he couldn't kill two human beings in cold blood. At the moment he was simply blocking off some of their air, and the worst that could happen was that they'd faint. But he didn't want *them* to know that, not when he hadn't yet gotten what he wanted.

"You're smart to understand that I'm more important to these people than two useless troublemakers," Lorand went on with the same small, cold smile. "I'm really tempted to get you out of my life once and for all right now, but luckily for you I have a job of work I want you to do. If you're interested in taking that job of work, tell me now."

Both men immediately nodded even as they continued to gasp and choke, and Lorand let his smile widen just a little.

"That's really very wise of you," he commended them. "It saves everyone involved a good deal of trouble. . . . Now, what I want you to do is find my friend Hat, and then bring him to me at my residence. If you hurt him in any way I'll know it and return the favor, but if you bring him to me unharmed I'll see that you get your gold. Are you still willing?"

By then Lorand had released the men to breathe freely again, needing to see their reactions when they weren't in a state where they would promise anything to be released. The man who had been standing now sat on the ground with his head hanging low, but Meerk glared at Lorand even as he kept dragging in air. Lorand met his glare with an unblinking stare, and after a moment the man dropped his gaze.

"Always thought that kinda thing was bullshit," he muttered, wiping his mouth with the back of his hand. "People bein' that strong, I mean. I'm real strong in Earth magic m'self, but ain't no way I coulda broke loose. Okay, you got yerself a deal. We dig out th' little drunk an' bring 'im t'you, an' you pay us. In gold, not in th' end a our lives."

He was back to staring at Lorand by then, and what he'd said was true. He *was* fairly strong in Earth magic, possibly even an unpracticed Middle, but he hadn't had a chance against Lorand's strength. He did, however, know the trick of monitoring someone's bodily signs to see if they were telling the truth, and that's what he was doing right now with Lorand. That said Hat had really believed the fantasy tale he'd told, but Lorand had no time to think about that now.

"You'll be paid in gold, even if I have to borrow the gold," he said clearly, making no effort to block the man's monitoring. "Does that satisfy you?"

"Guess it'll hafta," Meerk grudged, pushing away from the table to stand. "Don't know why you'd want th' little drunk, but if he's still here in Gan Garee, he's yours."

The one on the ground struggled to his feet, and the two walked unsteadily away. It was still possible that they'd killed Hat and hidden his body, but Lorand had done some monitoring of his own. As far as he could tell, Meerk had been sincere in accepting the offer. If Hat was still in the city, they'd find him and bring him to the residence. After that. . . .

After that, Lorand had no idea what he would do. In the middle of everything going on, what in the world would he do with a man who had turned into a perpetual drunk living in a fantasy world? Lorand didn't know, but he'd damned well better think of something fast. . . .

THIRTY-FOUR

After Mardimil left the coach, Vallant spent the few minutes until his own stop rearranging his thinking. He'd been depressed over the near certainty that he would lose the competition even if he were able to force himself to stay inside the building, and now, suddenly, he was *supposed* to lose. Never in his entire life had he ever done other than his best, but now. . . .

But now the circumstances were entirely different. If those people really were trying to find out just how strong they in the residence were, self preservation demanded that he and the others manipulate the results of the competition. Just the way he hoped the women were doing. . . .

Vallant exchanged wishes of good luck with Coll and left the coach, determined to think about "the *women*" and not one woman in particular. He no longer had anything to do with Tamrissa, and even his sense of physical attraction had faded. Tamrissa Domon was just one of the people in his residence, and he meant to keep matters just like that. She'd given up trying to talk to him rather easily last night, which meant whatever she'd wanted couldn't have been very important.

Walking through the entrance into the outskirts of the eating area showed Vallant a lot more people than he'd seen until now. That had to mean they were there for the competition, or at least most of the newcomers were. The rest had attended for their own reasons, and Vallant would have been happier if he knew for certain what those reasons were.

"Good morning, Dom Ro," a quiet voice said, and Vallant turned his head to see that a subdued Wimand had come up to him. It felt odd not to have the man making some nasty comment about Holter, and doubly odd not to have Holter right there with him. But then Vallant realized something.

"Good mornin'," he returned coldly and distantly, pleased to see the way the smaller man flinched. "Are they close to bein' ready to begin?"

"Very close," Wimand acknowledged, gesturing toward the building behind the exercise cubicles. "If you'll follow me, I'll take you there."

"Does that mean everyone has already arrived?" Vallant asked next as he began to follow the man. "Everyone includin' Holter?"

"Dom Holter is expected at any moment," Wimand grudged over his shoulder after something of a pause, carefully making his way through the crowd. "It shouldn't be long at all, and then the competition can begin."

"I think I'll wait for Holter outside the buildin'," Vallant decided aloud, watching for Wimand's reaction. "I'm too used to goin' to these things right along with him to change now, especially since I don't have to."

A flash of frustration showed on what Vallant could see of Wimand's face, but when the man glanced over his shoulder again, the emotion was masked.

"You may certainly wait anywhere you like, sir," Wimand allowed in a neutral voice. "The tardiness may well count against you, but as I recall you don't think of that as a consideration. Would you care for a cup of tea while you wait?"

"No," Vallant replied. "No tea, and I'll take my chances with the tardiness business. I'm too used to bein' at sea to feel comfortable inside buildin's, so the less time I have to spend in one, the better I'll like it."

Wimand quickly covered up his look of startlement, but not before Vallant caught it—as he'd thought he might. He'd wondered if those people knew about his trouble with being indoors, so he'd given Wimand a chance to try forcing him inside early. The competition couldn't start until all the participants were there, and what he'd suddenly realized was that Holter *had* to be one of the participants. The man had achieved his masteries and gotten his bracelet, after all, so it stood to reason.

And Wimand *had* tried to force him inside early with talk about tardiness. The fool must have said the first thing to come to mind, since his reasoning was even weaker than usual. You can't be tardy for something that won't start until everyone involved is there, only for something that starts at a particular time even if people are absent.

Vallant followed Wimand's stiffened back with a grim smile, wondering if the man realized yet just how much he'd let slip. He'd obviously meant to weaken Vallant's chances in the competition by weakening *him*, which probably wasn't part of his superiors' planning. By doing that he'd told Vallant just how much the testing authority knew about him, and had been caught off balance when Vallant had readily admitted what everyone apparently thought of as a secret.

But when a secret is used against you, it's time to let it out of the bag. Vallant stepped onto the path leading to the white resin building, relieved to finally be out from among all those people. Crowds weren't as bad as being inside someplace small and airless, but that didn't make forcing a way through them pleasant. If Vallant had hoped to win the competition he would have already been disturbed, but as it was he felt no more than slight discomfort.

"If you need me, sir, I'll be just inside," Wimand said, pausing right in front of the building. "And please consider what I told you about being tardy. If you look bad, I do, too—so think of it as self-interest on my part."

And with that Wimand walked inside, his expression now a bit more satisfied. Obviously he thought he'd given Vallant something to worry about, but that just showed how ignorant the man really was. His patchwork of supposed self-interest hadn't done a thing to plug the leaks in the logic of his tardiness story, but Vallant didn't mind his thinking that it had. It should keep him quiet and out of Vallant's way for a while.

It was another lovely day, so Vallant stood there and enjoyed it until Holter arrived. A number of people had passed him on their way into the building, but one glance at his clothing told them he wasn't one of them. That was a use for the distinctive clothing Vallant and the others hadn't considered, and he made a mental note to mention it at the next full meeting. The bracelets they wore were only one way of telling their status, and knowing that might come in handy later.

Holter appeared in about twenty minutes, silently following the supposed Adept Podon. He looked even more unhappy than usual, but his eyes widened when he saw Vallant.

"Thought I'd wait until you got here," Vallant said with a smile when Holter reached him, completely ignoring Podon. "I sort of got used to goin' to these things with you, and just because they moved you out of the residence doesn't mean I have to stop. Not yet, anyway."

Holter matched his grin at that, silently sharing the knowledge that the testing authority would certainly try to drive a solid wedge between them. Those people didn't want any friendships that weren't their own idea, but that didn't mean Vallant had to go along with them.

"It's good seein' ya," Holter said quietly, offering his hand. "It's always good seein' a friend."

Vallant took the offered hand with a nod, confirming for Holter that he was, and would remain, the man's friend. Then Holter started into the building, and Vallant took a moment to brace himself hard before following.

From the very first step inside, Vallant had to maintain a

rigid hold on himself to keep from bolting. Not only was the large building windowless and lit by lanterns, its size was greatly diminished by the number of people in it. And that didn't take into account the large glass tank filled with water which stood in the very center of the building. The air disappeared into countless lungs, leaving none over for his own lungs, which in turn caused the round walls to begin moving inward.

Ignoring all that was one of the hardest things Vallant had ever done, and even as he followed Holter he wondered how long he'd be able to keep it up. Panic shoved at him, determined and desperate to take over, making Vallant know it would be impossible to hold it off permanently. As soon as his strength failed the panic would take charge, and nothing in the world would change that. If only there was something to distract him . . . !

That was when Mardimil's suggestion came back, the one about adding water to the air. Vallant had no hope at all that it would do any good, but his desperation needed *something* to focus on besides running. Podon now led the way for both Holter and himself, with Wimand nowhere to be seen. They were being taken to a man who stood to the right of the glass tank, beside a double row of seats which were all filled except for the two on the near end. If something was to be done, it had to be done *now*.

So Vallant reached to the water in the large glass tank, the only real source of water inside that resin building. The water evaporating from the tank into the air should have added sufficient moisture, but somehow the resin of the building seemed to be absorbing most of that. Vallant pulled the moisture into an invisible oval in front of his face, and oddly enough, some of his discomfort vanished. Not all of it by any means, but now when the panic broke through it would be considerably more comfortable.

"Dom Holter, Dom Ro, allow me t'present Adept Arkow," Podon said as they stopped near the heavy, supercilious-looking man who stood beside the seats. "Adept Arkow is runnin' this here competition, an' he'll tell ya whut ya need t'do.''

"That's all, Podon," Arkow said without looking at the man, distastefully gesturing a dirty, smelly animal away from his vicinity. Podon, looking crushed, left immediately, but Vallant felt no pity for him. Anyone who deliberately involved himself with these people from the testing authority deserved whatever he got.

"How odd that you two arrived together," Arkow continued, speaking mostly to Vallant. "I was under the impression that you no longer shared the same residence."

"I got here first, so I waited for Holter," Vallant said, glad of the distracting conversation. "Was there any reason why I shouldn't have?"

"No, no, of course not," Arkow hastily assured him, obviously unused to people who defended themselves by counterattacking. "But now we're ready to begin, so please take your seats with the others. You'll be called up one at a time, and as soon as you've completed your performance you'll be conducted out of the building. I'll explain what's expected of you in just a moment."

The man turned away from them then, giving them the chance to sit down the way they'd been told to do. Vallant couldn't help hesitating, though, since sitting down wasn't what he most wanted to do.

"Don't give 'em th' satisfaction," Holter said softly, and looking at him showed that the smaller man knew just what Vallant's problem was. "It won't take long, an' then you c'n leave *without* givin' 'em whut t'laugh at."

Vallant nodded his thanks for the support, and then forced himself to go to a chair and sit. Almost everyone else there seemed totally unconcerned, and for Vallant that was a usual state of affairs. Everyone unconcerned but him. . . .

"Please settle down, everyone," Arkow suddenly called out to the room at large, holding up his hands. "We're about to begin, so I'd appreciate some quiet."

He got the quiet he'd asked for rather quickly, with those standing on the far side of the glass tank trying to edge around to hear him. Those people didn't seem to matter, though, as Arkow ignored them.

"I'd like to welcome all our distinguished guests to this occasion," Arkow continued, his smile more of a smirk. "We may be holding only a low level competition, but it still has its points of interest. Our participants will be required to do two things, both of them in this tank of water behind me. The first of those things is being prepared for right now."

He turned to glance at the two men who had climbed to opposite sides of the tank, something long held carefully between them. It took Vallant a moment to see that the something was a miniature suspension bridge, and it was being settled into place above and in the water. It was made of hardened wood, the way most bridges of that sort were, and looked extremely realistic.

"The bridge, although rather small, is quite sturdy," Arkow went on after a short pause. "Our participants will first need to use the water in the tank to destroy a good portion of that bridge, and then they will impress us with their strength by parting the waters and holding them apart for a moment or two. Their performance will be timed, of course, and those times will be announced later. Right now, let's have our first participant."

Vallant fully expected to be made to wait until the very end; after all, since they knew about his problem they'd surely want to take advantage of it. Being gestured to first came as more of a shock than a surprise, but Vallant was too relieved to worry about it now. He rose quickly and went to stand beside Arkow, suddenly more distracted than he'd expected to be. He couldn't quite remember the level of strength he'd decided on in case he *was* chosen to go first, and he only had a minute to bring the memory back.

"Please bear in mind that you may not touch the glass of the tank," Arkow said softly when Vallant reached him. "Beyond that, you may use your ability freely. Good luck, and do try to do your best. Many of the people watching can do you a great deal of good if they're properly impressed."

With that he walked away, supposedly leaving Vallant something exciting to think about. But the beads of sweat on Vallant's brow should have told the man that Vallant himself was beyond being impressed by anything but the chance to leave. It would be enough of a fight not to work as quickly as he possibly could, something that *had* to be remembered.

Opening himself freely to the power helped more than Vallant thought it would. It seemed to . . . expand his surroundings in some way—not enough to match the outdoors, unfortunately, but enough to give him some breathing room. That literal turn of phrase let him direct his attention to the problem, which wasn't as difficult as Arkow had made it sound.

During a violent storm, normally peaceful bodies of water had been known to wash out even a new bridge. The added strength of wind and crashing momentum allowed the water to do that, and the power enabled Vallant to add even more strength than wind and momentum supplied. The water would be a sledgehammer driven by a giant, and the bridge would not be able to resist.

But it did have to be allowed to resist for a *short* while. Vallant hated the need, but since it couldn't be argued with it had to be endured. He used his ability to get the water roiling more and more violently, and then he began to send it against the bridge. It couldn't take *too* much longer than it should normally, so the whole thing needed careful balancing.

When one section of the bridge finally gave way under the assault, there was a smattering of applause. Vallant knew he didn't particularly deserve that applause, so he ignored it in favor of tackling the next part of the exercise. This was really the harder job, and it had to start with calming the waters. Once that was done he inserted the fingers of his talent slowly and carefully into the water, then began to part it.

Spreading out widely enough to keep the waters from escaping was the biggest problem, but remembering all that practice in weaving let him accomplish it. For some reason the woven patterns spread out more easily and widely, so that the water in the tank parted neatly and stayed that way. After that, all Vallant could do was wait. He'd been told he would have to hold it apart for a time, and this was where a serious worry came in.

He couldn't pretend to be exhausted when he wasn't, not when any other strong talent would know better, so he had to hold the waters apart until he was allowed to release them. But that meant he couldn't hedge on this part of his strength, which might tell the watchers whatever they wanted to know. Hopefully it would only give them part of the answer, or even more hopefully turn all their results meaningless—

"Thank you, Dom Ro, you may release the waters now," Arkow's voice came, bringing Vallant back from distraction. His thoughts had drifted off, but his talent had held steady on its own. "Here is the gentleman who will accompany you out, and thank you again for participating."

Vallant turned to see a stranger waiting for him. It was such a relief to know he could leave that he wouldn't have cared *who* waited for him, but he couldn't simply rush out. He'd gotten support when he needed it most, and now it was time to return the favor. So he turned to look at Holter, gave the man a thumbs-up sign to show his own support, and only then left that place of torture.

Somehow Vallant kept himself from running, so it was forever before he got outside. He moved a number of steps beyond the entrance and stood there with his eyes closed, simply breathing. His insides still shuddered and twisted with what he'd gone through, but for the moment it was all over with.

"Are you all right, sir?" a voice asked, and Vallant opened his eyes to see the man who was supposed to accompany him. "Do you want me to call someone?"

"Once we get to an empty table, you can call a servant if you like," Vallant answered, running a weary hand through his hair. "I'm badly in need of a cup of tea, and maybe even a bite to eat."

"I'll do that, sir," the man agreed, then began to lead him

away from the building again. "Someone is already sending for your coach, and once it gets here you'll be able to return to your residence for some rest."

Vallant was glad to hear that, and even more glad to sit down at an empty table. There were still quite a few people milling around the area, although most of the crowd had gone to watch the competition. Vallant ignored the milling few, ordered his tea and a sandwich when the servant hurried over, then sat back to regather his physical strength.

No more than two or three minutes could have passed in peace and quiet before there were suddenly people stopping at Vallant's table. His first urge was to ignore them, but curiosity got the better of him and he glanced their way—only to stop and stare disbelievingly.

"Well, it's certainly about time," Mirra huffed, obviously insulted. "Did you see that, Daddy? He deliberately refused to look at us even though he surely knew we were here."

"You can't really blame him, child," Mirra's father, Dom Agran, said with a scowl of disapproval. "The boy knows how dishonorably he's behavin', so he's ashamed. That shows there's *some* hope for 'im."

"If it were me, Mirra, I'd never speak to him again," Mirra's mother put in with a sniff. "It's his good fortune that you still want him, but you'll have to put in a terrible amount of work changin' him into somebody decent. Are you sure you want to *do* that much work?"

"Oh, it won't be all *that* hard, Momma," Mirra returned with a laugh, moving her body back and forth rather slowly while she stared at Vallant. "He's real easy to handle at home, and once I get him back there I'll never let him wander away again."

"Now, see here, young man," Dom Agran began after clearing his throat for attention. "My daughter agreed to give you her hand in marriage, and now refuses to retract that agreement even though you've apparently changed your mind. That means you *must* honor your commitment, otherwise I'll be forced to—"

"That's enough!" Vallant said sharply, cutting the fool

off in mid sentence. "I don't know who let you people in here, but now that I'm over my shock at your intrusion, I might as well give you some hard truths. I *never* asked your daughter to marry me, we simply discussed the possibility. If she told you anythin' else, she's lyin' the way she usually does."

"How dare you!" Dama Agran gasped in outrage, but Vallant refused to let her get started on an hourlong tirade.

"Be quiet!" he ordered sternly, getting to his feet. "If you people hadn't indulged the girl so shamelessly while she was growin' up, none of us would have this bother now. I've *never* been engaged to your daughter, I say, and wouldn't have her to wife even if she were the only available woman in the world. Now take yourselves out of here before I ask somebody to have you *put* out."

Mirra stood sulking furiously while her father sputtered and her mother babbled. They might have stayed like that forever if Vallant's "companion" hadn't stepped forward with a scowl of his own. Dom Agran ended his sputtering, and glared at Vallant.

"There's nothin' wrong with a man dedicatin' his life to givin' his wife and daughter everythin' their hearts desire," the man stated flatly. "And keepin' hurt from them, which you made me miss out on today. You haven't heard the last of this, Ro, my word on that."

With that he took the women's arms and marched away, making no effort to look back. Vallant had no idea how they'd found him, but he sat down again silently cursing whatever method they'd used. They'd made the expected scene, but at least it hadn't been at the residence, where it would have upset—

Vallant found himself cursing again, only this time out loud in a mutter. Didn't he have enough problems to face, without needing the addition of all these women? No other man he knew could walk away from girl after girl and still be haunted by them in one way or another. What had made *him* so lucky . . . ?

Well, lucky or not, he'd sworn off all of them. And he *would* keep his word, he *would*!

THIRTY-FIVE

I exchanged good wishes with Jovvi and left the coach, feeling myself slip into the oddest frame of mind. For the first time I was worried about not failing a test rather than not passing it, and even that worry was muted by the decision I struggled with. Jovvi had been absolutely right to say that I had to decide what I really wanted from Vallant Ro before I tried to do anything about his coldness. His own intentions had been perfectly clear, and the idea still frightened me. Were all men so eager to have something permanent? Why couldn't they be satisfied with more casual relationships?

I sighed over that unanswerable question as I walked through the entrance, then stopped short only a pair of steps later. There were so many people here today, a lot more than I'd expected for what was really a very unimportant competition. And so many of them held themselves the way nobles do. . . .

"So . . . you're here," a strangely tentative voice said, and I turned my head to see that Soonen had come up on my right. "Do you want to have a cup of tea first, or would you prefer to go straight to the competitions building?"

This was a Soonen I hadn't seen before, one who had lost most of her arrogance and attitude. Now she seemed rather sullenly frightened, as though she really wanted to sneer at me again but didn't dare. It looked like yesterday's struggle with her and Gerdol had brought me more benefits than just a master's bracelet.

"Thank you, but I don't need a cup of tea," I responded politely but with no warmth at all. I didn't like Soonen, and probably never would. "Let's simply go on into the building."

She nodded jerkily, as though wishing she might say something pointed, then just turned and began to lead the way through the crowd. I moved along right behind her, letting her larger size get us through more easily, and wished I hadn't lied about the tea. I did need to sit down over a cup for a while, to decide what I would do if I happened to be called to perform first. Without knowing what the others were capable of, how would I know what I should do?

And then a thought suddenly came, strangely enough from something my mother had taught my sisters and me. Once, when we were still rather young, my sisters and I had been laughing over how stupid one of the boys at school was. Our mother heard what we were saying, and immediately stepped in to correct us.

"Girls, I never want to hear you saying something like this again!" she'd lectured severely. "That boy happens to be the eldest son of a very wealthy man, but that's beside the point. What you *must* remember is that *no* man is to be belittled, as one day he may end up as your husband. Until that time you will show as little intelligence yourselves in the presence of others as you can possibly get away with. Just enough to show that you're capable of managing a large household, and not a smidgen more!"

Back then I'd hated the idea of needing to pretend to be a moron just to soothe the ego of some male idiot, but right now the idea was exactly what I needed. I would use just enough strength to do whatever was required, and show not a smidgen more. I laughed shortly to myself, realizing that this was the first time I'd really been able to *use* something my mother had taught me.

It didn't take long to reach the white resin building the competition would be held in, but a large group of people was there ahead of us and moving inside rather slowly. Soonen seemed to be trying to decide whether or not to push ahead through them, but I knew she'd decide not to. Their clothes and bearing showed them to be of the nobility, and she wasn't likely to chance offending one of them.

"We'll be able to get inside in a moment, after they clear out of the way," she said after her hesitation, making the decision I'd expected. Then she turned to look directly at me. "Some people get really nervous during a competition, with so many important people watching. They try to control the nervousness but can't, and end up embarrassing themselves."

"I can see how that could happen," I granted her in the most neutral tone I was able to produce, beginning to boil on the inside. Soonen was afraid to insult me directly again, so she'd taken the opportunity to try planting seeds of doubt. I'd remember what she'd said about being nervous and then *I'd* be nervous, and after that I'd lose the competition. Well, I had news for *her* . . . !

The furious anger which had been building inside me suddenly collapsed, having discovered there was nothing for it to stand on. Soonen had just provided me with the best reason in the world for not winning the competition, and I almost felt like hugging her. Almost. The anger she usually produced in me was gone, but I still didn't like her.

The group of people took their time moving through the doorway, but eventually it was our turn to go inside. I did feel somewhat uncomfortable with so many people around who would soon be watching *me*, but thinking of them all as enemies helped quite a bit. That new idea frightened me instead, but being frightened was something I'd long ago gotten used to.

The inside of the building was one large, open floor, with lanterns on the walls which made it brightly lit. In the center of the floor was what looked to be a wide half circle of a wall made of clear resin. In front of that half circle were forms covered over with sheets, six of them arranged into a circle of their own. To the right of that arrangement was a double row of chairs with people in most of them, and a man standing beside the chairs. He reminded me of Gerdol, although he wasn't, and Soonen led me right up to him.

"Dama Domon, this is Adept Odrin," she said, her tone cold rather than polite. "Adept Odrin is in charge of the competition, and will tell you what to do next."

"Thank you, Sooner, you may run along now," the heavy man said without looking at her, obviously unaware of the way he'd mispronounced her name. "I'm delighted that you're here, my dear, as the wait was—uh—definitely worth it."

Odrin had stumbled over his attempted compliment, and that seemed to be because of something bothering him. His hands looked to be trembling with nervousness, there were beads of sweat on his forehead, and he'd only been paying half attention to what he'd said to me.

"I'm glad to *be* here," I murmured in answer, wondering if he'd hear me. "Is there anything in particular that I'm supposed to do now?"

"You'll be taking a seat with the rest of our participants in a moment, but first there are one or two things I must tell you," he said, and I couldn't decide if he were answering me or simply speaking a prepared speech. "You'll each be summoned one at a time to perform, and once you're finished you'll be escorted outside. You may refresh yourself while your coach is being summoned, and then you will return to your residence. When the competition is over a winner will be declared, and if that's you, a messenger will be sent with the notification and your gold. If you haven't any questions, you may now take your seat."

I parted my lips to ask what the competition would entail, but he'd already started away from me. Obviously, asking any questions would be a waste of breath, so I went to the chairs and sat in one of the empty ones.

A couple of minutes later a girl came and took the last remaining empty chair, and I couldn't help noticing how annoyed she looked. Realizing that she'd probably just gone through the same thing that I had with Odrin, I sympathized. The man was a moron, but apparently a lot of people supported my mother's rule about male morons.

"My lords and ladies, if I might have your attention," I just barely heard someone say in much too low a voice. I turned my head to discover that the someone was Odrin, now standing directly in front of the exercise arrangement. He seemed to be trying to get things started, but no one more than four feet away could have heard him.

Luckily for him, though, a big man of obvious importance stood within that four foot distance, and he projected in a deep voice, "Quiet, all of you!" That brought almost immediate silence, so he turned his attention to Odrin and said, "Speak loudly enough for everyone to hear you, or we'll find someone who can."

"Yes, my lord, of course," Odrin quavered, then got a good enough hold on himself to raise his voice. "We're about to start the competition, my lords and ladies, so I must tell you what it's all about. The participants will perform one at a time, and what they must do is produce invisible fire."

He gestured behind himself at the people who were undraping the hidden forms as though that was supposed to explain what he meant, but everyone seemed to be as confused as I felt. I'd never heard of "invisible" fire, and the blank looks on the woman across from me as well as on the two men who sat beside us, said they'd never heard of it either.

"As you know, invisible fire is quite a simple doing," Odrin continued, clearly unaware of the fact that we knew no such thing. "Each participant will need to start his or her fire on the *inside* of the various targets, and the flames aren't to show through until the entire inside of the object is consumed. How quickly the outside flares and goes to ash will tell us how thoroughly the inside has been reduced, and that will all be part of the timing."

"If that's what he calls simple, I'd like to see *him* do it," the girl muttered, her words only loud enough to reach those of us closest to her. I couldn't hold back a smile of agreement, pleased to see that someone else had noticed how incompetent those so-called Adepts were. I would also have enjoyed talking to the girl, but Odrin was still speaking.

". . . and the results of the timing of each performance will be announced later," he went on. "Now, with everything explained, it's time to present our first competitor."

I expected him to look toward us then, but instead he pulled out a slip of paper and squinted down at it. Hope flared inside me that it would be first come, first perform, but apparently good luck still attempted to avoid me. Odrin nodded after checking his list, then looked in my direction.

"Please come here, my—uh—dear," he said, obviously unsure of how words made sentences now that he no longer had something memorized to recite. I sighed as I stood and went to him, wondering who had the job of calling him in out of the rain.

"You must remember not to cross the white line," he said when I reached him, then he had to look around for a moment before he located the line he wanted to point to. Since it was painted on the floor right in front of the exercise setup, it was somewhat difficult for him to find. "And please don't forget that you'll be escorted from the building once you're through. Good luck, and you may begin as soon as you're ready."

After that he hurried away, probably afraid that I'd confuse him with one of the targets. With Soonen or Gerdol I might not have hesitated, but with him it would be easier to wait until he tripped over his own feet and fell and broke his neck. It was a miracle it hadn't already happened. . . .

All of which did nothing to help me start that exercise. I'd had a light touch on the power ever since I'd gotten here, so I started things off by opening myself wide. I felt the usual tingle as the power flowed through me, and suddenly I knew just how the exercise was supposed to be handled. It related to that weaving we'd done, but this time a different pattern was called for.

My attention went then to the six targets, each of which was in the shape of a four-foot post set in a flat stand. Each post was also constructed of a different material, and starting from the thick wooden one on the left they progressed to heavy leather, pulped wood, burlap, cotton, and fine thread.

But all six posts were exactly the same height and diameter, which meant their insides were completely different.

With the power flowing through me I felt tempted to start with the fine thread, which would be the hardest to keep from burning on the outside when its insides caught. Happily, though, caution was too strongly ingrained in my nature for me to do something that foolish, so I overrode the urge and started with the wood. I also deliberately took my time, since I wasn't supposed to win. Just enough strength and speed to do the job, and not a smidgen more.

The inside of the wooden post burned fairly evenly, and when the flames reached the surface of it there was only a bit of a roar before the whole thing fell to ash. The leather post burned more . . . lumpily, I suppose you could say, and there was less of a roar when the flames burst through. The pulped wood was easy, as was the burlap, but the cotton almost got away from me. The near miss showed me that my flames were too hot for the more delicate materials, so when I finally reached the thread I was able to do it properly. The outside of the post blackened all over before crumbling into ash, and the exercise was completely over.

"Excellent, my—uh—dear, really excellent," Odrin complimented as he came back to stand next to me, once again sounding as though he recited a—mostly—prepared speech. "That will certainly set the mark for the rest of the participants, and now you may retire. That gentleman there will escort you."

The man he referred to was rather grim-faced and certainly no noble, but I didn't mind leaving with him in the least. Odrin was beginning to get on my nerves, and with the power still coursing through me I might not be able to keep from saying so. So I followed my escort through the polite applause of the audience, and by the time we got outside I'd closed off all but a faint touch of power. It had gotten to be a habit to keep a touch on that minimal amount, and I felt a good deal better doing it.

It wasn't hard to find an empty table even with the greater number of people still standing around, and after ringing a bell for a servant, my "escort" positioned himself behind me. For a moment it felt as though I were being guarded instead of accompanied and I was startled, but then I realized that the thought of being guarded was comforting rather than disturbing. With the smaller flow of power my self-confidence had shrunk down to its usual low ebb, and the idea of being protected felt good.

The servant came quickly to take my order for tea and anything wickedly fattening that might be available, and then I sat back to relax until it came. If that girl happened to come out before I left I intended to talk to her, and if the coach had to wait then it would wait. Getting in contact with someone else in my position seemed a very good idea, and I wanted to—

"Good morning," a voice said, breaking into my thoughts. "Your performance was delightful just now, so I thought I'd come out and tell you so."

The man who spoke looked familiar, but for a moment I couldn't place him. A bit on the heavy side but of average build and looks, he was an older man with an air of easy authority to him. My "escort" stepped out to the left of where I sat, apparently ready to order the man away, but one look from the newcomer immediately silenced my guard. His expression said he suddenly recognized the older man and therefore wasn't about to challenge him, and an instant later I recognized him myself—with a gasp. He was the one who'd been there for my very first test, the test I'd almost died taking. He'd been much too attentive for my liking, and he'd said—

"I promised that we'd meet again," he said with an odd smile when he realized that I'd recognized him, sitting down as though he'd been invited. "You've grown into your talent a bit since we last saw one another, which I really do find quite delightful. There are a large number of women in our aspect, but few of them have a really decent amount of strength."

"But how can they survive that initial test without it?" I found myself asking, a question probably caused by the residue of power in my system. "We all do go through the same testing procedure, don't we?"

"Certainly we do," he agreed, that odd smile broadening just a hair. "The system would hardly be fair otherwise. But I was saying how thoroughly attractive I find you—"

"You know, a very learned friend of mine made an interesting point," I rattled on, pretending I heard nothing of a personal nature in his conversation. "He said that the nobility *had* to keep the testing fair, otherwise they would be the ones who were penalized. Exempting your children from having to prove themselves makes for weaker heirs, who then breed and raise even weaker ones. If the testing wasn't fair, my friend said it would eventually be difficult to find anyone in the nobility as strong as a Middle. Don't you agree?"

By then I had my hands in my lap to keep them from trembling. The man hadn't taken his eyes from me, and I silently cursed myself for having reworded what Lorand had told us. The man whose name I didn't even know wasn't amused, and there was no telling what he would do because of what I'd said. His eyes frightened me most, the unblinking stare of them terrifying, and I really wished I'd never said anything at all. He continued to stare for a very long minute, and then that smile was back.

"Of course I agree with something that sensible," he said, the words smooth and unexcited. "The same point was made by noble scholars quite some time ago, but with one small addition. They pointed out that although it was quite unthinkable, the problem could be solved by bringing in . . . new blood, so to speak, every once in a while. By using such women to bear his children, a man would be assured of healthy and *strong* offspring. But such a practice would be barbaric, don't you agree? I mean, the woman would be nothing more than a slave and brood mare."

I felt the blood drain from my face, leaving me faintly lightheaded and very cold. His smile had widened again, and those eyes. . . .

"I really would recommend against trying anything like that," something inside me made me say, the something not caring that the words came out a whisper. "I've had one very bad experience with a man, and if the circumstance ever arises again, I won't be the only one having it. Now please go away."

"You really are delightful," he said, actually chuckling as he stood. "Once again it's been a pleasure to meet you, and I sincerely look forward to . . . third time lucky? Do enjoy the rest of your day."

He walked away, and once he was gone the servant appeared. I had the distinct impression that the servant had waited to keep from intruding, but I didn't ask. I needed to give all my attention to steadying my hands, so that I might drink the hot tea and melt the ice inside me. *Not another one*, was all my mind could say, over and over. *Please, not another one. And why can't I find this ridiculousness funny . . . ?*

THIRTY-SIX

"But Delin, why did we have to come all the way into the city?" Bron asked as they walked into the establishment, sounding to Delin as though he were thoroughly annoyed. "What's wrong with the dining parlors in our own neighborhood?"

"Come on, Bron, you can't tell me you're even too lazy to get tired of eating at the same dining parlors all the time." Delin made sure his tone was very amused and just a little mocking, and Bron reacted self-consciously—and predictably—with silence. "Besides," Delin continued then, "it's safer to discuss certain things among you and Kambil and myself in a place where we aren't that well known. Less chance of someone deliberately trying to listen in."

Bron couldn't argue that point, and Kambil only looked as if he wanted to. When Delin had insisted that they three go out to dinner together, he hadn't told the other two exactly *where* they were going. He'd said he wanted to discuss certain things about the group, and he hadn't been lying. They would indeed discuss the ideas which had come to him, but their presence in that particular dining parlor had another purpose entirely.

The host came forward with a bow to conduct them to a table, and Delin allowed himself a moment of pure enjoyment. This establishment was one of the best in Gan Garee, offering silver eating utensils, beautifully delicate plates and dishes, crystal glasses, chandeliers boasting over a hundred candles each, and superb chefs who prepared exactly what each patron wanted. It had been much too long since the last time he'd been here, and he'd earned the treat—even if he hadn't been warned to be here tonight.

The host sat them at a fine table, off to one side of the room for privacy, but in a location which commanded a view of everything going on. Delin had paid good silver for that, and expected it to be worth every copper. They each placed their orders for food and drink, and once the host had left, Kambil leaned back in his upholstered chair and pinned Delin with a stare.

"All right, now you can tell us why we're really here," Kambil said in that calm and unaccusing way that he had. "You've been . . . bubbling over with excited anticipation since you picked us up in your carriage, so I think it's time you told us the truth."

"The truth is that I was *advised* to be here tonight," Delin admitted readily enough with a grin. "I happened to . . . *meet* a lovely lady whose husband is an investigator for the Advisors, and she told me about an extraordinary find that they'd made. It has to do with something we're all tangentially involved with, and the investigators mean to move tonight—which is why we're here.''

"You're not referring to the competitions, I hope?" Bron asked, immediately looking frightened. "If you are, then I should have been notified at once. I *am* leader of our group, after all, so—"

"No, it has nothing to do with the competitions," Delin replied with a laugh, his mood so good that nothing conceivable would be able to spoil it. "But it does have to do with something related to them, only I won't say what. I have a very strong suspicion, and I don't want to spoil the surprise."

Bron began to protest again while Kambil simply looked thoughtful, but their arrival at the parlor had been nicely timed. All protests and stares broke off at the appearance of a new group of four arrivals, each of whom fairly exuded personal power when they strolled in. The ladies on their arms were all beauties, and Bron, who faced the door, suddenly gasped low.

"That's Rigos with them!" he hissed, as though the man would have been able to hear him if he'd spoken normally. "Does *he* have something to do with the reason why we're here? Never mind, I don't care even if he does. Just cancel my dinner order, because I've completely lost my appetite."

"Rigos does have something to do with all this, but I can't tell what," Kambil said, studying Delin narrowly. "I'm even less happy to see the man, Delin, so I'd appreciate the courtesy of a full explanation."

"You'll both understand everything in just a little while," Delin assured them, soaring high on the unmatchable feelings brought about by the exercise of power. "Right now you'll have to trust me, since I don't really *know* anything. As I said, I have my suspicions about what will happen. Let's wait and see if I'm right."

The other two weren't happy about being put off, but Delin had made it all too obvious that he had no intention of saying anything else. A servant came then with the drinks they'd ordered, and Delin sipped carefully at his glass of light wine. He wanted to be clearheaded when *it* happened, so as not to miss a single moment.

They were brought a large plate of nibbles to keep them occupied until their food was ready, and Delin chuckled to himself when Bron immediately began to stuff them in his mouth. The fool had already forgotten what he'd said about losing his appetite, which showed again what a marvelous "leader" he made. Delin could hardly wait until the time came for him to announce that *he* was the real leader of the group. What a pity that that would not be happening until they'd won the Throne. Announcing it sooner would just be too risky, since there was always the possibility of someone finding out—

"What the—" Bron exclaimed, pulling Delin out of reverie. He turned to see what Bron already had, which was the arrival of two important-looking men leading a small contingent of guardsmen. They ignored everyone as they strode to the table where Rigos and his friends sat, not really all that far from Delin's table.

"Lord Rigos Baril, you're to rise and come with us," one of the important-looking men said, making no effort to keep his voice down. "Right now, if you please."

"Are you insane?" Rigos demanded coldly with his usual frown. "I certainly don't please anything of the sort. If you have some matter to take up with me, you may make an appointment with my secretary—during the day. Now you can get out of here."

"Rigos Baril, we're here to arrest you for the murder of Lady Elfini Weil," the same man went on, drawing gasps from almost everyone in the room. "Either get out of that chair and surrender yourself to the guardsmen, or they'll come over and pull you out of it!"

The outraged anger in the man's voice was extremely obvious, and Delin was delighted to see that Rigos just sat there staring with his mouth open. Obviously he couldn't believe what he'd heard, but his dark skin had still paled quite a bit. The man who'd spoken waited no more than a moment, and then he gestured to the group of guardsmen.

"No, what are you doing?" Rigos babbled as three big guardsmen began to circle the table toward him, his eyes widening even more. "I had nothing to do with the murder, so you can't treat me like this. Go away, I say, go away!"

Rigos's voice rose to a shrill scream with the last of his words, a delicious delight Delin hadn't dared to hope for. The icy poise and superiority Rigos always showed was broken at last, shattered when the guardsmen combined their strength in Earth magic and forced him to his feet. The heavy chair was nearly knocked over as Rigos screamed and tried to struggle, and everyone in the room seemed to be holding their breath. The other people at his table were as white as the lace cloth under their glasses and hands, and the beautiful woman Rigos had escorted in sat with her face turned away. She'd disassociated herself from him completely, and wanted everyone to know it.

It took another few moments before Rigos was dragged from the parlor, as his struggles would have done credit to a much larger—and more talented—man. He'd clearly lost all control of himself, and his terrified screams showed he hadn't a scrap of dignity left. One of the guardsmen watching finally lost patience, and then Rigos was bent forward and gasping in pain. Delin had felt the guardsman use Earth magic to squeeze Rigos's stomach from the inside, an action equivalent to a hard blow in the same place. After that they were able to force him out of the room, while another guardsman followed while readying chains.

"They're going to chain him to the arrest wagon!" Bron exclaimed low as the last of the intruders disappeared outside. "But he's a noble, just like the rest of us! How do they dare to treat him like that?"

"I'd say the Advisors decided to make an object lesson out of this," Kambil offered, his soft voice almost lost amid the shocked exclamations of everyone in the room. "He may be a member of the nobility, but so was the woman he murdered. Rather than arrest him quietly they did it publicly, so that everyone will eventually get the message: *no* one kills one of us and gets away with it. I certainly don't like the man, but now I pity him."

"Well, I don't," Bron said, all but taking the words out of Delin's mouth. "I agree with the Advisors, that no one can be allowed to attack one of us and get away with it. Just think: he could have come after one of *us* next."

"That's very true," Delin agreed, silently ridiculing the fool. Rigos hadn't a trace of talent beyond the basic level almost everyone was capable of, and they were all Highs. Only a moron would think for even a moment that Rigos could have a chance against any of them, but that was the whole point. Bron *was* a moron, if that didn't insult the intelligence of morons in general.

"Is that what you brought us here to see, Delin?" Kambil asked, his voice now filled with curiosity. "If so, how much of it did you know about beforehand?"

"All I knew was that Rigos was in trouble and that it had something to do with the murder investigation," Delin responded with the sort of smooth lies he'd always been capable of. "I thought he'd done something where Homin was concerned, and would be taken to task for it where we could witness his embarrassment. I never expected anything like this, but I'd be lying if I said I didn't enjoy it."

Kambil grunted and sat back, showing clearly that he still didn't agree with the way things had been handled. But Kambil was a fool in his own right, much too soft and forgiving. Delin, on the other hand, was precisely ruthless enough to achieve greatness, which his handling of the matter had proved conclusively. He'd buried the murder weapon with Rigos's traces all over it, then he'd sent a note with common traces and badly constructed language to the chief investigator. The note had suggested more than ordinary bad blood between Rigos and that slut Elfini, and hadn't said a word about searching the grounds of Rigos's estate.

Which, of course, was one of the first things they did. Delin sipped his wine again as he remembered how he'd kept track of what was going on, using his longstanding acquaintance with the chief investigator's wife. Her fear over what had happened to Elfini kept her after her husband to learn about any progress, and he'd kept her informed just to keep her from badgering him to death. She'd passed on everything she learned to Delin, which was how he'd known to be in the parlor tonight. They'd discovered Rigos's plans for being at dinner publicly tonight, and so had waited until now to arrest him.

"I've just realized something," Bron said suddenly, drawing Delin's and Kambil's attention. "Now that Rigos is under arrest, we don't have to worry about him any longer. This calls for a celebration, and it's just too bad that Selendi and Homin aren't here as well."

Delin saw a look of pain flash briefly across Kambil's face, and he knew exactly how the larger man felt. Bron seemed to make a career of pointing out how stupid he was, and this time he'd done it in more ways than one.

"Don't you think someone might have gotten the least bit suspicious if all five of us were here?" Kambil asked him gently, undoubtedly wasting his time in an effort to teach Bron how to think. "They'd know then that we'd been warned what to expect, and might even have our own reasons for wanting Rigos out of the way. We don't need that sort of suspicion, but I'm still curious about Delin's other reason for taking us to dinner."

"Oh, yes, he did say he had another reason, didn't he?" Bron remembered aloud, shrugging off the rest of what Kambil had said. "But if it has something to do with the group, the others should definitely be here."

"It most certainly does have something to do with the group, but you're the only one besides Kambil and myself whom I trust to handle it properly," Delin told Bron smoothly. "I've gotten an idea about the reception at the palace we'll be attending, the one where we'll be studying the groups we'll be going up against. I'd like to suggest something else we might do."

"I hope you're going to say miss the thing entirely," Bron complained, sprawling back in his chair. "But I can't possibly be that lucky, so go ahead and make your suggestion."

"What I have in mind is this," Delin said, easily ignoring Bron's newest stupidity. "You and I will search out any attractive ladies involved and show them how wasteful it would be to harm us, and Homin and Selendi will just mix with the peasant groups, leading them to believe that we'll be easy to overcome. Kambil here, though, ought to be doing something else entirely—like trying to find at least one member of each group who can be counted on to be . . . reasonable."

"What do you mean by reasonable?" Kambil asked before Bron put the confusion in his eyes into words. "If you're expecting some of them to take gold to ruin their group's chances in the competition, I'm afraid you're deluding yourself. Even an imbecile would understand that they'd be throwing away the chance to become the Seated Blending, something they have to be allowed to continue believing in."

"Yes, I'm well aware of that," Delin said with a smile, having expected the protest. "If I'd been referring to bribery with gold, you'd be completely correct. But what I'm talking about is bribery of another kind, namely the chance to join *our* group. You'll approach anyone in each group but the Spirit magic member, and engage them in conversation. Depending on what aspect they are, you'll point to one of the rest of us as someone much too weak to do the group good. The rest of the group will be eager to replace that one with *anyone* strong enough, and if we're told about the weaknesses of the others of *their* group, the place will be theirs."

"And they can't help but know that a noble group has a better chance of winning than any peasant group," Bron chimed in, finally understanding the idea and obviously loving it. "They may all believe that they really do stand a chance, but on the inside they'll know better. It's a perfect arrangement, and ought to get us all the information we need. You won't have any trouble doing it, will you, Kambil?"

"Well, no, I shouldn't," Kambil said with a frown, joining Delin in letting Bron continue to think that *he* was their leader. "What bothers me is the ethics of the plan, or I should say the lack of ethics. We all really are extremely strong, so there's no reason to believe we can't do this on our own. Why do we have to lie to and swindle a bunch of unsuspecting innocents just to steal ourselves a slightly greater edge?''

"That's the whole point, man," Bron told him with exasperation, letting Delin sit back and simply observe. "Whatever edge we can get will be worth any effort, considering what winning means. All the rest of us are willing to do whatever it takes, and this part of it is yours. If you refuse, you *could* be wrecking our chances to be the most powerful people in the empire.''

Kambil rubbed his face with one hand, obviously trying to make a decision. Delin sat quietly and sipped his wine, wondering if he ought to kill Kambil if the man refused to cooperate. That would leave them badly in the lurch, so first he would have to find a replacement practitioner of Spirit magic. Who that would be he couldn't imagine, but there had to be *someone* among the nobility with the same strength and more ambition—

"All right, Bron, I have to admit that you're right," Kambil said suddenly after taking a deep breath. "If we mean to have the omelet, we can't refuse to break a few eggs. I'll do it, and get us what we need."

"Good man," Bron said in approval, reaching over to clap Kambil on the shoulder. "When we have what we deserve, you'll be glad you weren't unreasonable. Now let's discuss what we might want to know about the peasants."

Kambil began to list the things that anyone but Bron could have thought of by themselves, so Delin stopped listening and returned to his own thoughts. Kambil had saved his life by agreeing with the plan, and Delin meant to use every bit of the man's talent to get them what they needed. But he still neither liked nor trusted the man, so he'd have to start thinking about when it would be best to get rid of him. The sooner the better, of course, but now he had the time to look around for a proper replacement.

And to indulge in some pleasure by picturing what Rigos must be going through. Delin chuckled to himself as he enjoyed another sip of wine, wondering if they intended to use torture to get a confession, as they sometimes did with peasants. Monitoring bodily reactions wasn't always reliable, not with the way some people were able to control themselves, so torture was often used in cases where the judge involved thought it was appropriate. If they did torture Rigos, the man was really in for it. He would need to face men of no talent like himself—except for the enjoyment they found in their work. In order to stop the pain he would have to confess to doing something he was innocent of, a delicious turn of events to Delin's way of thinking.

And maybe, Delin decided as their food began to arrive, just maybe he would find a way to observe some of the torture. It would be an experience of ecstatic delight, so he'd have to see if it might be safely arranged. Yes, he thought as he laughed to himself, he *would* have to find a way....

THIRTY-SEVEN

Jovvi's mind tried to jump around frantically with fear and panic, brought about by having been kidnapped by Allestine and her two henchmen. Allestine would take her back to the courtesan residence in Rincammon, and there she would stay until she was too old to attract patrons any longer. Then Allestine would probably have her killed....

Putting a hand to her head and sitting back on her heels where she knelt on the floor of the coach let Jovvi begin to exert control over herself again. Just a short while ago she probably *would* have been lost after being kidnapped, but now. . . .

"Oh, do get up and take a proper seat, girl," Allestine said, beginning to be annoyed. "Nothing will be done to you until we get back to Rincammon, and then your behavior on the trip will help to decide just how stern the punishment is to be. What a pity you now have to abandon all your personal possessions, which you would not have had to do if you'd been reasonable."

Jovvi could feel how much Allestine enjoyed that idea, and the two men, Ark and Bar, were almost as amused. They all enjoyed forcing people to do as they wished, especially supposedly helpless people.

"You really are a fool, Allestine," Jovvi said after taking a deep breath to restore her balance almost to normal. "You refuse to learn or think, and that's not the way to survive in the world."

"Neither is having a fresh mouth," Allestine growled, not in the least amused. "Bar, show her what happens to girls with fresh mouths."

Ark sat beside Allestine to Jovvi's left, and Bar sat to the right, next to where Jovvi herself was to sit. At Allestine's order Bar smiled with pleasure and raised one big hand, ready to slap Jovvi hard across the face. It would hardly be the first time he'd done that to a girl, and not only at Allestine's orders. Bar enjoyed hitting women, and indulged in the practice every time he could.

But not this time. Jovvi reached to him with her ability, but not to soothe and calm the way she used to. She'd learned an incredible amount about her talent since she'd come to Gan Garee, and now she touched Bar with fear. It was the sort of fear he usually produced in the girls of the residence, and his face twisted as he forgot about hitting her and cringed back on the seat with a sob. It was difficult for a man his size to huddle into the farthest corner away from her, but that didn't stop Bar from trying.

Not a single sound came in warning beyond Allestine's very soft gasp, but Jovvi didn't need warning to know when

Ark decided to knock her out. The man might be somewhat behind her as she looked at Bar, but the emotions of his thoughts were a scream in the silence. Jovvi hadn't been foolish enough not to keep a watch on him, and he didn't even get to fully raise his fist. His reaching the intention was enough, and an instant later he cringed back in his seat just the way Bar was doing.

"Do you understand yet why I called you a fool?" Jovvi asked, turning her head to look at a very pale Allestine. "Almost anyone else would have realized that I haven't yet failed any of the tests given me, which are meant to qualify applicants for High practitioner positions. And if you think I've done the worst I possibly can to them, you're even more of a fool."

"B-b-but this is illegal," Allestine stuttered, her mind clanging with shock. "If I report what you've done, they'll arrest you and put you on trial!"

"I don't know which part of that to laugh at first," Jovvi returned, finding it hard to believe that Allestine could be— and was—serious. "It's perfectly all right for you to kidnap me into what would have become slavery, but illegal for me to defend myself? I'd be curious to see just how a guard officer would take that."

Allestine's face twisted as she remembered why she *couldn't* report Jovvi, but Jovvi gave her no chance to comment.

"The other point you keep forgetting is that the officials of this empire consider *me* a good deal more valuable than you. Their interest is such that they'd probably look the other way even if I killed you, which I really could do. Those tests and exercises they've put me through are an incredible education. Call to the coach driver and tell him to stop."

Allestine was now almost cloud white, and she trembled as she leaned out the far window to call to the coach driver. But she hadn't hesitated to obey, which told Jovvi she'd gotten through to the woman to a certain degree. But not to a significant degree, not as stubborn and really rather stupid as Allestine was, so Jovvi waited until the coach had stopped before she spoke again.

"It's not difficult to tell that you'll decide later I was bluffing," Jovvi said as she prepared to turn and get herself out of the coach. "You'll talk yourself into believing that I'd never be able to kill anyone, and then you'll decide to come after me again. To save myself that trouble, I've decided to do worse than kill you."

"Worse?" Allestine quavered, for the moment almost as frightened as her henchmen. "What do you m-mean by—worse?"

"I mean I intend to report this incident to the testing authority," Jovvi answered with a mirthless smile. "I'll tell them exactly who you and those two are, and where you come from. After that you should be too busy trying to avoid arrest to bother me, that and worrying about what they'll do if they catch you."

"I—I'll tell them you're lying," Allestine babbled, sickness throbbing inside her. "I'll say you begged me to take you back and I refused, so you're lying to get even with me. They'll believe me, men always believe me."

"My testing authority representative is a woman," Jovvi commented, reaching back to open the coach door. "And I'd really love to see you try a story like that. Any person, man or woman, who believed I'd rather be a small-town courtesan than a High practitioner for the empire would *have* to be seen to be believed. It's too bad it has to end this way, Allestine, but try to remember that *I* didn't come after *you*."

"I'll leave!" Allestine blurted as Jovvi fought with her skirts while she climbed out of the coach from the floor. "I'll return to Rincammon, and you'll never see or hear from me again!"

"You expect me to give you a third chance at me?" Jovvi asked with a sound of scorn once she stood solidly on the ground. "Sorry, Allestine, but you'd better forget all about that, and I do mean *all* about it. As far as you're concerned, it just isn't possible. All right, driver, you can continue on now."

Jovvi slammed the coach door closed on Allestine's sudden stunned look, and then the coach began to move again. Once it was out of the way, she glanced around to see that she stood on the private road that led to the Fire magic and Spirit magic practice areas. But she was beyond both areas, almost to the road leading out of there. She also held onto Ark and Bar, finding it a bit harder than it had been for some reason, but that wasn't going to stop her. She meant to hold onto them until their coach went completely beyond her range. After that she would see about walking somewhere to get help.

It was possible for Jovvi to follow the coach with her talent for quite a distance, all the while holding the two men in their private worlds of fear. There was also something else involved, but it wasn't possible to resolve just what. Once she released the men it would take a short while for them to return to normal, but not being drugged like the test subjects meant they *would* return to normal. The farther away they were when that happened the better, so Jovvi held on as long as she could. When she finally *had* to let go, she was also finally able to tremble with her own reaction.

"So close," she whispered as she hugged herself against the inner chill. "They came so close to getting me back . . . and then the authorities would have been after *me* for trying to run away from the testing procedure. But I can't report her the way I threatened to do, so what *can* I do?"

Trying to find an answer to that made her head swim, so much so that the coach had reached her before she even knew it was coming. Stabbing fear made Jovvi look around wildly for someplace to run, but then she heard a blessedly familiar voice.

"Jovvi, are you all right?" Tamrissa called, then she continued, "Driver, please help her! She looks like she's about to faint!"

Jovvi did feel as though she were about to lose consciousness, probably because she'd pushed herself too far. The competition had been very tiring, and then the struggle with Allestine and the two men. . . . When the coach driver appeared next to her and lent a supporting arm, Jovvi leaned against him gratefully. She also needed his help to climb into the coach, and once she was on a seat it was Tamma who was there with a supporting arm.

"Please get us back to the residence as quickly as possible," Jovvi heard Tamma say to the driver. A moment after the door was slammed shut they were moving again, and a long moment after that Jovvi's head began to clear a little.

"Your color's beginning to come back," Tamma said then, touching Jovvi's cheek lightly and briefly. "Can you tell me yet what happened? When the coach reached me you weren't in it, and the driver said he'd been told that you'd taken a ride with someone else."

"I wasn't the one doing the taking," Jovvi managed to say, her head against the seat back. "Allestine and her bullies were waiting for me, and they tried to kidnap me. I had to use my ability to get away from them, and the effort really drained me. That means I'll be fine, so you can stop worrying."

"That means you'll be fine for how long?" Tamma demanded, obviously completely outraged. "This time you have to tell someone about that woman, and if you don't, I will."

"Tamma, please," Jovvi said with a sigh. "I'm really too exhausted to argue, but even though I told Allestine I meant to report her attempt, I simply can't do it. And I don't want *you* to do it either."

"But why not?" Tamma asked, clearly bewildered. "Are you trying to prove or disprove that old saying about the third time being the charm? You can't think you still owe her something, not after the way she's been trying to make you her slave."

"It has nothing to do with owing anything to Allestine," Jovvi said, wishing she had a cup of hot tea to sip from. "If I hadn't been beautiful she never would have taken me into the residence, and during my time there I more than repaid her investment in time and money. It's just that I . . . can't bear to report *anyone* to the guard . . . not after what I saw growing up.''

Jovvi had wondered if Tamma would understand without a detailed explanation, as something like that was beyond her at the moment. Happily Tamma remained silent for a moment, then she shook her head.

''I can't say I understand that attitude, but most people can't understand mine either,'' she said with a sigh. ''Someday we'll have to talk about it, but right now there are other things to discuss. You said you told Allestine you *would* report her, so maybe she'll believe you and go home. I don't particularly care *how* we get rid of her, as long as we do see the last of her.''

''That would work if Allestine were smarter,'' Jovvi said with a small headshake. ''But Allestine is a creature of emotions rather than rational thought, and as soon as she stops being frightened she'll become furious. No one has dared to refuse her slightest whim for many years, and if she goes back to the residence without me, all the girls will know I got away from her. That will give them ideas she doesn't dare let them entertain, and will also make her look foolish. No, she'll never leave here without me, and she certainly won't let herself remember what I can do.''

''So she's almost guaranteed to come after you again,'' Tamma said, sounding defeated. ''And if she tried it again at the house, she may decide again to add *me* in as well. What a pity if she does decide on that. I'll just have to tell her to get in line.''

''There's more behind that comment than just the urge to make a comment,'' Jovvi said with a frown, knowing the truth of that even with exhaustion waiting to take her. ''What happened, Tamma? And how did the competition go? With Allestine and her nonsense, I forgot all about it.''

''The competition itself went fine,'' Tamma said with a shrug, now very taken with watching her fingers twist about each other in her lap. ''I decided that my best chance would be to be only strong enough to complete the exercise, so I did but certainly lost the competition. They threw me out after my turn was done, so I don't know how anyone else did.''

"They don't want any of us knowing," Jovvi said, wishing she had the strength to send comfort to Tamma. "I thought of the same thing to do, so that makes two of us who didn't win. But you still haven't told me what else happened."

"After my performance I had a . . . visitor," Tamma admitted with strong hesitation. "There was a man present when I passed that very first test, and he said something about seeing me again. I'd forgotten all about it—until he sat down at my table just a little while ago. I tried to tell him to go away, but he isn't willing to do that as permanently as I would like. He . . . said something quite abominable, and then he strolled off smiling. I'm beginning to think I have a sign on me that invites men like him to come after me."

"We'll have to discuss the matter once I've rested," Jovvi said, reaching over to still Tamma's trembling hands. "In a manner of speaking you *are* wearing a sign, and we'll have to think of a way for you to remove it. Right now, though. . . ."

"You need to rest," Tamma finished for her, a strong pulse of self-annoyance coming from the girl. "You go through kidnap and escape, and here am I bothering you with *my* piddling problems. The last time I was the one who fell asleep, so now it's your turn. Just close your eyes, and I'll see us safely back to the house."

Jovvi smiled to thank her, then just *had* to close her eyes. There were so many things to do—and talk about—and worry about—but they'd all have to wait until later. . . .

THIRTY-EIGHT

Lorand was pleased with how quickly the coach came, and he simply sat back and relaxed until they reached the place where Ro was waiting. The big ex-sea captain climbed in quickly, his expression showing some sort of annoyance.

"About time this thing got here," he muttered as he settled into his seat. "I was just finishin' my third cup of tea when they told me it was approachin'."

"I barely had time to finish my first cup," Lorand replied with a frown, then he suddenly understood. "I'll bet they wanted to let the coach pick us up in order again, so they had to wait for me to finish performing. I was third, and there was a delay when the second participant had to be forceably put to sleep and carried out. He cracked under the pressure when he made a mistake, and tried to attack the Adept running things."

"You should have sent him over to *my* practice area," Ro came back, but with a bit less annoyance. "I could have found him a few people I would have enjoyed seein' attacked. So you went third. I was up first, happily, but I think I managed to lose anyway."

"If they know about your problem and we're right about this having been an evaluation, it makes sense that they called you first," Lorand commented. "They'd want to give you every break in order to judge just how strong you really are, just in case you find a way to use that strength in the more important competitions.''

''They do know about me, so you're probably right,'' Ro agreed, now looking thoughtful. ''My former Adept guide tried to get me inside too early, but I had the feelin' he was actin' on his own and tryin' to be vindictive. When I told him straight out that I was uncomfortable inside buildin's, he looked like somebody broke his toy.''

''What a shame,'' Lorand said with a grin, then joined Ro in interrupting the conversation while they picked up Mardimil. Rion looked his usual calm and easy self, and the first thing he did once he settled himself to Lorand's right was to turn to Ro.

''Were you able to complete the competition?'' he asked, clearly seriously concerned. ''Was my suggestion of any use to you?''

''Yes and yes,'' Ro answered with a smile. ''I completed the exercise, but mainly because addin' moisture to the air around my face made me more comfortable. But I'm fairly sure I failed, so my tryin' real hard didn't help.''

''Yes, alas, I'm certain I failed as well,'' Mardimil agreed with an easy grin, now apparently relieved. ''A young lady was called up before me, and despite my earnest efforts I believe she outdid me. And what fate did *you* find, Coll?''

''Sadly, the same,'' Lorand replied, but not as lightheartedly as he'd wanted to. ''As I was telling Ro, there were two people called up ahead of me. The girl did fine, but the man following her cracked under the strain. I could almost hear him thinking about how foolish he would feel if she bested him, and when it became certain that that would happen, he broke.''

''The man running our competition suggested there would be shame and worse for any male contestant whose efforts fell below those of the young lady, but I couldn't quite see that,'' Mardimil commented, his expression now puzzled. ''If the girl happened to be stronger, how would that become *my* fault?''

''It would be your fault because men are supposed to be stronger than women,'' Lorand explained, unsurprised that

Mardimil had missed the point. "I'm sure your mother never taught you that, but it's something every other man is taught. We're supposed to be stronger than women, and if we aren't then the fault is ours."

"You sound as if you wanted to outdo that girl," Ro put in thoughtfully, gazing at Lorand. "Was that your own idea, or did the one runnin' your competition do some 'suggestin' ' with you also?"

"Well, now that you mention it . . ." Lorand responded slowly, his frown back. "Lidim did make something of a point of it, which surely helped to drive that man over the edge. You think he did it on purpose?"

"It seems more likely than not," Ro decided, looking at Mardimil as well. "Both of you were told the same thing, and it happens to be somethin' that most men respond to. Bein' bested by a woman is shameful, and not the same as bein' bested by another man. A man has to be real sure of himself not to respond to that."

"Or determined to overlook it," Lorand said with a nod. "Or, as in Mardimil's case, not knowing about it in the first place. That seems to be another point in favor of our guess-work, that this 'competition' was really an evaluation. I wonder why the ploy didn't work with all the contestants."

"What do you mean?" Ro asked, joining Mardimil in looking at him. "What makes you think it didn't work with everybody?"

"I believe Coll is referring to something I noticed myself," Mardimil supplied when Lorand hesitated in trying to put a passing feeling into words. "Only the young lady and myself and two other men seemed actually interested in what they were about to do. The others appeared to be downright bored, which struck me as being odd."

"That's exactly right," Lorand confirmed. "Only the girl and the man following her—and me, of course—seemed to be there to compete. The others could have been waiting for a long-delayed ride home."

"Believe it or not, I think I noticed the same thing," Ro added, his gaze turned inward. "I was too busy fightin' the need to leave to really be aware of it, but most of those people in the seats were just markin' time. I wonder if that means they weren't goin' to be competin' at all?''

"Of course!" Lorand exclaimed, suddenly seeing the truth. "They were put there to pretend there were a *lot* of competitors, so the officials would have an excuse not to announce the results while we real competitors were still there. I can't imagine why they would want to do that, but I'm willing to bet that that was their aim."

"It might have something to do with the fact that they don't want us talking to or associating with any other competitor," Mardimil put in, not the least doubt in his voice. "I found that out when I tried to join the young lady who performed before me. My guard refused to let me go near her, claiming that 'fraternization' could 'compromise the integrity' of the competition. I took that to mean they're afraid we'll learn things from each other, and although I can't imagine what those things could be—or how we would locate other residences—it seems to be something we ought to consider trying to accomplish."

"I agree," Ro said as Lorand nodded. "I don't yet know how we'll do it either, but we ought to be thinkin' about it. The more we know that they don't want us to, the better off we'll be."

That had been obvious for quite some time, and Lorand remembered his earlier thoughts about a nightly meeting with the women. The idea seemed even more important now, as they might have seen or figured out something to satisfy all their unanswered questions. Lorand was about to mention the point, but a glance at Mardimil and Ro showed the two men sunk into thought. It made no sense to disturb them now, so Lorand decided to wait until they'd returned to the residence, and found thoughts of his own to occupy him.

The most compelling thing on his mind was the odd way he'd begun to feel. He'd responded to that deliberate attempt to make him try his hardest without even noticing it, which wasn't at all like him. Only men who were unsure of themselves would have responded, Ro had suggested, but Lorand had never before been unsure of himself. Unsure about using too much of the power and burning out, yes, but not unsure about *himself*.

So why had he responded to the point of being unhappy about needing to lose the competition? Lorand shifted on the coach seat, trying to understand the attitude that still hadn't left him. He'd started out being well and truly relieved that he wasn't going to *have* to win the competition, and had ended up disappointed that he couldn't do more. It was crazy to feel that way when worse than death awaited the careless practitioner, so what was wrong with him?

The question remained unanswered even when the coach pulled up at the residence, so Lorand dropped it with a sigh and joined the others in getting out. Maybe later, once he'd taken Mardimil's place with Tamrissa, he'd ask *her* for an opinion. He would have preferred to ask Jovvi, but still couldn't bring himself to face her.

The servant letting them in provided the information that the ladies had already returned, but both had gone to rest after having asked not to be disturbed. That left very little to do, since Mardimil went to his bedchamber and Ro announced he meant to use the bath house. Lorand took himself to the library instead, and spent the time until lunch reading a popular history about the empire.

Only Mardimil and Ro came to the dining room for lunch, and when they questioned Warla they found out what the ladies were doing. Jovvi, apparently, was sound asleep, having left word that she needed rest more than food. Tamrissa had asked for a tray in her apartment, also a bit too weary for a formal meal. Lorand and Mardimil discussed what might have happened to make the ladies so tired, but naturally could come up with nothing but guesswork. They'd have to wait until later to find out the truth, but Ro didn't seem as interested. He made no comment at all, and simply concentrated on his food.

After lunch Lorand decided to use the bathing house himself, but discovered he wasn't in the mood to soak. So he went back to his bedchamber and dressed again, then returned to the library. But not to read the same book. All that raving about how wonderful and perfect the empire was had begun to turn his stomach. If the empire was all that wonderful, it would hardly contain so many unhappy people.

Lorand was still trying to decide what to read when a knock came at the door. A moment later the door opened, and when he turned away from the shelves it was to see a servant.

"Excuse me, sir, but there's someone here to see you," the servant announced. "Shall I show him in here?"

"Yes, please," Lorand agreed, surprised that Meerk was back so soon. It couldn't be anyone *but* the tough, although he obviously didn't have Hat with him. The servant had said "show *him* in," not "show *them* in." Lorand hoped it wasn't bad news, but braced himself just in case. And then the servant returned leading the visitor, and Lorand was doubly glad that he'd braced himself.

"A representative from the testing authority," the servant announced, stepping aside to let the stranger in. Lorand simply stared, vastly surprised and instantly wondering if he weren't about to be ejected from the competitions after all.

"Dom Coll, congratulations," the man said with a smile as soon as he saw Lorand. "I've been sent to tell you that you're the winner of our competition, and to deliver your prize—in gold, of course."

The man held out a pouch Lorand had never expected to see, but all the lucky winner could do was stand and stare. He'd won? He'd *won*? How could he have made such a terrible mistake . . . ?

THIRTY-NINE

Vallant sat in a chair in his bedchamber, sprawled out in what should have been a comfortable posture but wasn't. He'd bathed and gotten into clean clothes, rested and had lunch, but some vague discomfort continued to disturb him. Part of it was the fact that the women hadn't come down to lunch, but that was more of a general concern. Apparently they'd had a much harder time of it than the men, but they'd also obviously survived without having been given any real harm.

So Vallant's discomfort had another source, and his thoughts were skittering around and making him feel as though he ought to be off and doing things. It finally occurred to him that if he were off and doing things he would have no time to think, so that was what his mind was trying to avoid: thinking, and obviously about some particular subject. One that he didn't *want* to think about. . . .

And just that easily the barriers fell, immediately making him wish they hadn't. Many people had envied Vallant's family life while he grew up, and there was no doubt that it had been incredibly happy. But once a boy becomes a man his interest turns toward making a family of his own, and in that Vallant had failed miserably. Mirra, the first woman he'd thought about sharing his life with, had proved to be in love with her own desires rather than him, and was more manipulative than he'd ever thought was possible.

So he'd left Mirra after swearing off women completely, and the next thing he'd known he was chasing after Tamrissa. He'd really believed it was possible to make a wonderful life with her, and foolishly, in his fantasies, still did. But Tamrissa Domon had made it perfectly clear that she wanted nothing to do with him, going well out of her way to prove the point. His attentions were unwanted, and he'd made a big hairy beast of himself in trying to press them.

The pain of those two experiences was more than Vallant would have been able to put into words, as they clearly showed there was something terribly wrong with him. He'd been seriously attracted to two women, both times the attraction had turned to disaster, and he'd never felt so lonely in his entire life. Or so like a loser. He was used to winning in everything, but that everything apparently failed to cover the most important aspect of his life.

Vallant closed his eyes, mentally searching for the will to try again, but for the first time in his life it wasn't there. He had no interest at all in trying again, not when associating with women brought such pain. And not when the picture of himself that he now carried in his mind was so distorted. A vain, shallow woman was determined to drag him into marriage, and a gentle woman with beauty both inside and out wanted nothing to do with him. What that said about *him* was an aching throb in his insides, and enough to make him deeply ashamed.

It was really too bad that grown men weren't supposed to cry, Vallant thought, his eyes still tightly closed. He hadn't even done much crying as a small boy. But now he felt a real need to cry, to sob his heart out the way women did when they found themselves helpless in some situation. Vallant was now just as helpless, but tears, like happiness, weren't permitted him.

Deep depression has a way of overcoming restlessness, so Vallant just sat in the chair and brooded. Even accomplishing something in the competitions had lost its urgency, especially now that they were all deliberately trying to lose. There seemed to be nothing left in his life to strive for, and he couldn't even care about *that*. What would the testing authority do, he wondered, if he simply walked away and went back to the sea? If they tried to reclaim him, he could always threaten to expose their slimy little arrangement. If he covered himself before making the threat, he might even be able to—

A knock at the door interrupted Vallant's thoughts, and when he called out his permission to enter, a servant opened the door.

"There's someone here askin' t' see ya, sor," the girl said shyly. "He says he's frum th' testin' a'thority."

Vallant frowned at hearing that, switching to unease from the dread he'd felt when he'd thought Mirra and her parents were back. That would have been bad enough, but this. . . . What could the testing authority possibly want? To tell him he was no longer part of the program? That would fit all too well with everything else which had happened. . . .

"I'll come down," Vallant said to the serving girl as he rose to his feet. No sense in hearing the bad news in private, not when his absence would be perfectly clear come dinnertime. And the others had been so sure that they were all going to be put into a challenging Blending.

When Vallant followed the girl downstairs, he found two men waiting rather than one. His first thought was that they were together, a precaution against the possibility of his arguing about being thrown out. But by the time he reached the bottom of the stairs he'd realized that the two men didn't know each other, and then the serving girl confirmed his speculation.

"That's 'im on th' right, sor," she said, pointing to the man before dropping a quick curtsey and hurrying off. The man on the right had noticed the exchange as well, and now came forward with a smile.

"Dom Ro?" he asked, and when Vallant nodded, the man's smile grew even broader. "Congratulations, sir! I've been sent to tell you that you've won your first competition. Here's your prize, which I'm sure you were expecting."

Vallant would have expected having the ceiling fall on him or a herd of wild horses trample him. Being told he'd won the competition and then being handed gold was a stunning shock, but his hand went out automatically to accept the offered pouch, and then the messenger bowed and left. Vallant would have also enjoyed moving the way living people are supposed to, but right now that seemed to be beyond him.

And then the second man at the door came to attention, and Vallant managed to turn his head to see Jovvi coming down the stairs after another serving girl. Jovvi wore a wrap and acted as though she'd been awakened from a sound sleep, but the second man didn't seem to notice.

"Dama Hafford?" he asked, and when Jovvi nodded to that, the man beamed at her. "You must be thrilled to be part of such an impressive residence. I'm not the first to say this, but that doesn't change the delight of it. Congratulations, Dama Hafford, on winning your competition. It's my honor to bring you the word of that, as well as your gold."

Jovvi seemed to be moving in her sleep as she accepted the pouch being offered to her, and Vallant knew exactly how she felt. The messenger bowed and left, and only then did she turn disbelieving eyes to Vallant.

"Am I still asleep and dreaming this?" she asked in a very soft voice. "I must be, since it wasn't supposed to happen."

"Let's go into the library and send for some tea," Vallant suggested, no longer too stunned to be able to think. "We can sit down and be comfortable, and incidentally congratulate each other."

"Yes, of course," Jovvi agreed in a normal voice, giving him a smile for reminding her about not saying anything she didn't want the servants to overhear. "Tea sounds marvelous, and so does the idea of sitting down."

With that settled they headed for the library, and Vallant used the pair of moments to try to figure out where he could have gone wrong. He hadn't been in any condition to notice much and he *had* gone first, but that shouldn't have won him the competition. The problem still nagged at him as he opened the library door for Jovvi, and then the problem instantly became more complex. Coll, Tamrissa, and Mardimil were there ahead of them, and each of them sat holding the same sort of pouch that he and Jovvi did.

"I don't believe it," Tamrissa said, staring at the newcomers. "You two also? I don't believe it."

"I believe the fact of it, but can't make sense of it," Mardimil said as Vallant and Jovvi went forward to join the group. "Tamrissa told us that the ladies came to the same conclusion we did, so this certainly makes no sense. Surely at least one of us would have attained the objective."

"Maybe our objective and the testing authority's were entirely different," Jovvi told him, glancing back at the door they'd left open. "Lorand, would you mind standing guard all alone? I'm not as exhausted as I was, but I'm far from being back to normal."

"I'd be glad to," Lorand responded, looking at her with clear concern. "The closest trace of human life is in the back hall and not moving this way, so tell us what you meant about different objectives."

"It's fairly obvious once you think about it," Jovvi said, letting Vallant seat her before he took a chair of his own. "In my own competition, we weren't allowed to learn what anyone's time was, including our own. Now we've been told that we won, but how do we know it's true?"

"Why would they lie?" Vallant asked, really wishing he'd been able to pay more attention to what had gone on around him. "If they're doin' this because they have too much gold and need to get rid of it, they could have just given it to us."

"There's no such thing as too much gold," Mardimil put in, obviously speaking seriously. "They've arranged this for a reason, and that's what we need to discover. I have the strongest feeling that we'll be badly at a disadvantage if we don't."

"I think Jovvi is right and they have to be lying," Coll said, decision strong in his voice. "I've been going over and over the competition in my mind, and although I *could* have done better than the girl who went first, I'm certain I didn't. Is that why they hurried her out so fast, do you think? To keep her from knowing that the prize went to someone with a slower time?"

"That would mean they chose *us* to win over everyone else who competed," Tamrissa said slowly, while Vallant and the others murmured in confusion. "I can't believe we're that important to them, not when they haven't done anything special for us until now. So the question arises: how do we know we're the *only* ones who were told they won?"

"You mean they lied to everyone?" Coll asked with a frown. "That sounds just like them, but what would be the point? All winners are supposed to go to that reception at the palace tomorrow night, and if the people we competed with show up, we'll recognize them."

"And they'd recognize us," Tamrissa agreed glumly. "I'd forgotten about that, but you're right. And yet I still have the feeling that my guess was close. We know nothing about the other competitors including where their residences are, and that can't be an accident."

"I agree completely," Jovvi said, rubbing at her forehead with one hand. "I have the same feeling, but I'm still too tired to think clearly. I need to get back to bed after I eat something, but first let's tell each other about what the competitions were like while we have the chance."

Everyone thought that was a good idea, so they took turns filling each other in. Vallant couldn't help noticing that Tamrissa looked faintly drawn and also seemed to be leaving something out of her story, but it was none of his business. She'd finally made that clear to him, and he'd made sure he would remember it.

Once all the descriptions were over, Coll, Mardimil, and Tamrissa went upstairs to get ready for that night. Vallant remembered Coll saying something about how he and Tamrissa were going to help Mardimil see some girl, but knowing that didn't help to make him feel any less left out. That meant he couldn't stand the idea of going back to his room alone, so he chose instead to join Jovvi in the dining room.

"No, I don't mind the company at all," Jovvi said when he put the question, giving him a warm, easy smile. "Or, to be more specific, I don't mind *your* company. There's some I'd prefer to do without even if I had to be alone for the rest of my life.''

''You sound as if you're referrin' to someone specific,'' Vallant said, leaning back in the chair he'd taken near her. Jovvi had already asked a servant for whatever happened to be left over from lunch as well as tea for the two of them, so they were alone in the dining room.

''I *am* referring to someone specific,'' Jovvi agreed. ''My former sponsor, Allestine, showed up at the practice area with her two bullies, and tried to kidnap me. I always knew she wasn't very bright, but believing she could simply drag me away without anyone official noticing. . . . I had to use my ability to get away from them after using it during the competition, and that's why I'm so drained.''

Vallant waited until the servant appearing with the tea had poured and left, and then he said, ''How did the testin' people react when you told them what had happened? I'd think they would send out guardsmen to arrest those fools right away.''

''I didn't report the incident, and also asked Tamma not to report it,'' Jovvi answered, looking at him with serious blue-green eyes. ''I can't explain *why* I don't want them arrested, but I'd appreciate it if you didn't say anything either. I'll think of an unofficial way to discourage them as soon as I've had enough sleep.''

''It's your decision,'' Vallant agreed, disliking that choice but feeling it wasn't his place to argue it. ''Now I understand why you ladies both look so strained. Kidnappin' attempts tend to do that to people.''

''Oh, Tamma wasn't there when it happened,'' Jovvi immediately corrected. ''She came by in our coach later, and picked me up. What's bothering *her* is that the man who was there after her very first test showed up again this morning, and said something that frightened her badly. I wasn't able to find out exactly what that was, but I will. I didn't want to add to her fright by saying the man is probably a noble, and if he's decided he wants her she could be facing a serious struggle.''

Vallant had to fight for a moment to keep from reacting to that news, but after the moment it became a good deal easier. If Tamrissa Domon had wanted his help she would have asked for it, and his continuing pain underscored the fact that she'd done nothing of the sort.

"What I said bothered you, but now the disturbance has changed," Jovvi observed, studying him over her teacup. "Does that mean you no longer care what happens to Tamma?"

"Not at all," Vallant denied, reaching for his own tea. "Dama Domon's well-bein' concerns me as much as that of everyone else in this residence. We all do have to stick together, after all. . . . So what do you think the testin' authority will try next?"

"Vallant, you're deliberately changing the subject," she accused, a very accurate description of his intentions. "I have no right to speak for Tamma, but I happen to know that she doesn't want to see you hurt. If she did something to make you change your mind about her, you have to remember what her life's been like until now. Encouraging a man goes against every sense of survival she has—even if most of her *wants* to encourage him. Be patient with her, and hopefully you won't be disappointed."

"I know how much she dislikes hurtin' people," Vallant said tonelessly as he got to his feet, remembering with a twinge how much Tamrissa had been prepared to sacrifice just to avoid hurting *him*. "I appreciate the goodness of her heart, but that's not what I'm lookin' for in a woman. Please excuse me now, I really do need to return to my bedchamber."

Vallant felt her sympathy and attempted comfort all the way into the front hall and to the stairs, but that just made everything worse. What he wanted in a woman was for her to love him, just the way he was prepared to love her. But he couldn't seem to inspire that even in someone who disliked giving pain, and pity was something he would *not* accept. Better never to be accepted at all, than to be accepted out of pity. . . .

He took the stairs two at a time, to avoid running into anyone else. He'd never be able to handle that now, any more than he could ease that blasted, everpresent ache. . . .

FORTY

It was only late afternoon, so I had plenty of time to dress for dinner. I spent a while in the bath house, soaking and trying not to think, but it was useless. My mind kept insisting that I go back over the scene when that man came to my table in the practice area, and consider what I would do about it. That part of it was downright funny, since there wasn't anything I *could* do. I hadn't mentioned my suspicion to Jovvi, but I was certain that the man was a noble. That made me doubly powerless if he turned out to be seriously interested in appropriating me, a thought that kept turning around and around in my head. Doubly powerless . . . doubly powerless. . . .

By the time I got back to my apartment, a realization had forced its way through the roiling. My position in the competitions, the very thing keeping my father currently at bay, had to be doing the same with that noble. That should mean I didn't need an immediate solution to the problem, only an eventual one. As long as I stayed in the running, that is, something I meant to do anyway.

Thinking the thing through that far made me feel a bit

better, so I went to my wardrobe to decide what to wear. Rion and Lorand would be dressed in their gray trousers and white shirts the way they usually were, but not because they had nothing else really appropriate. We wanted them to look as much alike as possible, and identical clothing would help the effect enormously.

I finally decided on my favorite party gown, very plain in design but classically rich. It was dark blue silk with long panels of cream lace, which matched the cream lace at wrists and throat. It was also nearly brand new, since I'd been able to wear it only once before my late husband's illness had forced him to stop going to parties. It was a bit dressy for what the men would be wearing, but the cloak Rion would have on—and would give to Lorand—should balance that.

When I found myself humming as I brushed my hair, I was surprised. I'd expected to be trembling over that scene with the awful noble for quite some time, but simply thinking about it for a while had let me dismiss it. I didn't understand why that was, but I had no intention of arguing. There would be enough to worry about in trying to keep up with the testing authority; I had no need of anything to add to it.

When I made my way downstairs, I found Rion waiting for me in the front hall. Lorand would have left some time earlier, following the directions I'd given him to the eating parlor. Rion looked very handsome in the black and gold cape he wore, and he smiled when he saw me.

"You look absolutely ravishing this evening, dear lady," he said, coming forward so that he might take the cloak I carried over one arm. "I very much appreciate your agreeing to celebrate with me tonight, and our carriage is here. As soon as I help you into your cloak, we can be on our way."

"That's good, because I'm starving," I said with my own smile as I turned to let him put the cloak around my shoulders. "I was too tired to eat much of the lunch I had sent up, and I remember how good the food is at that dining parlor we're going to."

Rion made a sound of amused agreement, and as soon as I settled the cloak around me I was ready to leave. Our little

conversation had been for the benefit of anyone who might
be listening, telling them why we were suddenly going out.
We'd decided to "celebrate" our getting through the first of
the competitions, but now we had something much more
tangible to celebrate.

Rion opened the door for me, but I got no farther than
two steps outside before I stopped short. My father and the
man he wanted me to marry, Odrin Hallasser, were on their
way in, and surprise stopped them as well.

"Why, isn't this convenient," my father said with a smile,
recovering his balance first—as usual. "Odrin and I were
coming by so that he might take you out to dinner, and here
you are, already prepared to leave. I'll just accompany you
two until we reach that stables with carriages for hire just a
mile or so down the street, and then I'll leave my daughter
and her betrothed alone."

"Yes, just the way you left me alone with Gimmis," I
couldn't help saying despite the pounding of my heart. "Real
fathers protect their daughters, I've learned, and every one
of them would spit on the sort of father *you* are. Now take
your disgusting friend and get away from my house."

"Struggle all you wish, child, but you won't escape me,"
Odrin Hallasser spoke up for the first time while my father
showed a flash of furious insult. The man's voice was deep
and smooth, and the dead look in his eyes glittered sicken-
ingly in the lamplight. "I make a practice of getting what I
want, no matter how difficult it is to attain. Our nuptials are
all arranged, so that once you're released from this testing
nonsense I'll be able to take my *wife* home."

"If it's a wife you want, fellow, you would do well to
seek elsewhere," Rion said suddenly and lazily, somehow
knowing I couldn't quite find the nerve to answer Hallasser.
"You lowborn peasants are all alike, believing that a bit of
gold makes you someone of importance, but it doesn't, actually. If you bother this lady again I'll have to speak to
some friends of mine, but right now she and I are on our
way to dinner. Why don't you go and do whatever it is you

people do for entertainment, and stay out of the way of your betters.''

I'd never heard Rion sounding like so much of a noble before, at least not since his very first days at the residence. His hand on my back guided me between two really furious and frustrated men, and a few steps later we'd reached our hired carriage. Rion handed me in and then followed, and once the carriage began to move I let out a very deep breath.

''Thank you,'' I told Rion very sincerely. ''That man frightens me down to my marrow, and I couldn't think of anything to say to him. What you said was absolutely perfect, and was probably the only way to reach him.''

''I detest his sort, so the pleasure was mine,'' Rion returned, an unusual hardness in his voice. ''And it strikes me that their appearance was too much of a coincidence. If you were in the house you could have refused to see them, so they arranged their arrival to meet you as you left. That suggests there's a servant in your father's pay, otherwise the timing couldn't possibly have been so good.''

''Is there a servant in the house who *isn't* in the pay of someone or other?'' I asked, finding the situation ludicrous. ''The only one I can think of is Warla, who isn't really a servant, so maybe I ought to have a talk with her. She's missing out on a lot of extra silver.''

''I'd be inclined to believe that selling information to outsiders is beyond her,'' Rion answered with a wry chuckle for my comments. ''Which really *is* too bad, since you're obviously correct about its being a thriving business.''

''Her main problem would be finding what to sell,'' I decided, enjoying the silliness of the topic. ''She's been put in charge of the house while it remains a residence, but she never pries. When I told her you and I would not be home for dinner tonight, she smiled and said she hoped we'd have a good time. A paid spy would have at least asked where we were going.''

''Very true,'' Rion agreed. ''And speaking about where we're going, I need to ask if there are any decent shops in the area. With five gold dins in my pouch ready to be spent, I'd like to buy Naran a gift.''

"That's a lovely idea, and I think I know just the place," I said, now feeling even better. "Just three doors down from the dining parlor is a shop with some beautiful things, and I've always wanted to go in there. Gimmis never allowed it, of course, because their merchandise wasn't expensive enough. He never bought anything that wasn't extremely expensive."

"A common error of those with more gold than taste," Rion said with a grimace, and then he smiled. "That shop sounds as though it will do perfectly, so let's indeed get you your first look at it."

By then the carriage was pulling up to the dining parlor, which was just as close to the house as I'd said. Lorand had decided against taking a carriage here himself, preferring to walk as though he intended to go only a very short distance. It would ease the suspicions of anyone watching, he'd said, and at the same time would give him the chance to get some exercise.

Rion helped me out of the carriage and paid the driver, and while he did so I glanced casually around. I expected to see nothing out of the way, but those following Rion weren't as subtle as I'd thought they'd be. A brown carriage pulled up and stopped a short way up the street, but no one got out. It was possible that the driver was simply waiting for someone to come out of one of the smaller houses nearby, but for some reason I doubted that.

So as soon as Rion finished paying off our carriage driver and returned to me, I put a hand on his arm.

"Oh, look, Rion, the shop I've always wanted to visit is still open," I burbled with enthusiasm as I pointed. "Would you mind terribly if we stopped for a few minutes before going in to eat?"

"Not at all, dear lady," he answered with a grin for my very obvious playacting. "Your slightest whim is my command. We shall browse for as long as you like."

He offered his arm then and I took it, and we went together

to "browse." I happened to have brought one silver and one gold din of my own along, never before having had the experience of being financially independent even for a single evening. I'd been curious about how it would feel, and now I knew: it was the headiest, most wildly exhilarating experience I'd ever had.

A bell on the shop door tinkled as we walked in, and an older woman came through closed curtains all the way at the back. She parted her lips, probably to tell us she was about to close, but then she looked at us again and simply smiled.

"Please take your time looking about, gentles," she said in a tone that told us she would never have done the same for anyone but us. "If you see something that pleases you, I'll be standing right here."

Right where she could see into the many mirrors arranged discreetly around the shop, she meant. Those mirrors would let her know if we stole something, without her having to be right on top of us. I'd learned all about that years ago, as a girl, but Rion seemed to know nothing about it.

"Decent of her not to hover," he murmured, obviously intent on looking at her merchandise. "I detest clerks who hover. . . ."

His voice trailed off as he drifted toward a case of jewelry on the right, but I went the other way. Attractive bolts of cloth were closest to the door with a riot of ribbons beyond them, but my eye had been caught by the blown glass ornaments just past the ribbons. I'd always loved things made of blown glass, but none of it had ever been expensive enough for Gimmis to buy. Now that I had money of my own, I could consider buying anything I pleased.

Half of the glass items were beautiful little animals, the facets in the glass making them gleam in the lamplight with all the colors of the rainbow. The rest of the glass had been made into variously-shaped perfume bottles, most of them delicately and carefully tinted or decorated in different colors. I immediately fell in love with everything on display, which was very depressing. How was I supposed to choose one—or at most two—of them to buy?

"I see you've found something to attract your eye," Rion said suddenly from my left, sounding amused. "We can return here in a moment, if you like, but now I would appreciate your opinion on something."

"Of course," I answered with a sigh, momentarily giving up on deciding among the little glass figures. Possibly once I helped Rion, I'd come back to discover that I'd made up my mind. I walked with him to the other side of the shop, where he stopped in front of the jewelry case to point.

"Which of those three brooches do you think Naran would like best?" he asked in a murmur. "I'll pretend I'm buying it for you, and then I'll take it with me."

"They're all beautiful," I granted him, and I wasn't lying. "That silver one with the diamonds is probably the most expensive, then the gold and ruby one, and then the silver and pearl. The workmanship on each is above average, but certainly isn't the product of a master jeweler. They'll probably be priced at more than they're worth, but if you really like one of them there's no reason not to buy it."

"Forgive my stare," Rion said automatically, and he *was* staring directly at me. "I find myself very surprised, and indeed a bit amazed. I've never heard a summation like that from anyone who wasn't a jewelry expert."

"If you think *I'm* good, you should try my sisters," I said a bit sourly. "Mother wanted us all well-prepared to gauge the value of any gifts given us, and to be able to know what to choose if the choice happened to become ours. I learned it all because I wasn't allowed not to, but what I learned most thoroughly was an indifference to all of it. I'd prefer gifts with less cost and more thought behind them."

"Less cost and more thought," Rion mused, glancing at the brooches before looking over to where the glasswork was. "Something tells me Naran may feel the same, so why don't we go back to what *you* were looking at."

I agreed rather happily, and led him back to what I intended to buy. Unfortunately I discovered that I still hadn't made up my mind, which was more a disappointment than a surprise.

"Madam, a moment of your time, please," Rion called, and the woman who was in charge of the shop came over looking less pleased than she had. She'd obviously wanted Rion to buy one of the brooches, but her expression said that any sale was better than none at all.

"Tell me something about these figures," Rion continued once she stood on the opposite side of the counter from us. "Do you have others that aren't out here on display?"

"Only near duplicates of the ones you see," the woman replied. "Even though they're all made by the same glass-blower, no two are exactly alike. That gives each piece a unique quality that many people envy when they see it."

"Unique is a quality that has always attracted me," Rion answered her sales ploy with a charming smile. "In fact, I really appreciate the concept of unique in quantity. Which of these pieces do you have the fewest number of left?"

"Why . . . I believe it's that one," the woman responded, pointing to a darling little seated cat. "That and this particular perfume bottle over here. If I recall correctly, I have only one more of each of them."

"Perfect," Rion said, still showing his charming smile. "Then I'll take this entire display, and the last two of the ones you pointed to. Please wrap the additional ones separately, as their rarity makes them especially valuable."

"Why, yes, of course, I'll certainly do that, sir," the woman exclaimed, clearly as startled as I was. "I'll wrap the more valuable ones first, and then return to do these. The price of the whole purchase is seven silver dins."

Rion handed over a gold din, and the woman went happily away to get the other figures and Rion's change. I sighed as I watched her go, feeling the old feeling that the world had passed me by.

"Is something wrong?" Rion asked as soon as she'd disappeared through the curtains. "Your sigh sounded rather forlorn."

"I hadn't realized that *I* could have bought all the figures," I admitted ruefully. "If I hadn't spent so much time trying to decide on one or two, all of them could belong to me. Now I can't even get the one or two, or the woman will start to wonder. You *are* supposed to be buying them for me, after all, and anyone questioning the woman later will become suspicious if I buy more of the same.''

''Your analyses continue to be extremely accurate, except for one minor point,'' Rion said, reaching over to touch my hand. ''I also expect someone to come here with questions, and that's why I gave the woman a reason for my buying duplicate figures. The two duplicates are what I'll be taking to Naran. The rest of the figures are yours.''

''Mine?'' I whispered, not quite believing my ears. ''You bought them for *me*? Why?''

''Perhaps because I saw how you were unable to decide among them,'' he replied with a gentle smile. ''Or perhaps it's because I've never before bought a gift for a friend. It's odd how delightful the feeling is, to give a gift to someone you care about. I often gave gifts to Mother because I was taught that they were expected, but giving them never felt like this.''

''Rion, thank you,'' I said, unable to rid myself of the whisper—or the tears which had begun in my eyes. ''No one has ever given me anything like this—''

I found I couldn't go on, not all choked up as I was. The little glass figures were the most wonderful things in the world right now, and it didn't even matter that I hadn't bought them for myself. Being able to buy them meant I no longer cared who actually did the buying. We stood there for a few moments with Rion grinning and me sniffling, and then the woman came back with a small box and Rion's change.

Rion put away his change and then took the box, holding it while the woman packed the rest of the figures into a larger box. She had paper trays with forms pressed into their surfaces to set the figures into, and then the trays went into the box one at a time with thick cotton wool between each layer. When she finally closed the box I was fairly certain the figures were protected from being broken, but there was a moment of awkwardness when Rion tried to take the larger box, too. He needed both hands to manage it properly, and one of his hands was already occupied.

So he did the only practical thing: he put the small first box into his cloak, and then his hands were free for the large one. His plan had been a clever one, but I'd almost ruined it by volunteering to take the small box before I realized he *wanted* to put it in his cloak. The people watching him would see only the one big box that he would give to Lorand. The second, smaller box would then be able to go with him.

We left the shop with the woman's warm invitation to come back ringing in our ears, and once outside I drew my cloak a bit more tightly around me. The evening was beginning to be chilly, and the short walk to the dining parlor made me eager for its warmth. We walked inside calmly and easily, closed the door behind us—and then all three of us went into a frenzy of activity. I held the big box while Lorand and Rion quickly exchanged cloaks in the dim entranceway, Rion took the gift for his lady and put it in his new cloak, and Lorand told Rion where the stables was and what arrangements he'd made. It couldn't have taken more than a minute, and then Rion was heading for the back door while Lorand relieved me of the box.

"And that should do it," Lorand said with a smile once Rion was gone. "Now all I have to do is remember to keep my back turned, and everything should be fine."

"I hope so for Rion's sake," I said with a headshake. "He really deserves to be rid of his mother's manipulations, and maybe this will be the start of it. And now you and I can get something to eat."

"About time, too," Lorand agreed, gesturing me ahead of him out of the dimness and toward the host's station. "I got here earlier than I expected to, and immediately began to get hungry."

Since the aroma of marvelous food permeated the air like teasing perfume, I could understand that perfectly. The host greeted us and quickly led us to a table, and we lost no time in ordering. Once the servant had brought us tea and small meat and cheese pastries to hold us until the food came, Lorand leaned back in his chair to study me.

"I wonder if you would mind helping me think about something I don't understand," he said, his fingers toying with one of the pastries that he hadn't yet tasted. "It isn't all *that* important, so if you aren't in the mood. . . ."

"Just remember what I said last time about wanting to give advice," I returned when his words simply trailed off. "If you ever hear me say I'm not in the mood, you'll know there's something seriously wrong with me. Now, what is it you don't understand?"

"It's . . . the way I felt today, after the competition," he said with a vague gesture, obviously groping for the right words. "I think you know how I've *been* feeling, which is . . . worried about the amount of power I've needed to use. When I got to the competitions building this morning, I was incredibly relieved that I wasn't going to have to push myself to win."

I nodded encouragement and agreement, glad that the pleasant background music covered most of Lorand's soft words. We were now discussing some things that others shouldn't know about.

"Well, while I was actually performing during the competition, I remember wishing the exercise could have been harder," he continued, now looking deeply disturbed. "Afterward I felt dissatisfied over having had to lose, and not in the least relieved. Now I'm afraid there's something wrong with me, and I don't know what to do about it. Whatever the condition is, it's dangerous."

"Because part of you is no longer worried about being burned out," I said with another nod, finding it surprisingly easy to see the point. "You've lived with the fear for so long, that you feel naked and vulnerable without it. I felt the same way at first about obeying my father. I'd done it for so long that stopping in order to save my sanity and life still felt wrong."

"But that's hardly the same thing," he protested, his soft

brown eyes troubled. "Breaking the habit of obedience did save you, but breaking the habit of intelligent caution does the exact opposite."

"Now I think you're getting to the heart of the matter," I said with a faint smile. "You said 'intelligent caution,' but is that what it really is? We're all now in a position where we have to be as strong as possible, or we could end up losing our lives in any number of different ways—most of which we don't even know about. Can something which interferes with that demand for survival need be called intelligent caution?"

He couldn't seem to find the words to answer, and again I found it easy to understand why. Pulling myself out of the deadly habit of blind obedience had been unbelievably hard, and I still hadn't accomplished it all the way.

"Our . . . situation is forcing you to rethink the beliefs of a lifetime," I continued gently, drawing his gaze again. "Without your crippling fear you're obviously a natural competitor, and now your true nature is trying to force its way through the bindings you've kept on it. It knows you need it in order to survive, so for the first time it's fighting the unnatural restrictions you've imposed. In my opinion there's nothing wrong with you, only something starting to be right."

"Even if ignoring the warning could get me killed?" he asked, still looking horribly uncertain. "Or, as it happens, worse than killed?"

"There are a lot of things worse than getting killed, but having your mind wiped out isn't one of them," I told him bluntly, forcing away thoughts of what waited to take *me*. "As long as you have no idea about what's going on around you, you might as well be comfortably dead. And if you think being dead isn't comfortable compared to . . . being appropriated and used like a slave, for instance, I have even more news for you. It is."

"You're probably right, but I'm going to have to think about this," he said after a moment with a sigh. "Maybe if

I can keep just a little of the fear, I won't do anything *too* stupid. . . . Thanks, Tamrissa, for listening to my problems again. You really are a good friend.''

"My pleasure," I said with a smile that didn't last very long. Both Lorand and Rion were good friends I really valued, but when my thoughts took off in a direction of their own, it wasn't either of them I thought about. Another man always seemed to be there, a man I hadn't had much luck in getting along with. It was a stupid waste of time, especially now when he wasn't even speaking to me any longer, but—

But I still couldn't wait to get home and go to my apartment. This was week's end night, the night I'd promised him, and maybe . . . just maybe . . . please . . . !

FORTY-ONE

Rion slipped out of the back of the dining parlor, excitement beginning to rise in him strongly. Now he was actually on his way to see Naran, something he hadn't fully believed he'd manage. He was so used to being thwarted at every turn rather than being helped. . . .

A quick glance around showed no one in sight, so Rion moved through the deepening darkness toward the stables where Coll had rented a horse for him. Traveling on horseback would be faster and easier than using a carriage, even though he would probably need a bath house after the trip. He hadn't been allowed to ride more often than was fashionable, but he'd been on horseback often enough to know that much.

The horse was saddled and waiting for him, and when the stableman said something about Rion's "brother," Rion knew approximately what Coll had told the man. It was fortunate that they two looked so much alike; a number of problems had been circumvented because of it.

Carriage traffic was light at that time of the evening, so Rion made good time finding his way to Naran's new place of residence. The street was an upper middle class neighborhood, meaning it was fairly wide but not comfortably so, and the houses had very little in the way of grounds around them. The houses themselves were also small, and the largest of them couldn't have contained more than four or five bedchambers. Rion had never visited a neighborhood like this, but for Naran he was willing to dare anything.

A large stable seemed to serve a good portion of the area, and that was where Rion left his horse. He felt tempted to ask directions to the house he sought, but instead took Naran's gift from his saddlebags, where he'd cushioned it with his cloak, donned the cloak, then left without asking. No one could have followed him, but discretion was the much wiser course.

Coll's dark brown cloak let Rion move invisibly through the darkness, and it wasn't long before he found the proper house. Feeling extremely proud of himself, Rion began to head for the front door—before he remembered that the fewer people who saw him, the better. Decorative lanterns lit the front of the house, and anyone walking up to the door would be visible to anyone who happened to be looking out of any of the neighboring houses.

So Rion took a lesson from Naran, and went looking for the servants' entrance. He looked all the way around to the back of the house, in fact, but the thing must have been on the other side of the house. All Rion found was a back door, dimly lit by a very small lamp, so he tried knocking there instead.

A very long moment passed, and then Rion heard someone

unlocking the door. Thinking it would be a servant, he began to put together a semi-coherent explanation of what he was doing there. The door opened and he parted his lips, but all explanations became suddenly unnecessary. It was Naran herself who stood there, dressed in a high-necked and long-sleeved gown of gold velvet, and her beautiful face lit up when she saw him.

"My lord, you came after all!" she exclaimed softly as she stepped back to allow him entrance. "I prayed that you would, and now I've been answered."

"Nothing short of death could have kept me away," he told her quite sincerely as he moved inside and closed the door behind himself. "I've thought of little else but this moment since you came to the residence, and now we've finally reached it."

"Yes," she breathed, moving into his arms, and then their lips were finally touching. Rion kissed her with all the growing hunger of his heart, and she seemed to respond in the same manner. They joined in a serious attempt to devour one another, and after a long, satisfying time she reluctantly eased back.

"What a terrible hostess I am," she murmured, touching her lips to his again very briefly. "Keeping you standing here in the hall with your cloak on, when dinner is all ready to be eaten. Are you hungry?"

"Yes, as a matter of fact I am," Rion replied with a bemused smile. He'd intended to take Naran to the best dining parlor in the neighborhood, but if she preferred to stay in he was not about to argue. "For the most part I'm hungry for you," he continued, "but also in that other, trivial way."

"Trivial," she repeated with that lovely tinkling laugh, and then she took his hand. "Well, let's see to the trivial first, and then we'll have as long as we like for the more important. You sit here, and I'll take your cloak."

"Aren't there any servants to see to that?" he asked, first removing the box from his cloak. She'd led him to what seemed to be a sitting room at the front of the house, only a ridiculously short distance from the back. "I brought you something, and I'd rather watch you open it than see you fuss with my cloak."

"I have only one servant, and she goes home at night," Naran said, her tone telling him that there was nothing unusual in what was, to him, such an odd practice. "And seeing to your cloak will only take a moment. There's a coatrack here in the side hall. . . . There, it's all done. Now may I see what you brought?"

Her request was polite and attentive, but Rion had the definite feeling that polite thanks was all she expected to feel. For some reason Naran seemed uninterested in what he'd brought, and Rion felt a moment of uncertainty. Would such paltry things as the glass figures tell her he had no real interest in her? Having no experience with things of this sort, he'd chosen the two figures which were most often purchased. Should he have bought her a full set instead, or perhaps one of the brooches?

"What I brought," Rion echoed her last words, looking down at the cheap paper box. It should have been silver or gold instead, and the figures the same. . . . "What I brought will probably bore you, so let's forget about it, shall we? Next time I promise to bring something that will truly take your breath away. Now—"

"Oh, please, my lord, please let me see it," she interrupted, her expression having suddenly changed. "There's something about it. . . . Please say you don't mind my opening it."

The earnest openness in her expression touched Rion, and before he knew what he was about he'd handed the box to her. He was convinced now that he'd made a grave error, and he watched with dread as she opened the box and began to remove the cotton wool it was filled with. She would be expecting gold and jewels, and all he'd brought was—

"Oh, my lord!" she said with a gasp, staring down into the box before reaching into it. "And there's something else beneath the glorious cat—Oh! How exquisitely lovely! I've never seen anything lovelier than these two—Oh, my lord, can you ever forgive me?''

"Forgive you?" Rion echoed for the second time, staring disbelievingly at her radiant face. "Whatever would I need to forgive you for?"

"Why, for believing even for a moment that someone as wonderful as you would bring an ordinary gift, like jewelry," she said with a laugh, carefully cradling the glass figures against herself. "You spent thought on me rather than gold, and I'll treasure these beautiful things forever. How can I possibly thank you?"

"You already have," he assured her, knowing his smile must look exceedingly strange. Spending thought rather than gold . . . when she and Tamrissa met, they would most likely become friends instantly. "Do you really like them? I must confess that I had help in picking them out."

"Listening to good advice is the mark of a great man," she said with a smile, and then she rose from the chair in which she had been sitting. "And no, I don't like them, I love them. I'll be back in just a moment."

With that she walked carefully out of the room, and when she returned in the specified moment, she no longer had the figures.

"I wanted to put them somewhere safe," she explained, then held out her hand. "Come, you've waited long enough for your dinner."

Rion rose and joined her, and she led him into the next room. It had to be the smallest dining room he'd ever seen, but with the tiny table set for two, he would have been happy even in a windowless pantry. Naran made him sit down, and then she went into the next room. Five minutes later she reappeared carrying a platter and a bowl, and that was only the first of it. An entire meal was brought out two plates at a time, and then she finally joined him at table.

"I made all this hoping you would be here," she said with a smile as she touched his hand gently. "If you hadn't come it would have gone to waste, but now it can be appreciated instead. Will you pour the wine?"

Rion smiled and touched *her* hand in answer, and then he poured the wine while she served the two of them. The food was extraordinarily good, or maybe it was just the company—and the fact that the two of them were alone in the house. Rion couldn't remember ever being entirely alone without even a single servant, and especially not with a beautiful woman. He swallowed his food and drank his wine while gazing at Naran, and she did exactly the same.

For dessert there was tea and cherry cobbler, and they sat a while after that just holding hands and gazing at one another. At last Naran smiled and rose, and Rion did the same without hesitation. He'd been waiting for her to be completely ready, and now he knew she was. She led him to yet another room on the ground floor which turned out to be a bedchamber, and its relatively small size almost went unnoticed by him. They were finally beginning what he'd been dreaming about, and Rion had no time for noticing the unimportant.

And being with Naran was just like a dream, only incredibly better. Rion removed her clothing slowly, reacquainting himself with her body as he kissed and touched her everywhere, and she moaned with pleasure, then returned the attention. By the time they merged they were both in a state of frenzy, and release came to them all too quickly. But then they were able to begin again, and this time the pleasure went on and on.

Hours went by, and at one point Rion even napped for a short time. He and Naran couldn't seem to get enough of each other, and when he used Air magic to increase her pleasure she laughed with delight. The time took hours but seemed like moments, especially when it was clearly time for him to go.

"I don't want to leave," he murmured, stroking her hair. She lay with her head on his chest and her arms about him as he lay on his back holding her, and his words were nothing but pure truth. "I want to stay here forever, and never leave you again."

"But you can't," she replied with a sigh of resignation, making no attempt to change her position. "You do have to go back, and I have my own duties and obligations. Don't be sad, my love. Wishing for what we cannot have will only ruin the pleasure we shared. I mean to treasure every moment we spent together, and will continue to dream of possible future moments."

"There will be *many* future moments," Rion told her firmly, taking her arms to raise her so that he might look her straight in the eye. "I've sworn that vow to myself, and now I swear it to you. We *will* share our lives until the end of them, Naran—unless *you* don't want to."

"I would give up breathing before giving up the hope of that," she answered quietly, putting one hand to his face. "I've loved you forever, my beloved lord, and will continue to do so. I even love you enough to let you go if you should ever tire of me, so—"

"Enough of that!" Rion ordered sternly, not in the least amused. "I will never tire of you, not in this lifetime nor any other, so I forbid you to speak like that again. Do you understand me?"

"Yes, my beloved lord, I understand you," she responded with a lovely smile, and then they kissed again. It was a kiss filled only with love and completely without passion, and when they reluctantly parted, Naran smiled again. "And now you must dress. Would you like some help?"

"No, or I'll be here all night," Rion replied with a grin as he sat up. "Your 'help' seems to have only a single purpose."

"Are you complaining, my lord?" she asked with arched brows, a teasing smile playing around her beautiful lips. "If so, then I'll certainly have to change my ways."

"If you change your ways, then I may have to begin beating you," Rion said, looking directly at her as he stood. "I would hate having to beat you, so. . . ."

"So I simply won't change my ways," she finished with a laugh. "I'll just sit here and watch you."

She sat with her arms wrapped about her knees studying him as he replaced his clothing. The process was entirely too short, and when it was over he leaned down to kiss her again.

"Don't bother getting up, I know where my cloak is," he said, only glancing at the glass cat and perfume bottle where they stood on a table beside the bed. "The next time I come, I'll bring you an entire glass menagerie."

"Bring yourself, and I'll be completely satisfied," she returned, apparently meaning what she said. "Be safe and happy until we meet again, my love."

"And you, my love," Rion said, delighting in speaking the words. "Until we meet again and forever beyond that."

They shared what really was a final kiss, and Rion quitted the bedchamber to find his cloak and leave the way he'd come in. Reluctance choked every movement and step, but he truly had no choice about returning to the residence. Outside the night was still and quiet, and he moved through the darkness to the stables where he'd left his horse.

The night in general may have been quiet, but the stables was the scene of organized chaos. Hire-carriages were lined up waiting their turn to be placed in a neat row before their horses were stabled for the night, and all the stabling workers seemed taken up with the chore. Rion considered interrupting to demand his mount, but he truly wasn't in a demanding mood. He chose to wait a short while instead, and leaned against the wall to enjoy the crisp cool of the night.

Rion's thoughts didn't have to return to Naran, as they hadn't yet left her. His memory was filled with the delight and . . . *completion* of being with her, and his reluctance to leave had increased. That was primarily why he had decided against asking for his horse immediately. Simply remaining in the same neighborhood with Naran for a few minutes longer was easier than riding away, not knowing when he would find it possible to see her again.

Rion began to brood about that, the uncertainty of the future where he and Naran were concerned. Between the testing authority and his mother, it could be weeks or even months before he was able to free himself again. The concept forever came up again, but this time in an extremely unpleasant way. If only he could simply stay with Naran. . . .

And that was when Rion realized that he really didn't have to be back to the residence before morning. No one would expect to see him before then, so returning just before dawn would accomplish the same as returning now. He could spend the night with Naran, sleeping while holding her in his arms, and then the coming separation might be a bit easier to bear.

Most of the hire-carriages had been settled into place, so Rion quickly left the stables before someone offered to get his horse. His heart pounded with what he was about, as staying out all night was another thing he'd never tried. He hurried through the darkness, picturing Naran's smile of delight when he appeared at her door again. She might well be asleep already, but if so, she would hardly mind being awakened.

The house looked just the same when Rion got there, the night lanterns keeping the front door well illuminated. Once again he made his way around to the back door, and then he knocked. There was a very long delay without an answer, so he knocked again. If Naran were asleep, which it seemed she was, she would need time to rouse herself.

The wait after the third knock produced the same nothing the first two had, bringing Rion a touch of worry. She might well be a heavy sleeper, but there was just the chance that something might be wrong. That thought made Rion reach out in frustration to try the doorknob, even though he knew the gesture would be useless. The door had a springed deadbolt, which he had set before leaving—

Rion froze when the door opened easily, but a heartbeat later he was in motion and running through the house. That door should have been locked, and the fact that it wasn't couldn't possibly indicate anything good. All the lamps were still lit, the dirty dishes still on the table in the dining room, but the bedchamber—The bedchamber was empty, of Naran and her clothing both. Not a single trace was left, not a stocking nor a handkerchief. . . .

The wardrobe and the chests were equally empty, and Rion felt completely dazed. It was as though Naran had never been there, but she *had* been there. And she was supposed to be living in that house; if that were true, then where were her personal possessions? Rion slowly went through the entire house including the upstairs chambers, but there was nothing. No possessions and no Naran.

After the search, Rion simply stood in the short, narrow hall in shock. He simply didn't understand what could have happened to her in the few minutes he'd been gone. If he weren't completely sure of himself, he might begin to doubt that she'd *ever* been there. He couldn't possibly have been hallucinating—could he?

The uneasiness of that thought brought to mind another so he strode back to the bedchamber where they'd shared themselves. It was just the same as it had been when he'd first returned, but this time Rion noticed that something else was missing. The glass figures that he'd given to Naran, the ones she'd put on the bedside table. . . .

They had disappeared as well, presumably having gone with Naran. But where, and even beyond that, why? In the name of every aspect, *why* . . . ?

FORTY-TWO

Jovvi filled her breakfast plate at the buffet and brought it to the table, but the appetite she'd come into the dining room with was quickly disappearing. The other four members of her group were already at the table eating, but the outward silence was in direct contrast to the whirling screams and shouts of their emotions. Every single one of them was badly bothered by something, and the emotional noise was so loud that Jovvi could barely hear her own disturbance. She no longer felt exhausted, but that had only been a minor, passing problem.

By closing her senses down as far as possible, Jovvi was able to give herself enough quiet to eat in. To her surprise she wasn't able to sever herself entirely from the power, not the way she'd once been able to do. Maybe the increasingly heavy use of power did that to people. She'd have to check with the others—later!—and find out if it was the same for them.

With no one dawdling over the food, breakfast was through rather more quickly than most meals. Vallant seemed ready to be the first to get up and leave, but his intention was interrupted when Warla appeared in the doorway to the hall.

"Excuse me, but Lady Eltrina Razas would like to speak to all of you," she announced in her usual, nervous way.

She also seemed about to add something, but the testing authority representative pushed her way past her.

"Good morning, all you lovely people, and congratulations," Lady Eltrina sang, obviously in the best of moods. "I came first thing to tell you how proud I am that each of you has won the initial competition in your respective aspects, and I'm very proud. But words are easy to say, so I'll show my pride in another way. Since you'll all be attending the reception tonight, I've brought you special outfits to wear. I guarantee that you'll be the most beautiful and handsome people there."

She clapped her hands then, and two servants holding large boxes came in. The boxes were put down on the floor and opened, and then the servants straightened up with their contents. The one on the left held a man's shirt in sequined silver with what looked like narrowly cut trousers in blue silk, and the one on the right held a gown. The gown had a sequined silver bodice and sleeves, and the skirt was blue silk.

"The colors are different, but that still looks like the sort of uniform we've been wearing to the practices," Jovvi deliberately observed aloud. "Will everyone else attending also be wearing a uniform?"

"No, silly, because it's a costume, not a uniform," Lady Eltrina answered with a laugh. "The Five have decided to make the reception a masked ball, and this way everyone will know who you are even behind your masks. You *do* want the Five to come over and congratulate you, don't you?"

"It's what I've been dreamin' about," Vallant replied when no one else did, somehow keeping the dryness out of his tone. "I do have a question, though. . . . You must have gotten our measurements from when we were fitted for the practice clothes, but how did you get these outfits made up so fast? None of us knew we would be goin' tonight until the messengers arrived yesterday afternoon."

"Were you expecting me to say that I had the dressmakers and tailors working all night?" Eltrina countered with a smile that should have taken a large bite out of Vallant. "Well, if so, you were being really silly. The truth is that I had these costumes made up days ago, when the Five decided on a masked ball. I had confidence in you, you see, and possibly even more confidence than you had in yourselves. The coaches will be by to pick you up at seven, so you have all day to relax before it's time to dress. I'll see you again tonight, at the palace."

She smiled around at them all again, and then she was gone with a wave and a flurry of skirts. Jovvi wasn't the only one who sat silently and watched the servants repack the costumes before taking them out of the room, but afterward she was the first to sigh and stir in her seat.

"Well, that takes care of my worry about what to wear tonight," she said brightly enough to capture everyone's attention. "With that off my mind, I think I'll spend some time walking in the garden."

"And I'll join you," Tamma said in agreement as she stood. "I could use some undisturbed fresh air."

"Well, if you ladies are going to stroll, I think I'll stroll with you," Lorand said, also getting up. "What about you, Mardimil, and you, Ro? Are you going to let two lovely ladies stroll about a beautiful garden with just a single escort?"

Both Rion and Vallant agreed that a decision like that would be out of the question, so they joined the other three as they headed for the back of the house. Jovvi knew that in a very short while the servants who were spying on them would grow suspicious about what was being said in private—if they weren't suspicious already—but there was no help for it. The group had to talk about what had just happened, and that no matter how suspicious it made people.

They walked well out into the garden, making sure not to hurry, and finally Jovvi muttered, "So now we know how they expect to get away with having everyone at the competitions think they won and therefore show up for the reception: masks, because it's also a masked ball. We'll be lucky if we recognize each other."

"But we won't have any trouble recognizing each other,"

Tamma pointed out. "We'll all be wearing the same outfits in the same colors. They'll know who *we* are, while we know nothing at all about *them*."

"But those outfits were made because she had *confidence* in us," Vallant said bitterly to everyone in general. "In a world of lies, that's one of the biggest. It was the testin' authority who had those things made, because they knew they would be usin' us."

"Wait a minute," Lorand said, looking around at them. "If those outfits were ordered by the testing authority, then they had to have made the decision about them well before we earned our masteries. One of my mother's friends once asked her help in putting sequins on her daughter's dress, and it took the two of them days to get it done in spite of the fact that they're both really good seamstresses. *No* one could have sequined up those outfits overnight, not even if they somehow found a way to use the power."

Everyone exclaimed over that, obviously agreeing, which brought Jovvi another thought.

"That in turn has to mean we were chosen as a group only because we 'qualified' in those first exercises at just about the same time," she pointed out. "The two people in our residence who didn't qualify then were moved elsewhere, but not dropped from the program. I think that says quite a lot about whether or not they want the very best for the important competitions."

"They probably would have taken Beldara and Eskin instead of me and Lorand if they could have gotten away with it," Tamma put in, also sounding horribly disillusioned. "All this competition business is nothing but a farce, and they'll end up giving all the positions to their nobles as usual. That means we're more than wasting our time doing as they ask, so why don't we show our contempt by picking up and leaving Gan Garee? Goodness knows I won't miss this place."

"Do you really think they'll just allow us to leave?" Rion asked, his own bitterness a bright and blazing torch. "They need a certain number of challenging Blendings to make their show look good, and if we try to ruin their plans they'll return the favor by ruining our lives. I haven't been really living long enough to want that to happen.''

"Then why don't we ruin their plans in another way?" Jovvi asked against the general ocean of dismay and disappointment and disturbance. "We've suspected for some time that they were using us, but now we can use them as well. If they teach us how to Blend and we work really hard, we might be able to best their noble Blending. Then *we'd* be the Seated Five, and there would be nothing they could do about it. What do you say? Are you all willing to try?"

There was a long moment of hesitation as they all considered her question, but nothing in the way of the full, instant agreement she'd been hoping for. The men had responded more positively to Tamma's suggestion of walking away, even Rion, despite his protests. Jovvi shared their lack of enthusiasm more than they could know, but she was certain that trying to run away would be deadly for them. She waited nervously, and finally Vallant broke the silence.

"I've never been one to just stand by quietly when people are tryin' to do me harm," he stated, not really looking at anyone. "It burns me to have to take it now, so if there's a way to strike back then I'm for usin' it. We may not win, but they'll surely know they were in a fight."

"I'll go along with Ro," Lorand said slowly, also not looking at anyone in particular. "I never let anyone push me around back home, and I don't see any reason to change that just because the bullies around here are bigger. Like Ro said: we may not win, but we *can* make them know they were in a fight."

"I don't like any part of this, but I *am* one of you," Rion said, his tone more depressed than supportive. "For that reason I'll agree to whatever the rest of you decide."

Jovvi nodded to Rion with a smile of thanks, then she looked at Tamma. The beautiful, innocent-faced girl knew it was up to her now, and her previous anger had drained away.

"I wish you could do it without me, but you can't," she

said, speaking mostly to Jovvi and showing a humorless smile. "I'd much rather turn and walk away, but I believe Rion when he says they'd never allow that. So I suppose that means I'm also in."

"You won't be sorry," Jovvi assured her with a warm smile, then she looked at the men. "None of you will be, and you have my word on that. We *can* win this thing—if we want to badly enough."

One or two of them nodded agreement, but all enthusiasm was conspicuous by its absence. Jovvi watched the group break up as most of them began to wander in different directions, and all she could do was hang onto her own inner balance. Realizing the truth of what the testing authority was trying to do to them had stolen all their previous feelings of pride and accomplishment. The master's bracelets they all wore had become meaningless, of no more importance than the identification cards they'd begun with.

But Jovvi herself *refused* to feel that way. She'd worked too hard to drag herself out of the gutter to let a pack of smug, useless parasites knock her right back in. Those nobles had had things their own way for much too long; it was time someone taught them that inheriting a title was nothing at all like having to earn it. The idea of becoming one of the Seated Five had been tarnished, but the next Seated Blending, no matter who they turned out to be, *would* be able to say they'd fought for and won their place.

Now all Jovvi had to do was get the others to feel the way she did . . . especially the one somebody she couldn't stop caring about even more than herself. . . .

Vallant began to move through the garden alone, enjoying the outdoors the way he always did. But that was all he felt able to enjoy, despite the decision he'd just made. Or maybe because of it. Fighting to keep from being left by the wayside was a reflex reaction with him, but this time it left him depressed. As badly as everything else was going, he had very little hope that their fighting back would accomplish anything. Besides making things worse, that is.

Vallant looked nowhere but ahead of him as he wandered, but that didn't keep him from being aware of the others. Or one of the others in particular. Once again Tamrissa was acting as though he were invisible, but he still hadn't figured out the trick of doing the same with her. In point of fact he'd slept very little the night before, struggling with all his strength to banish Tamrissa from his thoughts.

But his strength hadn't been enough, not against the awareness that that was the night he might have had her in his arms. If she'd had even the least interest in him . . . if there hadn't been something about him that insisted on attracting the wrong sort of women. Why hadn't he realized sooner that Tamrissa had fallen for his cute little joke because she'd wanted to be fair, not because she wanted *him*? In a definite way she was as bad for him as Mirra, but one small part of him refused to believe that.

And yet he had to learn to believe that, or he might as well drop out of the group right now. Maybe if he concentrated on winning. . . . Surely the idea of winning to the most powerful position in the empire would be enough to distract him from thoughts of a girl who was wrong for him anyway? It should be able to. . . . It had damned well better. . . .

Lorand moved away from the others to let the beautiful garden calm his mind, but for some reason it wasn't working. For some reason. It was embarrassing to think that even a small part of him would be that innocent, especially when the rest of him knew better. His agitation stemmed from what he'd committed himself to, a situation where his new ambivalence might well drive him insane. Half of him wanted to charge right out and challenge everyone trying for the Throne to individual combat, and the other half trembled in fear over what might happen if he ever did.

Running a hand through his hair also didn't help, but Lorand did it anyway out of habit. And out of weariness, since he hadn't slept much last night. After talking to Tamrissa over dinner, he'd very much wanted to run back to Jovvi and tell her joyfully that he seemed to be getting over his problem. He no longer lacked confidence when wielding the power, so she no longer had a reason to keep herself from him.

But Jovvi had been asleep again when they'd returned to the residence, so he'd gone to his own bedchamber to relax and do some thinking. No matter what lay ahead of them, he'd thought, Lorand Coll would no longer drag everyone down to his level of fear. He now had the confidence necessary for anything demanded of him, even if it threatened his very mind—

That was the point that Lorand had sat bolt upright. The end of that declaration of confidence had had a very familiar tinge of fear, one he'd thought he was done with. He'd worried about being too reckless now that his problem was gone, but suddenly he'd discovered that it wasn't gone. It still hung around his neck like a millstone, and it helped not at all that now it was just half a millstone. . . .

Lorand took a deep breath and let it out slowly, now grimly glad that he hadn't spoken to Jovvi. Anything he told her would have been a lie, and she deserved better than a liar. A crippled liar, crippled because he hadn't the courage to stand on his own two feet without trembling at shadows. He hadn't refused to join the others, not when he had nothing else to do with his life, but he didn't expect to be of much help to them. He'd end up fighting himself rather than the enemy, and if there had been anyone else to take his place he would have stepped aside without argument.

But there wasn't anyone else, so he would stay—and ignore the pain of knowing he'd never be the man the woman he loved both wanted and needed. . . .

It worried me for a moment that one of the others would come with me when I walked away from the group, but I needn't have bothered. Apparently most of them were as disturbed as I felt, and seemed to want the same isolation. But not for the same reason, *that* I was sure of. . . .

A thick bush caressed my skirt as I passed, but I barely noticed and didn't even check to see if there was a catch in the material. I seemed to have finally learned that Gimmis was dead and didn't have to be worried about any longer, but that didn't mean I had nothing to worry about. That stupid ultimate competition, and those awful, mean-spirited people. . . .

Disappointment hit me like a blow to the face a second time, only a shade less forcefully than the first. I'd actually thought I'd found a way out of the trap of being used, but I'd simply found other, more subtle people to do the using. I had no hope of winning a High practitioner position at all, and as for being a part of the winning Blending . . . of course I would be.

An old, small, broken branch lay on the ground near one of the trees, and I bent to pick it up. It looked very lonely just lying there after having been severed from the tree, but obviously it didn't know how lucky it was. The tree wasn't trying everything in its power to get the branch back, and certainly wasn't laughing at it for thinking it had escaped. The way my father kept laughing at *me*. No wonder he hadn't taken my status as an entrant seriously. He must have known the truth all along.

But when it came down to it, he didn't know the whole truth. He was still busily trying to sell me to Odrin Hallasser, when a member of the nobility had apparently "noticed" me. If that nameless noble was serious about claiming me for his own purposes, my father and his disgusting friend would find themselves out of luck. Considering what the noble wanted me for, I should have been terrified. But thinking about how angry my father and Dom Hallasser would be did a good job in chasing the terror away.

But not the depression. That had been hanging on since last night, even keeping me from sleeping very much. I'd been glad when Lorand hadn't wanted to dawdle after we'd finished our dinner, and I'd gone straight to my apartment once we were home and hadn't left it. That was supposed to be the night when Vallant Ro would come to lie with me, the night I'd been thinking about for what seemed like forever. I'd meant to tell him then that I'd decided to risk a relationship, even *with* all the hounds baying at my heels.

But Vallant Ro hadn't shown up, and hadn't even sent a note to say he wouldn't be there. He'd grown so cold and distant, but common courtesy should have come into play—unless he'd reached the point of caring nothing about me. I'd waited hour after hour, hoping and then praying for a knock at the door, but there had been nothing. I'd known the truth then, and I actually couldn't find it in me to blame him. By involving himself with me, he would have offended a large number of very wealthy and influential people. . . .

I felt tears start in my eyes, but there was really nothing to cry about. When every hope you have comes crashing down in ruins, you find yourself well beyond tears. I'd agreed to Jovvi's suggestion just to keep from needing to argue, not because I expected us to get anywhere. Being surrounded by ruin tends to take your belief away about building; I mean, if that's the way everything ends up anyway, what's the sense in bothering? There isn't any sense in it, so why not just go through the motions?

And that's what I was doing, going through the motions of living. It wouldn't be long now before every thread of the woven life we'd been leading began to unravel, but I couldn't make myself care. All I could do was hold a lonely little branch close to me, envying the peaceful death it had already found. . . .

Rion deliberately walked away from the others, in no mood to do anything but be barely civil. He'd gotten back to the residence late last night, but hadn't been able to sleep despite all the exercise he'd had. The question of where Naran could be demanded an answer, but he couldn't find one. She'd disappeared into thin air, and if there had been any signs of struggle he would have been worried as well as baffled to the point of insanity.

But he'd finally noticed last night that the bed he'd shared with Naran had even been neatly made, which seemed to rule out someone coming in and kidnapping her. She'd taken the gifts he'd given her and had left—but to go where? And even beyond that, *why*?

"Excuse me, sir," Rion heard, and looked up to see that he'd been stopped by a servant. "There's a gentleman at the door who has asked to speak to you. Are you available, or shall I send him away?"

"A gentleman?" Rion wondered aloud. He couldn't think of a single man who would come to speak to him, but the matter might just have something to do with Naran. "It's all right, I'll see him."

The servant nodded and turned back toward the house, and Rion followed with growing impatience. If the visit *didn't* have something to do with the woman he loved, he might well end up losing his temper. The front door stood closed, of course, and when the servant opened it before disappearing discreetly, Rion was able to see that the sloppily dressed visitor was a complete stranger.

"Are you Lord Clarion Mardimil?" the man asked, a sneer in his voice as he pronounced the name and title. "I'm not supposed to speak to anyone but him."

"The name is Rion Mardimil, not Clarion," Rion corrected shortly, ignoring the man's rumpled coat and trousers and well-worn shirt. "What do you want?"

"I have a message from . . . your mother," the man replied, sounding as though he'd meant to say something else entirely—until he'd realized how much larger Rion was. "I've only seen you from a distance, since I'm one of the ones working for the man who works for her . . . if you can follow that."

One of the ones watching his every move, Rion knew the man meant. But when he didn't comment aloud, the smaller man seemed to regain a certain amount of confidence.

''The message they want me to pass on is as follows,''
the visitor continued with now obvious relish. ''You didn't
fool us for long last night when you changed places with one
of your friends, and we know the neighborhood you went
to. It's only a matter of time before we also know which
house you visited, and then we'll have your little playmate.
Mommy says to tell you that she means to make the filthy
slut sorry she dared to despoil her precious baby, but if you
come home right this minute you might be able to talk her
out of it.''

The man's sneer was now completely visible, but Rion
was too confused to take offense. He'd managed to elude his
watchers only for a very short time, but the news of that
wasn't as disturbing as it might have been. If *he* hadn't been
able to locate Naran, these men would be lucky even to find
the proper house. He still didn't know why the girl had disappeared, but now he was heartily glad she had.

''I have a message for you to take back to my mother,''
Rion said after only a very brief pause. ''Tell her she might
as well forget about putting on her best corset, because I'm
not coming anywhere near her. And now I have a message
for you and your . . . associates.''

The man had lost his sneer rather quickly, but when Rion
used the power to push the man closer with a block of hardened air behind him, the fool actually went pale.

''In case you've somehow missed the point, I'm informing
you that I've earned a master's bracelet in Air magic,'' Rion
said softly, holding up his arm to display the bracelet. ''With
that fact firmly in mind, I'll now add that I truly *hate* being
followed around and spied on. From now on I mean to take
a very good look around every time I leave this residence.
If I happen to find someone following me, I expect I'll do
something . . . unpleasant about it. Now you can tell me what
you expect to do.''

The man swallowed hard, his dark eyes showing a good
deal of fear. When Rion had first used the power, the man
had tried to counter Rion's efforts. He seemed to be a rather

strong Middle talent, but next to Rion he might as well have been a talentless Guild member. Mother's agent must have sent this man in particular with the message, thinking he would be able to defend himself. It hadn't worked out that way, and the man was quick to admit it.

"Wh-what I expect to do is play it smart," the man stuttered in his haste to supply the right answer. "The others and I will find something else to do, and then you won't be bothered again."

"Wrong," Rion told him, using the block of air to push him another step closer. "What you will do is not mention any of this part of the conversation, except to the others who watch along with you. What you will tell them is that they'll now be earning easy silver, as they're to take their posts and then read or sleep. If I appear I am *not* to be followed, and you may make up any details for your reports that you like. Have I made myself clear?"

"Very," the man agreed with a gulp, but Rion could see the instant calculation in his eyes and decided against letting it pass.

"Don't think you can find a way around my orders," he said, suddenly but briefly blocking the air the man was currently breathing. "I mean to hold *you* responsible for the actions of all the rest of your friends, and if one or more of them follow me they won't be the only ones to experience my displeasure. Now what do you say?"

"Yes, all right, you've made your point," the man gasped out, finally able to breathe again. "I'll keep it quiet, and make sure the others do the same. In the name of the Unknown Aspect, how did you get so damned strong?"

"Practice," Rion answered dryly, then stepped back and closed the door in the man's face. Whether or not his orders would be followed was still up for debate, but at least he'd made *some* effort to increase his freedom. If it happened to work, all fine and good; if it didn't, he'd have to try something else.

But in the meanwhile, he had another question to ruin his

sleep: would Naran eventually return to that house and end up being found? He hoped not, or he would probably lose his head and do something horrible. He wished he knew where she was, and why she'd left like that. Where . . . and why, why, *why* . . . ?

Lady Eltrina Razas settled back in her seat as her carriage pulled away from the residence, which finally let her show the laughter she'd been holding in. Even the densest, most trusting member of all the groups would finally see the truth today, and none of the people she'd just left fit into that category. They were all smart enough to have grown suspicious about what the testing authority was doing some time ago, and this latest interview would have clinched matters for them. They might not have *all* the answers, but by now they ought to know that they'd be formed into a challenging Blending—and should also have decided to ruin things for the authority by seriously trying to win the Throne.

Eltrina laughed aloud in delight at such colossal naivete. She hadn't really believed that *all* the peasants would react that way, but Ollon Capmar had been absolutely right. He spoke from the experience of having gone through a previous twenty-fifth year, of course, so Eltrina wasn't as impressed as she'd pretended to be when he'd told her. But the idea of letting them think they'd learned things they weren't supposed to know was marvelous, no matter who had originally thought of it. It made the poor little things so much easier to manage. . . .

Another laugh escaped her, this time one of anticipation. She couldn't wait until all those naive little fools learned the real truth, only far too late for it to do them any good. And by then she would have all the power she needed to choose among the males for a toy or two, to keep her entertained for a while. But not too long a while. Lord Kagrin's father would begrudge her every minute she kept them, and Lord General Trepor Axtin wasn't a man to trifle with. He might refrain from criticizing her openly, but only if she were firmly seated in Ollon's place.

Sudden annoyance made Eltrina shift in her seat as it chased away her amusement. All her planning had gone extremely well, and she'd been poised on the brink of arranging Ollon's sadly fatal accident when circumstances had turned briefly against her. Ollon's sister had been brutally murdered, and Ollon's rage over the loss had caused the man to change his habitual actions. He had been spending most of his time haunting the investigators, demanding that they find the one responsible for killing his sister. Eltrina had known Elfini, of course, and personally couldn't see what the fuss was about. It wasn't as if someone *useful* had been killed. . . .

But Ollon raged on and on about the loss of his precious sister, leading Eltrina to suspect that there had been more between them than a sibling relationship. That part of it didn't matter in the least, but the fact that Eltrina was no longer able to *know* when Ollon would be in a particular place did. He hadn't even slept with her since the murder, and how was she supposed to arrange his accident when she never knew where he would be?

Eltrina took a deep breath to calm herself, hoping the rumor she'd heard this morning was true. Just before she left the house, her husband had mentioned that someone had been put under arrest for the murder. His informant had said it was one of their own, a member of the nobility, but no one seemed willing to believe that. A peasant, yes, but a member of the nobility? That was too ridiculous to consider.

But it really didn't matter *who* had been arrested, if the action served to return Ollon to his usual habits. She'd been the one doing all the work for the past few days, and that was definitely not part of her plans. Ollon was supposed to do the work before he died, not spend all his time looking for vengeance. If he wasn't careful, the Advisors would replace him before *she* had the chance to arrange his accident.

Time was growing very short, but Eltrina refused to abandon her ambitions. If Ollon wasn't there to oversee the final arrangements for the competitions, then Eltrina would just have to coax someone else into doing it and then take the credit for herself. She'd already had to pick a replacement for the entrant who had lost his mind during the first competition, and she hadn't enjoyed having to interrupt her own private schedule to do it. And now she had to drag herself to that tiresome meeting this afternoon in Ollon's place.

Thoughts of that meeting made her *very* tired, but the people involved were simply too important to ignore. She would be expected to report on the results of the measurements taken from the peasants, and would confidently tell them the truth: none of them was too strong to be easily handled, so the right people had nothing to worry about. The second part of it, though, concerning that idiotic worry about the Prophecies. . . . Ollon appeared to be just as concerned as their superiors, but *she* certainly wasn't that foolish.

So she would have to *pretend* to be concerned, no matter how ridiculous the pretense made her feel. Yes, we've had all the applicants closely watched, but no, not a single sign was seen to manifest. Big surprise, as though they'd have to look *hard* to see the signs the Prophecies spoke of. They were all fools, and maybe she would do well to consider taking one of *their* positions once she had Ollon's.

Well, that was for the future. Eltrina smiled again, pleased that she'd stuck to her determination despite all those ridiculous little snags. It meant she *was* destined for greatness, just as she'd always known. . . .

FORTY-THREE

Homin was actually the first to get to the new residence. When the servants who came out for his baggage told him that, it improved his mood to a small extent. And his mood needed improving, there was no doubt about *that*. Annoyance had been an unfamiliar emotion to him, but the past few days had begun to teach him a number of unfamiliar things.

It took only a few moments to follow the servants to his assigned quarters, where he left his coat and new hat. He'd been told that tea was ready before he'd come upstairs, so he went back down to the sitting room to have a cup. He'd only just gotten sugar added when he heard someone else's arrival, and turned in time to see Delin Moord enter.

"Homin, dear fellow, what an incredible surprise!" Delin exclaimed, obviously in a happily expansive mood himself. "You're actually the first of us to arrive, something I wouldn't have believed if I hadn't seen it with my own eyes."

"There are any number of things not to be believed around here," Homin replied with a grimace. "My apartment has only two rooms, Delin, and I seriously doubt if there are enough servants to see to our needs. Why couldn't they have left us where we were?"

"You can't join people into a Blending when they're scattered all over the landscape," Delin replied, now eyeing him curiously. "What's come over you, Homin? I scarcely recognize you from just a few short days ago."

"I'm no different than I was," Homin protested, knowing he spoke the truth. "It's simply that I've only just begun to . . . get things moving smoothly at home, and now they're forcing me to come here. I intend to suggest that we all move to my place, where we'll certainly be a good deal more comfortable."

"Your place," Delin echoed, still looking at him strangely. "You sound as though you've forgotten that it's your father's house, not yours, and I believe that's the key to your odd behavior. This is the first time you've been on your own, isn't it? There's no one at—'your place'—to tell you what to do, and on the contrary the servants have been taking *your* orders. Independence is a heady wine, isn't it, Homin?"

"Yes, it certainly is," Homin granted him grudgingly after gulping a swallow of tea. He *had* forgotten somehow that the house was Father's rather than his, and that Father could conceivably return at any time. Homin found that he disliked that idea intensely, especially since Father was almost certain to blame all his troubles on *him*. As though *he* were the one who had married that Elfini. . . .

"Well, it so happens I'm glad you've had a taste of that particular wine," Delin said, looking at him with the sort of approval Homin had never seen before. "You seemed to be the only one of us who didn't fully appreciate what our aim was, but now it's clear that you do. Our success will mean that you never have to go back to someone else's house, Homin. What you find around you will be yours, and you'll have guaranteed your independence for the rest of your life."

"How odd, Delin," Homin commented in surprise. "You're absolutely right, and I *didn't* realize that. Or wasn't able to appreciate it, just as you said. Now that I can, you can be certain of my full support and maximum effort."

"I'm delighted to hear that, old fellow," Delin said with a smile, then turned to see who was arriving now. It turned out to be Bron, who strode into the sitting room with a scowl on his face.

"My driver almost couldn't find this place," he announced as he headed for the tea service. "It's more than a little out of the way, and it's smaller than I expected. Do they seriously intend for us to live in each other's laps?"

"Homin and I were just discussing the fact that one must sometimes put up with minor annoyances for the good of more important aims," Delin told him smoothly with a wink behind Bron's back for Homin. "We'll need you to stress that point with the others, Bron, as they're certain to require your guidance. Not all of us understand these things as clearly as you do."

"That, old man, is why I'm leader of this group," Bron replied comfortably, turning with teacup in hand and scowl nearly gone. "And of course I'll explain the matter to the others, so you needn't worry. How soon will that new Advisory agent be here?"

"In about an hour," Delin replied, just as though he knew exactly what Bron meant. "Giving us time to get all settled in, I imagine."

"What's this about a new Advisory agent?" Homin asked, looking back and forth between the two larger men. "Has Lord Rigos been replaced? I never thought we'd see the day we were rid of him."

"Homin, where have you been?" Bron asked with that superior sort of amusement Homin detested. "Surely someone has told you that Rigos was arrested for—Good grief."

"Yes, discussing the matter with Homin could be somewhat difficult," Delin said when Bron stopped short in unexplained embarrassment. "What our leader began to say was that Rigos has been arrested for the murder of your stepmother. No one from the investigators or guard came by to tell you?"

"Possibly they sent word to Father," Homin suggested, his brows still high with shock. "*Rigos* killed Elfini? I knew there was bad blood between them, but I never would have expected *him* to—What reason did he give for doing it?"

"So far he hasn't even admitted to the crime," Delin said, speaking to Bron as well. "His father learned of his arrest almost immediately, and has actually been working to get

Rigos freed. All he's accomplished so far is to keep them from questioning our beloved former overseer, and rumor has it that that's about to come to an end. The Advisors want someone punished for that terrible crime, to be certain that no one loses himself to such an extent again."

"For once I agree with them," Bron said, sounding as though he meant it. "If we don't press our right to be untouchable in all ways, we could lose the right. A crime like this has to be severely punished, or one of us could conceivably be next."

Delin nodded sober agreement, but Homin simply drank his tea. He'd begun to feel extremely grateful to whomever had removed Elfini from his life, and it was odd to think of Rigos as the one. Was it now necessary to forgive the man for the way he'd treated them? Homin decided to try, but wasn't sure he would succeed.

The three of them sat down to drink their tea, and Homin was forced to admit that the chairs and couches were more comfortable than the ones in his father's sitting room. The house itself wasn't particularly new, but it had obviously been repaired and refurbished with fairly decent items and touches. The smell of fresh whitewash was enough to give one a headache, but that was better than the smell of rot and decay.

Delin and Bron continued to chat about Rigos for a time, and Homin had the impression that they knew something they weren't mentioning. After a while the sound of a new arrival came, followed closely by a second arrival. Neither of the newcomers appeared immediately, which presumably meant they'd gone to their apartments first. Another short while passed, and then Selendi and Kambil walked into the room together.

"That's one way to avoid being last," Delin commented with a grin. "Arrive at the same time someone else does, and then neither of you is last."

"I would never think to burden a lady in such a way," Kambil said solemnly, obviously teasing. "The onus of being last will rest squarely on *my* shoulders, to spare Selendi the ignominy of it all.''

''Not to mention the fact that he *was* last,'' Selendi put in dryly as she walked to the tea service, apparently not amused. ''But as far as being first to leave goes, that will definitely be me. Expecting us to live in this squalor is completely unreasonable.''

''Not when you consider what we're here for,'' Bron disagreed, just as though he hadn't said almost the same thing when *he'd* arrived. ''It will only be for a short time, and then we'll be able to move to *much* larger quarters.''

They all chuckled at that, realizing that Bron referred to the Five's palace. There were six wings on the palace, and only one of them was used for public functions of all sorts. Each of the others belonged to a different member of the Five, and he or she had the final word there. It was said that even the Advisors couldn't interfere with that prerogative, which sounded to Homin like absolute utopia.

''If living in a box drives me crazy, how far do you expect the rest of you to get?'' Selendi asked, turning with her tea to inspect each of them. ''The four of you need me, and you'd better not forget that.''

''The truth is that we all need each other,'' Delin put in smoothly before Bron could lose his temper and snap at the silly girl. ''Individually we're just a group of unimportant people, but together we're a force to be reckoned with. So which would *you* rather be, Selendi? Unimportant or a major force?''

The answer to that was too obvious to put into words, and Selendi didn't even try. Instead she sipped at her tea in a way that said she didn't care to discuss the matter any longer, and Delin acceded to her unvoiced wishes with a smile.

''So, Kambil, tell us if you've had any luck,'' he went on smoothly to another subject. ''No one seemed to know who would be put in charge of us in Rigos's place when I asked, so I've been hoping that your contacts are better informed.''

''I found out that the decision wasn't made until the last moment,'' Kambil said, coming over to sit down with the cup he'd filled. "Apparently there were people lined up from wall to wall who had been waiting for a chance like this, and they all descended on the authority together. They finally settled on the son of a man who was owed the largest favor, someone by the name of Hiblit Rahms. I think I've heard the name, but I can't quite put a face to it."

"I can, so take my word for the fact that you're lucky you can't," Homin said while everyone else frowned in thought or simply shook their head. "I was forced to attend social functions with Hiblit when we were both boys because his father and mine were working closely together at the time. The best thing I can say about him is that he made *me* look as handsome and charming as Delin, which should tell you something. I haven't seen him in years so there's a good chance he's changed, but whether for the better or the worse I don't dare try to guess."

"Now I can't wait to meet him," Delin said with raised brows, a curious amusement flickering in his eyes. "If he's really worse than you, Homin, we should have it made."

"Homin isn't as bad as I used to think," Selendi shocked everyone by saying, her gaze resting directly on an even more shocked Homin. "He seems like someone else now, even though I can't pinpoint what's different about him. I'll have to study the matter."

And with that she came to sit next to Homin on the couch he'd chosen, surprising him even further. He'd never expected Selendi to do anything but laugh at him, and he suddenly discovered that he was beginning to be aroused. Quite a lot of his thinking had changed in the past few days, each morning bringing new things for him to discover about the world, but this was far and away the best. He'd never even had the nerve to *pay* for a woman, but maybe now. . . .

"I know we're supposed to be close to one another, but this is ridiculous," Bron stated, staring darkly at Selendi. "Don't you think you'll be entertained well enough by the rest of us, *Lady* Selendi? Adding a probable virgin is almost an insult."

"He's jealous, so just ignore him," Selendi said comfortably to Homin, who was staring at Bron with burning hatred. "I happen to find the idea of a man who's never known another woman extremely exciting, so I hope he's right about that part at least. We'll have to talk about it later."

Homin looked back at Selendi to see the flames of need in her lovely eyes, and he shivered with excitement. He'd *never* had a woman look at him like that before, and suddenly he couldn't wait for the meeting to be over.

"Bron, Selendi is simply doing her part to prepare us for Blending," Delin said, his voice its usual smoothness. "The closer we are to one another the better a Blending we'll be, and as our leader I'm sure you know that. We depend on you to help us see things properly, and we could use some of that help now."

"Yes, well, sometimes it's hard to be a leader," Bron grumbled, then he took a deep breath and began to drone on in a repetition of what Delin had just told him. The fool sounded as though he thought no one else had heard Delin, and Homin suddenly realized that that wasn't the first time it had happened. In fact it happened *all* the time, only Bron never noticed. Delin used calling Bron their leader as a tool to lead the fool around by his nose, and Bron didn't know it! Homin found that very funny, but it wasn't the time to mention it. Maybe once Selendi stopped looking at him like that. . . .

"Aha, I think I hear the arrival of a carriage," Kambil said as he rose. "Since this sitting room is at the front of the house, I'll just take a peek out the window."

He walked over to one of the windows and glanced out, then immediately hurried back to his chair with a nod. That meant Hiblit had indeed arrived, and in a moment they'd see how he'd turned out. It was possible to hear a servant open the front door without the least need for straining, and then two sets of footsteps approached the sitting room.

"Lord Hiblit Rahms," the servant announced, then stepped aside to let the visitor enter. The man who appeared looked very much like the boy Homin had known, but he was no longer so fat that he made Homin look thin. He was of average size in both height and weight, but his face was almost gaunt. His clothes were obviously expensive, but he wore them as though they were filled with pins. Pins that stuck him at every step, Homin thought with a chill as Hiblit approached them. And there was something about the look in his very light eyes. . . .

"Lord Hiblit, welcome to our group," Delin said as he stood, charm pouring out like a falls. "We have only tea here, but I'll be pleased to send for anything else you might want."

"I'm not permitted to eat anywhere but at home," the man replied in a very soft voice without looking at Delin. "Please sit down, sir, and we'll soon be finished here."

Delin exchanged glances with everyone as he resumed his seat, most especially looking toward Homin. In turn Homin raised his brows and shook his head once, hopefully telling Delin that he had no idea what was wrong with Hiblit. It was obvious that something *was* wrong, but exactly what, Homin couldn't imagine.

"As I'm sure you already know, I've been given the task of taking over for Lord Rigos," Hiblit said once he stood in their midst, looking directly at none of them. "At the moment I have little to do but remind you about the reception at the palace tonight, where you'll have the chance to engage the lowborn challengers in conversation. They haven't yet been officially informed that they'll be put into Blendings, but you may assume that they're nevertheless aware of it. Use the time to find out as much as you can about them."

Hiblit paused then, as though to allow an opportunity for questions, but instead Homin and the others exchanged glances again. The man's voice had been very soft but also uneven, as though he were being forced to recite a prepared speech. Even Bron looked disturbed, and Delin had lost all trace of his charm.

"When you look in the wardrobes of your assigned apartments, you'll find your costumes for tonight," Hiblit continued when no questions were forthcoming. "There are matching masks, of course, since the reception is also a masked ball. The colors of your costumes are gold and orange, and the challenging Blending you'll face first will be dressed in silver and orange. Silver for the lowborn, gold for the high. You'll be given additional details about the challengers in orange once you've met and spoken to them, but not many."

"Why were we moved to this residence today rather than at the beginning of the next new week?" Homin asked when Hiblit paused again. He would hardly mind being answered, but that wasn't why he'd put the question. He wanted to see if there would be any recognition on Hiblit's part, especially since the man presumably knew Homin was there.

"The decision to move you over today came from my superiors without a supporting reason," Hiblit recited, still staring at the wall somewhere. "Two coaches will be sent to take you to the palace, and I've been asked to remind you that being fashionably late is unacceptable tonight. I'll be there as well, so if any questions occur to you later, you may ask them when we meet at the ball. Until later, then."

With that he headed for the door, his entire attitude showing that he didn't expect to be stopped. He was perfectly correct, of course, since everyone seemed as taken aback as Homin felt. They all sat in silence until the sound of a departing carriage came, and only then did it seem possible to breathe freely again.

"He didn't seem to remember you, Homin," Delin said at last, not the least trace of condescension or ridicule in the words. "Was he really like that as a child, too?"

"No, not in the least," Homin replied, his heart pounding in the same old way again. "I don't understand what's happened to him, Delin. He was badly overweight and very fidgety as a child, and most of the time it was impossible to get him to stop talking. He had a loud, raucous voice that would drive everyone insane, and occasionally he liked to play nasty tricks on some of the other children. But not when there was the chance of his victim finding out who had played the trick, never then."

"Are you sure he's still alive?" Selendi asked with a

shudder from beside Homin. "I've never felt such . . . *emptiness* in a man before, and I hate it. Do we really have to see him again? Emptiness like that makes me sick."

"It isn't emptiness," Kambil said in a strained voice, and Homin looked up to see that the big man was actually pale. A glance at Bron, who should have been ridiculing Selendi's comments, showed Homin that their supposed leader was too shaken to ridicule anyone, and Kambil looked at least as bad.

"Our new Advisory agent is quite full rather than empty," Kambil said into the troubled silence, his tone heavy. "Full of strict orders he's been given about everything, orders he doesn't dare even consider disobeying. They seem to cover everything including the proper way to breathe, or at least it feels that way. He doesn't seem prepared to do anything without thinking about it first, not even walk across a floor. I've seen repression before, but nothing to match *that*."

"Why would he watch himself so closely?" Delin asked with a worried frown. "And more to the point, is he also going to be watching *us* like that?"

"I don't know," Kambil admitted, his color only now coming back. "If he's told to watch us that closely, he will, but I think I made myself less than clear. He isn't doing that to himself, he's been trained into doing it. And whoever or whatever caused the condition, it's been going on for quite a long time."

"I think it has to have been his father," Homin said slowly, forcing himself to remember back to the unpleasant days of his childhood. "Hiblit had an older brother, and their father never missed a chance to point out how useless Hiblit was in comparison. Their mother was this nervous little woman who would pet Hiblit whenever she was near him, but who never stood up for him. I had the feeling she wasn't allowed to go near Hiblit's brother at all, and then the brother was killed in a freak accident. I never saw Hiblit again after that, since our fathers had gone on to different projects."

"Apparently Hiblit was forced to take his dead brother's place," Kambil said with a sigh. "If people understood just how dangerous that was, maybe they'd stop doing it. Hiblit is all control and proper action on the outside, but on the inside all those orders are making him scream. As long as he can keep the scream from escaping, there won't be any trouble. If it ever gets out of his control, though. . . ."

Kambil didn't finish the sentence, and Homin was extremely glad he hadn't. Whatever horrors Hiblit might be capable of, Homin would be happier not knowing about them. People had always pointed out the similarity in their names with a snicker, suggesting he and Hiblit were just alike, but that had *never* been true. Now, more than ever, he was delightedly glad of it.

"I've got to take a long walk," Kambil said suddenly, rising to his feet. "I need to be alone to clear my mind and regain my balance. . . . If I'm not back in time, don't hold lunch for me. I'll have something when I do get back."

They all nodded and watched him leave, Homin, at least, wondering how much harder that experience had been for Kambil than for the rest of them. He'd gotten so much from Hiblit, more than Homin had known was possible, and it must have been very painful. Kambil was usually so easygoing. . . .

"I think I'll go to my apartment until lunch is ready," Selendi announced suddenly, getting to her feet. "Homin, will you escort me there, please?"

"Yes . . . delighted . . . of course," Homin babbled as he struggled erect. "Please take my arm."

For a wonder, she did, and Homin could feel envious eyes on him all the way into the hall. Then he began to worry, and doubt himself, and wonder if she were really serious . . . and whether or not he would be ill. . . .

FORTY-FOUR

Delin watched Bron as Bron watched Selendi leave the room with Homin. Bron's scowl said he just might be thinking about following and interfering, so Delin leaned over to tap the other man's arm.

"I would recommend against doing whatever it is you have in mind," Delin said in his best coaxing tone when Bron's scowl was switched to him. "If I'm reading Selendi right, she's going after Homin only to get *your* attention. She wants to make you jealous enough to let her into your bed, but that's the worst thing you could do right now. She'll probably need some sort of encouragement to Blend with the rest of us, and promising to let her enjoy our leader might be the only thing capable of reaching her."

"She'll know about it when I finally do reach her," Bron growled, getting to his feet. "I hate the idea of that fat nothing touching her before I do, but she probably won't let him do more than walk her to her door. And he might not even be *able* to do more than that. Yes, of course, he won't be able to do anything but shiver and beg. She'll be sorry she ever spoke his name, but that's her problem now. I'm going for a soak in the bath house, and then maybe a rubdown."

Delin nodded and watched Bron leave, then he sat back in his chair with a smile. Bron fell for that same trick every time, but it might be wise to use it as little as possible from now on. If their ''leader'' ever managed to notice he was no such thing, Delin would have a good deal more trouble controlling him. Let the fool continue to believe as he was supposed to, and that would be one less problem to overcome.

The thought of problems erased Delin's smile, although there was only the new Advisory agent who currently fell into that category. The man chilled him as much as he obviously did the others, but on top of that Delin was also disturbed. He'd been hoping to get someone usefully manageable in Rigos's place, but instead they'd gotten someone who could prove to be worse. When a man follows the orders of certain others like a puppet, there was usually no reaching him.

And they needed an Advisory agent who *could* be reached, in one way or another. Once the group began to practice as a Blending, there would be no more pretense or half measures. They would have to do their absolute best at all times, and the effort would certainly be noticed by whichever servant was there to watch them. The watcher would report to the Advisory agent, which meant the agent would have to be someone who was willing to keep from passing on the report. Someone other than Hiblit, obviously. . . .

''Maybe he'll affect the other groups in the same way,'' Delin murmured to himself as he looked around at the very understated room. ''If so, we can all stand together and demand someone else in his place, and they'll have to accommodate us. If all they have left on competition day is their one chosen Blending, someone is very likely to notice.''

Delin chuckled at that as he got to his feet to stroll around the room, examining the accent pieces as he went. Using the other three groups similar to his against Hiblit was a marvelous idea, but not as good an idea as he would have gotten if Rigos were free of confinement. Providing another body which Rigos could be blamed for would be absolutely delicious, but as long as the former agent was kept locked up, Hiblit's continuing good health was assured. A pity that, since Rigos's supposed jealousy of the man who had taken his place would not even have to be pointed out. . . .

Delin puttered around for a while, then decided to do as

Bron had and go for a soak. The other man was gone so Delin was able to relax and enjoy himself, luxuriating in the temporary freedom from his father in the same way he luxuriated in the water. Now that he was out of his father's house he meant to stay out, no matter what the cost.

Everyone apparently chose to have lunch in their apartments, so Delin also had the rather small dining room to himself. The servants told him that Kambil hadn't yet returned from his walk, which made Delin think about the big man. Kambil had reacted so strongly to Hiblit's presence that Delin had been concerned, seeing more of Kambil's softness than he liked. There was no room for weakness in their group, so something would have to be done about the man. Delin did have one idea, but it would be a while before it was time to use it. . . .

The afternoon passed even more uneventfully than the morning, the only break in the boredom coming when Kambil finally returned. And the man didn't even have the decency to look around for any of his groupmates. Delin saw him speak to a servant on his way upstairs, most likely to order the lunch he'd missed, and then the man disappeared in the direction of his apartment. Standing to one side of the doorway of the sitting room, Delin decided that Kambil looked considerably better than he had. The change was a fortunate one where the group was concerned, but hadn't done anything to effect a similar change in Delin's plans. Once Kambil's active cooperation was no longer needed, Delin would make absolutely sure of his reliability in the best way possible.

When it was time to dress in his costume, Delin put it on and then examined himself in the mirror. Tightly fitted orange trousers were something he would normally never even be caught dead in, but as part of the costume they weren't bad at all. They went perfectly with the collared and long-sleeved shirt all done over in golden sequins, both together giving him the look of a dashing figure out of popular fiction. The mask that went with the outfit was also sequined in gold, with orange feathers adding to its size. His measurements must have been gotten from his tailor, but the clothing cer-

tainly hadn't been made by the man. Delin's tailor would
have screamed and fainted at the very thought of orange
trouser material or sequins on a shirt, an attitude Delin had
always approved of.

But tonight was a party, and even more importantly it was
time to find out about the peasants who would be facing
them. Delin had already been asking very proper questions
along those lines, and had had Kambil doing the same. The
big man might be weak, but he was the only other one in
the group who could be trusted not to make a mess of the
attempt. They hadn't yet had the time to compare notes, but
the ride to the palace ought to be long enough for that.

When Delin strolled downstairs with his cloak over his
arm, the others were already there. Bron and Kambil looked
almost as dashing in their identical costumes as he did, and
Selendi looked quite fetching in her orange skirt and golden
blouse. Homin was the only one of them who now looked
absolutely ridiculous, with his fatness and shortness emphasized by an outfit designed for the tall and slender. But
Homin didn't seem to *know* he looked ridiculous, and in a
moment Delin found out why.

"Homin and I will be sharing one of the coaches to the
palace," Selendi announced as soon as Delin had joined the
group. "We've discovered that we have quite a lot in common, and would like to continue our . . . conversation on the
way to the party."

Delin saw Homin stop himself from laughing aloud at the
word "conversation," and an easily defined difference now
marked the short, fat figure. Obviously Selendi had granted
him her favors after all, and the boy had finally been turned
into a man. But Bron's sneer suggested that he didn't see the
obvious, and the fool apparently still believed that Selendi
spoke only to taunt him and raise jealousy. That was fortunate, as Bron would be better off elsewhere when Delin and
Kambil talked.

"We don't mind you and Homin sharing a coach at all,"
Delin said amiably in answer to Selendi's announcement.
"In point of fact that sounds perfect, as Bron has already

said he needs to speak to you two again about what we'll be doing tonight. His presence should also make sure that your ... conversation doesn't cause you to arrive late for the party."

Bron looked smugly pleased with that idea, but Homin and Selendi weren't. The two began to protest the presence of someone else in their coach, but they must have remembered what Hiblit had said about being fashionably late—a memory that Delin's comment had been designed to elicit. They both fell silent again almost immediately, and Delin smiled around at them.

"That's all settled, then," he said with finality. "Now, does anyone know if the coaches have arrived yet?"

It turned out that the coaches had arrived a short while ago, so they all donned cloaks and went out to board them. Selendi went straight for the leading coach, of course, and Homin trotted after her with Bron strolling along in their wake. That was perfectly acceptable to Delin, who glanced at Kambil before going to the second coach. Kambil had smiled faintly when their eyes met, and then had followed Delin. As soon as they were settled and the coach had begun to move, Delin looked straight at Kambil through the darkness.

"I trust you're feeling better than you were earlier," he said, adding warm concern to the tone of the words. "Tonight we all need to be at our most alert."

"Yes, thank you, I'm feeling much better," Kambil returned, gratitude in his own tone. "And you're right about our needing to be alert tonight. Have you learned anything worthwhile in your inquiries?"

"One or two minor items," Delin agreed, pleased to see how quickly Kambil had gotten down to business. "I was commended for my diligence in preparing properly for the competition, but I also learned something I didn't care for. I wasn't the only one making inquiries, which means at least one of the other groups may have plans similar to ours."

"Or they may simply be doing what's expected of them," Kambil countered with a shrug in his voice. "In any event,

I can't see that it makes much difference. The chosen group will also be planning to win, and we haven't let *that* affect us."

"A nice point," Delin agreed, and he certainly did feel less concerned now. "With that in mind, I should tell you that Rigos did only fairly well with giving us the full picture. I was told during my inquiries that each of our groups will face one of the challenging groups of peasants, which will leave five winning groups after the first competition. One or two of those five could conceivably be peasant groups, and then *our* one or two strongest will stand to face them. That will leave either three or four winners, which at that point should be all ours."

"Should be," Kambil mused. "I wonder how they can be so certain of that. An objective view of the real world suggests that one lowborn group *might* be able to best most of ours. In that event *they'd* be the ones to stand in the final event, and then we'd *have* to oppose them with our best rather than those who were prechosen."

"You're not naive enough to believe that that would be allowed to happen?" Delin asked with true amusement. "Our noble leaders don't believe in leaving things to chance, my friend, so they've covered that point. Somehow all the peasants have been fixed so that they respond to specific orders at a specific time. That means they'll lose a competition if ordered to do so, and that order will be given to any group which makes it to a second competition."

"That's comforting to know," Kambil said, sounding as though he meant it. "So that could leave four of our groups to face one another. Two against two then, and the two winners left to face one another."

"That's supposed to be possible, but I don't believe it actually is," Delin told him, crossing his legs thoughtfully. "Damn these trousers. They're too tight even for comfortable leg-crossing. But to get back to the final number of groups which will be competing: my research showed that in the last hundred years, the first competition always eliminated three peasant groups and two noble groups."

"Leaving three noble groups and two of peasants for the next level," Kambil said, sounding thoughtful. "Yes, that would make sense, public imagewise. If the lowborn were all eliminated in the first round, the crowd would probably become hard to calm. But once they're eliminated in the second round. . . ."

"Then the other peasants accept their loss more easily," Delin finished with an automatic nod. "Yes, it does work out that way, as does the following level. Can you guess how they've arranged it?"

"With three groups left?" Kambil said. "Two of those groups would then face each other, with that winner being in the final confrontation. They probably hold their chosen group back until the very last, and then let them show their 'strength' by defeating the last group to challenge."

"You're almost right, but the plan is a bit more subtle," Delin told him with grudging approval. "They make sure to announce that the two *strongest* noble groups will face the peasants who are left, leaving the third noble group to stand there looking embarrassed. When the two 'strongest' groups stand triumphant over the peasants, it's then announced that they'll toss a coin and the winner will face the final noble group."

"And the final noble group somehow manages to defeat the stronger group they're made to face!" Kambil exclaimed, obviously understanding immediately. "It should drive the crowds wild, to see an underdog come out on top. They'll then be rooting for that underdog in the final challenge, and when they manage, against all expectations, to actually win, the crowds will be completely behind them. The prechosen Five will be a popular Five as well."

"Exactly," Delin agreed. "I admire the thinking that went into the idea, but I believe we can use the framework for our own purposes. We have to be one of the three last groups, of course, but that shouldn't be hard to accomplish. The Advisors don't care which of us is left after the first competition, as long as we number the requisite three."

"And then?" Kambil asked. "Do we win the coin toss

and go on to defeat the 'worst' of our groups?''

"Certainly not," Delin denied, beginning to be amused. Kambil was so *bad* at planning these things. . . . "If we defeat the underdog immediately, the crowds could very well turn against us. What we'll do is *lose* the coin toss, and then stand and watch our fellow winner be defeated. But instead of coming out belligerently to face the upstarts we're certain we can best, we'll come out frightened and humble, and we'll stand where the peasants' groups stood."

"So that the crowds will at least identify with us," Kambil said, again sounding thoughtful. "That might very well work, and then give us a matching acceptance when we just manage to win. We'll need the sympathy that just pulling it off will bring, but I do like the idea. I'm glad you can come up with these things so easily."

Delin made a modest sound in response to the compliment, doing nothing to disabuse Kambil of his admiration. The truth was that he'd awakened one morning to find the complete plan already formed in his mind, a product of the research he'd done. In that way the effort *was* his rather than a lucky outcome, so nothing *needed* to be said.

"I'm sure any of us would have thought of the same thing if *they'd* done the research," Delin nevertheless made sure to say. "And I wasn't the only one checking into things. What have *you* learned about our supposedly worthy opponents?"

"The first thing I learned is that they *are* worthy, at least a good number of them," Kambil replied. "As you probably know, the earliest competitors are sabotaged in some way in their final attempts at mastery. That lets the authority brush them out of the way to make room for those coming after. No sense in feeding and housing people all year, when they'll only be needed at the end of that year."

"So our opponents won't have had the chance to get to know each other really well," Delin said, pleased with the information. "What a tragic shame for their hopes and aspirations."

"Yes, I thought the same," Kambil commented dryly.

"The ones we'll be facing are all relative newcomers, and the various groups have been kept from meeting one another. They know only the members of their own residence, and won't even get to see much of each other tonight. Half of them were rated yesterday and the other half early today, but they were told the effort was a 'competition.' And then they were all told that they'd won."

"And I'm sure the fools believed that," Delin said with a laugh. "Peasants always want to win *something*, and never doubt you when you tell them they have."

"Especially when that victory allows them to attend a reception at the palace," Kambil agreed. "They've been told that their testing authority representative had such 'confidence' in their ability to win the first competition, that costumes were made for them even before they reached the competition. Being allowed into the palace is probably expected to make them forget any suspicions they might have."

Delin laughed, thinking that someone ought to write a play with such farce in it. Imagine, ignoring your doubts and suspicions because you're being allowed into a *building*.

"I made sure to speak to many of the people who worked with the entrants as guides," Kambil continued. "They aren't very good judges about how strong the entrants really are, since in too many cases their own strength was barely above the level of ordinary. And a curious fact came to light: they allowed more entrants to qualify for Blending status than are usually allowed to do so, but they claimed there was nothing strange about it. It simply happened by error, they insisted, since they worked in pairs against all entrants they meant to eliminate."

"And it would clearly be a matter of their inadequacy to do the job properly if it *weren't* a simple mistake in counting," Delin said, appreciating the point. "That means they must have been lying, and some of the entrants are *considerably* stronger. Were you able to find out which?"

"Since nothing unusual happened, the guides had no one to point to," Kambil reminded him. "I tried gold on one or two of them, but those I picked were honest about having nothing to sell. Looking for the ones who did could take longer than we have before we *need* the information.''

''So we'll have to get it in a different way,'' Delin decided. ''I'll think about possible methods and let you know. Were you able to get access to the test results?''

''Yes, and it didn't even cost me anything,'' Kambil replied with a chuckle. ''When I heard that the entrants had been rated, I asked with full innocence if the results were going to be made available to *all* the noble groups. I was told that no, all our groups would *not* be given the results, only the ones who were intelligent enough to ask for them. And then I was given an already prepared copy of who did what, color coded with tonight in mind.''

''I'll want to see that as soon as we get back,'' Delin said, faintly annoyed that Kambil hadn't already shown it to him. Another annoyance to be laid at the feet of that fool Hiblit. . . . ''What were the results of the entrants marked as orange?''

''I checked that before we left, and found that our first opponents are one of the two strongest groups,'' Kambil told him, now speaking slowly. ''The other will be wearing blue, and none of the remaining three really need to be worried about. Just orange and blue, with orange having scored fractionally higher.''

''I'll bet that bastard Rigos arranged that before his . . . fall from grace,'' Delin growled, heavy anger flaring inside him. ''We're scheduled to face the best of the peasants, which means we're expected to lose to them. Can you imagine what that would do to our social standing if we hadn't made up our minds to do more than simply participate?''

''Yes, I have a very good imagination,'' Kambil said, sounding just as angry. ''The loss would also ruin our chances at any political position we might be under consideration for, no matter *who* tried to support us. So much for the promises Rigos made when he asked me to spy for him.''

''Well, now he's in no position to laugh at the gullible fools he lied to,'' Delin said with a good deal of satisfaction. ''But let's forget about him and think over what we mean to do tonight. We'll have to concentrate on the group in orange, but the ones in blue also need to be investigated. If they make it past the first round they *should* be neutralized in the second, but I dislike depending on the doing of others to keep me safe and happy. I'll feel much better if we find out as much about them as we can."

"I agree, so I have some good news," Kambil said, his tone now grimly pleased. "The blue group has a member who turns out to be someone I know. I have no idea why he's there, but it's Lady Hallina Mardimil's son Clarion—who's now calling himself Rion."

"*That* clod?" Delin asked with immediate derision. "I also know him, at least in passing. He's the laughingstock of our peer group, and if it weren't for Lady Hallina's incredibly high social position—which leads me to wonder how they managed to get away with putting him in with peasants."

"She must have offended someone even higher," Kambil replied, and Delin could hear the shrug behind his words. "She's far from a pleasant person, and embarrassing her like that must have gained someone a large number of points, politically speaking. But none of that is as important as the fact that Mardimil is right there in the middle of the blue group. And he and I were briefly—but pleasantly—friendly at one time."

"Which means that he won't hesitate to tell you all about the peasants," Delin pounced happily. "Especially when you point out—What aspect is Mardimil? I'm almost afraid to ask. . . ."

"Believe it or not, it's Air," Kambil supplied. "And by now he must be furious over having been ignored by the two females in his group. Since I'm certain he's never had any experience with females, they might even have laughed at him."

"So he won't hesitate when you offer him Selendi's place in *our* group," Delin finished, beginning to feel drunk on good fortune. "He'll tell you all about the blue group, and then will sit back to wait for his shift to *our* group. No need to mention that I wouldn't have him with us even if we had to do *without* Air magic. In many ways he's worse than Homin, who's certainly the least of us."

"Then you'll see personally to the orange group?" Kambil said, slightly less enthusiasm in his voice than had been there a moment ago. "I'd been thinking maybe I ought to approach them—"

"And waste that Aspect-sent rapport you have with Mardimil?" Delin interrupted smoothly. "We wouldn't be foolish enough to do *that*, would we? You'll see to Mardimil and I'll see to our primary opponents, and later we'll fill each other in."

"Yes, I suppose it makes sense that way," Kambil agreed after a moment with a sigh. "But later we *will* have to fill each other in."

"Certainly," Delin agreed with heavy warmth and sincerity. "We'll each know everything the other does."

Or almost everything, Delin amended silently as he made himself more comfortable on the coach seat. Only the true leader of their group needed to know absolutely everything, so Kambil would just be out of luck. Once he spoke about everything concerning the blue group, he would be told only what directly concerned him regarding the orange group. It was for his own good, after all. Burdening so weak a man with too many details would never do, not while they still needed Kambil. . . .

FORTY-FIVE

"I . . . think I'm impressed," Rion heard Tamrissa say, the darkness in the coach keeping him from seeing her as well. "The palace has always been the one place in Gan Garee that my father and his friends could never gain access to no matter how much gold they accumulated, but *I'm* almost there. And it looks so . . . so. . . ."

"Big," Jovvi finished for her in a gently amused voice. "Palaces are supposed to be big, I'm told, so I try not to let myself get carried away with awe. But if you feel you have to be impressed, go ahead and do it. Just try not to forget what we have to do tonight."

"How *can* I forget?" Tamrissa returned ruefully. "It was partially my idea. But to be honest, I still don't understand why I suggested that we try to get in touch with the other entrants. Even if we do, how will that change anything?"

"We won't know until we've done it," Jovvi pointed out, the gentleness firming. "Exchanging information can't possibly hurt, and on the plus side it's something the testing authority doesn't *want* us to do. It would be worth trying for that reason alone."

"If you say so," Tamrissa agreed with a sigh, sounding even more depressed than Rion himself felt. "But right now I'd like to ask—Rion, have *you* ever been here to the palace before?"

"Once or twice, many years ago," Rion answered after the briefest hesitation. "Mother does happen to know some of the Blending, but exactly what the relationship is, I have no idea."

And whatever it is, Rion thought, it wasn't enough to keep someone from having *him* put in with a low class group of applicants. He'd done a lot of thinking during the hours just past, and he'd come to the inarguable conclusion that he could well lose Naran because of that fact. If he were still in his proper position he could hire people to search for her, as it was a virtual certainty that his peer equals involved in the competitions had *not* been cut off from their personal funds. But he *had* been, and the piddling few pieces of gold allowed him were all but useless.

Rion couldn't yet see the palace from where he sat in the coach opposite Jovvi and Tamrissa, and was in no mood to turn around and look. The fact was that he would have stayed at the residence if that had been possible, partially in the hope that Naran would get in touch with him again. For the rest, he felt a great reluctance to be in a place where he just might run into someone he knew. His feelings of helplessness put him at a great disadvantage, but he would never again be the innocent fool he once was. If someone he knew came over to play the game of bait-the-victim, he'd probably cause a scene.

The ladies continued on with occasional comments, but happily none were directed at him. He'd volunteered to be the one to accompany them in their coach, as he'd really had no stomach to keep up his corner of a conversation with the other men. He was there in case the other coach was somehow delayed, as having two ladies arrive at the palace unescorted was unthinkable. None of them had known that, of course, not having had experience with the palace before this. Protocols were incredibly inflexible, and the ladies would have been left standing on the approach despite their invitations if they had arrived unescorted.

Rion and the other men hadn't told the ladies that, however, as there had been enough disturbance in everyone's mind without that point. Where only a short while ago they had all been members of a close-knit group, now they'd somehow withdrawn into their individual selves. Jovvi, apparently the only one left with any sort of enthusiasm for continuing on, had somehow gotten them all to agree to try to reach members of the other groups. Rion had agreed as well and would keep his word to make the attempt, but it remained to be seen how successful it would be.

All too soon their coach pulled up to the near approach, so Rion got out and turned to help the ladies. Behind him the palace blazed with the multicolored light of hundreds of lanterns, and other invitees could be seen arriving in coaches and carriages. All of them were costumed and masked just as Rion and the others were, but not in the *same* costumes and masks. Jovvi had been quite correct to say that they'd been marked for some purpose, and that fact simply added to Rion's depression.

The ladies held Rion's arms as they all strolled up the approach toward the main entrance, Ro and Coll following right behind. Their coach hadn't been delayed by anything after all, so the group would be able to enter *as* a group. Those who stood about the approach and on the verandah talking or waiting for friends stared at them, then began to exchange low-voiced, excited comments.

"Isn't it nice that so many people are impressed by our arrival?" Jovvi murmured. "After a single look they know exactly who we are, and they're *very* impressed. Now why would people like them be impressed by a group which has 'won' only a single, low level competition?"

"Possibly because they know something that we supposedly don't?" Tamrissa murmured in answer from Rion's other side. "Like the fact that we'll be competing in more than that single, low level competition? Why do they know all about it while nothing has been said to *us*?"

"They're all members of the nobility," Rion supplied, knowing it for a fact. "Apparently word has spread about our status, so they may make a general announcement tonight. Or not, just as it pleases them."

"I should mention that they're also faintly afraid of us,"

Jovvi said, much more soberly. "I wonder if they'll be just as afraid of our noble counterparts."

"Probably not," Rion told her when Tamrissa failed to venture an opinion. "Our counterparts will be considered civilized human beings and known quantities, while we. . . ."

"Are neither," Jovvi finished with a nod when Rion let the sentence trail off. "Yes, I quite understand."

Rion was certain she did, but not quite as thoroughly as he did himself. She hadn't grown up among these people, or at least on the fringes of them while being taught the same values. . . .

"Look who's waiting for someone just inside the entrance," Tamrissa said as they mounted the stairs to the verandah. "And without a mask, to be certain we recognize her."

"Lady Eltrina Razas," Jovvi supplied with distaste. "At least *she's* delighted to see us. Not a trace of fear in the woman, unless it's due to the possibility of someone showing up in the same costume. But that's hardly likely, considering the number of roses outlined in sequins on her skirt and bodice. There couldn't be enough roses left in the empire to *do* a second costume like that."

Tamrissa giggled over the comment, and even Rion was forced to smile. He disliked Lady Eltrina even more than they did, although the disparaging comment about her costume would have been laughed at by the woman. She'd obviously spent a fortune having it made, and that would be all that concerned her.

"Yes, let that group through, they're my people and expected," Lady Eltrina was saying to the guardsmen on duty as they reached the huge, double-doored entrance. "I'll take charge of them, and show them where to go."

The head guardsman nodded and spoke softly to his men, so no properly engraved invitation was demanded of them. Those guests at the entrance before them stepped aside to allow them through, and Lady Eltrina gave them a wide, pleased smile.

"You're right on time," she told them approvingly. "Just

follow me, and I'll show you to the ballroom.''

She turned and moved off then, sailing along without turning back even once, and Jovvi murmured, ''I wonder how she recognized us. We *are* wearing masks, after all. No, Rion, let's *not* hurry after her.''

Rion discovered that he'd unconsciously begun to increase his pace to match Lady Eltrina's, and was therefore glad that Jovvi had brought it to his attention. Hurrying in that woman's wake was the last thing he wanted to do, even if it ruined Lady Eltrina's good mood. *Especially* if it ruined her mood.

So they strolled up the central hall as though they really belonged there, with both Jovvi and Tamrissa looking around at the uninterrupted carvings on the marble walls twenty feet to either side of them. The ceiling was carved as well, Rion knew, but it was really too far above them to be easily seen at night. Jovvi looked at everything with only moderate interest, but Rion was amused to see that Tamrissa all but gaped. She was such an innocent child, to be impressed with her surroundings like this. She would certainly learn better eventually, but for now it was kinder to allow her the innocence.

Eltrina eventually discovered that they weren't right behind her, and her annoyance was clear when they finally caught up. She'd stopped at the entrance to an enormous ballroom, which seemed nevertheless to be well filled with people. They could hear music playing and see that some people were dancing—at least until Eltrina blocked their view.

''Now isn't the time to go sightseeing,'' she lectured, looking at Jovvi and Tamrissa sternly. ''I have to get you settled inside, as there are other things I must do. Please try to keep up this time.''

Once Eltrina turned away to continue on into the ballroom, Rion exchanged an amused glance with Jovvi. It had felt good to annoy the testing authority representative, but it proved impossible to repeat the performance. There were too many people standing about for Eltrina to resume her sailing stride, and in order to keep from following closely, they would have had to stop walking altogether.

Eltrina led them a good quarter of the way around the extremely large room, having moved to the right once they were all inside. They were only a couple of steps behind her when she stopped and turned to them again, at the same time gesturing to a nearby servant.

"I'm going to assign this servant to fetch whatever you may want in the way of refreshment," she said, addressing all five of them. "You are *not* to move from this spot unless I return and tell you to, or the consequences will be much more serious than you can imagine. When the Blending decides it's ready to have you introduced to them, they won't be amused to get here to discover that you've wandered off. Do you all understand what I'm saying?"

"You may not think so, ma'am, but we *are* used to speakin' and hearin' the language," Ro told her in a drawl. "But if you still doubt that, you could start lookin' around for an interpreter."

"An excellent suggestion, Dom Ro," the woman returned immediately, a faint blush in her cheeks. "The only problem is, I'd never find one in this particular crowd. I'll be back to check on you all in just a little while."

With that she swept away, leaving a group of grimly satisfied people. Despite the masks, Rion could tell that the others had enjoyed Ro's comments just as much as he had.

"This turns out to be a rather interesting place for her to have left us," Coll commented in a voice too low to reach the servant who now hovered just a short distance away. "Am I mistaken, or are those people down there wearing almost the same costume we are? Their sequined parts are also silver, but the rest is yellow. And all the way beyond them—is that a group wearing silver and brown?"

"I think I also see silver and green all the way down near the far doors," Ro put in, confirming Coll's observations. "That makes four groups of us, so unless we just aren't seein' one, there's a group missin'."

"That could be the 'business' Eltrina talked about," Jovvi

murmured. "Meeting the last group of us to arrive. But that's not the only interesting thing about our position. Has anyone yet glanced *across* the room?"

Rion did his glancing in the same casual way the others accomplished it, but he couldn't hold back a faint sound of disgust.

"That group across the way is wearing *gold* and blue, and down a bit to the right is one in gold and yellow," he said. "Apparently we've been positioned for the benefit of our noble counterparts."

"I'm sure it's nothin' but an accident," Ro said after making the same sound Rion had. "But isn't this a little too obvious even for those fools at the testin' authority? How are we supposed to miss seein' that we're here for them to look over?"

"Maybe the point will be that we're supposed to look *them* over as well," Jovvi suggested. "If we don't take advantage of the opportunity it won't be *their* fault, not when we ought to be bright enough to have figured it out for ourselves. So I don't know about the rest of you, but if any of them come over here to 'chat' with us, I'm going to be doing some definite looking."

Murmurs of agreement came in answer to her suggestion, but Rion wasn't certain he cared to add his own. He detested the idea of being looked over as though he were a horse or a bolt of cloth about to be bought, which was undoubtedly the way those heavy-handed fools would manage it. Ah well, he'd already resigned himself to the probability of being a part of an unpleasant scene. . . .

"I believe I'll ask for a glass of wine," Rion said to everyone in general. "Would any of the rest of you care for something?"

They all decided they did, so the hovering servant was summoned and given their drink orders. The man bowed and hurried away to fetch them, returning rather quickly with the drinks and a platter of fried cheese bits. The snack seemed rather cheap—until one tasted the breading on the outside and the seasoning within. The cheese bits had been prepared by a High artist of a chef, possibly a chef of one of the Five themselves.

Only a short while went by while they sipped their wine and devoured cheese bits, and then suddenly there were people joining them. The people only just happened to be wearing costumes of gold and blue, and they all seemed to be rather amused.

"I was told I would be impressed," one of them, a woman, drawled as she looked around with obvious scorn. " 'They're to be your opposite numbers,' they said, 'and you'll find them formidable adversaries.' So I checked your test results and now I'm over here looking at you, but somehow I'm *not* impressed. You lowborn fools won't stand a chance against us."

"Stand a chance against you in what?" Jovvi asked, really emphasizing her pose of wide-eyed innocence. "The only thing you're clearly capable of is showing bad manners, but I think we'll prove to be better even at that."

"Watch how you speak to us, woman," a man in gold and blue growled while his female groupmate gasped in insult. "If no one has ever taught you how to address your betters, it isn't too late for you to be taught right now."

"Oh, we already know all about that," Ro put in at once, smiling at the man without the least sign of amusement. "And as soon as people better than us start showin' up, we'll be glad to demonstrate."

"I *told* you it would be a waste of time to talk to these peasants," another woman in their group announced huffily. "They have no idea how much weaker they are than us, and it was a mistake to think they'd be grateful if we told them we planned to be gentle. Now I don't *want* to be gentle, even if they decide to give us no reason to hurt them during the competition."

"But we did have to try, my dear," the man said, sounding as though he scolded her mildly. "Those in our position have a certain duty, and it would have been dishonorable if we'd simply overwhelmed them. Now we'll do as we must with a clear conscience, knowing they flatly refused our offer. Come, let's return to where we belong.''

The five nobles turned with almost the same toss of the head, and then they were strolling back to where they'd come from. Rion was as silent as the others as he frowningly watched them go, and then Jovvi clicked her tongue.

''What an absolute shame that we've now lost our only chance to get through the competition without being hurt,'' she commented then. ''With people so much stronger than us, we should have been exquisitely polite and thanked them sincerely for their big-hearted offer. I wonder if it's too late to accept it after all.''

''If we did some beggin', there's a small chance they'd change their minds again,'' Ro answered dryly. ''That has to have been the worst actin' I've seen in a long while, not to mention the dumbest idea. Were we really supposed to have agreed to 'givin'' them no reason to hurt us?' Just because *they* said they're stronger?''

''They still expect the ploy to work,'' Jovvi answered him. ''The lowborn are supposed to take the nobility at their word, so that's what they expected to happen now. They're pleased with how well they've frightened us, and probably think we'll accept their offer by the time we reach the competition.''

''But we're not supposed to know that we'll be facing them,'' Tamrissa pointed out with disturbance in her voice. ''If *they* know we know, so should the testing authority. And how could they believe that we're afraid of them? Didn't they have their Spirit magic member checking us over?''

''Not as far as I could tell,'' Jovvi responded, still staring at the retreating nobles. ''They apparently did no more than assume we would believe them, and thereafter made no attempt to check. Even the way that woman started an argument with us was part of their plan, but—I don't like the rest of it. They *shouldn't* have told us as much as they did, not without the least feeling that they were giving away secrets. I'm going to have to think about this.''

Rion exchanged disturbed glances with the others, also

disliking the implications. The group of people who had approached them were mindless fools, but they knew things that Rion and the others didn't. Were those things important enough to mean an absolute defeat in the competition? If they weren't, how could people raised in the midst of political backstabbing and social intrigue be so unconcerned?

And even more importantly, was there any chance that he would survive what lay ahead of them even so far as to *see* Naran again? Somehow, he was beginning to doubt that. . . .

Lord Kambil Arstin stood at the fringes of his group, watching his peers in gold and blue walk away from their counterparts in silver and blue. His fellow nobles were fully convinced that whatever they'd said to their future opponents would bring about the desired result, but Kambil knew better. If their Spirit magic user had bothered to check, he or she would have felt the same anger/derision/stubbornness/refusal that Kambil did.

But it seemed that their Spirit magic user *hadn't* checked, so they all rode a cloud of happy accomplishment that was meant to turn into openly acknowledged victory. Kambil still found it hard to believe that supposedly intelligent people could *assume* success at something without making more than a token effort to cause it to happen. He found it hard to believe, but knowing the way most of his peers had been raised, he also didn't doubt it.

And yet, that made *his* chore a good deal easier. He'd gently felt around the group in blue and silver with his talent, and had already located Clarion Mardimil. Or Rion Mardimil, as he now called himself. Being on the receiving end again of the same sort of contempt he'd gotten all his life from his supposed peers would disturb Mardimil even more, and Mardimil's disturbance would be Kambil's advantage.

Waiting until Mardimil had taken a step or two away from his group, Kambil began to make his way toward the man. Delin had told him to wait until after he'd spoken to their own opponents before going after Mardimil, but this was too good an opportunity to miss. Their opponents in orange hadn't yet arrived, and if Kambil waited it was likely that Mardimil's mood would change to one a good deal less usable.

As Kambil moved, he readily admitted to himself that he disliked the idea of what he was about to do. If he'd had any choice at all he would have done something else entirely, but being a part of his particular group left him *no* choice. He'd simply have to go through with it, and worry about possible consequences at another time.

Mardimil's distraction wasn't so deep that he didn't realize Kambil deliberately approached him, so Kambil nodded as he came in speaking distance.

"Yes, I recognize you, but I don't expect the recognition to be mutual," he said as he came to a halt. "I'm Kambil Arstin, and we knew each other a number of years ago."

"I remember the time," Mardimil replied after a brief hesitation, displaying a great deal of surprise. "But as you said, it's been a number of years. How did you happen to know who I was?"

"I'm sure you realize there's nothing involving 'happen to' about it," Kambil replied with a smile of wry amusement. "Even if we'd been meeting fairly often at receptions and things, tonight we're both masked and costumed. But at that, *my* costume should be enough to answer your question."

"You're a part of one of the groups who will be contending as a Blending," Mardimil obliged him, making no attempt to play coy. "You probably noticed my name on a list somewhere, and that way knew I'd be here tonight."

"Absolutely correct," Kambil agreed, also refusing to play coy. "And I came to speak to you with a particular purpose in mind, but first I'd like to ask an intrusive question: what in the name of the Highest Aspect are you doing with *them* rather than with us? You don't belong here any more than I would."

"Someone apparently disagrees with that point of view," Mardimil returned evenly, but Kambil was able to feel his continuing sense of having been betrayed. "I was put where I currently am and wasn't permitted to argue, so someone

rather powerful must be behind it. Who that would be, I have
no idea."

"Neither do I," Kambil muttered, letting the man see that
he seriously considered the question. "It could be any one
of a dozen people, and we would find out which only if he
or she wanted us to. It doesn't pay to pursue the matter, at
least not directly. But if you would be interested in some
oblique payback . . . ?"

"What do you mean by oblique?" Mardimil asked, his
slowly appearing interest completely real. "And how is it
possible to repay someone whose identity you don't know?"

"You don't have to know who they are in order to ruin
their plans," Kambil pointed out. "They obviously want you
to stay right where you are, so the best thing you can do is
move. Which brings me to the favor I came over to ask:
would you *please* take a moment to consider leaving this
group and joining mine? You have no idea how badly you're
needed."

The clang of shock in Mardimil's mind was so loud and
strong that Kambil would have felt it from the other side of
the room. It was exactly the sort of reaction he'd been looking for, but he made certain to keep nothing but desperate
hope in his manner.

"You want *me*?" Mardimil demanded in a choked voice,
bewilderment now rising up. "All my life I've never been
good enough for anything but to be laughed at. How can I
suddenly be the answer to someone's prayers instead?"

"None of us was *allowed* to do anything but laugh at
you," Kambil replied with the one point Mardimil was likely
to believe. "Your lady mother always placed you in a position where you would be an object of ridicule, and we were
all too young to do anything but give her the reaction she
wanted. Now it would be different, but by now you've undoubtedly lost your taste for associating with your peers."

Mardimil remained silent, but his emotions betrayed him
by loudly denying the contention. The man positively
yearned for acceptance by his peers, a truth it took no talent
at all to know.

"You asked if I would be *willing* to change to your group," Mardimil said at last, his emotions now spinning. "Have you forgotten that it wasn't my idea to be here in the first place? Making decisions that you haven't the power to put into effect is useless."

"It isn't useless when we need you as badly as we do," Kambil countered at once. "I'm sure you know that the real contest will be among the challenging Blendings from *our* people, but in order to have any hope of winning you need someone decent in *all* of the aspects. Our biggest lack is in the area of Air magic, but we've been told that there isn't anyone else available to replace our current member. All those with really decent strength are already part of other groups."

"And you believe they'll let you choose *me* to round out your Blending?" Mardimil asked, his emotions still roiling. "I consider that rather unlikely—"

"You're wrong because I've already checked," Kambil interrupted the reluctant protest. "If *you're* willing to agree, they'll get it done no matter who dislikes the idea. Everyone wants the strongest Seated Blending possible, so they'll help us in any way they can to produce another viable group. What do you say? Will you at least *consider* the idea?"

"I'll be glad to consider it," Mardimil agreed after taking a deep breath, but the promise was a lie. The man had *already* made up his mind to agree, and would say so in just another moment or two. Kambil had won, then, so there was no reason not to continue to the end he'd come over to accomplish.

"I know you'll make the right decision," he said with as warm a smile as he could manage. "The girl we now have in *your* proper place is just a girl, and as incompetent as they all are. You must have had your hands full with the ones in your own group, and I can't wait to hear the stories you must have. Just imagine, a *girl* trying to get somewhere with Fire magic, the position that requires the most strength in a Blending. You'll have to tell me just how womanly weak she really is."

Mardimil smiled and parted his lips, about to tell Kambil exactly what he wanted to know. Kambil could feel it, and that brought him a sense of triumph. Despite even his own misgivings, he'd actually managed to pull it off!

FORTY-SIX

Rion felt lightheaded and delirious over the offer he'd been made, one he'd been longing for ever since that business of testing had begun. He'd be part of a group with his peers, among people who had, until now, wanted nothing to do with him. He smiled and parted his lips, ready to tell Arstin all about Tamrissa's little quirks and problems—

—until he remembered the touching way she'd confided in him after they'd lain together. She'd also said something about not being used to having friends, and that now she finally understood how friends kept each other's secrets. To say anything about her at all would be a betrayal, much more of one than simply leaving the group.

"Our Fire magic user is a lovely lady," Rion said instead, looking at Arstin levelly. "But rather than talk about *her*, tell me how soon I'd be able to transfer to your group."

"Why, I'm sure it can be arranged by next week's end," Arstin replied, a flash of frustration showing very briefly in the man's eyes. "If that means you've decided to join us, I couldn't be more pleased. But don't you have *anything* you'd like to say about the lady of Fire? Surely she's joined the others in treating you quite intolerably?"

"As a matter of fact, they've all treated me rather well,"
Rion told him, suddenly and belatedly suspicious. It would
take an entire week to arrange something Arstin claimed
everyone wanted? When people had previously been shifted
out of the residence in half a day's time or less? "And I'd
like to know why you keep asking about Dama Domon. One
question on the subject can be considered casual conversation; two questions in as many minutes is not in the least
casual."

"I merely thought you'd enjoy discussing the outrage
you've been made to suffer through," Arstin replied sooth-
ingly—just as Rion became aware of the man's talent trying
to accomplish that soothing as well. "Talking about things
which disturb us lets us finally put those things out of our
mind. We need you to be as relaxed as possible when you
join us, after all, so why not take advantage of a friendly
ear? Begin by discussing one of the others instead, and return
to Dama Domon when you feel more comfortable discussing
her."

"Your friendly ear doesn't seem to hear very well," Rion
observed, forcing himself to face the unpalatable truth. "I
told you that I was treated well, but you ignored that in an
effort to get me talking. You and your group don't want *me*,
you simply want the information I can give you."

"I'm sorry you choose to see it that way, Mardimil," Arstin said with a sigh, now sending the emotions of regret and
uncertainty. "My offer was a good one, and nothing but your
unnatural suspicions are ruining it. It still isn't too late for
you to change your mind. . . ."

Arstin let his words trail off in a coaxing way, as though
waiting for the regret and uncertainty to make Rion more
easily manipulated. But Rion understood what was happening now, and simply showed a faint smile.

"You know, Arstin, I'd actually forgotten how everyone
of our class loves to control and use others," Rion told him.
"You have my thanks for reminding me, but that's all you'll
have when you walk away from here. Which you would be
wisest doing right this minute."

The flash of frustration in Arstin's eyes was stronger this time, and the man's head came up as though he were indignant over having been discovered at his little game. But he wasn't foolish enough to try adding any more words. He simply nodded curtly, turned on his heel, and walked away.

"I hope you don't mind if I say how well I think you handled that," a soft voice murmured, and Rion turned his head to see Jovvi beside him. "I noticed him come up to you and begin to touch you with his talent, so I . . . helped out."

"Helped out," Rion echoed, perplexed for a moment before understanding came. "So that's why I was aware of what he tried rather than being affected by it. What did you do?"

"I'm not really sure," Jovvi admitted, a small frown creasing her beautiful brow. "I wanted to protect you by letting you know what that man was trying to do, and suddenly it was happening. Just exactly what I did. . . . I'll have to think about that for a while before I make any attempt to describe it."

"Take all the time you need," Rion said, smiling at her fondly. "But you must also take my thanks for keeping me from making a fool of myself. I wanted so very much to believe Arstin—after having conveniently forgotten that my . . . 'own kind' can't be trusted not to betray even the people they consider friends. I expected to feel bitter disappointment over having lost an opportunity, but what I feel instead is relief. It's you and the others who are 'my kind,' not them."

"I'm glad you now see it the way the rest of us do," Jovvi replied with a smile filled with warmth that couldn't be doubted. "You earned your place among us even before you helped Tamma so much, so I'm just glad I was able to do my part. But what did that man want from you? I know he was trying to make you believe something, but I don't know exactly what."

"He tried to make me believe that he and the others of his group wanted me to be one of them," Rion answered, anger coming to him in place of hurt. "I've spent all my life on the outside looking in, and he offered to unlock the door to acceptance. But the price of the key was betrayal of the rest of you, which I should have realized would not have gotten me inside. If I left at this stage of things, there would be no one to take my place. So why would information on everyone's shortcomings and problems be at all important? Without a full Blending, none of you would compete.''

"Someone else in your position would not have seen that,'' Jovvi said, putting a gentle hand to his arm. "I spent a long enough time alone on the streets to know how strong the lure of acceptance is, and I'm not sure I could have been as strong as you were. You're wonderful, Rion, and I'm proud to be part of something with you.''

For once Rion was at a loss for words, but it was a very pleasant loss. He returned Jovvi's smile as he briefly put his own hand over hers, feeling—no, *knowing*—that words were his only loss. He had more with these people than Arstin and his group could ever provide, and even the thought of Naran no longer disturbed him. His real friends would help him to find her again, just as they'd helped him to see her in the first place.

Rion's gaze found Arstin as the man stalked back toward his group, and all thoughts of warmth and happiness disappeared. Those very insistent questions about Tamrissa . . . would that gentle, damaged child really turn out to be the most important one in their Blending? The point was one he'd have to discuss with the others, but until then he'd worry about it all by himself. . . .

Vallant was far from comfortable. The room they stood in was more than large, but the number of people in it turned it into something the size of a middling box. And the fact that they'd been told not to leave the area they now stood in. . . . Only the absence of a locked door had kept Vallant from bolting. As long as whether or not he stayed put remained his own idea, it also remained somewhat tolerable.

Looking around at the people attending the ball wasn't very interesting, but it had the benefit of being something of a distraction. Everyone seemed to be inspecting the fascinating animals who had been dressed up in distinctive, color-matched costumes, even those nobles who were pretending to dance. Staring alternated with whispering, and Vallant might have been curious about what they were saying if their behavior hadn't filled him with so much disgust and outrage.

So he looked away from those staring at him, only to find that one of the five people in silver and yellow was also staring at him. Indignation flared immediately, that someone in his own position would be as rude as those so-called nobles, but then Vallant's mind began to work in place of his emotions. The man who stared at him was on the small side, and he stood at least two steps away from the rest of his group. . . .

"Holter, that's got to be Holter," Vallant muttered to himself, the obvious having finally come to him. "And what was that Jovvi said about us gettin' in touch with other groups . . . ?"

The idea appeared fully formed, so Vallant lost no time acting on it. Holter must have been told the same thing about not wandering around, but there was one instance where leaving the area *had* to be permitted. He gave Holter the thumb-up sign they'd exchanged more than once, and the small man returned it immediately—and almost eagerly. He couldn't have been certain that he was looking at Vallant or that he himself would be recognized, but now he knew he'd achieved both.

Once recognition was established, Vallant moved on to the idea he'd gotten. After glancing around casually to be sure no one was watching too closely, he gestured at himself and went into the small, brief dance that young children sometimes did when they had to relieve themselves. Holter stared for a moment with his head to one side, but then he nodded with understanding and turned away.

That was the signal for Vallant to also turn away, in order to find the servant assigned to them to ask directions to the nearest sanitary facilities. The man looked as though he were prepared to lead Vallant to them, but before he could make the offer he was called by Tamrissa. Frustration flashed briefly across his face before he turned to point out a door to Vallant, and then he was off to find out what Tamrissa wanted.

Vallant took immediate advantage of not being accompanied, and made for the door which presumably led to the sanitary facilities. As he approached he saw one man go in and another two come out, all of them dressed like nobles rather than participants. Looking around for Holter would have been stupid, so Vallant simply walked to the door while silently hoping. Holter *could* be sent to a different facility, as it was unlikely there would be just one. . . .

The door led into a smaller, narrower corridor than the one they'd used to reach the ballroom, and a short distance down on the left was a door with the standard sign for men. On the right and a bit closer to the ballroom was the sign for women, which was only to be expected. There were no women going in or out, though, while the men's facility had fairly brisk traffic.

Vallant stepped into the outer room casually, but there was nothing casual about the response of the other occupants. All eyes were suddenly on him, and he didn't need Jovvi's talent to tell that most of the men were frightened. The rest were at least uncomfortable, and in a moment they were *all* heading for the way out. Vallant smiled to himself as he pretended not to notice, instead enjoying how large the facility entrance room was. With everyone else leaving, it was actually almost bearable.

A minute or two after the room emptied, the door opened again and Holter came in. Vallant had used the time to see that at least two of the small facility rooms in back were occupied, so he gestured silence to Holter and led the smaller man to the far side of the entrance room. The place was beyond the line of small tables holding wash basins and stacks of towels, just in front of a large, clearly comfortable couch.

"They don't want any of us talkin' together, so we'll have to make this fast," Vallant said softly once Holter stood beside him. "Jovvi thinks we all *should* talk, so we're tryin' to find out the locations of the other groups. What do *you* think?"

"I think th' lady's right as rain," Holter said with a slow nod. "We gotta do somethin' t'keep 'em frum gittin' us, but th' fools in m'new residence prob'ly won't go along. I'll tell ya where I am, but first I gotta tell ya 'bout th' new Earth magic user we got. Three guesses who he is."

"Eskin Drowd," Vallant answered promptly, remembering what Lorand had said. "I take it he still doesn't have much in the way of ordinary manners."

"An' never will," Holter agreed with a nod, pushing at his mask. "This damn thing's too tight, but we ain't allowed t'toss it. . . . Man who wus in Drowd's place t'start with never come back frum that there first comp'tition. They said he's sick 'r sumthin'."

"Lorand said he went crazy when he messed up durin' the competition," Vallant supplied, unsurprised that the people in the man's residence hadn't been told any details. "They had to put him to sleep by force, then he was carted off somewhere. But Drowd hadn't yet qualified, or so Lorand also said. Did he manage to get through the tests, or did they just throw him in without requirin' it?"

"Drowd ain't tellin', so there's no way a knowin'," Holter replied with a shrug. "He's just walkin' around smug as ever, makin' trouble ever' time he opens his mouth. But what's happenin' with this here thing t'night, an' how cum yer here? They said *I* won th' comp'tition."

"We think they told that to everyone," Vallant said, "and your bein' here confirms the guess. They probably want the noble groups to get a look at us, and maybe even pick up a hint or two about defeatin' us. The group we'll be facin' came over and tried a fool's trick to make us afraid of them, but all it did was get us annoyed."

"Gotta tell ya sumthin'," Holter said, the visible part of his expression looking worried. "Ran inta a old friend th' other day, an' she ain't worried none 'bout whut I kin do. So we talked some, an' she said there's lots a gold floatin' around in bettin'. Coulda guessed that, but th' other part ain't so good. None a th' gold's on any a *us*.''

"And at least some of it should be," Vallant put in, suddenly very worried. "There's no way of knowin' one of our groups won't get lucky—unless things are arranged so that none of us *can* get lucky. Any idea about what the arrangement can be?''

"Nobody's sayin'," Holter denied with a headshake. "M'friend's tryin' t'find out, but prob'ly she ain't gonna get very far. All she culd tell me wus that th' gold's been agin us all along.''

"Which might or might not mean somethin'," Vallant acknowledged as he nodded. "I'll tell the others, and if we come up with any ideas I'll pass them along. How do I get in touch with you?''

Holter gave him an address which meant nothing to Vallant, but he memorized it with the hope that Tamrissa would know where it was. Then Holter added, "I'll ask m'friend t'see if'n she c'n get th' other addresses. Meanwhile *we* gotta keep in touch.''

"If you don't hear from me in two or three days, see if you can sneak back for a visit," Vallant said, again agreeing. "But don't let any of the servants see you. Some of them have got to be watchin' us for the testin' authority—but you already know that. Just take care of yourself, and don't let Drowd get to you. Chances are he didn't pass the sort of tests the rest of us did.''

"I mean t'say thet durin' breakfast t'morra," Holter replied with a grin. "Th' sonuvabitch awready got t'me, an' now it's my turn. You take care, you an' th' others.''

Vallant simply nodded in an effort to ease the man's very obvious embarrassment, as though there were anything wrong with being concerned about people you liked. Holter matched his nod and then left, clearly reluctant to return to his new group but having no choice in the matter. Vallant had almost offered to trade places with him, but there was no sense in disturbing the man even more. The testing authority would never allow them to switch places, even though Vallant wouldn't have minded in the least.

Or at least wouldn't have minded much. His mood wasn't likely to lighten no matter what he did, so there was no sense in not helping out a friend. Ah well, it would probably all be over soon for all of them. . . .

Vallant waited another moment before following Holter out, having no more use for the facilities than the smaller man had. If that servant had known Vallant's talent was Water magic, he would certainly have wondered why Vallant needed to *go* to the facilities. Simply knowing where they were would have been enough, but some Water magic users were too fastidious to relieve themselves the easy way. He could always have claimed to be that sort. . . .

Taking a deep breath before stepping back into the ballroom didn't help, but Vallant did it anyway. All he wanted to know at the moment was when they'd be allowed to leave. He wanted out of there, even if it meant leaving the ladies behind. Neither of them really needed him, especially not that particular lady, so there was no reason to feel reluctant. No, he would not be abandoning her—*them*; not in the least. . . .

Delin saw Kambil making his way back to the group, and it was fairly clear where the man had been. A touch of annoyance fleeted through his mind at having been disobeyed, but maybe Kambil had had a reason to approach Mardimil sooner than he'd been told to. Delin would wait to hear what Kambil had to say before pointing out the man's error.

"Well, my part of it is finished," Kambil said once he stopped beside Delin. "Mardimil has changed since I knew him last, and he actually figured out what I was doing. Needless to say, he parted with no information beyond the contention that the commoners have been treating him extremely well."

"As if we believe that," Delin returned with a sound of ridicule. "But possibly you would have gotten a bit farther if you'd waited until later to approach Mardimil. As I suggested earlier.''

"I thought the same at first, but a moment's consideration changed my mind," Kambil countered with a dismissive wave of his hand. "I approached him to begin with because of the unstable state of mind he happened to be in, but it turned out to be something other than a general unstability. Generally he's gained a remarkable amount of self-control, and that ridiculous stuffiness he always used to show has disappeared entirely. After speaking with him, I'm sorry we *can't* find a way to make him a member of our group.''

"I find it hard to believe that the man has changed so much," Delin said with a frown, partially diverted from his annoyance. "His attitude of superiority used to be unbearable, especially since there was nothing to base it on. You believe he would do more for our efforts than Selendi could?''

"There's no doubt about it," Kambil said, his nod very certain. "I had the impression that 'good enough' would never satisfy him the way it does her, and he could very well be stronger. I wonder if there's any way we could have him transferred to us that wouldn't arouse everyone's suspicions. Seeing him just thrown away disturbs my habit of avoiding waste.''

"I'll think about the problem and let you know," Delin promised, then the last of what Kambil had said really came through. "But what did you mean about him being wasted? Being part of a challenging Blending isn't quite the same as being thrown away.''

"In this instance it is," Kambil disagreed, gesturing behind himself. "Didn't you see who will be facing Mardimil's group first? I missed the point myself to begin with, but his turning me down made me think about it. It seems that the testing authority is taking no chances with the second strongest group of commoners.''

Delin followed the gesture to see the group in gold and blue, but for a moment the sight meant nothing. Then he noticed that most of the group's members were women, and that meant—

"It's Adriari's group," Delin blurted, surprised in spite of himself. "They're putting Mardimil's group up against their pet Blending!"

"Which means the poor sods can't possibly get past the very first competition," Kambil agreed, also turning to study Adriari's group. "The authority can't be counting on an honest win, not with the opponents chosen for them, so they'll be using their unmentioned edge. If Mardimil stays in that group, he'll go down with the rest of them."

Delin nodded, knowing Kambil spoke nothing but the truth, which probably meant there would turn out to be no possible way to shake Mardimil loose. The authority had everything arranged, and they really hated having their arrangements disturbed . . . unfortunately for that predoomed group. . . .

The Chronicles of
Fionn Mac Cumhal
Prophet, Poet, Warrior, Outlaw

☺ ☺ ☺

by Diana L. Paxson
& Adrienne Martine-Barnes

MASTER OF EARTH AND WATER
75801-6/$4.99 US/$5.99 Can

Safely hidden from the world of men, an ancient warrior will teach the child called Demne many things—but never speak about the boy's mysterious parentage.

THE SHIELD BETWEEN THE WORLDS
75802-4/$4.99 US/$6.99 Can

Now the time has come for Fionn to assume his tribe's mantle of leadership—to restore his fian to its former greatness.

SWORD OF FIRE AND SHADOW
75803-1/$5.99 US/$7.99 Can

It is the bitter twilight of a noble hero's life as enemies mass on all sides, waiting to strike the killing blow. But from the terrible wreckage, he will arise victorious once more.